Alienation of Affection

Based on the True Story of the Sensational 1911 Murder at Denver's Richthofen Castle

ROBERT HARDAWAY

WESTERN REFLECTIONS PUBLISHING COMPANY®

Montrose, Colorado

© 2003 Robert Hardaway
All rights reserved in whole or in part.

ISBN 1-890437-93-X

Library of Congress Control Number: 2003107456

Cover painting: The Necklace by Thomas Wilmer Dewing
Cover and text design by Laurie Goralka Design

First Edition
Printed in the United States of America

Western Reflections Publishing Company®
219 Main Street
Montrose, CO 81401
www.westernreflectionspub.com

Dedicated to
Judy Swearingen

"Oh, what a vileness human beauty is,
Corroding and corrupting
Everything it touches."

Euripides

PREFACE

A s a law professor, much of my writing relates to obscure and arcane areas of the law. It so happened that a research project into the legal history of an all but forgotten legal remedy, the tort of alienation of affection, coincided with a quite remarkable walk I took with my golden retriever, Rambo. Late one summer evening near my home in Denver, Colorado, I found myself at the intersection of Twelfth and Pontiac streets, a peaceful middle class neighborhood through which I had never walked before. There I came upon an imposing brick wall with wrought iron gates. There were several signs hanging from the wall warning trespassers to keep out and to beware of the dog. Curious, I peered through the gates and saw moonlit, behind thick foliage and shrubs, the outline of an imposing stone mansion that seemed quite out of place in a middle class neighborhood. At that moment I heard footsteps behind me and turned to see an elderly gentleman in red Bermuda shorts and tennis shoes. He was also walking his dog, a small black boxer.

Observing that I was curious about the mansion, and without bothering to introduce himself, he launched into a history of the house. He informed me that it was known as the Richthofen Castle, built in the 1890s by the famous Richthofen family. One member of that family later became the Red Baron, the German fighter ace who shot down a record number of allied planes in World War I. Although I was intrigued, it was getting late, so I thanked him for the history lesson and turned to walk back home. Sensing that he was about to lose his history student, the man cut to the chase. The spot on which you are standing, he said authoritatively, is the very spot on which the most notorious murder in Denver's history occurred ninety years ago.

The man in the red Bermudas now had my attention, and for the next hour he engaged me with a tale so extraordinary and so rich in details of scandal that I could only conclude that it was the product of a fertile imagination. When I asked where he had heard the story, he said his father had told it to him when he was a young boy, but he had deleted the more scandalous details. Over the years, he gleaned the details from neighbors who were his father's contemporaries. Dismissing the more fantastic aspects of his story, if not the actual fact of a murder at the very gates of this house,

The Richthofen Castle at Twelfth and Pontiac Streets in Montclaire
section of Denver, Colorado, circa 1911. Denver Public Library
Western History Department, #20068.

I was nevertheless fascinated by one aspect of the tale, which related to the research I was pursuing on the common law tort of alienation of affection.

Alienation of affection was a common law remedy brought by an aggrieved wife or husband against a person who had alienated (i.e., stolen) his spouse's affection. Courts often awarded considerable monetary damages to the injured party in such cases. At the turn of the nineteenth century, the remedy of alienation of affection was considered to be a necessary deterrent to adultery. The tort of alienation of affection was abolished in Colorado in the 1930s by legislators convinced that the remedy was ineffective in deterring adultery and was the instrument of much mischief, particularly blackmail. Most states have agreed, with one notable exception — South Carolina. A court in that state recently awarded a verdict in the millions of dollars against a young and attractive secretary who allegedly stole the affections of her employer.

My curiosity thus piqued, I asked students in my civil procedure class at the University of Denver College of Law if any of them would be interested in researching the historical records for any information on a murder which occurred at the Richthofen Castle in 1911. One of my most enthusiastic students, Denise Stott, came forward after class. From her first day in law school, Denise had pursued her interest in criminal law, and particularly in great criminal trials, hoping to make a career as a criminal trial attorney. She would have made a good one. She was an active student in the law school clinic, in which she zealously represented indigent clients in court under the supervision of a clinical professor. She loved to argue and debate and could keep a discussion going for hours. I cautioned her that the case might be nothing more than the creation of one elderly gentleman with an exaggerated imagination. Nevertheless, she committed eagerly to the task of tracking down any evidence of such a case.

Several weeks later she came to my office with an immense portfolio of newspaper clippings from the November 1911 issues of five Denver newspapers — most notably the *The Daily News, The Denver Post,* and *Rocky Mountain News.* Proudly, she laid out on my office floor a set of organized and indexed scrapbooks containing clippings of the Gertrude Gibson Patterson murder case. I learned later that one of Denise's many passions (which also included scuba diving and musicals) was "scrapbooking." Indeed, she was a co-owner with her parents of a scrapbook shop in her hometown of Salt Lake City, Utah.

I looked at her scrapbooks with quiet astonishment. For several hours I pored over them, slowly realizing that every shocking detail related to me by the old man in Bermuda shorts was documented in front-page headlines about Denver's most notorious murder trial. For over two entire months in 1911, all the Denver newspapers filled their entire front pages, and a good part of the interior pages as well, with stories of the murder trial of Gertrude Gibson Patterson, a beautiful young woman charged with the cold-blooded murder of her once dashing but then sick and tubercular husband, Charles Patterson. It was a rare front page that did not include large photographs of the accused and endless descriptions of "the beautiful young woman, delicate in appearance as a rare cameo carved in white against shell pink." Entire issues of the paper were dedicated to diagrams and maps of the layout of the Richthofen Castle, scenes of the unruly and passionate crowds of young women who demonstrated their support of Gertrude each morning at the West Side Court, and endless representations of the daily scenes of high drama in the courtroom. Supplementary back-page stories delved into the scandalous subplots of the murder, while daily columns rhapsodized on the defendant's extraordinary beauty (one entire section of the Sunday edition was devoted to pictures and descriptions of the defendant's hands and ankles).

Daily editorials and columns philosophized about the role of beauty in society and in the justice system. Debate concerning the latter continues to this day. In Nancy Etcoff's 1999 best-seller, *Survival of the Prettiest,* the author cites a scientific study showing that for a beautiful woman the average man is willing to "help move furniture, donate blood, donate a kidney, swim a mile to rescue her, save her from a burning building, and even jump on a terrorist hand grenade. (The only thing they seemed reluctant to do for her was loan her money.)" Challenging Naomi Wolf"s thesis in the *Beauty Myth* that the notion of beauty is culturally ingrained, Etcoff cites studies showing that even babies look significantly longer at attractive faces than unattractive ones and concludes that "we face a world where lookism is one of the most pervasive but denied of prejudices."

What I found most astonishing about the Patterson trial was that an event that had so completely captured the imagination not only of Denver but also of an entire nation in 1911 had somehow been so totally lost to the collective memory. I asked Denise to look for any books that might have been written about the trial, believing that there must be some, and perhaps even dramatizations and films made about so extraordinary and colorful an event in American history. After scouring the databases of every library she could access, Denise found only one very brief chapter about the trial in a 1946 book called *Denver Murders* by Frances Wayne and a 1948 Sunday supplement article in the *Rocky Mountain News* by Frances Melrose. After reading these two short pieces, I realized that the events described were not within the memory of the authors and that the case had already by that time faded from the collective memory.

Because court records of the trial were not available, our first task was to assemble a complete transcript of the trial from the newspaper clippings. (After each day of the trial, every word uttered at the trial was recorded verbatim in the inside pages of all the Denver newspapers.) I studied the transcript with the idea of using it as a case study in my upcoming trial practice class that I teach at the University of Denver College of Law and also as a topic for an upcoming symposium on the development of legal doctrine and trial practice at the turn of the century. I concluded that the great Denver trial of Gertrude Gibson Patterson in 1911 surely eclipsed, in drama and notoriety if not in enduring fame, the New York murder trial, some six years before of Harry Thaw, charged with the murder of the architect Stanford White. That trial too had featured a legendary beauty, Evelyn Nesbitt, and had to that date earned the appellation of Trial of the Century. Of course, as anarchist Emma Goldman observed at the time, "there were ninety-five years to go."

Later trials of the twentieth century, such as the Lindbergh trial, and more recently that of O.J. Simpson, pale in scandalous comparison with that of Gertrude Gibson Patterson, at least in the press coverage.

Frances Wayne's chapter on the trial in "Denver Murders," while vague on the facts of the case itself, was most useful in recreating the notoriety surrounding the trial:

*Blaring headlines informed all of the latest violation of the
Sixth Commandment and the citizenry, regardless of station, race, color or culture was agog over the circus poten-
tialities of the deed. Here were all the elements of sizzling,
thrilling melodrama. Newspapers gave a go-the-limit
orders to editors, reporters, artists, cartoonists and special
writers, to fill not paragraphs, not columns, but entire
pages of every edition of Denver's five daily newspapers,
and warned that the punishment for being scooped would
be unlimited leisure. This order held for almost two
months, as church clubs and organizations such as the
Women's Christian Temperance Union and the Women's
Citizen League adopted resolutions denouncing the publication of 'sordid nauseous details' of this notorious 'crime
passionel.' A voice howling into an empty barrel would
have been as effective. The public demanded to know how
'Gertie did it,' even to the smallest detail, and who Gertie
was and had been.*

In the end it was Denise's persistent ferreting out of old, decaying
newspapers that provided the material for this book. Invaluable as this
assistance was, she made an even more substantial contribution. In one
of our earliest discussions about how best to present the extraordinary
story of Gertrude Gibson Patterson, Denise asked me if I had ever read
Theodore Dreiser's first novel, *Sister Carrie*. I recalled having read the
book in college, vaguely remembering something about a depressing turn
of the century tale about a young woman's travails in the big city. The city
was Chicago, Denise reminded me, and Dreiser's fictional Carrie arrived
in Chicago on the train in the same year as our real antiheroine, Gertrude
Gibson Patterson.

Denise suggested that I reread *Sister Carrie*, paying particular attention to some of Dreiser's thoughts about the human condition and how his
descriptions of Carrie might be helpful in understanding Gertrude's story. In
many ways, Denise observed, Gertrude Gibson Patterson fit Carrie to a tee.

I was heavily involved in other projects at the time and recalled that
Sister Carrie was not light reading. I did not follow up on her suggestion at
the time.

Then, on January 14, 2001, came the most shocking and sad news.
Denise, flying back from a parachuting expedition with her devoted fiancé
and seven others, was killed when her small plane crashed into the Great
Salt Lake in Utah. The news was utterly shattering to all who knew her.

It was several months before I was able to return to the project on
which we had collaborated. Her scrapbooks and clippings remained on my

living room floor, daily reminders of Denise, her passion for the law, and her interest and contributions to this project. I resolved to complete the project as my personal memorial to Denise.

My first act of re-entry was to read the original, unedited version of *Sister Carrie*. Like Denise, I was struck by the eerie similarities between Carrie and Gertrude — each trying to make her way in a cold and insecure world using the one weapon available to them — beauty, which armed them for life's battle in a cold world of laissez-faire but also left them peculiarly vulnerable.

It briefly occurred to me that Gertrude's notorious murder trial might even have been the model for Dreiser's Carrie, just as a sensational murder case was the inspiration for Dreiser's 1925 novel *An American Tragedy*. It was oddly a strange relief when I realized that that was impossible, since *Sister Carrie* was published in 1900, eleven years before Gertrude gained the national notoriety that would have brought her to Dreiser's attention.

Nevertheless, in the story that follows I could come up with no better description of Gertrude than Dreiser's description of Carrie who, like Gertrude, found herself at age eighteen on the train, bound for Chicago, to make her fortune:

> *Self-interest with her was high, but not strong. It was nevertheless, her guiding characteristic. Warm with the fancies of youth, pretty with the insipid prettiness of the formative period, possessed of a figure promising eventual shapeliness and an eye alight with certain native intelligence, she was a fine example of the Middle American class — two generations removed from the emigrant. Books were beyond her interest — knowledge a sealed book. In the intuitive graces she was still crude. She could scarcely toss her head gracefully. Her hands were almost ineffectual. The feet, though exquisitely small, were set flatly. And yet she was interested in her charms, quick to understand the keener pleasure of life, ambitious to gain in material things. A half-equipped little knight she was, venturing to reconnoiter the mysterious city and dreaming of some vague, far-off supremacy, which should make it prey and subject — the proper penitent, groveling at a woman's slipper.*

Nor can my description of Gertrude's train trip in Chapter 4 compare in literary merit with Dresier's description of Carrie's same trip:

> *When Caroline Meeber boarded the afternoon train for Chicago, her total outfit consisted of a small trunk, a*

> *cheap imitation alligator-skin satchel, a small lunch in a*
> *pepper box, and a yellow leather snap purse containing*
> *her ticket, a scrap of paper with her (relative's) address,*
> *and four dollars in money.*

Sister Carrie, like Gertrude's trial, was an insult to the times. Harper Brothers rejected it outright on grounds that it was not "sufficiently delicate to depict without offense to the reader the continued illicit relations of the heroine." When Doubleday eventually published it with great trepidation, it sold fewer than seven hundred copies and created a reputation for Dreiser that E.L. Doctorow, in an introduction to the 1992 Bantam Book edition of *Sister Carrie*, has described as that of the "naturalist-barbarian." According to Doctorow, the reason for the early rejection of *Sister Carrie* was that Dreiser did not view the business of the writer to be the creation of an "idealized picture of human beings for the instruction or sentimental satisfaction of readers, but rather to portray life as it is really lived under specific circumstances of time and place, and to show how people actually think and feel and why they do what they do."

It was only later that the brilliance of Sister Carrie was recognized. The *Newark Sunday News* was among the first to see genius: "The impression is simply one of truth and therein lies at once the strength and horror of it."

In the end, Dreiser's work was heavily edited — Dresier claimed that it was "bowdlerized" — in order to make it palatable to the moralistic, if hypocritical, Victorian reading public at the turn of the nineteenth century. As Doctorow recounts, the particular concern of the editors was that Dreiser not "leave the reader at the end of the book with the impression that Carrie was to be rewarded for her life of illicit relation."

The editors, of course, missed the point. It was one thing to moralize, indeed admirable to do so; it was quite another to tell the truth.

In what follows, I have endeavored only to tell a remarkable story as I myself found it. I have used the less than modest literary abilities generally allotted to the academician, and a lawyer at that. What lessons might be learned from Gertrude's story, both from a standpoint of understanding human behavior — that is, "how people actually think and feel and why they do what they do" — or understanding the evolution of American justice during a time of dramatic revolution in legal thinking, I leave to the reader. If nothing else, the story that follows reveals the role of gender and race in the administration of justice during a period when gender and race played a far different role in society at large.

The story that follows is told in narrative rather than documentary style. I have made every effort to adhere to documented historical facts. In the narrative, every word spoken at the trial is taken from published transcripts, as are the published public statements of all those involved. Although the events leading up to the trial are described generally in the transcript of the trial, they are referred to only sketchily. Because it is these events that form the greater part of the narrative that follows, I have found it necessary to create some conversations, locations, events, and minor characters as a means of providing continuity to the narrative. With regard to the events leading up to the trial itself, the narrative is "based on a true story." Inevitably, I found it necessary to adopt one of several possible versions of those events that were vigorously disputed at the trial; I therefore covered the most disputed events only generally in the narrative. I have left it to the reader to judge the guilt or innocence of Gertrude Patterson based on the actual verbatim trial testimony set forth in the final chapters. Although it has been necessary to edit the testimony (which at the trial ran to hundreds of hours), I have made every effort to include the evidence and testimony most crucial to each side.

To further assist the reader in this task, I have prefaced some chapters with actual newspaper accounts and photographs from the Denver newspapers and relied heavily on the headlines, stories, and columns of *The Denver Post* and *Rocky Mountain News*. Alice Roche of the *Rocky Mountain News* wrote a daily column on the Patterson trial, and her reflections are liberally cited. All of these citations are direct quotes, and from them it may be possible for the reader to adopt a version of events that differs from those set forth in the narrative. In the spirit of Denise's insightful comparisons of Gertrude to Dreiser's Carrie, I have prefaced some chapters with passages from *Sister Carrie*.

The latter proved to be an invaluable source in other respects as well. Although traditional history books provided information and details about locations and events that provide the background for the story, it was difficult to find books that described the slang, or "lingo," in common usage at the time. The dialogue in *Sister Carrie* is rich in the vernacular of this period, therefore most helpful. (Without it, I would never have known that the common term for an apartment in turn of the century Chicago was "flat" or that fashionably dressed dandies were called "drummers.")

Another reason that I have included actual newspaper accounts and photographs is that without them there would be a temptation to dismiss the fantastic story that follows as fiction. It is also hoped that the juxtaposition of the headlines to the narrative will serve to highlight the contrast between the cardboard character cutouts depicted in newspapers and tabloids in cases of national notoriety and the very complex human beings that lie behind those headlines, whose characters inevitably come in shades of gray.

Finally, I wish to thank Madeleine Kriesher for her research assistance about Chicago, Carmel-by-the-Sea, Fontain-bleau, Paris, and the great ocean liners, including the Titanic; my friend Stanley Brady for his often brutal, but nevertheless very helpful literary criticism; my friends and colleagues at the University of Denver College of Law, too numerous to mention, who offered many helpful suggestions; to Dean Mary Ricketson, whose personal and moral support, as well as official support for all my endeavors at the College of Law is most gratefully acknowledged and appreciated; and especially to Denise Stott, without whose dedication and enthusiasm this story would never have been told.

Robert Hardaway
Denver, Colorado
June 2003

1

In 1858, Green Russell stopped to pan for gold near the confluence of the South Platte River and Cherry Creek at the gateway to the Rocky Mountains in Colorado. He found little gold, and he and his fellow prospectors soon moved on to the mountains. Other fortune-seekers soon followed and occupied the site, among whom was a part-time preacher named William Larimer, who saw riches not in the elusive gold, but in the land itself. He bought much of the land surrounding the camp, subdivided it into lots, built several cabins, and called the site Denver. He modestly named the rutted trail that ran between his cabins Larimer Street. Larimer's venture soon fell on hard times. Six years after its founding, the entire city of Denver burned to the ground. The next year, after the cabins were rebuilt, Cherry Creek flooded and washed away what was left of the city. In a second resurrection of Denver, miners who had struck it rich returned to build grand Victorian mansions and open businesses and factories with their new-found wealth.

Nevertheless, Denver's prospects looked bleak indeed when, in 1870, the Union Pacific chose to lay its transcontinental line through Cheyenne, Wyoming. Determined to avoid becoming an irrelevant backwater, Denver's civic fathers raised money to build a connecting line to Cheyenne, thus saving Denver from oblivion. In the ten years after the building of this critical line of communication to the rest of the world, Denver's population increased from five thousand to thirty-five thousand people.

High rollers now flocked to the Queen City of the Plains — mining tycoon John Campion, cattle baron Dennis Sheedy, and brewer John Good. New mansions were built on Capitol Hill, and office buildings sprang up in central Denver.

Denver was still to be dealt one final blow. The collapse of the silver market in 1893 brought down Denver's elite and with them the hardworking shopkeepers and workers who toiled in the factories. Oysters were no longer served at Mr. Pell's restaurant, and the champagne dried up at Charpiot's.

Yet again, Denver recovered when gold was discovered in Cripple Creek. Like the rough cabins that gave way to magnificent mansions, sin too became more refined. As in Denver's earliest days, one-third of all men over the age of twenty-five had syphilis, but rough and tumble whorehouses evolved into magnificent pleasure palaces. Dusty wagon ruts were transformed into lush boulevards, trees were planted with irrigation from Cherry Creek, and empty tracts were replaced with parks, flower gardens, and fountains by Denver's energetic mayor, Robert Speer.

Several newspapers survived the competition — most notably the *Rocky Mountain News,* started in an attic in 1859, and *The Denver Post,* purchased by F.G. Bonfils in 1895 and turned in to a flagship of yellow journalism, which loudly proclaimed its banners: "No good shall lack a champion" and "Evil shall not thrive unopposed."

By 1890, Denver was the third largest city in the West, bigger than the cities of Washington, D.C., Kansas City, St. Paul, and Minneapolis. Women outnumbered men — a far cry from Denver's earliest days in which men outnumbered women seven to one — and the wealthy from around the world flocked to the Queen City to find relief in the dry climate from such ailments as asthma, emphysema, and the scourge of day, tuberculosis. Many of these newcomers stayed to carve out a new life and add to the business and cultural life of the city.

Culturally, the railroads cast Denver as two cities — Auraria in the west, which became a city of railroad men, complete with hundreds of saloons, breweries, mills, and flourishing parlor houses, and Curtis Park, to which Denver's more refined citizens commuted along the newly built street railroads (later called trolleys). These same trolleys later supported even more fashionable neighborhoods in the prairie to the west and north, which resisted the expansion of the saloons and passed local dry ordinances. Only to the south did saloons continue to flourish, prospering with the extension of the South Broadway streetcar carrying customers to Pop Wyman's Roadhouse, Fiske's Beer Garden, the Cottage Grove Dance Hall, and the Overland Park Racetrack.

By 1911, Denver's core of Auraria and South Denver, saturated with saloons, taverns, and dance halls, was surrounded by dry and more refined suburbs. Denver itself now had more than five hundred saloons, more saloons per capita than Boston, Baltimore, St. Louis, or even New Orleans. Saloons even took over the stately mansions of the city's elite, who moved to such newly fashionable neighborhoods as Cheesman Park and Capitol Hill. The Williams Daniel mansion at 1422 Curtis was remodeled as the Inter-Ocean Club, and the Tremont Boarding School on Broadway became the lavish though notorious Navarre Saloon, to which high-society customers gained entrance through a secret tunnel from the Brown Palace Hotel. Most infamous of all was the California Hall, across from city hall, which was finally closed for "allowing immoral, vulgar and blasphemous females to assemble in said place for the purpose of attracting customers."

In 1902, Governor Peabody led his "crusade against depravity," sending agents to the pleasure palaces and saloons. Results of his intense campaign and investigation revealed "bums, dirty and disreputable in appearance and with bloated faces." Most shocking, according to the final report, was the sight of "a drunken white woman being drug into the wine rooms by (African-Americans), all using the most vile and obscene language." It was alleged that young boys were the victims of "unnatural" and "unspeakable crimes not to be named among Christians."

Such campaigns against sin were firmly resisted by organized labor. Bill Haywood, editor of *Miners Magazine,* called the crackdown on saloons a capitalist plot to maximize "profits through greater physical efficiency and endurance on the part of the slaves." A letter to the magazine asserted that the saloons were essential to the survival of the working man "because it supplies a want — a need. It offers a common meeting place. It dispenses good cheer. It ministers to the craving for fellowship. To the exhausted, worn out body, to the strained nerves — the relaxation brings rest."

It was not until 1886 that Denver was incorporated as a self-governing municipality. James Flemming, an oilman turned mining magnate, contributed his mansion at 1520 South Grant Street as a city hall, which was convenient because he also served three terms as Denver's mayor. By 1911, many of these more refined neighborhoods, including Park Hill, Highlands, Globeville, and Valverde, had been annexed to Denver. Park Hill had been platted by a transplanted aristocrat from Germany named Baron von Winckler.

Not to be outdone, Baron von Richthofen, a close friend and fellow aristocrat, decided to establish his own empire farther to the east on a prairie plat he called Montclair. According to his prospectus for the new town, Montclair was destined to be the most "beautiful suburban town of Denver," with "as pure a moral atmosphere and one as beneficial to society as the bracing air of Colorado. Montclair will be a club of families of congenial tastes united for the purpose of excluding all that might destroy their peace or offend their better tastes."

In 1886, Baron von Richthofen built a castle in the middle of his empire, the then empty prairie subdivision of Montclair. The castle's central feature was a tower, on which was carved in red sandstone the bust of Frederick Barbarossa, the legendary medieval Holy Roman Emperor. Below the bust was the Richthoven coat of arms — two lions placing a crown on a judge's head.

In 1903, Edwin B. Hendrie, the son of the founder of Hendrie and Bolthoff Manufacturing Company, bought the castle and grounds and spent more than two hundred thousand dollars to remodel it with stones from the Castle Rock quarry that he reopened for the purpose of matching the castle's rhyolite stone.

In 1910, Hendrie's son-in-law, William H. Grant, moved into the castle. One year after Grant moved in, there occurred at his front gates an event so extraordinary, a crime so notorious that it shattered the illusions of a city, a nation, and an era.

2

"Frenzied Mob Struggles to Get Into Court, and Women Have Teeth Trampled Out and Clothing Torn From Bodies in Wild Riot."

"Hundreds Jam West Side Court to Catch Glimpse of Beautiful Slayer."

(Headlines from *Rocky Mountain News,* November 20-21, 1911)

Those spectators who fought and bled to get into the courtroom to gaze upon this slight, blue-clad, beautiful defendant were peevish at being cheated of a moment's morbid pleasure. Yesterday, the craze of the curious railbirds reached a fever heat. One woman, in fighting her way for admission was struck in the mouth and several teeth knocked out. In spite of her protests that she wanted to get in, an ambulance was called, and she was taken to city hall to be treated. Another woman, whose hair, false and otherwise, was torn from her head, whose clothing was torn, and who was so badly mauled that it was thought she was seriously injured, was so persistent that she was finally escorted to a good seat.

"Any woman who is so crazy as you are to see this trial," said the bailiff, "can get in."

(*Rocky Mountain News,* November 21, 1911)

The riot at the Denver West Side Criminal Court began at 9:45 a.m. when the bailiff opened the back door of the court. In the face of the surging crowd, the bailiff pleaded for order.

"Ladies and gentlemen, if you do not step back, no spectators will be allowed in the courtroom! Now you must line up in an orderly fashion!"

Gertrude Patterson on her way to court on the first day of her trial, November 23, 1911. (Denver Post, November 24, 1911)

An eager crowd awaits admission to the Patterson murder trial. (Denver Post, November 24, 1911)

As the throng continued to push forward, two deputy sheriffs blocked the entrance and began to push the crowd back. It was twenty minutes before the crowd began to form a semblance of a line.

Deputy Sheriff George McLachman bellowed into his megaphone: "The Judge has ordered that anyone who enters the courtroom will not be permitted to leave the building once admitted — until there is a recess!"

Alice Roche, the society columnist for the *Rocky Mountain News,* scribbled her notes for the next edition: "The curious belong to no particular class. There are clubwomen who have pledged their moral support to the defendant, and plain, everyday housewives who haven't had anything in months to disturb the monotonous tenor of their cramped lives."

There was also a contingent of young men who had come to feel their hearts skip a beat at the sight of the beautiful prisoner. A group of nine University of Denver law students, more than half the entire student body, had been invited to observe the trial as an academic exercise. They waited patiently for admission.

There was a sudden hush as the prisoner approached the entrance, accompanied by her attorney, O.N. Hilton, and Deputy Sheriff George McLachman. In awe, the crowd hushed and opened a path.

Alice Roche pushed her way to the front to get a better view of the prisoner and feverishly scribbled her description of the defendant in her pocket notebook:

She wore a suit of dark blue, nicely tailored and giving sinuous, willowy lines to her slender figure, harmonized with the toque of dark blue velvet relieved in front by a touch of Persian trimming. Her tiny, patrician feet were encased in black suede shoes with slender spooled heels. She wore no veil. Her hands were ungloved, and the slender, long artistic fingers, lifted every now and then to the table beside which she sat, had a mute appeal in them.

Four weeks before, a Denver coroner's jury had signed the following verdict: "We, the jury, find that said Charles A. Patterson came to his death in front of the Richthofen Castle at 7020 East Twelfth Avenue, in the City and County of Denver, State of Colorado on September 27, 1911, about 10:25 a.m. from result of a gunshot wound through the heart, and was fired by his wife, Mrs. Gertrude Gibson Patterson, with felonious intent."

The *Rocky Mountain News* headlines the next day reported the verdict:

"Slew Sick Husband As He Writhed on Ground Crying 'Oh, My God.'"

"While Consumptive Struggled to Regain Feet Beautiful Wife Fired Final Bullet Through Heart."

"Mrs. Patterson, She of the 'Ruinous Face,' Shot Her Husband Twice in the Back."

Dr. Harry C. Brown had testified at the inquest that "both shots which had entered Patterson's body had gone through the back." The victim, Charles Patterson, a once robust football player, had been severely ill with tuberculosis at the time of the shooting and weighed no more than 112 pounds.

An eyewitness to the shooting, Charles E. Logston, had testified that he was driving a grocery wagon at Eleventh Avenue and Olive Street when the firing took place. "I saw two people bending toward each other and then saw the man fall."

Lawrence Fleckenstein, a motorcycle racer, saw the woman standing over the man after the shots had been fired, crouch down over him, and place a gun under his body.

Adie E. Shugart, who was the first man on the scene, said he saw Gertrude Patterson holding the gun, and heard Charles Patterson crying, "My God! My God!" immediately after being shot. He rushed to where Patterson lay moaning and found a gun hidden under his body.

Louis Schramm, a stableman working at the Richthofen Castle, testified that he first saw the Pattersons together in front of the house. He then returned to his work in the barn and heard four shots. Immediately after he heard the shots, he looked out and saw Mrs. Patterson running through the castle gates toward the house screaming that burglars had killed her husband.

A servant, Mrs. William Shaughnessy, answered the front door and let Mrs. Patterson into the parlor. When Mrs. Shaugnessy asked what happened, Mrs. Patterson answered, "He shot himself." Alma Boding, another servant in the Hendrie household, heard Mrs. Patterson say, "My husband has committed suicide." The household cook, Nora C. Brown, who also came into the parlor, heard Mrs. Patterson say, "My husband shot himself."

The first policeman on the scene, Police Sergeant Joseph McIntyre, testified that "the only feeling Mrs. Patterson showed after the killing was when I told Mrs. Patterson that I would have to take her to the police station. 'Oh, for God's sake, don't take me near him,' she told me." Upon further questioning, however, she stated that her husband had brought a pistol with him to their meeting and had threatened her with it, whereupon she

Post *artist re-creation of the shooting of Charles Patterson by his wife, Gertrude on September 27, 1911. (September 29, 1911)*

Denver Post sketch showing Gertrude Patterson and her husband, *Charles; walking to the gates of the Richthofen Castle where Gertrude is depicted shooting her husband after an argument on September 27, 1911 at 10:25 A.M. (Sept. 29, 1911)*

had grabbed it away from him and in the struggle had accidentally shot him. When confronted with evidence that the gun was hers and that she had brought it with her in her pocketbook, she changed her story yet again, admitting that she had done all the shooting but that she had shot him in self-defense because he had been abusing her.

Gertrude Patterson did not appear at the inquest on the advice of counsel and received the news of the coroner's verdict without emotion. "I wonder how long it will be before they try me," she responded calmly.

Several days after the coroner's jury verdict, information was filed against her, charging her with first-degree murder and seeking the penalty of death by hanging. She was removed to the county jail, which adjoined the Denver West Side Court House.

At the county jail, she was immediately taken under the wing of the jail's matron, who, apparently taken with the fair-faced ingenue, installed Gertrude in her own spacious and secluded cell away from the other inmates. She permitted Gertrude to bring several trunks containing her extensive wardrobe to her cell, as well as several items of comfortable furniture, a blue-enameled bathtub with gold fixtures, and a large vanity mirror. Curtains were hung over Gertrude's cell bars to ensure that she could dress and bathe in complete privacy. Special arrangements were made for gourmet meals to be brought over from the Brown Palace Hotel, and a hairdresser was permitted to visit every morning to fix Gertrude's hair and attend her toilet. When Louise Scher, a reporter for *The Denver Post* went to the jail on October 7 to interview Gertrude, she first met with Gertrude's sympathetic matron.

"Poor soul," said the matron to Louise Scher in the reception room, "she doesn't look as though she could harm a kitten, much less a man — she's so sweet looking."

Louise Scher was the first to be granted an interview with Gertrude. Although the interview lasted over three hours, Louise's full-page story in the following day's *Denver Post* focused on Gertrude's fashionable appearance:

> Gertrude Gibson Patterson, beautiful as a Brinkley girl and as lithe and willowy, with dark brown eyes and pale brown hair, her face white, with only the red of her Cupid's bow mouth to relive the paleness, sits and stares at the gray surroundings of the county jail in the women's ward, and wonders about the things to come. On her head she wore a smart tailored hat of white and coronation blue, the new Kurzman shape, with a band of black fur and a bit of silver trimming. Her suit was plain dark blue serge, heavily braided with black. Her tiny shoes and gloves were of black suede. Over her hat and face was draped a large widow's veil of black.
>
> Her large brown eyes were heavily fringed with lashes. It was during the matron's absence that I had a splendid opportunity to study Mrs. Patterson. In her room are a leather couch, a small table, two pictures, and a looking glass. For a few minutes she sat and carelessly rocked back and forth in her chair, glanced about the room and then down at some books which she brought with her. There were two. She chose the Ballad of Reading Gaol, opened the book, read for a second, and then got up and walked to the looking glass. She stood and gazed long at herself, then thrust back a wisp of her hair which peeped below her hat. She just stood and studied her own pretty face for some time.
>
> 'Is it true' I asked, 'that Mr. Strouss is on his way from Chicago to aid you in this trouble?' For about three seconds her gaze never faltered from mine, then in the sweet, soft voice of a gentlewoman, she answered me. 'It's just as false as it can be. I haven't seen Mr. Strouss in — let me see,' and here she brushed the back of her hands before her eyes and thought, 'It will be just three years in February, I saw him in Chicago. I do so hate to talk of this thing.'

Louise Scher's article merely whetted the appetite of Denverites who could now not get enough details about Gertrude Gibson Patterson. With little actual news between the time of the coroner's verdict and the first day of the trial, the columnists took over the front pages with their impressions, predictions, and endless interviews with anyone even remotely connected with the case. After the spectacle of the women who had their "teeth trampled out and clothing torn from their bodies in wild riot," Denverites began to choose up sides, and reactions were furious.

On November 23, Mrs. R. K. Blyles, President of the woman's Christian Temperance Union, submitted the following resolution to *The Daily News:*

> *Whereas a particularly vulgar and revolting murder trial is now in progress in our criminal court; therefore be it resolved that:*
>
> *The W.T.C.U requests the newspapers of this city to refrain from publishing the details of this trial.*

To the *Rocky Mountain News* was sent the following demand:

> *The board of the Denver circle of the Colorado Congress of Mothers, realizing the influence of the press*

One of the many newspaper photographs of Gertrude Patterson which were splashed on the front page of the Denver newspaper before, during, and after Gertrude's notorious murder trial. Interior stories about Gertrude rhapsodized about her beauty, and columnists gave running commentaries on everything from Gertrude's fashionable clothes and hats to obsdervations of her physical characteristics, including her eyes, ears, nose, hands, and feet. (Denver Post, November, 1911)

*upon the child, the home, and the community at large
protests against the publicity given to the vulgar details
of the Patterson murder trial now before the courts of
Denver, and earnestly beseeches it to curtail such reports
and pictures.*

Mrs. Fred Dick, President

The Sunday *News* published on its front page a poem by R.J. Riley
entitled "A Woman Who Dealt Out Death." Whatever the poem lacked in
literary merit, it more than made up for in the inflaming of passions:

*Call out to the open spaces, and summon the Furies from
Hell,
Give to their eager vision a sight they shall love full well.
A great and majestic city stands waiting with bated breath
To Watch the passing of one who slew —*
A Woman who dealt out death.

*What watered blood runs through its veins, that all can
stand aside,
To watch a blood-stained woman pass in strange mis-
shapen pride;
Weaving around her every act, and through each broken
sigh,
A garbled story of grim romance —*
With every word a Lie.

*Call out to the Gods of Laughter, for nothing can please
them more,
Than watching these crowds of women that surge around
the courtroom door,
Perhaps to show their virtue, as such only can be shown,
By whispered comments as She goes by —*
The woman whose sins are known.

*Surely the vultures have bred this tribe. Their souls are lit-
tle and mean,
They camp themselves in the open court to listen with
minds obscene.
But as they drench themselves anew in one pale Woman's
shame,
Far down in Hell the 'Devils laugh —*
And note down every name.

3

"Accused Beauty Send Luring Glances At Men in Jury Box."

"Drama of Sex Staged in Gloomy Court Where Gertrude Patterson Battles With Only Weapon She Possesses."

"Woman of the Ruinous Face Appears Not to Realize Gravity of Murder Charge Against Her."

"Mrs. Patterson Gay at Trial as any Matinee Girl."

"Jail Her Till Her Beauty's Gone — Boy's Mother."

"'Put Mrs. Patterson Where Her Poisonous Beauty Can't Ruin Others, Parent of Her Victim Asks."

"Mrs. Patterson, Beside Mourning Parent, Laughs."

(Headlines, *Rocky Mountain News,* November 11-21, 1911)

The psychology of beauty is the subject now open for study in the West Side Court. The jury is being selected, and already that subtle thing, feminine charm, is sending its sex waves vibrating across the courtroom. That ineradicable thing, wom-

anly beauty — a beauty that lures and gains its ultimate desire — is on one side of the counsel table and the waves emanate from a pair of woman's eyes that look softly, sweetly, appealingly, significantly, invitingly, understandingly into those of the men in the jury box.

An irreverent reporter suggested to Prosecutor Benson yesterday afternoon about the twelve people who are to decide the fate of Gertrude Patterson had been chosen that if he desired a conviction he would have to put blinders on the jury. The remark merely shows how thoroughly the element of feminine beauty enters into the trying of a murder case and how irradicable it is regarded. The jury in the Patterson case is composed of young men. One here is the brother-in-law of a budding newspaper writer whose sympathies have been strongly aroused by the sight of a young and beautiful woman in a tragic role. Prosecutor Benson, however, appears to have no regard for this fact, as he believes an intelligent jury of thinking men has been secured. Mrs. Patterson, her exquisitely molded profile outlined against the green paneling of the court wall, as pure, as appealing as in Ingres painting, shot luring glances into the faces of the talesmen. The light that lies in woman's eyes will illuminate the West Side Court this week, gloomy as the atmosphere in this murder trial may be.

With all due respect to the legal talent that will be displayed in the Patterson case, there is the feeling that the real struggle, the real battle will be fought by this slight, slender woman with the flower-like face. There is no law on earth that can prevent the most strong-minded and honorable man from feeling the appealing charm of beauty.

There is not the slightest insinuation against the integrity of the twelve men in the jury box, but there is a more subtle power than argument and evidence at work in the West Side Court. It is the charm of feminine beauty — a charm that in big murder trials has often amounted to a spell. Whether or not it will gain its end in this court depends entirely upon the men in the jury box and the counteracting influence of the prosecutor, who will endeavor to tear aside this exquisite mask of superficial loveliness and lay bare the soul beneath.

(Alice Roche, *Daily News*, November 11, 1911)

As the spectators, lawyers, and potential jurors awaited the entry of Judge Allen, Gertrude Patterson appeared to be the most unconcerned person in the courtroom. Sitting comfortably in a large leather armchair that had been provided for her, she chatted amiably with Deputy Sheriff George McLachman who sat beside her, attentively filling her glass of water and replenishing her pitcher.

In the third row of spectators, Alice Roche recorded her observation of the defendant as one who had the "air of a woman attending an entertainment, conscious that she is smartly dressed and well groomed."

Minutes before Judge Allen entered, a small drama unfolded in the courtroom. An elderly woman, veiled and dressed in black, entered the courtroom, walked slowly down the aisle, and took a seat directly opposite Gertrude. A whisper went around the reporter's table: "It is the mother of the dead man."

Alice Roche, who was sitting in the third row of spectators, recorded her observation in her notes:

> *It was a moment when one could expect even this emotionless woman of the delicate beauty and the remarkable nerve to show just a faint sign of feeling, whether it was surprise, or shock or interest. But Gertrude Gibson Patterson gave the mother of the man she had murdered a cold calm look. Then she turned away and then again she looked at the little black-clad figure sitting opposite her, a silent protest and reminder of the one whose soul had been sent into eternity on the morning of September 25. Several times Gertrude Patterson looked calmly, coldly, but with no emotion whenever upon that figure clad in black. Later, while that other woman sat, a figure of grief in front of her, she laughed in sheer amusement at some of the answers given by the jurors on voir dire.*

But Horace G. Benson, the prosecutor assigned to the Gertrude Gibson Patterson capital murder trial, had a problem. Determined to seek the death penalty, he faced the task of seating a jury willing to inflict death on the fair-faced ingenue in the dock.

During voir dire, (the questioning of potential jurors), both Mrs. Patterson's attorney, O.N. Hilton, and the prosecutor, Horace Benson, questioned jurors closely as to whether they had formed an opinion about the guilt or innocence of the defendant.

When potential juror Phillip J. Leavitt was called to the stand to be questioned, Benson asked if he had any opinion about the defendant's guilt.

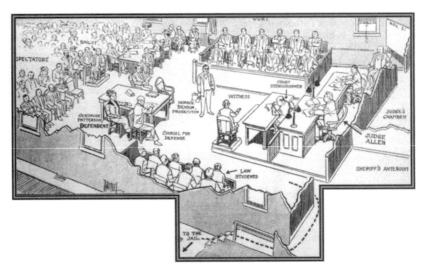

Daily News *sketch of the courtroom in the Patterson murder trial.*
University of Denver Law School students, who observed the trial as
an academic exercise, are seated as a group (shown seated at the
bottom middle of the diagram). (November 24, 1911)

"Yes, I have," Leavitt said, "but it is purely superficial."

In the end, only six of the twelve men seated in the jury box had declared that they could impose the death penalty upon a woman. The others had simply not been asked.

These twelve chosen jurors were described by *The Daily News* as "clean-looking, intelligent-appearing business men and from the standpoint of the business world are representative: two real estate men, two grocers, two mining engineers, two manufacturers, an assayer, a hat dealer, a clerk, a fruit dealer, and a salesman who on voir dire had given his name as F.S. Perry.

Gertrude glanced at all the men in the box. She caught the eye of F.S. Perry as he was casting a furtive glance at her silk-clad ankles. Red-faced, he quickly looked away when she returned his smile.

It was a sunny, crisp November morning, and the sun's rays filled the usually gloomy West Side Courtroom with an eerie, luminous glow. As they did so, she of the "Ruinous Face" — that is, a face so beautiful that it seduced, enslaved, and ruined men — retreated inwardly from the nervous commotion and activity which surrounded her, fixed her gaze on the window through which came the glow, and became lost in her thoughts of the long road that had taken her to this place.

4

"When a girl leaves her home at eighteen, she does one of two things. Either she falls into saving hands and becomes better, or she rapidly assumes the cosmopolitan standard of virtue and becomes worse."

Theodore Dreiser, *Sister Carrie* (1899)

Twelve Years Before
June 27, 1899

G ertrude Gibson ignored the furtive glance from the young man in the brown Jaeger suit who was seated across the aisle from her in the second-class rail car, curled herself tightly against the window, and gazed serenely at the crimson sunset dipping into the passing amber fields of Illinois farmland.

She had been to Chicago once, five years before when she was only thirteen. Even then she had longed to leave her home in Sandoval, Illinois, where her father was a mining engineer. Her family had not been exactly poor, but neither had there been many refinements in her life — indeed, none as she saw it. She lived with her parents, James and Jane Gibson, and younger brother in a modest wooden house near the coal mines. The year before, her sister Evelyn had married and gone to live in St. Louis. Every morning Gertrude awoke to the whistles of the mines and watched the miners, their hard, lined faces permanently blackened from coal dust, bent over from years of bone-cracking labor, trudging along the dirt path by the house on their way to the pits. Although she had been to Chicago once before, she had not seen it. She had only gotten as far as the station at the mouth of the Chicago River near the Great Prairie Exchange before she and the young man with whom she had eloped, a saloon keeper named Link (she didn't even remember his last name) had been intercepted by the sheriff. Even before she had arrived, her father, James Gibson, had telegraphed the sheriff, who promptly escorted Gertrude and Link back to Sandoval. From then on, her father had almost literally kept her under lock and key.

Nor had the aborted elopement been Gertrude's first scrape. Two weeks before her elopement, she had been expelled from her school at the request of her teacher for having been caught in a closet with a lustful male adolescent. The boy had been given only a private reprimand because he was considered to be the innocent victim of Gertrude's shameless allure. It was feared that other boys too would not be able to resist her physical attractions, and the only solution was to remove her entirely from the presence of the opposite sex. So it was she who had been suspended, humiliated, and sent home to spend her time studying her lessons alone, babysitting her younger brother, and doing chores.

The elopement had been her intended means of escape from the drudgery and isolation that seemed to have no end. Link had seen her walk every day by the saloon on Main Street on the way to school. He would come out to flirt with her, flatter her, carry her books, and give her little trinkets. At seventeen, he too had few prospects — not that the other boys who followed her had any better, but Link was a handsome and robust creature in his own right. Nevertheless, Gertrude paid him little attention until she was cast out from the society of her schoolmates and exiled to her life of dreary isolation at home. By day, she would spend any idle hours reading *Cosmopolitan* and *Ladies Home Journal,* poring over the pictures of the fashionable young urban women in their afternoon dresses of the new S-curve fashion, the silk crepe-de-chine skirts with high-waisted swath bodice and transparent sleeves of thin silk decorated with embroidered braid and gold thread, court-style shoes of glaćé kid, brocades, and soft leathers, and most of all the new Watteau style hats of lace and tulle. By night she would sneak out of her bedroom window and see Link. When it became apparent that he would do anything for her, Gertrude made him an irresistible offer. If he would take her far away from the mud pits of Sandoval to Chicago, the city of her dreams, the city of bright new electric lights, night life, shopping, excitement — then she would be his. She nursed no illusions about his prospects, but he was a fine specimen of a male, and she knew life must be taken in steps. The first and biggest step was to get to Chicago.

As the last of the sunset disappeared from view, Gertrude sat back and gazed up at the rail car's ceiling, thinking wistfully of that first aborted attempt five years before to free herself from the stifling bonds of her small town life. This time would be different. There would be no sheriff at the station to put her back on the train to Sandoval. She was going to Chicago with the blessing of her father, who saw in his beautiful eighteen-year-old daughter one who could never be happy living near the mudpits. Having no desire for her to remain in an unhappy state, he reached an accommodation with her shortly after she had been returned: If she would stay at home until she was eighteen, help care for her brother, and assist her mother with household chores, he would give her twenty-five dollars, a train ticket to Chicago, and assist her in finding a situation there.

She had agreed, with resignation, to defer her adventure in life, recognizing the folly of her elopement and the hopelessness of leaving Sandoval without her father's approval. Over the past few years, her father had even sent her on several excursions to St. Louis to visit her sister Evelyn and had recently given Gertrude pocket money to buy a new hat. When Gertrude turned eighteen, he had lived up to his part of the bargain in most respects. He had supplied her with twenty-five crisp one-dollar bills, a second-class rail ticket to Chicago, and a contact with whom she could stay, at least for a time. The contact was a young woman named Bonnie Lipshutz, whom Evelyn had known briefly in St. Louis. Bonnie had left St. Louis for Chicago several months before with her fiancé who had gotten a job with the Pullman Company. Evelyn's father had tried to do better, as he knew little about Bonnie, and Evelyn could tell her father little about her because she had only known the woman for a short time. He had also been unable to find a position for Gertrude in Chicago (his contacts being primarily in the mining industry), and the job market was difficult in the aftermath of a recent depression. Evelyn had suggested to her father one potential employment contact that her sister might pursue in a pinch — a Mr. Emil Strouss, who had met Gertrude at an art gallery opening to which Evelyn had taken Gertrude during her last visit to St. Louis. Evelyn had described Strouss to her father as a tall, dark, prematurely balding man in his mid-thirties (though he looked older), who had made a fortune in the clothing manufacturing business. Strouss had followed Gertrude around the art gallery like a lap dog, intruding awkwardly into conversations between the two sisters and their friends, and had obviously been quite taken with Gertrude — a display which Cynthia, one of Evelyn's closest friends, had later confided appeared quite disgusting. In Evelyn's presence, Strouss had practically begged Gertrude to look him up if she ever came to Chicago. Unfortunately, Strouss was not attractive or even charming, and he had made little impression upon Gertrude. Evelyn had only recently heard that Strouss was very wealthy, and it had not occurred to her to mention this fact to Gertrude. Understandably, their father had not been impressed with this description of an older man, despite the man's alleged wealth, whom he assumed was lecherous and uncouth — not the type to whom his youngest daughter should be beholden even in a pinch.

"You know how pretty little sister is," Evelyn had written to her father, "and I've always been so envious of her. But if she insists on going to Chicago, she will surely be preyed upon if she is not protected. You must alert her to all the dangers that await her there. Please, Father, help her understand, for you know how much I love my little Gertie."

Gertrude sat up, wondering what time it was and how long it would be before she arrived at the station. She considered asking the time of the young man across the aisle, as she noticed a gold watch chain hanging from the side pocket of his Jaeger suit. She thought better of it, remembering her father's last words to her: "Do not talk to strangers, especially men. They have only one thing on their mind, and they will try every trick, every contrivance, and all manner of flattery, to gain your confidence. Don't be taken in by them, or your adventure, sweet daughter, will end badly. Find a good Methodist church, meet the right people — God-fearing people who will not lead you astray but will have your best interests at heart. Know that your mother and I will always be here, and you can always come home. Will you promise?" Gertrude, feeling a tenderness she had never felt before for her father and holding back real tears, had nodded and kissed him on the cheek. Somehow it had been so much harder to leave home this time than five years before when she had wanted only to escape both her home and parents. Now she felt a deep sinking in her stomach, and she was not yet on the train.

It can't be more than an hour before the train arrives, she thought to herself. She opened her well-worn leather purse and took out a small mirror. Nothing gave her more confidence or pleasure than looking at her reflection — the big brown eyes with thick dark lashes, the perfectly turned nose, the naturally red lips, the cameo complexion which she had nurtured every morning and night with cream for the past five years. She was just as pretty as the fashionable women in the magazines — no prettier, she thought. But they had one thing she had always lacked — fine, fashionable clothes, gowns of lace and silk embroidery, the latest pointed shoes with waisted heels with a bar across the top and closed with a button, the new colored stockings of artificial silk made by such fashion houses as Courtaulds, and the new Juliet caps decorated with beads and pearls.

There was another reason she could not ask the young fashionably dressed young man for the time. She was ashamed of how she was dressed — in a plain and well-worn long black woolen skirt; a graying though clean and meticulously pressed shirtwaist; a light wool jacket; and lace boots, which, though laboriously shined and tightly laced, could not hide the heel ground down from years of walking through the mud and dust of Sandoval.

Gertrude was ashamed, and ashamed that she was ashamed. She put away her mirror, pursed her lips, and felt one tear roll down her cheeks. Then, she wiggled her nose in response to a strange, distinctly unpleasant sensation. At first, she didn't realize what it was. A few minutes later she knew it was a smell — not just a smell, but a stench, a sickening odor viler than she had ever endured living near the mudpits. Instinctively she opened her purse and almost frantically began searching for her handkerchief. Then she realized she had packed it in her satchel that now rested on the overhead.

"May I offer you a handkerchief?" said the pleasant male voice from the other side of the aisle. The young brown-haired man in the Jaeger suit produced a large, pristinely white and neatly pressed handkerchief and held it out to her.Gertrude looked at him and hesitated, but she took it and held it tightly over her nose and mouth. "We're just coming to the stockyards," he said matter-of-factly. "Pretty strong if you're not used to it." Gertrude gasped. "Thank you," she said. "What is that smell? Surely it isn't just from cattle and pigs." The man smiled sympathetically. "I guess you don't want to know, Miss. It's not something that should be described to a pretty young lady like yourself."

Gertrude ignored the compliment and looked out the window, but it was too dark to see anything. "How much longer before we . . . "

"Get to Chicago? Or get away from this exquisite aroma?" he said with a grin.

Gertrude laughed, and peered over the handkerchief that she still held to her face. "Both, I suppose."

"We're about six miles from the station now, so we should be there in about ten or fifteen minutes. We're going by the processing plant buildings now, so we're past the worst of it. It'll be better when we get to the yards proper. Look, you can see the cattle under the arc lamps up ahead." He pointed through Gertrude's window.

Gertrude peered again out the window. As far as she could see there were yards filled with bellowing cattle. The backs of the bellowing cattle glistened in a light rain under the high arc lamps. She wondered why she couldn't remember having this unpleasant experience when she had come to Chicago with Link five years before.

"I've been to Chicago before. It wasn't this bad then," Gertrude said.

"Oh, it's always been this bad, Miss. You probably came in from the south and probably went to the Van Buren Street Station over by the Great Prairie Exchange."

"Where will you be staying in Chicago?" the man asked, hoping to keep the conversation going.

"I'll be staying with a friend of my sister. She's to meet me at the station."

"Will you be seeking a position in Chicago?"

Gertrude hesitated, concerned that she might be giving out too much information to a complete stranger, but he seemed pleasant and presentable enough, even prosperous. Besides, who was she to be standoffish, given that it was she who was so obviously down in the heel.

"I hope to get a position at Marshall Field's Department Store. I hear it's a wonderful store," Gertrude finally said.

"Yes, it's quite a store, although you know they hate it when you call them a department store. They insist that they are a dry goods store. It has a magnificent collection of top-flight merchandise — the best. It's far surpassed the Boston Store in recent years, which has really gone down hill if I may say so. You're quite right to seek a position at Marshall Field's. You know what they say here."

"No, I don't."

"You know, the ditty 'All the girls who wear high heels, they trade down at Marshall Field's. All the girls who scrub the floor, they trade at the Boston Store.'"

"My friend works at the Boston Store," Gertrude said, not amused, and aware that it might end the conversation.

Undaunted, the man, who had hoped to compliment Gertrude for her good taste but now had unintentionally insulted Gertrude's friend, pressed onward.

"Let me give you my card," he said hopefully, taking out an embossed card from a gold cardholder and handing it to Gertrude. "The job market is quite difficult now in Chicago, I'm afraid; you know, the recent financial panic. It's very hard to land any kind of a decent position unless you know someone. But you know someone now if you'd ever like to work for my company."

Gertrude took the card and examined it closely. "Armour and Company, Mr. Nelson Mayweather, Assistant Accounts Officer."

She looked up at Mayweather. "You mean, you — "

Mayweather smiled sheepishly. "Yes, I'm afraid so. I work for the stockyards. But not in the meatpacking end of the business, I assure you. The accounting office is on the other side of the stockyards, and the aroma isn't bad at all there. My department is just like any accounting office in downtown Chicago. We keep all the records for the company, which is doing quite well now I should say."

Gertrude was appalled by the idea of ever working anywhere near the stockyards.

"Gertrude Gibson," she said, handing back the card. "I don't think I should like to work in that business at all, but thank you."

"No please, keep it," Mayweather said, holding up his hand. "If the position at Marshall Field's doesn't work out, perhaps you might reconsider. Marshall Field's is a pleasant place to work, but shop girls get only three dollars a week there, hardly enough for any young woman to live on. In my department, we pay our girl clerks four dollars, which can rise to five dollars after two years."

"And what do the *boy* clerks get?" Gertrude asked.

For a moment young Mr. Mayweather was tongue-tied.

Gertrude put the card into her purse. "We're slowing down. I think we're coming into the station," she said, standing up to get a better view of the lights in the distance.

"Why, yes we are. Early, in fact. I say, may I help you with your grip?"

Again, Gertrude hesitated, but she did think it would be nice not to be heavily laden as she tried to find her way through the station to find Bonnie."

"Very well, thank you," she said, pointing to the brown canvas satchel on the overhead.

Moments later, the train stopped at Grand Central Station. Mayweather, laden with Gertrude's satchel as well as his own, led Gertrude to the car's exit, stepped down, and took her hand to assist her down from the platform.

"I say, if you're not too familiar with the city, I'd be very happy to show you around," Mayweather said, as he accompanied Gertrude down the platform toward the huge glass-and-iron concourse.

Gertrude hardly heard what Mayweather was saying, struck as she was by the tremendous cavern of light she saw ahead and the tumult and crowds milling about the station. Added to the noise from within the station was the thunder of the streets outside, which reverberated and echoed throughout the great vestibule. It was overwhelming, and quite different from what she remembered of the Van Buren Street station some five years before.

Enthralled, Gertrude began looking about. "My friend should be here. But I don't know what she looks like, except she'll be wearing a red coat and holding a sign I think."

After falling behind Gertrude who was walking briskly, Mayweather, breathing heavily, caught up with her.

"You know," he gasped, "there are many things to see here — there's Lakefront Park, the Palmer House, State Street, and they have double-decker steamer rides every evening from the Clark Street Bridge. If you like biking, Lincoln Park has some wonderful paths. I belong to the Viking Bicycle Club, and we have outings every Sunday during the summer. If you like shows and opera, you must go to the Auditorium. Magnificent architecture! The best opera in the world, better than New York and Paris. Do you like Gilbert and Sullivan? I think *The Mikado* is playing there now."

Gertrude, pushing forward, had not heard a word. She was looking about in every direction for Bonnie, concerned now that she might miss her in this vast cavern. Then, at the entrance to the carriage hall she saw a young, petite, blond woman in a red wool coat, holding a paper sign that read: "Gertrude G." Waving madly, she rushed up to the young woman.

"Bonnie? Bonnie Lipshutz?" asked Gertrude excitedly.

"Gertrude Gibson?" responded the woman, throwing down the sign and holding out her arms.

"You've come! You're really here! I can't believe you're here." The two embraced as if they were lifelong friends.

"Evelyn has told me so much about you!" Bonnie gushed. "Little sister! She told me how pretty you were, and you are! You know I'm to take good care of you! I do so hate living alone. Oh, it shall be grand having a roommate. There are ever so many things we can do together. I'm so excited! Little sister Gertrude!"

Suddenly remembering Mayweather who was standing patiently nearby with the bags, Gertrude turned to introduce him to Bonnie.

"This is Mr . . . " But she had already forgotten his name.

"Mr. Nelson Mayweather," he said, holding out his hand to Bonnie. "Well, I see you have found Miss Gibson, and she is quite the enchanting fellow traveler, I must say. Had a bit of difficulty as we passed the stockyards, though. I say, would you care to share a hansom?"

Both women looked at each other dubiously, not sure of how the other might respond. Bonnie hesitated because she knew the cost of a hansom and doubted if the prosperous looking man lived in the same neighborhood as she. Gertrude too said nothing as she was beginning to resent Mayweather's intrusion and thought it quite enough to get to know one stranger at a time — though Bonnie, being her sister's acquaintance, was not strictly a stranger.

"I thank you, Mr. Mayweather," Gertrude finally said, "but I think it best that my friend and I get settled together. You were quite kind to help me with my bag."

"Is there a place I might call upon you later, that I might inquire if you need further assistance in the city?"

Again, Bonnie and Gertrude looked at each other warily, both hesitating to give out Bonnie's address to a stranger, pleasant though he appeared to be.

"I have your card and telephone number," Gertrude finally said. "Perhaps we shall need assistance, and I might call upon you."

Trying to hide his dejection, Mayweather bowed. "Very well. Please do not hesitate to call upon me if you wish any help with a position, or if I can be of any service."

Mayweather turned and walked away, thinking he had been so close. It was not every day that one came upon a woman so pleasing to look upon as Gertrude, and now he doubted whether he would ever see her again. An image of her in a lavish low-cut gown, bedecked in glittering jewels, and himself dancing with her in the grand ballroom of the Auditorium flashed across his mind. He was now convinced that the ditty about the Boston Store had done him in. So close, he thought.

"This way," Bonnie said after Mayweather had taken his leave.

She pointed toward three great alabaster arches that led out to Harrison Street. Gertrude had been hoping that Bonnie would take her into the glittering carriage court where they might get their own two-horse hack, but she did not inquire as to what transportation arrangements Bonnie had made. As the two walked through the middle arch, the chaos suddenly became overwhelming — the racket of the streets, the cacophony of the clatter of iron-shod horses and the shrill shouts of their drivers, the clang of gongs, and the distant bells of a fire wagon. Amazed, Gertrude looked up at the tall buildings about her and saw the clock tower looming above her.

"Oh, watch out!" Bonnie cried.

In front of them in the gutter was a putrid dead horse, its open eyes gazing upward. Gertrude had almost tripped over it as she was looking up at the clock tower. Pedestrians were walking around the decaying carcass as though it was nothing unusual, and indeed it was not. More than ten thousand horses died on Chicago's streets in 1899, and it was sometimes several days or even a week before the hard-pressed sanitation crews in municipal carts came to pick up the overworked and often abused animals who collapsed under the horsewhip in the middle of the streets. Horse manure too was thick on Harrison Street, filling the gutters in its liquid form with a foul brown stream and in its pulverized form blowing into the faces of pedestrians and riders alike. The aroma was only mildly less pungent than that which surrounded the stockyards.

"Oh, oh!" cried Gertrude in shock at the sight, instinctively pulling up her long skirt.

Just then an electric streetcar came careening by at a speed of twenty miles an hour, far faster than the cable cars of a few years before which had never exceeded nine miles an hour. In horror, Gertrude watched in amazement as the streetcar slowed only slightly for an omnibus that lay astride its tracks at an angle. The omnibus could move neither forward nor backward, hedged in by carriages in all directions. The streetcar, its conductor outraged by the trespass on its tracks, slowed only enough to make the impact endurable to its own passengers, and then violently pushed the trespassing omnibus out of the way. There were shrieks, shouts, and much commotion, but this incident too was not unusual in a city where there was an average of three deaths a day from encounters with streetcars and railroad cars.

"Look for the car saying 'Maxwell Street,'" Bonnie shouted over the din.

Gertrude hid her disappointment that they were to take one of the hideously overcrowded streetcars. She could see passengers hanging on precariously to the pole on the streetcar's rear platform. She did not see how any of the streetcars she saw passing by could accommodate even one more passenger, let alone the two of them with a bag in tow. As many as eighty passengers were crammed into cars designed to carry no more than thirty — courtesy of the notorious Chicago streetcar tycoon, Charles Tyson Yerkes who explained to his shareholders that "it is the people who hang to the straps who pay you your big dividends."

"There's one coming!" Bonnie shouted over the din as she saw a car approaching from Franklin Street. "Just follow me!"

"Bonnie," Gertrude shouted back, "Couldn't we take one of the . . . "

Bonnie was not listening, but instead had walked fifteen feet past the streetcar stop, the better to beat the crowd waiting to get on the nearing car. With a screech the car stopped, and Bonnie jumped on the rear platform, squeezing her way between a very large man and an elderly woman.

"Hand me your bag!" Bonnie shouted.

Gertrude handed her the bag, which Bonnie shoved between the crowded passengers into the interior of the car.

"Now jump on!" cried Bonnie.

But Gertrude saw no place on the platform on which to jump, and the streetcar was already beginning to lurch forward.

"Here, grab my hand!" shouted a dapper young man clinging to the rear pole. Desperate that the streetcar, along with Bonnie and her bag, might leave her behind, Gertrude grabbed the man's hand. Holding her tightly as she dangled in the air struggling madly to find a footing, the man pulled her aboard.

"Here, move on in," he said, pushing Gertrude through the mass of bodies toward her companion.

"Oh my, oh my," said Gertrude breathlessly.

"It'll take about forty-five minutes to get home," Bonnie said when she saw that Gertrude was safely aboard.

"Where is Maxwell Street?" Gertrude shouted over the noise.

"The South Side," Bonnie said, declining to elaborate further on their destination.

Forty-five minutes later the streetcar came to the end of the line. There were only a handful of other passengers riding in the car by this time, and Bonnie and Gertrude sat together in the front seat of the car.

"We have to walk from here," Bonnie said, leading the way.

Mercer Street was even more chaotic than Harrison Street, but unpaved and lined with run-down pine cottages, saloons, and seedy rooming houses. They saw no dead horses, but at almost every corner there was a dead dog, cat, or rat. The municipal carts came only rarely to Mercer Street, and dead animals often rotted for weeks or even months in the summer heat. The stench was as bad as the stockyards. Unsavory, wraith-like characters walked along the dark, gloomy street.

"Hey, little girlies, what'll two bits git me tonight?" an inebriated man in ragged clothes called out from behind them.

"Just look straight ahead and keep walking," Bonnie whispered grimly to Gertrude. "It's only two more blocks."

They quickened their pace, ignoring the cacophony of catcalls and taking pains to avoid any man standing near a saloon door. Gertrude, now terrified as well as horrified, could only hope that Bonnie's room would be better than the surroundings suggested, but her heart sank when Bonnie took her up the back stairs of a saloon and opened the door to a small room.

There was a single bed, a dresser, one soiled divan, and two well-worn wooden chairs.

"I know it's not much." Bonnie said apologetically. "I hope to be able to move soon uptown. Johnny, my fiancé, lives in a workers' dormitory in the town of Pullman, up north. He's saving his money so we can be married. The company says in another year he'll be eligible to buy one of the company townhouses. This is all I can afford now. I get paid three dollars a week, but the streetcar is five cents each way, so I have only two dollars forty a week after paying carfare."

Gertrude tried to hide her disappointment and shock. She was speechless. "There's only one bed," she finally managed to say.

"Yes, I know. I was going to explain. You see, I thought I would sleep on the floor and you could have the bed. Or maybe you wouldn't mind sharing the bed. Later, I thought you and I could pool our earnings and maybe get a bigger room closer to downtown."

Gertrude put her bag down on the bed and sat down beside it. For the moment all she could think was that living in this hellhole for even a day was out of the question.

"What is the rent here?" Gertrude asked.

"It's a dollar fifty a week, so after carfare and rent, I have only ninety cents a week for food and other necessities. Sometimes Johnny helps me out if I'm in a pinch."

Gertrude sighed, looked around the room, stood up, and gazed out the window at a brawl between two drunks. She suppressed a shudder.

"I have some money," Gertrude said, suddenly realizing that the twenty-five dollars in her purse was now the only thing that stood between her, Mercer Street, and Sandoval. "I think we should go to a hotel tonight. Tomorrow we can look for another room closer to downtown."

"Oh Gertrude, I'm so sorry it's not better. Together we can get a much better room. That's why I'm so thankful you're here. But it's almost midnight now, and the streetcar is shut down now. No hansoms come down here at this time of night, and we can't walk very far. It's only for one night. Tomorrow we can look for another room."

With a sigh, Gertrude slumped down on the divan.

"One night then," she said with resignation, her illusions of life in the big city now shattered. How could Evelyn have been so ignorant of poor Bonnie's plight? What had she and Father been thinking?

"One night, then."

Gertrude wanted to cry.

5

"I was determined not to remain poor."

(Marshall Field, in response to Theodore Dreiser's
question, "What drove you to become successful?")

Gertrude, who had not removed her clothes before falling on the bed
beside Bonnie, slept fitfully.

The early June sun peeking through the window and the bustling
sounds of Mercer Street woke her early. Disoriented at first, Gertrude stood
up and looked in the mirror above the dresser.

"Frightful!" she gasped as she cringed at the sight of her matted hair
and crumpled shirtwaist. "Simply frightful!"

With this, Bonnie awoke, and sat up. "What shall we do now?" she
asked plaintively.

"Pack your things," Gertrude said. We'll go find a better place. You
don't work today, do you?"

"No," said Bonnie. "Today is Sunday, my day off."

Within the hour, Gertrude had hailed one of the few hansoms
cruising Mercer Street on this early Sunday morning. The driver, who had
ventured to Mercer Street only to deliver a passenger, was only too
delighted to procure a respectable customer for the return uptown. He
stopped immediately.

"Can you tell us where is the nearest clean hotel with hot running
water?" Gertrude asked the neatly dressed hansom driver.

"Depends on how much you want to pay, mum" he replied. "The
Bancroft Hotel up near Wolf Point is one I recommend — very clean, good
service, and close in to shopping. Nothing fancy, mind you, but it will still
cost you two dollars a night."

"That will do," Gertrude said. "How much to take us there?"

The driver smiled. "For you two lovely ladies, fifty cents."

Gertrude was not sure if she was being overcharged, but she was in
no mood to haggle. Getting away from Mercer Street was her first priority.

"Can you afford this, and the hotel?" Bonnie whispered to Gertrude
as the two settled in to the comfortable leather seat of the hansom.

"It's just for tonight," Gertrude said. "We'll leave our bags at the hotel and spend the rest of the day looking for a room."

It was a fresh, beautiful summer morning, and Gertrude relaxed, enjoying the breeze in her face as the hansom weaved between the slower carts and wagons. The seedy pine buildings of Mercer Street soon gave way to the paved thoroughfare and stone buildings lining South Water Street.

The hansom drew up to the Bancroft Hotel, a sturdy four-story brick building wedged between South Water Street and River Street near the Kinzie Street Bridge. Moments later Gertrude and Bonnie were soaking up the relative luxury of their new, if temporary, accommodations.

"Look, you can see the cutters and clippers on the river," Bonnie said with excitement as she looked out at the Chicago River clogged with watercraft of a variety of types and sizes.

"Come," said Gertrude. "We must find ourselves a room."

Six hours later the pair had found a third-story flat overlooking Twenty-first Street that delighted them both. It was a small suite of three rooms, including a tiny but tidy living room, a modest, tastefully decorated bedroom furnished with two comfortable single beds and matching maple dressers, and a small kitchen with a gas oven, an eating table, and ample cabinet space. Its lights were gas, however, because none of the flats in this price range had electric lights.

"It's wonderful," Bonnie exclaimed. "But can we afford it?" The rent was four dollars and fifty cents a week, and Gertrude had not yet found a position.

"We shall have to," Gertrude replied, determined not to settle for anything less. "If you can't pay two twenty-five, I will lend you the difference until you can."

"Well," said Bonnie hopefully, "we're ever so much closer to the Loop, and I suppose I could walk to the Boston Store from here, although it might take a half hour. That would save me sixty cents a week in carfare, so I think I could manage two twenty-five if we don't eat much. I'm due to get a raise to three-fifty next month."

"Then it's settled. We shall move in tomorrow, and I shall go to Marshall Field's and secure a position."

In 1899, Marshall Field's was the largest retail dry goods store in the world. Its entrance, the store advertised, was adorned with "monoliths rivaling those in the temple of Karnak." Its twelve stories of polished stone contained no less than fifty-three of the latest Otis elevators, and the store boasted its own hospital, post office, delivery system, and the most modern telephone switchboard in the world. Billed as a "Palace of Desire," with splashing fountains and glittering floor displays lit with electrical lights that rivaled those of the Columbian Exposition, it lived up to its reputation as "the modern woman's paradise."

The store consisted of two mammoth buildings — the older Parisian style building which faced State Street, and a newer building built to complement the Columbian Exposition at the corner of Washington and Wabash.

It was nine o'clock sharp on Monday morning when Gertrude Gibson, fresh as a peach and beaming with excitement and high hopes, appeared at the monoliths of Karnak.

Stepping into the glittering threshold, Gertrude wandered first among the linen handkerchiefs and Parisian-made kid gloves displayed in the handsome mahogany display cabinets. An unctuous sales clerk immediately attached himself to her, extolling the quality of the new imported gloves.

"What is the price?" asked Gertrude, feigning slight interest.

"Twelve dollars fifty, ma'am. The finest gloves made in the world, and I daresay, they would look exquisite on you. Would you like to try a pair on?"

Gertrude smiled, pleased that despite the drab and common clothes she wore, the salesman thought her a potential purchaser of such a luxury item.

"I think I shall wait until fall, when it is cooler," Gertrude said airily.

She had intended to ask where the employment office was, but having been mistaken as a store customer, she was embarrassed to ask. Instead she walked to the adjoining department, in which the latest silk evening gowns from London were displayed. These were the dresses that in her daydreams she had imagined herself wearing. Reluctantly she moved on, avoiding the approaching clerk whom she was sure would recognize her for what she was — a common wage seeker.

Gertrude continued to wander through the massive store, conveniently putting out of her mind, for the time, the unpleasant task she had come to perform — that of presenting herself, a commonly dressed woman with little education and no experience, for a position as a clerk in the world's most fashionable dry goods store.

Having spent the entire day gazing in awe at the variety of luxurious merchandise, she stopped in the restaurant for an ice before she realized that it was only half an hour before closing. She inquired of a clerk in the perfume department where she might find the employment office and was directed to the twelfth floor of the new building.

As she exited the elevator on the twelfth floor she encountered an elderly, well-groomed man in a single-breasted round-cut sack suit sitting behind a desk.

"May I direct you, Miss?" the man asked without looking up from the ledger in which he was busily making entries.

"Do you need any help?" Gertrude asked timidly, losing all the nerve it had taken her to come this far.

"Shop girl?" the man asked, still not looking up.

"Yes, sir," Gertrude replied even more softly.

"Speak up, please!"

"I wish to inquire about a position," Gertrude said, her voice rising but cracking in the middle of her sentence.

The man handed her a form, clipboard and pencil. "Fill this out and wait inside. I don't know if anyone will be able to see you today. The office closes at six thirty."

"Thank you."

Gertrude took the form and entered the waiting room. Inside were eight or nine fashionably dressed young women busily filling out their forms on the clipboards. If these women could afford such clothes, Gertrude wondered, why would they be interested in positions that paid no more than three or four dollars a week? In fact, she was soon to learn, most of these women lived at home and sought employment at Marshall Field's for the glamour and relief from a life of domesticity. Three or four dollars was merely pin money to such women.

As Gertrude sat down, a young woman wearing a waist petticoat of crepe de chine, with a white cotton bosom amplifier and lace and ribbon trimming, looked at her disdainfully.

As she met the woman's gaze, Gertrude wanted nothing more than for a large hole to materialize so that she could fall into it and hide her miserable, manure-soaked frock and three-year-old soiled shirtwaist. Suddenly she realized that she would have no chance competing with these ladies for a few scarce positions at Marshall Field's. She would have to first acquire a wardrobe.

Gertrude excused herself to those sitting next to her, put the clipboard on the chair, and rushed out. Taking out her purse, she feverishly counted her money. She had spent two dollars for one night at the Bancroft, fifty cents for the hansom, and four dollars and fifty cents for the first week's rent. (She had agreed to pay for the entire first week's rent at the new flat because Bonnie had had to forfeit the rent she had already paid for the Mercer Street room.) Another seventy-four cents had gone for meals out during the past two days. In all, she counted seventeen dollars and twenty-six cents in her purse.

Gertrude rushed to the fourth floor of the Parisian Building where she had earlier been looking at women's day dresses. With only moments before closing, she chose a tucked full-sleeve blouse of sateen and percale of stripes with detachable collar and cuff, a velvet-bound jacquard skirt of taffeta and moiré, and a seal belt. She had no time to look at shoes. She knew that there was no way she could afford what she really wanted — a short-jacketed walking suit with a band of satin and flared at the hem. Such fine suits cost at least fifty dollars. As it was, her new skirt and blouse cost eleven dollars and forty cents, leaving her only six dollars and fifteen cents.

Nevertheless, Gertrude began to regain her confidence as she tried on her new outfit. Although far from the glamorous ensembles worn by the young ladies on the twelfth floor, her new outfit had at least enabled her to shed her drab small-town image. Buttressed by the compliments of the sales clerks who said she was the perfect Gibson Girl, she returned to the flat on Twenty-First Street in good spirits.

Gertrude was in front of the dressing mirror fixing her hair in the new "Nestle" style, when Bonnie returned from her long day at the Boston Store.

"Sister Gertrude! You look absolutely gorgeous! Where did you get that outfit? I love the velvet trim!"

"Do you like it?" Gertrude said, spinning around. "I got it at Marshall Field's. It was a good price because they're moving their summer stock early."

"You got the position, then?" Bonnie asked.

Gertrude sat down. "No," she said hesitantly. "All the other girls applying wore the latest fall fashions. I knew I had no chance with what I was wearing. So I bought this outfit to give me a better chance tomorrow when I make application."

Bonnie sat on the edge of the bed. "Gee, Gertie, I don't know how much money you have. It's a beautiful outfit, and you look wonderful in it, but don't you think you should get a position first? I mean, what if you run out of money before you get a position?"

Gertrude too had considered this unpleasant possibility and didn't need Bonnie to remind her.

"I won't buy anything else until I find something," Gertrude promised. "I just wanted to give myself every chance of getting a position at Marshall Field's. I do so want to work there."

"And certainly you shall," Bonnie said, returning to her upbeat mood.

"It's a beautiful evening," Gertrude said. "Let's go down to the Loop and get something to eat."

"We could make something here," Bonnie said opening a paper bag. I bought a loaf of bread and some fish."

"Tomorrow we shall eat the fish," Gertrude said. "Come, I want you to show me this famous Loop I've heard so much about."

The Loop was as exciting as Gertrude had imagined when she had read the magazines about life in Chicago. Arc lamps lit up the entire area, which was filled with restaurants, clubs, theatres, and hotels. Most of all, Gertrude was impressed by the people — so many men and women in the latest fashions. Even the shop girls, walking together in groups of four or five, laughing and talking gaily, were dressed in fashions in which they might be mistaken for upper-class women.

"You must show me the Auditorium," Gertrude pleaded. "Is it far?"

"It's on Michigan Avenue. We can walk," Bonnie said.

"Nonsense. We'll take another of those exciting streetcar rides."

When Bonnie hesitated, Gertrude took her by the wrist. "It shall be my treat, and in return you shall be my guide!"

Relieved that she would not have to part with another precious nickel, Bonnie relented.

Being a weekday evening, the streetcar was not as crowded, and each got a seat in the open air "summer car." Excited by the sight and sounds of gaiety and sublime chaos, Gertrude's spirit's lifted. She would make it. Somehow, she decided, she would make it.

The Auditorium was everything she had imagined. The theatre crowd was milling about in front, and elegant hansoms and carriages crowded Michigan Avenue.

The pair slipped by a uniformed security guard who was checking tickets and entered the opera house lobby. In awe, they looked up at the high ceiling, decorated with gold leaf and reliefs inlaid with carbon-filament lamps and supported by majestic arches. From there they walked up the magnificent alabaster staircase. From one of the doors to the forty-three-hundred-seat theatre they stood for a moment and peeked into the interior. Never had Gertrude imagined so much glamour, and so many beautiful people in one magnificent place.

"Your tickets please," came the voice of an officious theatre usher, immediately suspicious of the two woman, and in particular of the one wearing the typical shop girl clothes sold by the lower class department stores.

"We're waiting for someone. We'll come back later," Gertrude said, pulling Bonnie away to leave.

"*The Mikado,*" Bonnie said wistfully as they sat on the last street-car of the evening to go to Twenty-First Street. "I wonder what it's like. Something about a Japanese emperor I think."

"Hmmm," said Gertrude, not really listening. She was thinking of that whole world she had seen in the Auditorium — a world that she was determined to someday enter.

6

"After staring at photographs of very attractive faces, men show less desire to date an average-looking woman. (This) most certainly is one reason why beautiful women have a tougher time holding on to female friends."

Nancy Etcoff, *Survival of the Prettiest* (1999)

Despite returning late the night before, and with but a few hours sleep, Gertrude, meticulously groomed and dressed in her new outfit, appeared on the twelfth floor of the Parisian Building at nine sharp. She was the first to be called in for an interview.

"I see you are interested in a position as a shop girl," the middle-aged man with slicked-back black hair said as he perused Gertrude's application.

"Yes sir."

The interviewer looked up and gazed intently at Gertrude. As he did so his demeanor appeared to soften. Her confidence in her own appearance and appeal rose as she recognized a look of appreciation and eagerness on his face — a look with which she was not unfamiliar and had long come to expect when making contact with a member of the opposite sex.

"I'm afraid we have a backlog of over three hundred applications for such positions," he said apologetically. "Can you tell me what experience you have?"

"None, sir. I have just arrived in Chicago, you see."

"We do have a few positions open for stenographer-typists, and the pay is considerably higher, eight to twelve dollars a week, depending upon skill and experience. Would you be interested in these positions?"

"Oh no, sir," Gertrude said, suddenly realizing the inadequacy of her qualifications.

Shaking his head, the interviewer seemed genuinely sorry that he could offer nothing.

"Here," he said, handing Gertrude a pamphlet. "Take this. It is a pamphlet by Elyce Rotella titled "From Home to Office" and has some useful information about office and sales work. Read it, so that when a position becomes open you will be well acquainted with today's office requirements. We may have some filing clerk positions opening up in the next few months."

Distressed and embarrassed, her hopes dashed, Gertrude now wanted only to make her exit as gracefully as possible.

"Thank you, sir," she said, taking the pamphlet as she rose from her chair and turned towards the door.

"Miss . . . " the interviewer said, looking down at the name on the application, "Miss Gibson?"

"Yes?" Gertrude said, turning around hopefully.

"As I said, we have no shop girl positions at the present time. However, if you have no plans for lunch, perhaps we could discuss what other opportunities might become available in the near future."

Gertrude considered this offer for only a moment. Noting a wedding ring on the man's finger, and feeling strongly her humiliation in being rejected for a job she so desperately sought but which paid but five dollars a week, she experienced a consoling sense of satisfaction in returning the rejection.

"I think not," she said coldly and shut the door behind her with just enough force to communicate her frustration and anger.

"You did what?" Bonnie asked in consternation.

The force of her rebuke took Gertrude, who had never seen Bonnie this way, quite aback. She realized that she should never have told Bonnie the details of her unsuccessful interview, particularly the interviewer's solicitous invitation to go to lunch with him. Already deeply depressed, Gertrude had spent the afternoon in the flat reading "From Home to Office" and its contents had not encouraged her: "Women are especially suited as typists and switchboard operators because they are tolerant of routine, careful, and manually dexterous. A woman might make an ideal filing clerk but the head of a filing department should preferably be a man."

"He had no position to offer," Gertrude insisted, "and I saw no reason to waste my time or his."

Bonnie slumped down in her chair. "I suppose you did the right thing."

There was a long silence as each woman considered what to say next.

"What about the rent next week?" Bonnie finally asked softly.

Gertrude pursed her lips. "I have six dollars," she said. "If you can pay your two dollars and twenty-five cents, I can pay mine for at least two more weeks. That will give me time to find a position."

Relieved, Bonnie's good humor returned. She appeared lost in thought. "You could apply for a position at the Boston Store!" Bonnie said as if surprised she had not thought of it before.

"I don't know," Gertrude said. She was not yet prepared to give up her hopes of working in a fashionable dry goods store. She had visualized herself meeting beautiful people and selling elegant gowns, silk purses, and fine leather goods — not cheap goods from the Boston Store's bargain bazaar.

"Gertie, there are too many girls applying for positions at the fancy stores. Even at the Boston Store they're turning girls away. But I could talk to my supervisor, Mr. Turnage. I think he likes me."

Gertrude remained dubious.

"You could still look for another position, but in the meantime you would be bringing in something," Bonnie said with renewed enthusiasm.

Gertrude sighed, but she realized that Bonnie was right. It might be weeks before she found a position that suited her, and in the meantime the rent had to be paid.

"Very well, if this Mr. Turnage will hire me, I will work there. But only until I find a position that suits me."

"Then it's agreed. Come with me tomorrow, and I will introduce you to him. I'm sure he can help you."

With this matter settled, the two prepared a meal of fish and bread.

"Next Sunday, I'm to visit my Johnny up in Pullman," Bonnie said as she picked up the dishes and took them to the sink to wash. "It's a lovely little town. Come with me, won't you? I want you to meet Johnny," Bonnie smiled mischievously. "And he has some friends who might like to meet you."

Gertrude was noncommittal. She had thought of going back to the Loop the following Sunday or visiting Jackson Park, the site of the Columbian Exposition. Visiting a company town and meeting some laborers was not high on her agenda. Nevertheless, Bonnie had been a true friend, and Gertrude had no desire to be alone on the weekend.

Gertrude nodded. "Sure," she said. "I'd like to meet Johnny. But no friends! Promise me."

Despite Gertrude's fears of an even more humiliating experience at the Boston Store, Mr. Ralph Turnage took one look at Gertrude and decided she would make an ornamental addition to the shirtwaist department. Setting aside a waiting list of shop girl applicants, he hired her on the spot for three dollars and twenty five cents a week."

"Why, Miss Lipshutz, you've outdone yourself in bringing me such a prospect as Miss Gibson here."

Turnage turned to Gertrude, eyeing her appreciatively. "Now, young lady, can you start tomorrow morning?"

"Yes," said Gertrude, most pleasantly surprised. It was not the job she wanted, but it relieved her immediate anxieties about paying the rent.

Even Bonnie was surprised by the ease with which Gertrude had taken a position — and at a wage higher than she.

That evening the pair celebrated Gertrude's success by eating an antelope steak dinner at a diner near the Loop.

"You see," Bonnie said, "good fortune has finally smiled on us. We shall pay the rent and eat antelope as well!"

Gertrude's first days on the job went smoothly. To Abernathy's great pleasure, she sold more than her expected quota of shirtwaists. However, the twelve-hour days on her feet were exhausting, and after one week Gertrude found herself totally spent.

Sunday brought a welcome respite. The early morning train to the company town of Pullman was packed with Sunday day travelers. Bonnie and Gertrude were fortunate to find two seats together.

Bonnie stood up and shielded her eyes from the sun as she peered out the window looking for Jonathan.

"I see him!" Bonnie said excitedly as the train lurched to a stop in the Pullman central railroad station. Bonnie and Gertrude stepped down from the car and fought their way through the crowd.

"Over here!" Bonnie shouted, waving to Jonathan as she stepped off the platform.

Jonathan saw her and rushed over. He picked her up in his arms, kissing her and twirling her around in circles.

"Jonathan!" she cried. "I want you to meet someone."

Jonathan put Bonnie down.

"This is my dear friend Gertrude. She came to Chicago last week, and we are sharing a flat."

"Pleased to meet you, Miss," Jonathan said, extending his hand and taking Gertrude's hand firmly.

Jonathan was a stout and brawny man with thick blond hair. He wore his working blue overalls, and his soiled shirt had a distinctly pungent odor.

"Please excuse me," he said. "I just got off the night shift and didn't have a chance to change."

"I've packed a picnic lunch," Bonnie said, apparently not disturbed by her fiancé's appearance and odor. "I thought we could have an early lunch in the park."

It being a pleasant day, the Pullman Park was packed with other picnickers. The three found a spot under an oak tree, and Bonnie spread out her blanket.

"This time next year," Bonnie said happily, "Johnny will be eligible to buy a house from the company and he can leave the workers' dormitory. Then we shall be married!"

Jonathan smiled and nodded.

"Gertrude," Bonnie said, "we must show you our little house. It's only three blocks away. It is so adorable!"

"After that," Jonathan said, "I have a little surprise for you."

"Oh, I just love surprises!" Bonnie said.

"Close your eyes, then." Jonathan said.

Jonathan placed three tickets in her hands. Bonnie opened her eyes.

"Tickets! To a concert!" she said excitedly.

"Not just a concert, but a concert on the lake. The Michigan Queene sails tonight at 6 p.m. from the Clark Street Bridge. It's a double-decker. They have the best ragtime band in Illinois."

With great excitement the two lovebirds led Gertrude down Pullman Avenue to a neat row of redbrick townhouses and pointed out the third house from the corner.

"Oh, Johnny, I just adore it!" Bonnie exclaimed when she saw it. "Can't we go inside?"

Jonathan shook his head. "No, it's against the rules. Not until my promotion to supervisor is approved and the closing is completed. Just one more year."

As Bonnie stepped forward to gaze lovingly at the home more closely, Jonathan turned and gave Gertrude a suggestive glance. As it fastened upon her, she felt a vague sense of discomfort. She turned away just as Bonnie stepped back.

"I have tickets on the 4:00 p.m. train," Jonathan said. The steamer leaves at six and returns at nine. Then we must part, as I will take the train back to Pullman, and you can take the streetcar from Clark Street Station back to your flat."

On the train back to Chicago they were able to find three seats together. While Bonnie chattered on, Gertrude looked out the window at the lake, conscious that Jonathan's eyes were again fixed on her. Gertrude reddened as she noticed his furtive glances at her ankles, and she self-consciously covered them completely with her skirt. She could only hope that Bonnie was not noticing these attentions by her fiancé.

There was great commotion at the Clark Bridge Street Station, and great crowds were milling near the steamer ticket office. All tickets for the evening cruise were sold out, and scalpers were shouting offers to sell their twenty-five cents tickets for thirty-five cents.

Gertrude was struck by the difference in the Michigan Queene passengers and the glamorous people she had seen at the Auditorium

Opera House. Although most of the Michigan Queene passengers were dressed in their Sunday best, they constituted a distinctively lower middle-class clientele. Gertrude recognized one of the women as a fellow shop girl at the Boston Store, dressed in an outfit of summer white and stiff straw hat of the type that Gertrude sold at the Boston Store. It occurred to Gertrude that the glamorous men and women who attended the Auditorium Opera did not patronize cheap excursions on the lake. Although Gertrude was dressed in her new outfit, she knew that she did no better than meet the standards of dress on the Michigan Queene — and that only barely.

It was a soft summer evening on the Lake, with warm soothing breezes from the East. The three stood along the crowded railing to wave at the throngs on the pier as the steamer slowly departed. Ten minutes into the voyage, the band on the second deck struck up a ragtime waltz, and couples began dancing. Jonathan brought Bonnie and Gertrude a sarsaparilla, and himself a beer.

"Look, she's doing the new Jennie Cooler Dance," Bonnie said looking at a young woman dancing the latest steps. "A friend at work showed me how to do it. Come one Johnny, I'll show you."

"Now you know I can't do those new-fangled dances," Jonathan protested, but Bonnie pulled him out onto the dance floor.

Jonathan glanced back at Gertrude and shrugged his shoulders, as if to communicate to her in an intimate way that he would prefer to dance with her.

Gertrude turned away, determined not to provide any pretense for Jonathan to neglect his devoted fiancé, who also happened to be Gertrude's only friend in the world.

Gertrude watched the pair struggle through the Jennie Cooler steps and decided to explore the steamer on her own. She had not gotten very far when several young men approached her. The first to arrive was a dapper young man in cheap imitation spats smelling heavily of perfume.

"Care to try the Texas Tommy?" he asked cheerfully.

"I'm afraid I don't know those dances," Gertrude said shyly, appreciative of the attention, but unsure of the appropriate response.

"Well, you can two-step, can't you?" the young man persisted.

At that moment, Bonnie, trying to get Jonathan to follow her lead, noticed that he was looking in the opposite direction. "Jonathan, please pay attention!" Bonnie cried over the loud music.

"I think some mashers are bothering our little friend Gertrude," Jonathan returned as he awkwardly began tripping over his own feet.

Bonnie, who was still moving to the ragtime beat, turned around. "Maybe she'll meet someone. I hope she does. She hasn't met a single young man since coming here."

"Well, she doesn't want to meet those drummers. I know their type," Jonathan said, breaking off the dance.

"Jonathan, come back here," Bonnie protested as Jonathan left her standing and approached the young men now surrounding Gertrude.

"She's with us!" Jonathan yelled to the young men, pushing them to the side. "Leave her alone."

"Who are you? Her old man?" the young man responded testily. "You ain't dancin' with her." He began to shove back.

A scuffle, or worse, might have ensued had Bonnie not intervened.

"I'm sure my sister would love to dance with one of you gentlemen, later after dining," Bonnie said sweetly. "Come back then, won't you?"

Assuaged, the young man and his friends tipped their straw hats.

"Thank you ma'am. We'll come back then, and your sister can dance as she likes." They smiled at Bonnie but gave Jonathan a parting look of contempt.

After they had left, Bonnie turned and glared at her fiancé.

"I want to talk to you, Jonathan. Alone."

As Bonnie took Jonathan to the side, Gertrude discreetly slipped away. She went back to the railing on the starboard deck, gazed out at the Chicago skyline in the distance, and sighed.

She was thinking not of the fatuous young men who had approached her or of the Michigan Queene or of the needless complications that her best friend's fiancé was threatening to introduce in to her life.

She was thinking: "I don't belong here." She was thinking of the Auditorium and the life she had seen there.

Bonnie and Gertrude sat in total silence on the streetcar ride back to Twenty-First Street. Each knew what the other was thinking, but neither wanted to broach the subject first. For Gertrude, Jonathan's attentions had been most embarrassing. She considered trying to convince her friend that Jonathan had merely been solicitous of her, as Bonnie's friend; but Jonathan's furtive glances at her on the train had been all too obvious and his attentions awkwardly transparent. The evening had been capped by the spectacle of Bonnie's inebriated fiancé insisting upon a dance with Gertrude. Gertrude wanted to tell her that she was not in any way attracted to Jonathan, and that in any case, as Bonnie's devoted friend, she would never encourage his attentions. But she could not think of appropriate words. When Gertrude instead tried to take Bonnie's hand and comfort her, Bonnie withdrew it coldly.

"I have only one thing to say to you, Miss Gertrude Gibson. Stay away from my Johnny, or I swear you'll wish you never came to this terrible city."

Bonnie's eyes became thin slits.

"I mean it."

7

"Beauty has a downside."

Nancy Etcoff, *Survival of the Prettiest* (1999).

In the weeks following, Bonnie and Gertrude continued to walk together to the Boston Store every workday morning. Nothing more was said about Jonathan or the disastrous evening aboard the Michigan Queene. Bonnie even made gestures of reconciliation. But it was apparent to Gertrude that their friendship could never be the same, and each found it an effort to make even light conversation on their long walks to and from work. Gertrude could not forget Bonnie's virulent outburst, which Gertrude felt to be most unfair; and Bonnie would always see Gertrude as a threat to her own dreams of a long and happy life with Jonathan. Although they each worked in the same building and had the same lunch hour, each found an excuse not to meet for lunch as they had always done before.

The pair's friendship became strained further by the failure of their joint financial circumstances to improve. Although both were now earning a wage, it was barely enough to pay for their flat and food. The stake that Gertrude's father had given her was now consumed, and though they managed never to be late when the landlady came by for each week's rent, they did so by only the scantiest of margins.

Even Gertrude's new outfit was becoming rapidly worn out, because she wore it every day and had no other suitable clothes to wear to work. The long twelve hour days on her feet, in the stifling summer heat of the Boston Store's top floor, had become unbearable. When she came down with a severe flu and high temperature, she dared not miss even one day of work, knowing that she would be docked and find herself unable to make her full contribution to the rent. The pair made no further efforts to plan Sunday outings, since both of them found themselves too exhausted at the end of the week. Instead they lay in bed almost the entire Sunday restoring their strength for the next seventy-two hour week.

At first, Gertrude made every effort to be polite even to the rudest of her customers. By the end of each long day, however, as her clothes and hair became wet with perspiration, she found it more difficult to be accommodating to the demands of the young women customers, most of whom were of no higher station than herself, and who no doubt took delight in making demands on someone who was obliged to cater to them. In such a way, Gertrude was convinced that these women compensated for their own long days of labor in which they, in turn, had to cater to the demands of their own stern taskmasters.

Gertrude had asked Turnage for a transfer to a department that catered to men, thinking that the opposite sex might treat her with more deference. Turnage had not denied this request but, without giving a reason, had put her off, stating that he would try to accommodate her at some time in the future. There had been the slightest hint in his manner that she should expect to provide something to him in return for such an accommodation.

In fact, she had ignored a series of such hints over the past several weeks, including several invitations to join him on one pretext or another — one day, for lunch to discuss a transfer, on another for a tête-à-tête to discuss her suggestions on how to reorganize her department. It had now become obvious to her that he had lecherous intent, and every day brought new challenges in how to avoid him.

One late Thursday afternoon just before closing, Gertrude was folding shirtwaists on a display table when she was confronted by the last person she wanted ever to lay eyes upon again. It was Jonathan.

"Hi Gertie," he said innocently, as if it was pure coincidence that their paths had crossed again.

"Jonathan!" Gertrude stammered, shocked by his sudden appearance. "What are you doing here? Bonnie works in the bargain department in the basement."

Jonathan smiled mischievously. "I didn't come to see Bonnie."

Gertrude turned away, but Jonathan clasped her wrist and held her.

"You must know it's you I want. I think you know!" he said in a loud whisper.

Gertrude pulled herself away from his grasp. "I am not to be had for the wanting! And even if I were, Bonnie is my dearest friend. What would she say if she knew you were here?"

"Tell her then. If you don't, I will. I want you! I can't help it!" Jonathan's loud whisper had now become a plaintive bellow, and nearby customers turned to listen to the commotion. "You're all I think about! I just want to talk!"

"No! Don't you dare tell her any such thing! Now you must go!"

At this point, Gertrude was saved from any further disturbance by the most unlikely source.

"Miss Gibson, I'd like to see you in my office," came the firm voice of Ralph Turnage from across the room.

Jonathan looked around, distracted, and finally turned heel and headed down the nearby staircase.

Gertrude followed Mr. Turnage, who led her upstairs to his office.

"Please sit, Miss Gibson."

"Yes, sir," she said, sitting. "You see that man was bothering me and I . . . "

Turnage put up his hands, as if to say he was not interested in the details.

"Miss Gibson, I'm sure you know the rules about socializing on company time. When you are socializing you are not selling shirtwaists. And if you are not selling shirtwaists, then the company is not making the profits it needs in order to pay your wages. I'm sure you understand."

Gertrude saw that it was hopeless to try to explain further. It was easier to simply comply.

"Yes sir. I understand. It won't happen again."

"Please see that it does not."

Turnage now took, for the moment, a more agreeable tone. "While you are here, Miss Gibson, I should tell you that I have been working on a new work schedule for the shop girls. I was trying to accommodate your request to work in the men's department, although I have reservations."

"Reservations? What kind of reservations?"

"Let's just say that," and here Turnage paused to touch the tips of the fingers of each hand with the other, "let's just say that your tendency towards socializing might be an even greater hindrance in that department."

Flustered, Gertrude rose from her chair, weighing the consequences of saying what she truly wanted to say.

Seeing her discomfort, Turnage held up his hands.

"Nevertheless, Miss Gibson, I may be in a position to help you if I can expect some cooperation from you in the future. But it's late. We can discuss it tomorrow. Please come in first thing in the morning."

Gertrude stood, glaring at Turnage but saying nothing.

"That will be all, Miss Gibson, until tomorrow morning."

The long walk home that evening with Bonnie was even more awkward than usual. On the one hand Gertrude wanted to tell her friend that her fiancé was a cad and not worthy of her affection; on the other, she was quite sure that any recitation of Jonathan's appearance in the shirtwaist department that afternoon would give rise to a jealous fury that Gertrude was deliberately trying to steal her fiancé away from her. Gertrude also wanted desperately to consult with her friend about how best to handle Mr. Turnage, but she could not think of the right words with which to bring up the matter.

"We're going to be fifty cents short on Friday," Bonnie finally said glumly as they approached their flat on the walk home that evening.

Gertrude stopped and pulled out a dollar bill from her purse. She had been saving it for just such an emergency.

"Here," she said, handing it to her friend.

Bonnie took it and put it in her purse. "Thanks."

"Bonnie," Gertrude said softly, hoping to find the words to say what was weighing so heavily on her mind.

"Yes?" said Bonnie, looking at her with more curiosity than interest.

"Nothing."

Both women slept fitfully that night, and both stifled tears. Bonnie was tormented not only by thoughts of losing Jonathan but of losing her life's dream. Gertrude had a foreboding about the following day.

"Well, Miss Gibson, have you thought about what we talked about yesterday?"

Mr. Turnage appeared particularly well groomed, and his jet-black patent shoes were exceptionally shiny.

"About my request to transfer to another department?"

"No, Miss Gibson. About your promise to cooperate with me."

"I'm sure I don't know what you mean, sir," said Gertrude looking down, but now, hearing his tone, fearing the worst.

"Come here," he said, waving his hand. "I want you to look at my new schedule."

Gertrude approached, but stopped several feet from his desk and looked over at the document he had spread out.

"Closer," he said. "You can't read it from there."

As she drew closer, Turnage rose from his chair and came up behind her, putting his hands around her waist.

"You see," he whispered into her ear as he drew her closer, "I have assigned you to the men's department and raised your wage to six dollars a week."

Gertrude turned around sharply, moving away.

"Please, sir!"

"Please sir, what!" Turnage growled.

"Please don't . . . "

Turnage took her again about the waist and pulled her close.

Gertrude pulled away and slapped him across the face with the back of her hand.

Stunned, Turnage released her and stood back, stroking his face with his hand. Gertrude, appalled at what she had done, put her hand to her mouth.

"Why, you little whore!" he hissed. "Get out! Get out right now before I call the police!"

He grabbed her by the wrists and pushed her toward the door. As she stumbled out, he pursued her from behind and shoved her toward the stairwell door. Then he opened the door and roughly pushed her. Gertrude grabbed the railing to avoid falling, and turned around.

"My purse! My things! They're in my locker. I have to get them!" she cried, holding back her tears.

Turnage glared at her and pointed his finger.

"Wait there, you little strumpet! Don't move! Wait there!"

He turned back through the stairwell door and returned moments later. He had her purse and scarf in his hand. Violently, he threw them both down the stairs. The scarf floated in the air, and the purse and its contents spilled out on to the stair landing. In tears, Gertrude knelt to gather them.

"Get out!" Turnage yelled again. "And don't ever try to get a job as a shop girl in this city! Nobody wants a fuckin' whore!"

Still shaking and hiding her tears, Gertrude staggered out to the street. Her head down, ignoring all around her, she made her way through the early morning crowds back to the flat. Her distress was exceeded only by her heightened fears and anxieties. How would they pay the rent next week? How would they even have money for food? Her mind recoiled at the thought of having to return to Mercer Street. No! She swore to herself. She would never return to Mercer Street! With every dream shattered, she would have no choice now. She would have to return to Sandoval, to the mudflats, to the wretched little town that hated her. She had to accept the fact that she was just a woman — with no skills, no purpose, no task, no utility. In short, she had nothing to offer anyone. She was an insignificant peon who could drop dead on the sidewalk without anyone caring — except perhaps the municipal workers who would be annoyed that they had yet another body to throw into the cart with the other dead animals. If she did so, Gertrude was now convinced, Bonnie would be relieved that she was no longer a threat. Her parents would mourn for her, perhaps even light a candle one night in her remembrance, but their lives would not really change. Certainly no one else in Sandoval would mourn her. Gertrude indulged in a momentary lighter thought that perhaps Link would think kindly of her, perhaps even grieve for her.

Back at the flat, she threw herself on the bed and buried her head in the pillow. She was still lying in that position when she heard Bonnie at the door. She had not expected Bonnie to return from work until that evening, by which time Bonnie would surely have heard of her dismissal. She rose from the bed as Bonnie entered.

"You're back so early," Gertrude said, pulling back her hair and determined to maintain a dignified front in the face of her own personal disaster.

Bonnie slammed the door and entered the kitchen without saying a word.

"Bonnie, I have to tell you something."

Bonnie opened a cabinet and took out a teapot, slamming it down on the stove.

"Bonnie, I need to talk to you. Something terrible has happened."

Bonnie turned around and gave Gertrude a fierce gaze.

"I have something to tell you, Gertrude Gibson! I got the sack today too! Because of you! Oh, I knew I should never have tried to help you! What did you do? What did you do? Oh, what shall become of us now? It's all your fault!"

Bonnie broke into tears and pushed Gertrude aside as she stalked into the bedroom and flung herself on the bed.

Gertrude followed, sat beside her, and placed her hand on Bonnie's shoulder to comfort her.

"Oh, get away!" Bonnie cried. "You're just no good, Gertrude Gibson! You're no good! First you try to steal Johnny, then you insult my boss and get me sacked! You're no good! You've been nothing but trouble ever since you came here! You're just evil, evil, evil!"

With Bonnie in such a state, Gertrude saw that there was no use explaining what had happened. She went to the sitting room and sat in the chair, looking out at the street below. After waiting for twenty minutes until the sobbing subsided, she returned to the bedroom and stood by the door.

"Bonnie, please understand. Mr. Turnage accosted me. He tried to . . ."

"What did he do?" Bonnie sat up on the bed. "Did he ask you to go to lunch like the man at Marshall Field's? Oh heavens no, you couldn't ever do anything like that! No, you're Gertrude Gibson! You're too good to do anything like go to lunch with a man!"

Mortified, Gertrude was silent.

"You had to insult him!" Bonnie continued, her voice now a shriek. "Did you consider that he was just trying to help you? And did you think about me? What about me? Was it worth it, Miss Hoity Toity? Well, I'll tell you something. You need friends in this city, or you won't survive. Any other girl at the store would have been flattered to have some attention, to have just a little help. It wouldn't have killed you to be just a little nice! But not you! Not Miss Goody Two Shoes! Miss Prim and Proper! Well let me just ask you this! How do you plan to pay the rent next week? Did you think about that? Mercer Street was too good for you! Well, I hope you have a plan, because next week we're both on the street. Mercer Street was a paradise compared with where we're headed now. Do you know what that means? Do you know what that means?"

Bonnie threw herself back on the bed, her sobs renewed.

Gertrude tried once more to comfort her.

"Go home, Gertrude Gibson! Go, and never come back! Go back to the coal mines you came from! " Bonnie cried, pushing her away. "Go home and leave me alone!"

Gertrude realized it was hopeless to reason with her estranged friend or to make her understand. She pursed her lips stoically and turned away. She looked into the mirror, but she did not find there the usual consolation. She looked truly awful. Her eyes were red, her face puffy, and her blouse dirty and soiled. She turned to pick up her purse and left the flat, closing the door quietly behind her.

At the bottom of the stairwell she turned and rested with her back against the wall. To her own surprise, Bonnie's outburst had not deepened her depression and anxiety. Instead it had filled her with a great resolve. She would not go back to Mercer Street. She would not go back to Sandoval. *She would not be defeated.* Whatever it took, whatever she had to do, somehow she would survive.

Early the next morning, Gertrude would set out for the streets to search for a job — any job that would pay enough to meet the next week's rent. After that, she could look for something else. But first she had to pay the rent.

Before noon she had tried her luck at four establishments — a shoe factory on lower Jackson Street, two restaurants on State Street, and a glove factory on Kinzie Street near the Chicago River. By midafternoon, she had walked many miles, her hair was oily and dirty, and her clothes were drenched in perspiration. She had become hardened to rejection. Even the curt "Get out! We don't need help!" heaped upon her at the glove factory failed to curb her resolve.

By early evening her persistence achieved a small reward. A machine operator at the Pentagon Shirtwaist Factory located in the loft of the McKenzie Building on River Street offered her encouragement.

"I'm Hector Potter," the machine operator said in heavy brogue. "Yeh see, Missy, the company don't hire workers. It just contracts with us machine operators, and we negotiate with the company for the rates to be paid on each piece. We then hire girls to do the sewin'. I 'ave seven girls working for me, and that's all I need now. But one didn't come in today. She looked a bit sickly yesterday, so she might not be comin' back. I tell you what, Missy. Yeh be here tomorrow mornin' at six in the mornin'. If the lassie doesn't show up, yeh can take her place. But I can't promise yeh anything."

"May I ask the pay, sir?" Gertrude asked.

"Yeh get paid by the piece. A penny for each sleeve you sew to a bodice. I'll expect yeh to work at least thirteen hours a day — six to seven, six to four on Saturday — and we don't work on Sunday. If yeh learn to work fast, you can make four, maybe even five dollars a week. I had a lassie last week who made six — of course, she worked until ten each evening."

"I'll come," Gertrude said firmly.

"You'd better think about it, Missy," Hector went on. "I'll not lie to yeh. It be hard work, and if you're not careful yeh can get hurt. Last week a girl lost her thumb in one of the machines. Got tired and wasn't paying attention. Yeh come ten minutes late, and I'll get someone else to replace yeh. Lots of young missies like you, come in from New York just off the boat, wanting work. Now, yeh still want to come?"

"Yes," Gertrude said.

It was dark when Gertrude returned to the flat. She found Bonnie curled up in bed. Gertrude started to light the gas lamp.

"Leave it off," Bonnie sobbed.

"Oh, Bonnie, please don't cry. I got another job. I start tomorrow. We'll pay the rent, I promise."

In the dim light from the streets that poured through the bedroom window, Gertrude saw that Bonnie clutched a crumpled piece of paper in her fist.

"I don't care about that," Bonnie said, heaving and suppressing yet another heavy sob.

"But we can stay here," Gertrude said, sitting beside her. "We'll pay the rent."

Bonnie now broke into uncontrolled convulsions of tears.

"What is it?" Gertrude asked. "What's in your hand?"

Bonnie slowly released the paper from her fist as Gertrude took it. It was a letter from Jonathan. Gertrude went into the sitting room and turned on the lamp. When she had finished reading it, she returned to sit next to Bonnie on the bed.

"I'm so sorry," Gertrude said.

"He says he was caught unionizing and given the sack. Says he's going to California. To make his fortune, he says."

"He says he'll come back for you," Gertrude added hopefully.

"He won't be back. He doesn't care about me. I know that now. He just wants you 'cause you're pretty." Bonnie buried her head in the pillow to suppress her sobs.

"Bonnie, you're pretty too."

"Not like you, and you know it," she said gritting her teeth in rage. "Now just go away!"

"Bonnie, please don't think I had anything to do . . . "

"Please," Bonnie said softly. "Please just go back to Sandoval. Everything was fine until you came." With that she curled up and pulled the spread over her head.

Gertrude sighed and went into the sitting room, softly closing the door to the bedroom. She took a piece of paper from the bureau drawer, sat at the table, and began to write a letter:

Dearest Evelyn,

> *I never thought I would have to write you like this, but I very much need your help. I have lost my job, though not through my own fault. I may have found a new one working in a shirtwaist factory, but my twenty-five dollars from father is gone, I have no decent clothes and have not eaten for two days. If you could wire me a few dollars by Western Union I would be ever so grateful. Please don't tell father, as he would come and fetch me back, I know it.*

Your loving sister, Gertie

Gertrude folded the letter, sealed it in an envelope, and put it in her purse. Then she changed into her nightgown and lay down beside her still suffering roommate.

8

"Oh the shame at merely being a woman, with no task, no utility."

Elia Peattie, *The Precipice* (1899).

The loft of the McKenzie Building was filled with a hundred and ten sewing machines arranged on four parallel rows on forty-five foot tables. Working at the tables were a handful of operator foremen, a dozen or so male cutters, and a hundred and eleven young girls, some as young as twelve and thirteen. The cutters, exclusively male, were skilled workers who piled up layers of fabric. A cutter placed a pattern on the fabric and cut the fabric in jigsaw fashion. His skill was to place the patterns in the most efficient manner so as to minimize the amount of wastage of fabric. The actual cutting was done with a short stubby knife. After a sleeve or bodice was cut out, it was hung on a wire in the manner of a housewife who hung out her family's laundry. On each side of the long table perpendicular to the cutting tables were twelve young women working feverishly at the machines.

Gertrude arrived early at the Pentagon Shirtwaist Factory loft. She had taken great care to wash and iron her Marshall Field's outfit, arrange her hair in Nestle style, and polish her boots.

"I see you've come, little Missy," Hector Potter said. "Lily!" he barked over the loud clacking of the machines.

A rail-thin, raven-haired girl of fourteen with acne got up from her machine and came over.

"Yes, Mr. Potter."

"Take this Miss . . . " He turned to Gertrude. "Gibson is it?"

Gertrude nodded.

"Take this Miss Gibson over to your machine and show her how to use it."

"Yes, Mr. Potter," Lily said obediently.

Gertrude sat next to Lily by the machine.

"Just watch me," Lily said. "You take a piece from this pile and lay it under the needle, just so."

It was afternoon before Gertrude felt she could perform the stitching on her own. When Lily inspected her first product however, she found it unsatisfactory.

"No, no," Lily said. "The stitching has to be even along the edges. Here try it again."

By late afternoon Gertrude had produced here first passable shirt-waist.

"Well, you've earned your first penny," Hector said with a touch of sarcasm when he came by to monitor her progress. "Are you sure yeh can do this, Missy?"

"Yes, sir," Gertrude said confidently. "I've got it now. Tomorrow I can do a lot."

"I hope so," Hector said. "If yeh can't do at least seven shirts an hour, you're no good to me, and yeh won't earn enough to buy your own lunch."

The next day, with Lily's help, Gertrude managed to produce a total of thirty-seven shirtwaists over the course of the day. Hector, however, rejected nine of them as unsatisfactory, leaving Gertrude a credit for only twenty-eight.

That night, Gertrude nursed her hands, which were cramped and numb from the hours of toil on the machines. At the rate of twenty-eight cents a day, she would have only a dollar sixty-eight by the end of the week — not enough to pay the rent. Compared to this job, she now recalled her job at the Boston Store as being idyllically effortless.

She considered urging Bonnie, whom she found lying in bed every evening when she came home, to find a similar job but thought better of reminding her of why she had lost her job at the Boston Store. In any case, Gertrude had increased her production of shirtwaists to fifty-six by her third day, of which only three were rejected.

By the end of the week she had earned three dollars and sixty-five cents. Exhausted one night after she had come from the factory, she laid the money by the table next to the bed.

"It's not enough," Bonnie said testily.

"Give it to the landlady when she comes," Gertrude said. "Tell her I'll have the rest in three days."

"Then we'll be short the following week," Bonnie said abruptly.

Gertrude pursed her lips, as she always did when weighing the consequences of saying what she wanted to say. "Bonnie, I know how you are suffering, honestly I do. But now you have to help me. I found this job, and you can find one too."

"Working thirteen hours a day in that slave-shop? All because you got me sacked at the Boston Store? How long do you think you can work there before your hands get cut up? Look at them now. Just go back home. Go back home while you still can."

Gertrude looked at her hands and saw that Bonnie was right. She couldn't continue at this pace. But she had to buy some time, and she couldn't go back to Mercer Street. *Or to Sandoval.*

Although the thought of returning to the Pentagon factory sickened her, Gertrude was determined to buy the time she needed. Sensing that her only chance to obtain a more suitable position was to again make herself presentable, she reverted to wearing the street clothes she had worn on the train from Sandoval. She carefully cleaned and ironed her Marshall Field's outfit and meticulously folded it in her bureau drawer. She would wear it only when applying for a better position elsewhere. Potter didn't care what she wore to the factory, and everyone who worked there was bathed in sweat at the end of the day.

Every day during her twenty-minute lunch break Gertrude hurried to the Western Union outlet on Franklin Street to see if any money had arrived from Evelyn. She mentally calculated the number of days it would take mail to arrive in St. Louis and for her sister to read the letter, obtain the funds, and send them. She wondered if she had adequately explained her dire straits in the letter. But nothing had come yet.

The following week, there was a disturbing incident at the factory. One of the girls who worked at a table across from Gertrude got her hair caught in her machine. It had pulled her face up against a flywheel connected to the leather belt attached to the rotating axle, severely lacerating her face and cutting her eye open. With cries of "get her out of here," the foremen, concerned that the girl's hysterical screams and the sight of blood spurting across the tables would distract the other girls from their labors, had the unfortunate girl ushered quickly from the premises. She never returned.

Gertrude earned four dollars and thirty cents that week, but she had to work each evening until ten o'clock. She now realized that she was rapidly reaching the limits of her endurance. After subtracting enough money to buy a small amount of bread and cheese, the rent money was again short.

On the fourth morning of her third week at the factory, Gertrude was dressing in the flat when she opened her drawer and noticed that her Marshall Field's outfit was missing. She woke up Bonnie who was still sleeping.

"Bonnie, do you know where my blouse and skirt from Marshall Field's are?"

Bonnie yawned, smiled mischievously, and slowly turned over.

"Oh, didn't I tell you? The landlady said she wouldn't accept less than the full rent two weeks in a row. Your little Marshall Field's outfit," and here she mouthed the words "Marshall Field's outfit" in an affected high-pitched voice, "was the only thing of value in the flat she would accept for the deficiency."

Gertrude was so stunned she could hardly speak.

"You gave her my . . . "

Trying to hide her fury, Gertrude turned on her heel and slammed the door. At the bottom of the stairs she burst into tears. All was truly lost now, she told herself. All was lost.

Walking to the factory at a furious pace, Gertrude made an irrevocable promise to herself. She would work only one more morning at the shirtwaist factory and procure her wages due. Then she would make a final roll of the dice.

She stopped at the intersection of Clark and Van Buren streets where a crowd was waiting for an omnibus to pass. She opened her purse and took out the card that read "Armour and Company, Mr. Nelson Mayweather, Assistant Accounts Officer." At the bottom of the card was a telephone number.

Darting into a small hotel on Clark Street, she asked for the nearest telephone. After inserting her last coins into the box, she dialed the number on the card.

"Mr. Nelson Mayweather, please," Gertrude said in as authoritative voice as she could muster.

"Just a moment, please," came the pleasant voice at the other end.

Gertrude held her breath.

"Nelson Mayweather here. May I help you?"

"Mr. Mayweather?"

"Yes?"

"Mr. Mayweather, this is Gertrude Gibson. We met on the train some weeks ago?"

"Miss Gibson," replied Mayweather cheerfully, obviously delighted. "How wonderful to hear from you. How is the city treating you? Well, I hope?"

"Well, I am having some difficulties, actually," Gertrude said trying to disguise a tone of understatement. "I was wondering if you still had an opening for a position in your office."

"I'm sure we could find something for you," Mayweather said, wondering himself how he might manage to fulfill his earlier promise to Gertrude of a position in light of the long waiting list of applicants now sitting on his desk. "Would you care to come down and see our office?"

"Yes, I could do that. You see, I will be leaving another position this afternoon, but I could be there later in the afternoon."

"Splendid. I shall look forward to seeing you."

Mayweather gave Gertrude directions to get to the Armour Company stockyards by streetcar.

"Just check in at the reception office at the main gate and give your name. They will have someone escort you to our offices on the other side of the stockyards."

"Thank you, Mr. Mayweather. I shall see you this afternoon, then."

Gertrude now decided to go to the shirtwaist factory for the sole purpose of procuring her back pay. It relieved her tension considerably to know that she would never again sit in front of those dreadful machines. Although she expected some difficulty in procuring her back pay on the very day she announced that she was leaving, Hector was pleasantly accommodating.

"I must say, I never thought yeh suited for this work, Missy," he said amiably.

Hector, who had taken a liking to Gertrude, was in fact relieved that he would be spared the thankless task of sacking her. "Here's two dollars eight-five and an extra fifteen cents I'm throwin' in — three dollars. Yeh worked hard, Missy, but you just didn't take to it. Good luck to yeh now."

9

"I pack everything but the oink."

Philip Danforth Armour (1896).

It took Gertrude the better part of an hour, and three streetcar transfers to make the six-mile journey to the imposing stone gate of the Union Stock Yard. The trip had taken her through a dreary section of the city, cobwebbed with two-story pine-framed buildings and saloons, criss-crossed with hundreds of rail crossings, and lined with gray factories belching giant clouds of smoke that gave the sky a perpetual overcast. Having become accustomed to the pungent odors of the city, Gertrude found the smell of the stockyards not as overwhelming as it had been five weeks earlier when she passed by on the train.

As she approached the infamous gate, the sounds of bleating, squealing, and bellowing livestock blended with the sickening odor of raw meat, butchered viscera, feces, urine, and blood.

A crisply uniformed Armour Company guard greeted Gertrude at the stone gate.

"I have an appointment with Mr. Nelson Mayweather," Gertrude announced.

The guard looked in his company directory. "Yes, Miss. Accounts Department?"

"Yes, sir."

"Wait here one moment please. I'll have a runner take you there."

The guard called on the telephone for a runner. Moments later a young sandy-haired youth in gray overalls appeared at the gatehouse.

"Escort this young woman to the accounting department."

"Yes, sir," said the runner, turning to Gertrude. "Just follow me, ma'am."

Gertrude thanked the guard and followed the young man who was to guide her.

"Have you been here before, Miss?" the runner asked with a mischievous smirk.

"No. I've only seen it from the train."

"Well, it's the biggest show in town. People come from all over the world to see this place. Why, just last year, Sarah Bernhardt visited us, called it a 'magnificent spectacle.'"

A more direct route to the accounts department wove around the periphery of the yards, but the runner choose to guide his pretty visitor through the very heart of the plant. Had Gertrude noted his smirk more closely, she would have discerned that he got his twitters from watching the reaction of genteel visitors, particularly women, to this "House of Blood."

He led her first up several flights of stairs to the visitor's gallery. Below, in the pens, were hundreds of terror-stricken pigs scurrying about in helter-skelter fashion, squealing and grunting so frantically that one eminent visitor would later conclude that the ill-fated hogs must have "had a vision of the approach of the horrible machines, from which there could be no more escape than a doomed man whose head lies on the guillotine."

The killing machine was a huge medieval-looking wheel with clanking chains hanging from its rims. One by one, a man attached the hind legs of the hogs to the wheel that jerked the terrified animals into the air upside down, thrashing, kicking, and biting. At the top of the wheel, an aerial tramway carried them, still upside down and flailing about, to an executioner in a leather apron. The latter slashed violently at the animal's neck, from which came a spout of jet-black blood so strong that it spurted as far as ten feet, drenching the executioners who failed to avoid it. More often than not, the cut did not kill the twitching animal, which was now passed over a cauldron of scalding water, dumped, and boiled alive.

Bloody as the slashing spectacles were, it was the sight of the terrified, squealing pigs being hoisted into the air by the giant wheel that was most apt to cause faintness in young women visitors. Grinning, the runner looked over at Gertrude as the wheel did its terrible work. He was not disappointed. Gertrude, holding a handkerchief to her mouth, was indeed faint and about to wretch as she held on to the railing for support.

"Please," she said, her voice barely audible amidst the cacophony of squealing, "take me back."

"We're almost there Miss," the runner said, ignoring her plaintive request. "There, you can see the admin building just across the way."

The runner left Gertrude in the waiting room of the accounts department. Still trembling, Gertrude sat for some time as she tried to recover from the trauma of what she had just witnessed. A harried desk clerk paid her no notice. Having decided that under no circumstances could she ever work in such an environment, even as a filing clerk, she was trying to work up the courage to make her way back to the stone gate. She was about to leave when Nelson Mayweather appeared.

"Miss Gibson," he said with surprise. He came over to her and held out his hand. "I didn't expect you until later this afternoon."

Gertrude put away her handkerchief and looked up.

"Good afternoon, Mr. Mayweather. It is nice to see you again."

"Well, won't you come in to my office, and we can talk about finding you a position."

"Mr. Mayweather," she replied, "I think I was mistaken to have come here. You see . . . "

"We can talk about it," Mayweather interrupted. "Since you are here, won't you come in?"

"Just for a few minutes, since I am here, but . . . "

"This way, Miss Gibson."

He led her into a modest windowless office and ushered her to the chair in front of his desk.

"Are you all right?" he asked, observing that she was in some distress.

"I saw the pigs, the . . . "

"You mean they took you through the plant?" Mayweather said with exasperation. "You should have called me when you arrived, Miss Gibson. It was not necessary to take you through the plant."

Mayweather now understood and made a mental note to track down the runner who had so traumatized the woman whom he had hoped to ingratiate.

"You see, I couldn't possibly work at this plant, I . . . "

"I understand completely, Miss Gibson," Mayweather again interrupted. "Of course, here in accounting we have no contact with the plant operations."

Gertrude shook her head. "No, I couldn't."

There was a silence as Mayweather considered what tack to take. He recalled the desperation in Gertrude's voice when she had called him, and he noted that her clothes were even more dull and drab than when he saw her on the train.

"Miss Gibson, I do have some contacts with other companies — restaurants, wholesalers, hotels, with whom we do business. Is there any possibility that you might be able to join me for dinner this evening? I would very much like to help you if I can."

Gertrude thought for a moment. She had three dollars in her pocket and had not eaten properly for weeks. The alternative to accepting Mayweather's invitation would be to spend yet another unpleasant evening with Bonnie."

"You are very kind, Mr. Mayweather, but I'm afraid I'm not dressed for such an occasion and I . . . "

"Miss Gibson, you would look lovely in any dress, and I would consider it an honor if you would accompany me this evening."

Gertrude smiled for the first time in weeks.
"Yes, I would be happy to dine with you.

It was agreed that Mayweather would call for her at 8 p.m. at her flat. Splurging on a seventy-five cent hansom ride back to Twenty-first Street, Gertrude's immediate regret was that there was little she could do to improve her appearance for the evening. She had one change of frock back at the flat, but it was no more suitable than the plain one she was already wearing. She was still furious that Bonnie had given up her eleven-dollar outfit from Marshall Field's to satisfy a one dollar and twenty cents rent deficiency. She could take a bath, freshen up, fix her hair, and apply some lipstick, but that was all.

She had the hansom stop by the Western Union office to see if there was any money from her sister. There was not. When she checked her mailbox, however, she was delighted to find a letter from Evelyn. She tore it open with great anticipation. It read:

Dearest Gertie,

I have received your letter of the 29th, and am so sorry to hear of your difficulties. I talked to Michael about finding some money to tide you over. Unfortunately, we are quite strapped ourselves these days, what with the steep mortgage payment on our house and some business reversals, but I sold a bracelet Michael gave me before we were married (he doesn't know), and it fetched seven dollars from our local pawnbroker. It's worth more, but that is all he would give me. I can't get out of the house this week to go to Western Union, but Michael will be out of town on a business trip next week and I will wire you the money then.

I wish there was more I could do to help. If you are truly desperate, I have one idea that I am reluctant to convey to you. Do you remember the art gallery opening that you and I attended when you last visited St. Louis? You may recall a man who quite inappropriately followed you around that evening, a Mr. Emil Strouss. When you mentioned that you might one day go to Chicago, he encouraged you to look him up if you ever came to the city. I have since learned that he is quite wealthy and owns a textile business in Chicago named Strouss, Eisenradth & Company. Of course, I cannot vouch for him in any way, but he did seem quite taken with you and might be able to help you. If you do look him up, please be careful, as I have no idea what type of man he is, and he did not impress me.

As you requested, I have not mentioned your difficulties to father, although he asks about you quite frequently. You really should write him more often as you know how much he cares for you.

Your devoted sister,
Evelyn

Gertrude, elated that her circumstances were improving, put the letter in her purse and ran up the stairs to the flat. She put her key in the door, but the bolt was latched from the inside.

"Bonnie?" Gertrude called, knocking at the door.

After several moments with no response, Gertrude knocked again.

"Bonnie, I need to come in. Bonnie, open the door!"

"Go away!" Gertrude finally heard from within.

Gertrude pounded on the door.

"Bonnie, you must let me in! I have to get some things!"

A disheveled Bonnie opened the door a crack and peered at Gertrude through the opening.

"Come back later. I'm busy now," Bonnie said hoarsely.

"Busy?" Gertrude said with exasperation as she pushed open the door. "How can you be busy?"

As she stood at the threshold, Gertrude beheld an appalling sight. Standing at the bedroom door was a middle-aged bearded man, stark naked, frantically trying to put on a pair of grimy coveralls.

"Oh my God!" Gertrude cried. "Who is that?"

As Gertrude looked on in astonishment, the man buckled his coveralls, hastily put on his shirt, and stuffed his feet into his heavy shoes without bothering to tie the laces.

"Here," he said, throwing two quarters on the table, "you didn't tell me we'd have company. I ain't paying a dollar for this."

With that he shuffled out and slammed the door.

For a moment the two women stood looking at each other.

Bonnie crossed her arms. "What are you looking at, Miss Princess Primrose? How'd you think we were going to pay the rent?"

Gertrude was still too dumbfounded to speak.

"I can make five dollars a day while you make your stinkin' pennies scraping your fingers raw at that slave shop."

Gertrude remained speechless.

"Oh, I forgot, the princess is too good for this! Well, you weren't too good to seduce Johnny, were you? It's because of you that I'm doing this!

You're the one who made me leave Mercer Street. I was fine there. It's all your fault! Do you hear me? It's all your fault."

Stunned, moving in a fog, Gertrude went to the closet and fetched her bag. Bonnie followed her as she went to the bedroom and began stuffing her bag with personal effects.

"That's right, just go! Just get out! I don't need you now! It's you who's the whore! Good riddance!"

Bonnie slammed the door hard as Gertrude made her exit.

10

"Man admires and often tries to exaggerate whatever characteristics nature may have given him."

Charles Darwin

Kinsley's Restaurant on Adams Street, the most elegant eating establishment in Chicago, was known as the "Delmonico's of the West." Before the Great Fire, it had been located in Crosby's Opera House. After the destruction of the opera house in the fire, H.M. Kinsley built a five-story Moorish castle in which diners could choose from the French or German café, the Ladies and Gentlemen's Restaurant, or the Gentleman's Restaurant.

Nelson Mayweather was not a wealthy man, but neither was he a poor one. His salary as head of the accounting department at Armour and Company was adequate for his needs, and he supplemented his income by facilitating contacts between Armour customers. He maintained a comfortable set of rooms in a new building of flats near the New Tremont Hotel and could afford the latest men's fashions in order to present himself most advantageously.

Determined to make a favorable impression upon Gertrude, with whom he had by now become infatuated, he had made reservations to take her to Kinsley's Castle. He was prepared even to take her to the extravagantly elegant Ladies and Gentlemen's Restaurant, but decided on the German Café as an establishment where Gertrude would not feel as out of place in her modest frock.

After her abrupt exit from her Twenty-first Street flat, Gertrude had realized that she could never return there. With but two dollars in her pocket, she knew that unless Mayweather could find her a position quickly she could not stay in Chicago more than a day or two — perhaps as long as a week if she received Evelyn's seven dollars very soon. The long list of personal calamities that she had experienced since coming to Chicago — the Mercer Street horror, the incident with Jonathan on the Michigan Queene and the subsequent hateful alienation of Bonnie, the mortifying circumstances of her sacking at the Boston Store, the crushing servitude of the shirtwaist factory, the revolting exhibition at the stockyards, and finally the shocking spectacle of Bonnie's self-destructive abasement — had resigned her to forsaking her dreams and returning to Sandoval.

Evelyn's suggestion to contact the less than appealing Emil Strouss (whom she could barely remember meeting in St. Louis) had seemed of doubtful potential, and she placed little hope on Mr. Mayweather other than to provide her with a decent meal and a pleasant evening to help her forget the miseries of the summer.

Gertrude had not had time to freshen up or bathe before her abrupt departure, and as she stood at the bottom of the stairwell, dressed in her sweatshop attire and holding in her small canvas bag all her worldly possessions, she knew that she presented a piteous figure. It was only six o'clock and Mayweather was not due to call until eight. Not wishing to stand at the bottom of the stairwell for two hours, nor wanting to risk a confrontation with Bonnie should she leave the flat, Gertrude walked across the street to a small café. There she procured a small table by the window and watched for the arrival of Mayweather's hansom. She wanted to be sure to intercept him before he walked up the stairwell to call for her at her flat.

At five minutes to eight, Gertrude saw Mayweather exit from a smart hansom across the street. Carrying her bag, she waved and called to him.

Mayweather turned around.

"Miss Gibson!" he said, as much in surprise as delight at the sight of her.

As she crossed Twenty-first Street, dodging an omnibus and gasping for breath, Mayweather took her bag.

"Miss Gibson, please let me take that." He wanted very much to compliment her on how she looked, but given her scruffy appearance he feared it might be construed as sarcasm. Except for her features, she looked like a typical factory girl.

"You must forgive me, Mr. Mayweather," Gertrude said breathlessly. "You see, I've had to leave my flat, and I . . . "

"Come, get in," Mayweather said with an indulgent smile. He escorted her to the waiting hansom. "You can tell me all about it at dinner."

Gertrude sat self-consciously. She was seated across from Mayweather at a cozy corner table of the German Café. Looking around, she saw other well-dressed couples and felt deeply the inferiority revealed by her appearance.

Nervously, she looked over the menu. Although desperately hungry, she recognized few of the items on the menu. Many of the entrees were in German, and others suggested exotic dishes with spicy sauces. It was the prices, however, that caused her to gasp. Roast chicken was a dollar fifty, tenderloin steak two dollars, prime rib three fifty and pheasant four dollars.

"Are you hungry?" Mayweather asked.

"Yes, very," Gertrude replied softly. "There are so many items . . . "

"Would you permit me?"

"Yes, of course, whatever you recommend."

Mayweather waved for the waiter, who appeared instantly.

"The lady shall have the pheasant."

"Yes, sir, a fine choice for the lady," the smart, uniformed black waiter responded with approval.

After ordering fish for himself (not wanting to remind Gertrude in any way of the stockyards and their products) Mayweather dismissed the waiter, sat back, and smiled.

"Tell me, how is your friend you introduced me to at the station?"

Gertrude paused uncomfortably. "I'm afraid we had a bit of a falling out. You see, that's what I was going to tell you. I haven't been able to find steady work, and unless I find work soon I shall have to go back home."

"You mean home to your family?"

"Yes."

"I see. But you've hardly been here a month. I'll help you find something."

"I just couldn't work at the plant, you understand."

"Yes, yes. I take it that Marshall Field's did not work out."

Gertrude hung her head. "No, they didn't have anything."

"Well, it's just as well. What do they pay there? Four or five dollars a week? You can't live on that, can you?"

Gertrude was too embarrassed to tell Mayweather about her job at the Boston Store where she earned even less than that. "Yes, it's difficult, but with a roommate to share the rent . . . "

"Even so, what kind of life is that? You can do much better. We'll find you something better. In the meantime where will you be staying?"

"Well, that's just it, you see. I can't go back to my flat, what with our falling out; and I don't have enough money to stay here more than a few days."

"Miss Gibson . . . might I call you Gertrude?"

"Yes, of course."

"Gertrude, I was hoping you might permit me to help you a bit until you find a suitable position. I live a few blocks from the New Tremont Hotel, and I know the manager there. I think you would find it quite comfortable there, and I know the manager would give you the best rate."

"Oh, no, I couldn't . . . " Gertrude protested.

"It would be just a loan, you understand. You could repay me from the earnings from your future employment, and I have no doubt that we can find you something suitable. Then, when you are settled in your new position, you would find your own flat, of course."

"I don't know," Gertrude stammered, trying to calculate whether any position for which she might qualify would pay enough to repay such a loan. She also thought of the words of her father, who had cautioned her about becoming obliged to men who inevitably wanted something in return.

"You don't really want to return home, do you?"

Gertrude sighed. "No."

"Then you must let me help you."

"Why?" she asked innocently.

Mayweather looked puzzled.

"Why do you want to help me?" she repeated.

Mayweather stiffened slightly, then sat forward.

"I think you are a most charming young lady, and I believe you have a wonderful future in Chicago. You have only to find a situation worthy of you. I have the means to help you, and therefore I want to. Will you trust me?"

Gertrude nodded, not asking herself why she should trust someone she hardly knew.

"Then it's settled. Tonight I shall procure a room for you at the Tremont, and you shall repay me when you are able. Now, the next question is, how we shall go about finding you a suitable position. Would you be terribly offended if I took the liberty of giving you some advice?"

"No, please."

"It might offend you."

"No, please tell me what you think I should do."

"Well, Gertrude, it's your, your . . . "

At this, Gertrude turned crimson. "You mean my clothes, don't you?"

"Please, don't be offended. You look charming, I assure you. But if you want to get a proper position, I would suggest . . . "

Gertrude shook her head, feeling even more deeply the shame in how she looked. "I know, I know. I am so embarrassed." She looked up at him defensively. "I told you I had nothing to wear this evening."

"No, no, I am not thinking of this evening. I am thinking of how you might best present yourself to prospects at the firm I have in mind."

Gertrude did not need to be told how drably she was dressed and, despite her promise not to be offended, felt resentment at his observation. Was he so obtuse as not to understand that she did not choose to be dressed like a factory girl but was reduced to such a lowly state by her lack of money?

As tears began to well up in her eyes, Mayweather realized that he was taking the wrong approach.

"I say this only because I want to help you in this regard as well. If you will permit me to make an advance on your future earnings, I would like very much for you to purchase a new wardrobe."

"Oh, no, Mr. Mayweather, I couldn't let you do that . . . "

"It would just be a loan. I would expect you to pay me back when you are able."

"Oh, I don't know." Gertrude was genuinely torn between her overwhelming need to improve her station and her conscience, which told her that there was something not right about accepting his help.

"Gertrude, think about it, please. What can you do by yourself without help? It would make me very happy if you would let me assist you."

"It would make you happy?" she asked, only to eager to find a respectable reason for accepting his kindness.

"Yes, it would make me quite happy."

There was a long silence as Gertrude considered her alternatives. She knew very well that Mayweather was right — she could never find an advantageous position dressed as a factory girl, or even a shop girl. There was no future for her in Sandoval, and she lacked the means to stay much longer in Chicago unless she went back to a place like the shirtwaist factory to earn a subsistence wage and perhaps break her own health.

"What would you say to this?" Mayweather added. "Tomorrow morning I will open an account for you at Marshall Field's. I will put enough in your account for you to buy what you need."

Marshall Field's! Gertrude thought to herself delightfully — and she as a customer not a common wage-seeker. She replayed in her mind the dazzling array of dresses, gowns, shoes, purses, petticoats, laces, and ribbons which she had seen that first day in the store.

"Perhaps I shall go look," Gertrude said cautiously, wondering, but not daring to ask, just how much might be in the account. "Well, perhaps I will just go look."

Mayweather clapped his hands together softly. "It's settled then. Look, here comes your pheasant!"

11

Dance light, little maid, in your old-world gown,
*   In your high-heeled slippers and dark brown hair;*
Small wonder 'King Louis turned to look'
*   If the real marquise was but half so fair.*

With outstretched, patient, beseeching hands
*   Poor Pierot follows you through the world,*
And you care less for his hopeless love
*   Than for one bright lock on your dark brow curled.*

Would you treat one so if the play were real?
*   Or is gay coquetry part of the dress,*
With the satin slippers and silken train
*   And laces, light as your lips' caress?*

The years are swift and the play is short,
*   But jest and earnest may ofttimes meet,*
And, in jest or earnest, I pray you dear,
*   Dance light, for my heart lies under your feet.*

Grace Goodale, "Dance Light for My Heart Lies Under Your Feet"
(Cover song for the Maxfield Parrish painting on lithographic crayon
"At An Amateur Pantomime," 1898).

Luxuriating in the clean linen and firm mattress of the canopied bed in her room at the Tremont, Gertrude considered sleeping the entire morning. Instead, she rose early, took a long hot bath, and prepared to go out.

Gertrude had promised to look, and so she decided to do so. She would have gone directly to Marshall Field's, but she remembered that Mayweather had said he was to open an account for her in the morning. She would have to allow several hours for him to do so.

It was 11:00 a.m. when she arrived at the monoliths of Karnak. She went first to the hat department, and asked the shop girl to set aside a Juliet cap so that it might be available should she later decide to purchase it. Taking the elevator to the third floor she next viewed accessories. From there she looked at petticoats and undergarments, eyeing in particular the straight-fronted corset with the latest "Neena" inserts, and a sueded tricot corset with lace trimming. By midmorning she was in the dress department, and she quickly fell in love with a suit of moiré, consisting of an elegant velvet jacket trimmed with braid, and a silk skirt with flared flounces. She could not resist holding before her a crushed strawberry satin evening gown with silver and mauve embroidered bands, though she knew its cost greatly exceeded any amount Mayweather could conceivably have deposited in her account.

She made her final selections in the shoe salon, where she picked out a pair of black patent leather, buttoned-bar walking shoes with high vamps and a silver buckle, and pumps of beige suede with pointed toes and high waisted heels.

As she enjoyed coffee in the tearoom, she made a list in her mind of the dresses she would try on before the mirror. She spent the afternoon trying on her selections; it took an entire hour to try on the moiré suit, complete with corset, hat, gloves, shoes, suspenders and inserts. By a coincidence that smacked to her of fate, the suit fit perfectly.

Once she saw herself before the mirror, she possessed the suit completely in her own mind and could no more have given it up than if it had always been hers all along and someone were trying to steal it from her. For the first time since coming to Chicago, she beamed with delight, and the color came instantly to her cheeks. In those few moments before the mirror she became a woman she hardly even knew, a woman known only from the cover of the *Ladies Home Journal*.

She would have the suit and the gloves and the hat and the stockings. She would have them all — if the account had one hundred dollars.

It did.

At dinner with Gertrude that evening at the Tremont Hotel Restaurant, Mayweather was astonished by Gertrude's transformation. Even in his fantasies, he had not dreamt of such beauty. After showering her with compliments, he presented her with a gift — a gold stickpin with a pearl on the tip.

Basking in his admiration, Gertrude made only the mildest protest and accepted graciously. However, she could not help wondering how long her besotted wooer could maintain such patronage. He was, after all, only a salaried company man for whom a hundred dollars had to be a considerable sum. For all she knew, his funds might even now be close to depletion. So when Mayweather, despite his generosity, could report no progress in securing her a position — though only a day had passed — she felt a vague disquietude and began to question where her dependency might lead. Despite her fine clothes, comfortable lodgings, and satisfied belly, she still had no money. She could be back on the streets within a day at Mayweather's whim. For this reason there could be no harm in pursuing other opportunities, such as the prospect Evelyn had mentioned in her letter — to wit, the infamous Emil Strouss.

With the memories of Mercer Street and her days of insufferable servitude at the mercy of others still etched vividly in her mind, paramount in her vision of her future was the notion that on no account could she regress. Her conscience was dealt with summarily by a simple thought: Mayweather had said it would make him happy for her to allow him to help her. And so she had. It was thus for his sake, not her own, that she had accepted his generosity. Along these lines she also considered whether her acquiescence could be morally rationalized by the simple expedient of returning his affection.

In was in this regard that she considered him closely that evening. The fact was that he was at least ten years her senior and she knew little about him. Certainly his appearance was pleasing, and his meticulous grooming had impressed her. This evening he was smartly dressed in a gray worsted three-piece lounge suit and gray spats over black shoes. He had as yet made no demands upon her modesty or shown dishonorable intent. When and if he did so, she told herself, she could deal with it as it came.

During the course of the evening, as she listened to his chatter about business dealings in which she had no interest, she realized that she was not physically attracted to him. Certainly he posed no challenge to her. There was also something vaguely disquieting about him that she could not yet identify — perhaps nothing more than his association with the stockyards. Perhaps it was something more. In any case, she had little to risk in her present circumstances by giving him time to find a position for her, even as she pursued other opportunities.

On Monday morning, Gertrude enjoyed a luxury she had not enjoyed since coming to Chicago. With nothing in particular to do, she spent an hour dressing and styling her hair. After a brief lunch that she charged to her room, she checked at the front desk for any messages from Mayweather. There being none, she inquired about the location of Strouss, Eisenradth & Company. Recognizing Gertrude as the same woman who, in factory clothes had checked in two nights previously, the desk clerk obliged.

"Yes, Miss, let me look it up for you in the business directory."

He flipped through the pages of the directory.

"Yes, here it is. Strouss, Eisendrath & Company on Kinzie Street. It's near the river."

"How far is that?" Gertrude inquired. "What would be a fair hansom fare?"

"It's about two miles. Don't pay more than 45 cents."

"Thank you."

Gertrude stepped out into the street and hailed a hansom.

In 1899, there were 4,007 millionaires in America. Emil Strouss was one of them. He was the owner of Strouss, Eisendrath & Company, which was a gray, sprawling complex of buildings covering a six-block area along the Chicago River. The executive offices of its owner, Emil Strouss, were in a three-story building on the south side of the complex overlooking the river.

When Gertrude arrived at the reception area of the executive offices, she found the large desk vacant. She sat down to wait for the secretary to return.

After twenty minutes, she stood up and began to pace, wondering if any one was about. As she waited, she noticed a detailed model of a textile machine on the receptionist's desk. Curious, she walked over to the desk to get a better look. Lying next to the model, she noticed an elaborate engraved invitation that read:

The Chicago Opera Company Requests the Company of Mr. Emil Strouss at a Benefit in the Grand Ballroom of the Chicago Auditorium. Thursday, August 11, 1899. Suggested Contribution: Twenty-Five Dollars.

"May I help you?" came a husky voice. It was Emil Strouss' secretary, a sturdy middle-aged woman standing in the doorway to an adjoining office.

Startled, Gertrude turned around.

"Yes, I was wondering if it would be possible to see Mr. Strouss?"

"Mr. Strouss is very busy. Do you have an appointment?" the secretary asked testily.

"No. I met him last year in St. Louis, and he suggested I come see him if I was ever in Chicago."

"I see," said the secretary, scowling with transparent skepticism. "Well, Mr. Strouss is in New York at the moment and will not be returning until tomorrow morning. Shall I inform him who called when he returns?"

Gertrude shifted nervously. "No, that's all right. Perhaps I shall return some other time."

"Very well," said the secretary as she sat at her desk and busied herself in paperwork. Gertrude nodded timidly and took her leave.

Later that evening, it occurred to Gertrude that perhaps her trip to meet Strouss had not been completely unproductive. She remembered the date of the benefit, Thursday, August 11, which was three days hence. It occurred to her that since it was a fund-raising affair, it might not be difficult to procure an invitation. She had no way of knowing whether Strouss would attend, but it was at least possible since he was returning the following day. A benefit ball might provide a more suitable setting for meeting Strouss than a visit to his factory office. At dinner that evening with Mayweather, she decided to bring the matter up.

"I went to see about a position today," Gertrude mentioned casually as she sipped her wine.

"Oh, where?"

"At the Strouss, Eisendrath & Company on Kinzie Street. I met the owner, Mr. Strouss, at a social affair in St. Louis last year. My sister recently wrote me, reminding me of our meeting. She suggested that I see him for help in finding a position. However, he wasn't in so I didn't see him."

Mayweather was not thrilled by this news. He had already made a substantial investment in Gertrude and was not pleased by the prospect that she might now find a position without his help.

"Well, you know I'm working very hard to find you a position, and just today I made a promising contact with a large accounting firm, Larson and Myers. Of course, I have heard of Strouss Manufacturing, but it — Mr. Strouss I mean — doesn't have a very good reputation in this town. He's successful — in the financial sense, that is; but he pays his workers practically nothing and works them night and day because the workers are mostly unskilled and aren't unionized. From what I hear, Emil Strouss is a textile tycoon of the worst kind. And socially he's not the sort to be invited to dinner with Pullman, McCormick, or Marshall Field."

Gertrude shrugged. "Perhaps you're right. But I need to find something. I can't keep relying on your kindness."

"I hope to have an interview set up for you next week at the accounting firm."

"What type of work would it be?"

"Filing," he finally replied.

"Oh," said Gertrude without enthusiasm.

"You know," said Gertrude, changing the subject, "I have heard that there is to be a benefit ball for the Chicago Opera Company at the Auditorium on Thursday. Have you ever been to such events?"

"Why, yes," said Mayweather, still eager to make an impression on Gertrude. "I read about the opera benefit in the Times. Would you care to go?"

"There is a requested contribution of twenty-five dollars."

"Oh," said Mayweather, mentally calculating whether his bank account could withstand yet another major withdrawal. This concern was balanced by his vision of being seen at such an event with a woman of Gertrude's comeliness.

"It would be for a worthy cause. I shall procure an invitation and would be pleased to escort you."

"That would be wonderful!" gushed Gertrude. "There is only one problem."

"What is that, my dear?"

"The clothes you bought for me at Marshall Fields are simply exquisite. But as for a gown, suitable for such a ball . . . "

"Never you mind about that. Tomorrow you shall go back to Marshall Field's and purchase a suitable gown."

Gertrude smiled. She had a particular gown in mind that would be quite suitable indeed.

12

"Beauty is a greater recommendation than any letter of introduction."

Aristotle

O n the evening of the Chicago Opera Grand Benefit Ball, Gertrude, dressed in the low-cut strawberry satin evening gown of silver and mauve, displayed neck plump and full and skin like satin.

Mayweather felt himself the object of envy as he and Gertrude made their appearance at the ballroom fountain. It was around this central fountain, washed in electrical lights in the rainbow colors, that the Chosen of Chicago society paraded their array in a grand promenade while the full opera orchestra on the balcony above played the latest Strauss waltzes.

Mayweather himself wore black tails with silk lapels, braid trouser seams, slippers, and top hat. The purchase of this ensemble, along with Gertrude's strawberry gown, had finally depleted his reserves. Only by pawning his gold watch would he be able to keep Gertrude at the Tremont for another week. He had hoped that a business deal he had been pursuing would enable him to play the protector for some time longer, gaining more time to win Gertrude's affection. But soon, he realized, he would face the moment of truth when Gertrude would have to accept him for what he really was — a modestly salaried company man. If he found work for Gertrude as he had promised, there might still be hope.

Somehow Gertrude had sensed that Mayweather, despite his confident front and protestations, was being played out. She had been willing to take him at face value because the alternative was to believe that she was being deceived; and if she were deceived, no one could fault her if she broke her bonds of dependence.

Gertrude now saw two visions of her future — the first, a modest life with Mayweather, who adored her but for whom she nursed only a feeling of gratitude; and the second, a distinctly different vision of herself as an object of admiration among the truly rich and prosperous men who surrounded her at the ball.

Excusing herself to powder her nose, Gertrude made discreet inquiries: Had anyone seen a Mr. Emil Strouss? On her fourth such inquiry, she was directed toward a group of men standing near the grand staircase. There, among the group, standing and chatting amiably, was the man whom she only faintly remembered. Not sure if it was he, she came closer, feigning confusion, and caught his eye. Several others in the entourage also looked her way. At his second glance, Emil Strouss recognized her. Excusing himself, he broke off his conversation and came over to her.

"Miss, Miss . . . "

Gertrude fanned herself briskly and looked away.

"Miss Gibson, isn't it?" Strouss said.

"Why yes. Do I know you, sir?"

"Are you not Gertrude Gibson of St. Louis, and did we not meet there last summer?"

"Why, I do not recall, sir."

"I am sure we met — at an art exhibition I believe. Mr. William Weller introduced us, and I had met your sister Evelyn on a previous occasion."

"You know Evelyn?"

"Yes, indeed."

"Oh," Gertrude said, looking away nervously and fanning herself with renewed vigor.

"May I offer you a glass of champagne, Ms. Gibson?"

"Well, I am here with an escort, though for my life I can not find him."

"An unforgivable offense, to misplace so charming a young lady."

She looked away again, annoyed that the man upon whom she had placed such expectations had not the grace to disguise his awkward stare at her décolletage. He was, as she remembered, distinctly unappealing — balding, rotund, with a sagging double chin. Yet at this instant, she made a fateful decision.

"Perhaps one glass, then."

Gertrude Gibson Patterson awoke from her reverie and glanced down at the counsel table as she remembered the fateful words she had uttered that night at the Auditorium Ball. Would she be here today, in this court-room, charged with murder in the first degree, if she had turned away and returned to Mayweather? She thought of the countless, infinite number of decision points in her life that could be traced to that one moment — to those few fateful words.

Her counsel, Mr. O.N. Hilton, was at the bench arguing a motion about an obscure point of law. She gazed back up at the window, and re-entered her private world of memories.

"Perhaps one glass, then."

"Splendid! We are having a soiree in the Lincoln room off the mezzanine. Won't you join us?"

Gertrude followed Strouss up the grand staircase, looking back for Mayweather. She did not see him.

"Gentlemen, I would like you to meet Miss Gertrude Gibson," Strouss announced to an assemblage of prosperous looking business men in fashionable evening wear who had congregated near a center table in the oak-paneled Lincoln Room. "Her sister is a dear friend of mine from St. Louis."

All approached her, taking her hand in turn amid a cacophony of "charmeds" and "delighteds."

"Gentlemen, you must excuse us," said Strouss interrupting. I have a lot to catch up on with Miss Gibson. I haven't seen her for over a year."

He turned to the server at the nearby champagne table.

"A glass of champagne for the lady," Strouss instructed the white-aproned server.

Gertrude took the glass and sipped it slowly.

"Now, you must tell me how Evelyn is getting along," Strouss said as he directed her to a large leather chair in front of an alabaster fireplace.

"She and her husband are well, thank you," said Gertrude, sitting.

"Unbearably hot down there in St. Louis this time of year."

"It's quite hot enough here," Gertrude said fanning herself.

"That is a beautiful gown you are wearing this evening, Miss Gibson. You look absolutely enchanting."

"Thank you, Mr. Strouss."

"Now tell me how you happen to be in Chicago."

"I have come to find work, but without much success I fear."

"What kind of work are you looking for, may I ask?"

"Anything, really. Except in the stockyards. I shouldn't want to work there, I think."

At this Strouss broke into a long and hearty belly laugh, his double chin quivering in a most unappealing fashion.

"I should think not! Not a pretty young lady such as yourself."

Gertrude took a sip.

"Have you thought about the textile business?" Strouss asked.

Gertrude considered telling him about her unpleasant experience at the shirtwaist factory but decided it would be better not to reveal the lowly station to which she had been reduced.

"I have heard the work is terribly hard."

"Yes, but it's honest work. And machines have made our workers the most productive in the world."

Gertrude nodded.

"It's in the business end of textiles that you might have more interest, I think."

"Business end?"

"Yes. Producing the cloth, the woolens, and the dry goods is only half of what I do. I must sell my products for the best price to make a profit. I spend much of the year abroad negotiating with customers — wholesalers mostly, but some retailers."

"It sounds terribly exciting, Mr. Strouss. Where do you go abroad?"

"To France, Paris mostly. Have you ever been there?"

"Oh, no. Except for two trips to St. Louis to visit my sister, I've never been out of Illinois."

"Looking at you, Miss Gibson, I would say that you and Paris were made for each other."

"Do you think so?" she asked innocently.

"Yes, I do most certainly."

Gertrude gazed into the fire.

"You know," said Strouss, picking up the conversation, "my greatest difficulty in selling my products to customers is the language. I speak only a few words of French, and am at the mercy of my customers' interpreters. This puts me at a great disadvantage. What I really need is an interpreter I can trust. Tell me, Miss Gibson, have you ever thought about studying the French language?"

"Oh, no sir. But I think I would very much like to learn. It is a beautiful language, is it not?"

"Indeed. Did you learn French in school at all, Miss Gibson?"

Gertrude sighed. "I fear that my education has been deficient."

"What if you could return to school? Would you want to?"

Gertrude laughed and threw her head back in such a fetching way that Strouss was visibly entranced.

"I should love to learn French, I think."

"Is that all?"

"And art, and philosophy, and music, and . . . I should like to play the harp, I think."

"The harp?"

Gertrude nodded.

Several minutes passed as Gertrude looked into the fire, and Strouss pretended to. Gertrude felt his gaze on her silk-clad ankles, but she did not cover them; instead, she crossed them so as to expose them fully.

"Miss Gibson?" Strouss asked, breaking the silence.

"Yes?"

"Have you heard of the Standard Club?"

"No, I've been in Chicago but a short time."

"It is where I live, on Michigan Avenue downtown. I don't live in a house because I travel so much and have no wife and family. If you truly have an interest in going to school and learning French, I would very much like to show you some brochures I have of French schools. Would you also be interested in seeing some photographs of Paris?"

"Why, yes, I would. Do you mean this evening?"

"Yes, yes," Strouss replied, grateful that he had not needed to be explicit. "This evening, yes."

Gertrude hesitated. "I would have to let my escort know."

"Of course," he said rising.

"No, please wait here," she said, touching him lightly on the shoulder. I will return in a few minutes."

Gertrude smiled to the men who had kept a discreet distance during her intimate conversation with Strouss.

"Excuse me, gentlemen."

The men bowed in appreciation as she passed through.

As she reached the bottom of the staircase, Gertrude saw Mayweather standing by the fountain and frantically looking about.

"Oh, there you are!" he said with relief as Gertrude approached.

"Nelson" she said with excitement. "I think I may have found an excellent opportunity for a position."

"Here?" he asked.

"Yes! You will never believe who I met — Emil Strouss! It was an extraordinary coincidence. I think he may have a position for me."

"But Gertrude, what about your interview with the accounting firm next week?"

"I can still do that if this doesn't work out."

Mayweather looked crestfallen.

"You wouldn't want me to pass up this opportunity, would you?"

Mayweather wondered if she remembered anything he had told her about Strouss. "No, no, of course not. It's just that . . . "

"See, he wants to tell me some things about the position this evening . . . "

"This evening!"

"I think I should look at what he wants to show me. He may forget about the whole matter tomorrow. You understand, don't you?"

"Why can't you just go to this factory tomorrow? It will be late tonight when you . . . "

"Nelson, please understand," Gertrude said, stamping her feet in exasperation. "I can't let this opportunity pass. If you cared about me you would want me to do this!"

Mayweather knew he had lost this battle, and deep within he knew he had lost her as well.

"Sure," he said. "I'll call you tomorrow in the morning to see how it went."

"Late in the morning would be better. I must go now!"

Mayweather nodded as Gertrude turned heel. He watched her as she held up her gown and walked up the staircase. She did not yet move with the grace of a princess, but he had no doubt that she soon would.

He sighed with regret as he realized he would never see it.

He had been granted one week of bliss, and it had cost him all that he had.

13

"Money — it has no meaning without a woman to spend it on."

John Paul Getty

The chauffeur of the Woods Electric Hansom stepped down from his perch on the hansom when he saw his employer, Mr. Emil Strouss, exit the Michigan Boulevard entrance of the Auditorium Building. He was surprised to see a young lady with him. He held open the door of the hansom.

"Thank you, Herbert," Strouss said as he approached the vehicle.

"Herbert, I want you to meet a most charming young lady, Miss Gertrude Gibson."

Herbert tipped his hat. "Good evening ma'am."

Strouss held Gertrude's hand and helped her into the crushed velvet interior of the vehicle. Strouss followed, and Herbert closed the door behind them.

The Woods Electric Hansom looked in all respects like the familiar horse-drawn hansoms that plied the most fashionable streets of Chicago — that is, with the driver sitting at the top and rear of the carriage — with one remarkable exception: There was no horse. It was the first model of an electric car made by the Woods Electric Vehicle Company, and a lithograph of it graced the spectacular color cover of the company's 1899 catalogue. In all of Chicago, there were only ninety electric cars, and none as sumptuous as the Woods Electric Hansom. There were also fifty-five internal combustion vehicles licensed in Chicago, most produced by the Duryea Company. However, none of these primitive internal combustion contraptions were enclosed since they vibrated so severely that any enclosed carriage built on such a chassis would be torn apart. This feature rendered them unsuitable for fashionable or even comfortable city transportation. The Woods Electric Hansom, on the other hand, was completely quiet and enclosed and furbished with the luxurious interior of the plushest horse-drawn carriages.

Gertrude had never seen such a vehicle before. She gazed at the lush interior trappings with quiet amazement and softly stroked the velvet seats and silken coverings.

"My," she said, visibly impressed. "What kind of carriage is this?"

"The newest electric model," replied Strouss, pleased by her reaction. "Do you like it?"

"It's wonderful. And so quiet."

Strouss detached an ivory voice tube. "The Standard Club, Herbert."

The Standard Club on Michigan Avenue was the swankest residential apartment building in Chicago. Its closest rivals were the elegant Palmer House and the Congress Hotel, an Auditorium annex connected to the Auditorium by a tunnel under Congress Street.

Strouss' seventeen-room suite covered the entire seventh floor of the Standard Club. Strouss had selected it because, unlike the Palmer House and Congress Hotel, it made no pretensions of catering to social or racial pedigrees. Its sole requirement for residence was an ability to pay the eight thousand dollar annual lease payment, the three thousand dollar a year club fees, and a fifty thousand dollar initiation fee.

The rooms were lavishly decorated with French furniture and art, including an original Renoir over the center fireplace in the living room, and an original Reubens in the dining room.

Gertrude gazed in wonderment as Strouss gave her a tour of the apartments. Entranced, she stopped to look at each piece of art and sculpture.

"What is this?" Gertrude asked, pointing to a sculpture of a naked figure in the garden room.

"The Venus de Milo," Strouss replied. "I wish I could say it was an original, but it's a replica sculpted by a very talented artist I met in Paris some years ago."

"Hmmmm." Gertrude murmured. "She's beautiful."

"Not half as beautiful as you, my dear. Perhaps some time you might permit my sculptor friend . . . "

Gertrude smiled, and cut off his thought. "What a lovely painting in the hallway," she said, pointing to a Rubens.

The tour ended in the study, which was lined with bookshelves.

"Please have a seat, Miss Gibson," Strouss said as he opened a polished oak cabinet. "Can I offer you a nightcap?"

"Why, thank you, Mr. Strouss," said Gertrude, sitting on the brown leather divan in front of the fireplace. "I'm a little unsteady as it is from the champagne. This is all so overwhelming."

"Emil, please. Call me Emil."

Gertrude smiled obligingly and nodded. "Emil, then."

"Perhaps an ice tonic, then?"

Gertrude nodded.

Strouss fixed her drink, handed it to her, and then went back to the cabinet and opened a lower drawer from which he removed a dark mahogany box. He brought it to her and sat down beside her on the divan.

"Open it."

Gertrude slid off the lid. Inside were pictures and brochures written in French.

"Oh," she said, taking the contents out and laying them on the coffee table.

"That is the Eiffel Tower," Strouss said picking up one of the photographs. "And this is the Louvre."

Gertrude picked up each photograph and scrutinized it closely. "How beautiful. I have always longed to see such places."

Strouss sat back and watched Gertrude as she pored over the pictures. He had thought of her often ever since he had met her so briefly in St. Louis. Now, as he watched her, he realized that he had never known a woman so enchanting and beguiling — and beautiful.

"Miss Gibson," he said, picking up a brochure and handing it to her, "these are pictures of Madame Sophie Loreac's finishing school in Paris. It is one of the most respected schools for young ladies in Paris. It has educated princesses and heiresses from all over Europe. I have a close acquaintance with Madame Dorleac, a wonderful woman whom I met some years ago in Paris."

Gertrude took the brochure and looked at pictures of the school's façade and gardens. "Such beautiful gardens. But I can't read it. It's in . . . "

"French. Yes. But would you like to? Be able to read it, I mean?" He looked deep into her eyes.

She felt the passion, ardor, and adoration in his gaze. As she did so she experienced a sudden thrill, a surge of power over a man who was transparently infatuated with her — a man who she was sure had the power to gratify her desires.

"Yes," said she, crossing her ankles so as to expose them completely. "I would like that very much."

"Would you like to go to such a school?" he asked, his lips quivering.

"Oh, yes," said she, still not sure if Strouss was merely making conversation or in fact offering to send her to school in Paris.

"If you are truly serious about going back to school and learning the French language, then I would certainly have a position to offer you as my interpreter."

"Your interpreter?" Gertrude thought for a moment. "But surely it would take several years for me to learn. What would you do for an interpreter during that period?"

She wanted to ask about how her expenses were to be paid while she was at school, but it occurred to her that since Strouss knew her circumstances, his offer implicitly included the payment of all her expenses.

"I shall have to make do with what interpreters I can find, who to date, I am sad to say, have not proved satisfactory."

"I don't know what to say, I . . . "

"It is perhaps not the sort of position you were looking for?"

"Oh, no. It is a position that I think would suit me very well — if I could learn French, that is."

"You needn't decide now. But the position I am offering would be satisfactory?"

"Oh, yes."

"Then why don't you think it over? Perhaps you should talk to your parents."

"Yes, I should talk to them. For how many years would I be in school?"

"It is four years to earn a degree in the arts, but you would not have to stay that long if you did not wish to."

"I should wish to earn a certificate." She thought for a moment. "But four years in Paris. It must be terribly expensive."

"You would leave that entirely to me, Miss Gibson."

"But why? I mean, why would you do this?"

Strouss broke into a wide grin. "Because I have much need for a good interpreter. I would ask only that you put your mind to the task of learning the French language."

It did not need to be said that his reason surely went beyond his need for an interpreter. She would consider later what might be required for her to give in return, but for now all she could think of was Paris.

"I have plans to sail to France in six weeks. If you decide you would like to join me, I will cable Madame Dorleac, and I am quite certain she will find a place for you in the fall class."

Gertrude put both her hands across her breasts. "I can hardly believe it, Mr. Strouss! It sounds like a dream! Paris!"

Strouss took her hand and held it.

"Emil," he corrected her.

"Yes, Emil," she said, leaving her hand in his and sensing his excitement.

"Would you like to see a brochure of the *Campania?*"

"The *Campania?*"

"It's the ship I will be sailing on to Paris — and you too if you decide to go."

Gertrude spent several minutes poring over postcards and brochures and sighed. "I suppose I should be getting back. What time is it?"

She had sensed that by departing now, she could heighten his desire. At the very minute she spoke, the grandfather clock in the hallway chimed two.

"It is late, my dear, I had no idea," Strouss said. He picked up a small bronze bell from the table and rang it. Edgar, the butler, appeared moments later.

"Edgar, would you go down and have Herbert bring the Woods around to the front."

"Yes, Mr. Strouss," Edgar said, bowing slightly.

Strouss stood and extended his hand.

"Now where is home, Gertrude?"

"The Tremont. For the time being at least."

"Ah yes, the Tremont." He seemed about to make a comment about it or ask a question, but then did not.

"Miss Gibson, might I make a suggestion?"

"Yes, please."

"I don't know how many nights you are booked at the Tremont, but I have an apartment I maintain at the Auditorium. I use it to entertain clients here in Chicago. It is empty now, and I have no immediate plans for its use. Perhaps you would find it convenient to stay there after your booking at the Tremont expires. It is closer to the Standard Club — should we need to discuss further the terms of your future position."

The Auditorium Hotel! Gertrude could not conceal her excitement at the suggestion.

"I . . . "

"It's called the Congress Hotel, but it's part of the Auditorium complex. I'm sure you would find it quite comfortable."

"Oh, I know I would! But . . . "

"Your things?"

"Yes, I would have to fetch them first."

"We could simply drop by the Tremont now, and Herbert could help you fetch your bags. Then we could go directly to the Auditorium, and you could stay there tonight, if you like."

Overwhelmed and excited by the prospect of actually living at the Auditorium, Gertrude readily agreed.

It was three o'clock in the morning when Strouss opened the doors of the Auditorium suite. Gertrude stood in awe at the sumptuous surroundings. There were four rooms, consisting of a spacious living room and bedroom, a boudoir with giant closets, and a bathroom finished in granite. In the living room were several Louis XVI chairs, a delicately embroidered divan, a marble fireplace, brass electric light fixtures attached to mirrors, and paintings. The centerpiece of the bedroom was a gigantic canopy bed fully enclosed with transparent silk.

"Oh, it's just beautiful!" Gertrude effused.

"I trust you will be comfortable, my dear," said Strouss.

"Oh yes, quite." Gertrude held out her hand.

Strouss took her hand, kissed it, and bowed. "Until tomorrow, then. There is a telephone, and you may call me anytime." He handed her a card with his number.

"Thank you, Mr. Strouss. You have been so generous."

"It is my pleasure, I assure you."

After Strouss left, Gertrude stood for a moment and gazed in reverence at her new surroundings, scarcely believing herself within them. Too excited to go immediately to bed, she went about each room, closely inspecting each fixture and covering.

Finally she plopped herself on the bed, arms outstretched, and gazed at the ceiling. For some time she reflected on whether it was all too good to be true, and for the briefest moment considered what price she might have to pay for all of this. Would it be a price she would be prepared to pay?

She recalled Strouss' attentions over the course of the evening and felt again the surge of power she had felt earlier in the evening — a power which she was confident she could use to set her own conditions.

And then she thought of Paris.

14

"Fashion dies very young, so we must forgive it everything."

Jean Cocteau

Gertrude spent the following three weeks acquiring a suitable wardrobe for Paris. Strouss retained a maidservant to serve Gertrude. Her name was Freda, and she was an expert in back combing, or French combing as it was called.

Gertrude spent her afternoons at Marshall Field's. The latter was a major customer of Strouss, Eisendrath & Company, and Strouss discreetly settled all of Gertrude's purchases by offsets in his business accounts with the dry goods store.

Gertrude's new wardrobe included ensembles for every conceivable occasion, from balls and the theatre to bicycling, tennis, swimming, and riding. These included a bolero suit with embroidered matching top and overskirt, basqued jackets with high revers and high Medici collars, several sports coats of crepe de chine and silk, and Ulster summer overcoats, capes, and paletots. Her tennis outfits were cut princess style, with embroidered bodice and cuffs, blouses with turned down collars showing from a V-necked front, and scarves worn around the collar. Tennis, Strouss had informed her, was a major sport at Madame Loreac's school, for which she would be well advised to practice before she arrived in Paris.

In the weeks that followed, Gertrude adapted to her new life of privilege as smoothly as she shed her clothes from the sweatshop in favor of those in Marshall Field's windows. Within a few short few weeks, her previous life of deprivation had become a distant memory. She had, it was true, suffered several bouts of conscience when she thought of her treatment of the besotted Mayweather, but her chief anxiety now was what Strouss might expect in return for what he was giving her. Thus far he had made no demands on her whatever; indeed he catered to her every whim. Perversely, however, his impeccable behavior towards her only increased her anxiety. She knew that soon — very soon — it would be necessary to articulate their relationship. In the meantime, she was content to accompany Strouss to restaurants and the theatre.

Several evenings a week Gertrude accompanied Strouss to the theatre — to *The Mikado* at the Auditorium on a Friday and to Cyrano de Bergerac (featuring the "Divine Sarah," Sarah Bernhardt) at McVickers Theatre on a Saturday. The latter play had received considerable notoriety in the press as a result of extensive litigation initiated by a certain Samuel Gross, who claimed that the essential elements of his play The Merchant Prince of Cornville (including a character with a large nose who wooed a beautiful woman by standing beneath a balcony and impersonating a handsome but colorless suitor) had been purloined by Edmond Rostand.

It was after this latter evening at the theatre, followed by dinner at the Standard Club dining room, that Gertrude brought up the subject of what was to be the terms of their relationship. She had tried on several previous occasions to bring up this same matter, but Strouss had always managed to avoid the issue by making some humorous reference that changed the subject. With but three weeks before the Campania sailed to France, Gertrude was determined not to wait another day.

Gertrude was dressed in a red low-cut gown and a pale gray redingote. Strouss, dressed in the same black tails he had worn at the Auditorium Charity Ball, stood silently as the private elevator took them to his Standard Club suite. She followed him to the study, where she took off her jacket, kicked off her shoes, and curled up on the divan in front of the fire. Strouss sat dutifully beside her. Gertrude knew it would be her task to raise the matter of terms.

"Emil," Gertrude opened, turning toward him.

Strouss did not respond but took her hand and kissed her little finger. He had kissed her hand many times before, but never quite so passionately.

"Emil, you must listen to me," she said, withdrawing her hand.

The ungainly but physically imposing textile tycoon, feared by his competitors and held in awe by his vast army of workers, hung his head submissively like a chastened schoolboy in the close presence of the object of his desire. He would have preferred that his relationship with Gertrude remain ambiguous, so that it might progress unhindered by preset rules. But the man known as the toughest negotiator in the textile industry was now prepared to agree to any terms that might keep Gertrude by his side.

Gertrude, sensing her advantage, began with a scolding.

"Emil, at Honore Palmer's dinner party last Thursday evening, you introduced me as your fiancée. Do you think that was proper, given that we have been seen together for but three weeks and have never even discussed what we are to each other, never mind marriage?"

Strouss shifted uncomfortably. "You are quite right to be offended, my dear. I spoke hastily, mindful of how Chicago society views such matters."

"Then society does not permit a man to escort a woman to dinner unless they are to be married?" Gertrude pressed her advantage.

"No, not at all, that is to say . . . "

"Is that the way it's to be then, that you may present me in any way you wish, regardless of my desires?"

"Gertrude, I only wish to make you happy."

Gertrude sighed. She put her hand on his neck and gently caressed it. "I know you do, Emil, and I am ever so grateful. Please believe that. But there must be an understanding between us."

Enthralled by her caress, Strouss was rapidly entering a state of apoplectic desire. Had Gertrude asked him at that moment to chop off his own head, he would have done it without question and thanked her for the privilege.

"I will not be your mistress," she said firmly. She had already decided that it was within her power to insist on a non-meretricious relationship.

Strouss nodded blankly, revealing nothing about what had been his expectations.

"Do you understand? I will not be your mistress."

"Gertrude, I would never ask you to," said he, as if such an idea had never crossed his mind.

Gertrude had expected Strouss to resist on this point, and his acquiescence left her for the moment speechless. There was a long silence as she considered how to make her next point, which she felt would require more delicacy.

"You must also not think that we can ever marry."

At this suggestion, however, Strouss could not hide his distress.

"It would never be possible?" he asked plaintively. The idea of marriage to Gertrude was not inconceivable to him. Some years before, President Cleveland, in his fifties, had married a girl of seventeen in an elaborate White House ceremony. Strouss was but thirty-eight to Gertrude's eighteen years, a not ridiculous age difference for the period.

For an awkward moment, Gertrude considered that she had overplayed her hand. It occurred to her that perhaps she had to at least offer hope. Although it was inconceivable to her that she could ever marry a man to whom she was not sexually attracted and for whom she felt no romantic impulses, she could not exclude the possibility that her feelings, or lack of them, might change. She had long had her own vision of the man she would marry — a dashing man with handsome features, an athletic build, thick flowing hair, and for whom she would experience the most intense sexual desire. She was not prepared to give up this idea if she did not have to. Nevertheless, she could not deny that she had developed feelings for Strouss of a different kind — feelings that went beyond mere gratitude. It was a feeling that she could not articulate, even to herself, but which lay somewhere in the Netherland between friendship and romantic desire. It was this undeniable feeling that caused her to relent on her last point.

"I cannot say it would never be possible, Emil, for one cannot know the future."

Strouss took her hand, and this time Gertrude let him kiss her fingers one at a time.

"Emil, you may kiss my hand, but you must understand that you must go no further."

With no little apprehension, she waited a long moment to see how he might respond to this restriction.

He looked at her with a blank expression, judging the degree of advantage she had over him, and calculating that it was considerable. "Will you come with me to Paris?" he asked softly.

Gertrude nodded. "Yes, if you agree to what I have asked."

At this, Strouss visibly brightened. "Yes, yes, I agree!"

"Then I should be ever so happy to come with you to Paris. It would be a dream come true for me, but . . . " and here she held up one finger as if addressing a recalcitrant child, "to learn French so I can be your interpreter."

Flashing a dazzling smile, she held out her hand for him to kiss. He took what she offered and held her hand to his cheek.

With the bargain struck, the tension which had been building since they entered the study dissipated. It was like a great weight had been lifted, and they both reacted with good humor and playfulness.

"Is there no other part of you I may kiss?" he pleaded in mock submission.

"We shall see," said she teasingly, raising her naked foot, and twisting it back and forth playfully. "But for now, you big stupid ogre, you must ask for nothing more!"

Standing up, she roughly pushed him away, took his neck tightly in both her hands, and pretended to strangle him. As he fell back on the divan, Gertrude fell on top of him, as if to test their agreement. Strouss howled with laughter but held his arms and legs up in the air like a gargantuan overturned turtle, making the point that, as agreed, he would not embrace her.

Thus was their agreement sealed. He would play the beast to her beauty and would give her everything while making no sexual demands; and she would accompany him to Paris. In what was to prove the cornerstone of their relationship, both believed the bargain equal.

With the major provisions of the agreement now arranged, the pair settled down to a game of backgammon, the rules of which Strouss had only recently taught her. Gertrude sat cross-legged on the floor before the fire, while Strouss lay down across from her, elbow on the floor, propping up his head with his hand. Gertrude was winning handily by virtue of a near miraculous succession of double sixes and fives.

"Not again!" he cried playfully as Gertrude rolled yet another pair of sixes.

Proudly, Gertrude removed her last pieces from the board, clinching the victory. Strouss rolled over on his back in a mock pout over the loss.

"May I bring up a very practical point?" Strouss asked. There remained the matter of details in their agreement.

"Of course," said Gertrude, sipping from her wine glass with one hand while recording her victory in a small black notebook in the other.

"You know that I have reserved a suite for us on the *Campania*, which sails on the twenty-sixth of next month."

Gertrude, now curled up on the divan, nodded.

"It was necessary for me to register us as man and wife."

There was a long pause as Gertrude reflected. In 1899 Victorian America, there was no need to explain the reason.

"I understand," she finally said.

"Have you talked to your parents?" Strouss asked.

"No," Gertrude replied. "I am afraid they would not consent."

"Would you let me talk to them?" Strouss asked.

"Would that be wise?"

"If you will trust me, I will send them tickets to come to Chicago and talk with them here. Herbert can pick them up at the station in the electric. Will you trust me?"

Gertrude nodded. Since she had made up her mind to go to Paris, perhaps it would be best.

The meeting of James and Jane Gibson with Emil Strouss in his library at the Standard Club began as a stiff affair. Gertrude, dressed primly in a cotton smock with high collar sat demurely on a high-back chair, and her parents sat together on the divan. Strouss sat in a heavy leather chair next to the divan.

"As we understand it, you propose to send Gertrude to Paris in order to further her education," James Gibson said, sipping the tea which Edgar served them on a sterling silver tray.

"That is correct, Mr. Gibson. As majority owner of Strouss, Eisendrath & Company, I conduct considerable business in Europe, especially in France. I am in great need of an interpreter on whom I can rely. It is my hope that Gertrude, in addition to her other studies at Madame Loreac's school in Paris, will become proficient in the French language."

"But surely, Mr. Strouss," James Gibson responded, "it is not necessary to send a prospect to school for four years in order to retain an interpreter."

Gertrude's father was getting to the heart of the matter — namely Strouss' true intentions. Strouss was prepared for the question and had rehearsed his response at length with Gertrude.

"Mr. Gibson, I have asked for your daughter's hand in marriage, and, with your approval, she has conditionally accepted."

Neither James nor Jane Gibson had been prepared for this news, and they looked at each other with surprise.

"Conditionally accepted?" James Gibson inquired, looking over at Gertrude.

"She wants to earn her certificate in the liberal arts before marriage, and I support her fully in this endeavor."

James Gibson took a deep breath and struggled for words to tactfully express his dismay, which lay chiefly in the general appearance of unsuitability in such a match, given Strouss and Gertrude's differences in age, religion, and background.

"Mr. Strouss, I must confess I have none of the traditional objections that a father has to a daughter's marriage — that is, I do not doubt your ability and capacity to provide for Gertrude. Indeed, she has already told us of how you have generously provided for her. Nevertheless, four years seems an excessively long courtship."

"Your daughter and I have both decided it is best to give priority to her education."

"Yes, yes, of course," said James Gibson, conceding this point.

The conversation was interrupted as Edgar served cakes.

"This voyage on the *Campania*," Mr. Gibson continued. "May I inquire about the accommodations?"

Gertrude and Strouss had also anticipated this question and were prepared with an answer that Strouss had ensured could not be checked.

"I have obtained a first class cabin for Gertrude and my chambermaid, Freda, who will accompany Gertrude as her traveling companion."

"And in Paris?"

"Gertrude will reside at the school in Paris, and I have ensured that she will be provided with the most comfortable accommodations. In the summer, she may return for visits to the United States if she likes."

Gibson turned to his daughter. "This is what you want, Gertrude?"

"Yes, Father. It is a wonderful opportunity, would you not agree?"

Gibson considered asking to speak to Gertrude alone, but thought better of it. Given his daughter's bleak prospects just a few months before, she could do far worse. With reservations he kept to himself and gave his blessing to his daughter's venture.

15

"What it all adds up to is a silent sermon in good taste."

Cunard Line publicity brochure describing
the *Campania* (1899)

The *Campania* was designed to surpass in magnitude and power
every steamer of the past. So great was its size that it had to be
launched diagonally since the length of it was longer than the width of the
river Clyde on which it was built. This floating metropolis established the
Cunard line as the premier carrier on the Atlantic. In magnificence and
luxury it was only to be exceeded thirteen years later by the *Titanic*.

On the morning of the twenty-sixth of September, 1899, Gertrude
Gibson and Emil Strouss arrived in New York City on a private Pullman car
fitted with separate bedrooms, salon, and dining room. Freda, who served
as Gertrude's hairdresser and maidservant, accompanied them. Upon
arrival at Grand Central Station, Strouss escorted Gertrude by carriage to
Delmonico's for a late breakfast, while Freda and a retinue of day laborers
escorted six trunks containing Gertrude's wardrobe to the *Campania*
docked on pier sixteen in New York Harbor.

Strouss and Gertrude arrived at the docks later in the afternoon in a
hired electric. Making their way through a festive crowd, they embarked on
the *Campania* and registered as "Mr. and Mrs. Strouss" in the Riviera suite
on the First Class deck. The ship was bound for LeHavre, France, with a
stop in Southampton, England.

Gertrude, dressed in a bright blue single-breasted bolero jacket and
skirt and wearing a brimless toque, was delighted with the accommodations. The suite was composed of a private salon, a servant's cabin, a
boudoir, and two separate bedrooms. All the rooms, except the servant's
cabin, were finished in mahogany and satinwood. Gertrude's room, the
master, was furnished with a polished brass bed covered with silk, hang-
ings, tapestries, and a large mahogany wardrobe. All the luxury suites
shared a private promenade. A complement of five members of the ship's
staff, including a waiter, valet, maid, chambermaid, and steward were
assigned to serve the suite's occupants on an exclusive basis.

After watching the bon voyage festivities from the windows of the Palm Court, Gertrude retreated to her bedroom to rest before dinner, while Strouss retired to the smoking salon.

In her cabin Gertrude grasped the bedposts firmly as Freda untied her corset.

"Can you breath in just a bit more, m'um?" Freda entreated.

Freda was still struggling to learn the trick of unfastening the hooks on the stylish new "Neena" corset that Gertrude had recently purchased for herself. This fashionable undergarment was designed to perform the triple task of thrusting the bosom forward as a bust improver, while at the same time pushing out the posterior at the back, and reducing the appearance of circumference in the waist by the use of padding on the back, hips, and chest. Through the use of the device, Gertrude was able to reduce her already slim waist to but eighteen inches.

Gertrude exhaled completely, then inhaled and held it. With a final pull, Freda unhooked the fastening and opened the corset.

Gertrude took a deep breath.

"Isn't it exciting, m'um?" Freda said as she removed the corset. "I've never been away from Chicago, and now we're off to France. I can't hardly believe it, m'um."

Gertrude turned and sat down on the bed. "Except for two trips to St. Louis to visit my sister, I too have never been out of Illinois. I'm just as excited as you, Freda. I have a trunk full of books about Paris, which you are most welcome to read in your spare time."

"Thank you, m'um." Freda did not know how to read, but she would enjoy looking at the pictures.

"May I ask a question, m'um?" asked Freda, helping Gertrude into her sleeping gown.

"Of course, Freda. What is it?"

"Do you know where I shall be in Paris? I mean, will I be with you or Mr. Strouss?" Freda knelt down to slip on Gertrude's sleeping slippers.

"Hmmm." Gertrude said, snuggling under the covers. "I shall have to ask Emil about that. I shall be going to school in Paris and living there. I don't know if they will permit me to have my own servant at the school. Emil's apartments are nearby, so I imagine you shall live in his quarters. But I shall need you quite often for my hair, I think."

"I hope I shall be with you mostly, m'um" said Freda, who was growing quite attached to her pretty mistress.

Gertrude sat up while Freda brushed out her hair.

"Thank you, Freda. I don't know what I would do without you."

"Will there be anything else, m'um?"

"No, you may go, Freda. Wake me up in two hours to do my hair for dinner. I shall want a full Nestle."

"Yes, mistress Gertrude. What will you be wearing, m'um?"

Gertrude thought for a moment. "I understand the dinner tonight is not formal. I shall wear the white court dress and the court shoes with the high Louis heels."

"Yes, m'um."

The first class dining room lay under a glittering thirty-five-foot Tiffany dome that gave the illusion of natural light emanating from above. The crystal chandeliers were of the latest electric design, and marble columns graced the entire length of the room. A thick Persian carpet covered the floor. Smaller tables for two or four lined the outer perimeter of the room; the center tables seated eight.

Gertrude and Strouss were seated at a center table. While they considered the menu for the twelve-course dinner that was to follow, their fellow passengers introduced themselves. Next to Strouss sat the banker, Mr. John Phipps, and his wife. Seated next to Gertrude were the Viscountess Lee of Fareham and her American sister, Miss Faith Moore. Seated across the table were Captain Edward DeLemar and his daughter, Natalie, and Mrs. Juliana Armour Ferguson and her twenty-one-year-old son, Percival Ferguson. The latter, a third year student at Harvard, was traveling to Oxford for the summer rowing races. He was traveling with his mother under protest. He would have preferred to travel the following week with his teammates on the Imperator, but his mother, who was visiting relatives in London and did not wish to travel alone, had insisted upon his company.

After these awkward introductions, the conversation abruptly ceased as the waiter poured the wine.

"I say, have you seen those frightening bands of young women on the second class deck?" Mrs. Ferguson chimed, breaking the awkward silence.

"With the ice broken, Captain DeLemar picked up on the observation with gusto. "Courtesy of Mr. Thomas Cook, I should say. Devil's dust tourists, tribes of unlettered Americans coming over in waves."

"Well, I don't want to be harsh, but they appear quite crumpled-looking, don't you agree?" returned Mrs. Ferguson, pleased that Captain DeLemar shared her concern about the philistine horde of young women swarming about on the second- class deck.

"I daresay they injure our credit, not to mention our character." DeLemar agreed. "Give a terrible impression. Travel everywhere in Europe for a hundred dollars, I hear. Bring their own pillows and camp stools."

Captain DeLemar turned to include his daughter in a conversation that had not yet drawn in the other passengers at the table.

"What do they call them, Natalie? Kansas peaches, Kentucky Belles? Whatever they're called, they create quite a false image of the younger generation, don't you think, Natalie?"

Natalie, a vivacious and mischievous ingénue who was quite aware of both her class and allure, shrugged her bare shoulders as she helped herself to butter for a croissant. "I really wouldn't know, Father. I have no interest in watching second-class passengers."

There was another awkward silence.

Gertrude took a sip of wine and looked down to avoid the gaze of Percival Ferguson, who had been looking at her ever since they had sat down. Percival had been prepared to pout the entire voyage, but the sight of Gertrude, radiant and angelic in her white court dress, had altered his demeanor considerably. He had been disappointed to learn that she was married and shocked that the large and repulsive creature sitting at her side was her husband.

Natalie, accustomed to being the center of attention of the opposite sex, was visibly annoyed at Percival's attentions to Gertrude. She had eyed Percival as suitable partner for a romantic interlude to relieve the boredom of the voyage, and now saw Gertrude, married or not, as a rival to be thwarted.

It occurred to Gertrude that but three months before a hundred dollars would have seemed a fortune and that she would have envied anyone fortunate to have such a sum and be able to visit the capitals of Europe.

"I've read that the ship's greatest profit comes from the second-and-third class passengers," Gertrude ventured cautiously. "Perhaps we should be grateful that they have purchased tickets and subsidized our passage."

Strouss beamed. He was delighted that Gertrude had the verve and moxie to hold her own with even the most pretentious scions of high society.

"Bravo!" Percival exclaimed with approval, raising his glass bombastically in a toast to Strouss. "I am most impressed, Mrs. Strouss! Tell me, Mr. Strouss, where did your delightful wife acquire her knowledge of business economics?"

"My wife is most talented in a wide variety of endeavors, Mr. Ferguson," Strouss said reservedly. "She is largely self-taught."

"Extraordinary!" Percival returned. "Have you considered sending her to Radcliffe? I daresay she could make the most charming contribution to that venerable institution."

Strouss had never had much use for society brats, and there was a taunting tone in this brat's voice. It was presumptuous for Strouss to be rich, Percival's tone said, and even more so to have a young beautiful wife who would be far more suitable match for a handsome Harvard gentleman. Strouss had heard the same tone many times in his business dealings with those who tolerated him only because of his financial power and acumen, while rejecting him socially because he was a Jew.

"My wife is planning to further her education in Paris," Strouss said, and left it at that.

Mercifully, Mr. John Phipps changed the subject to the Universal Exhibition, which would open in Paris on the Esplanade des Invalides the following April to celebrate the new century.

"The Great Wheel will be the biggest in the world, and there is talk of a moving sidewalk. Have you ever heard of such a thing? They call it an escalator," Phipps said, now monopolizing the conversation. "On the Ecole Militaire they will show the first electric searchlight, and an enormous colored electric light display. It will be three times that of the Columbian Exposition, they say."

The subject of the Paris Exhibition continued to dominate the conversation until the crepe suzettes were served in the final course. This conversation between the others at the table did not inhibit Percival from transparently flirting with Gertrude from across the table, showering her with compliments about her dress and asking about her plans to attend the dance in the Grand Salon later in the evening.

"Yes, Emil and I plan to attend for a short time," she said.

The Grand Salon was even more lavishly furnished than the dining room. A full orchestra played the latest Strauss waltz, "The Blue Danube," and many couples were dancing the new "hesitation waltz" steps. Percival stood to the side and watched Strouss and Gertrude dance. As the evening wore on and the older passengers retired, a younger set began to predominate on the dance floor. The orchestra accommodated them with the latest ragtime sensation, the "Maple Leaf Rag," by Scott Joplin. As Strouss and Gertrude sat at a table, Percival approached them.

"Mr. Strouss, may I have the honor of dancing with your charming wife?" Percival asked, bowing slightly.

"Perhaps you should ask her," Strouss said.

"Madame? Would you do me the honor?"

Gertrude looked over at Strouss, who indicated by his expression that the decision was hers alone.

"We were about to retire, but perhaps one dance, Mr. Ferguson." Gertrude had taken an instant dislike to Percival at the dinner table but thought it impolitic to decline.

Percival took Gertrude immediately in hand and twirled her around the dance floor in an energetic two-step.

"How long have you been married?" he shouted above the music.

"Long enough, I assure you, Mr. Ferguson," Gertrude replied.

"I mean you look so young, Mrs. Strouss."

"I know what you meant."

"Why I believe I'm older than you are."

"I'm sure you are, Mr. Ferguson, and that you have the manners not to inquire about age."

"I wanted to say that you looked beautiful tonight."

"You already told me that at dinner."

"No, I told you that your dress was beautiful."

"I know what you meant," Gertrude repeated. She was beginning to feel uncomfortable and looked over to the orchestra to see if the musical number was about to end.

"I mean, are you really married?"

Gertrude stopped dancing abruptly. "Whatever do you mean, sir?"

Percival held up his hands. "I meant no offense. I just mean that a married woman usually wears a wedding ring and I couldn't help noticing . . . "

Gertrude resumed dancing and responded nonchalantly. She had not thought of the need for a ring, but the reason for having one was now apparent. "My wedding ring is being repaired if it is any of your concern."

"On board ship? I didn't know we had a jeweler aboard."

Annoyed with this little cross-examination, Gertrude looked away in silence.

"I was wondering if you would care to meet me later topside for a drink or two. Perhaps on the first class promenade."

"Certainly not!" Gertrude replied indignantly. "My husband and I will be retiring after this dance."

"You're not really going to bed with that old hoot, are you?" Percival asked, smirking impishly.

Gertrude again stopped abruptly and stepped back. "How dare you!" She wanted to slap this arrogant drummer hard across the face. Only a concern for causing a scene restrained her. She turned away and walked back to the table.

"Emil, I'm quite tired. May we go?" Gertrude pleaded.

"Of course, my dear," Strouss said, looking back at Percival, who stood in the same place Gertrude had left him.

"Emil," Gertrude said after they returned to their suite.

"Yes, my dear."

"May we talk before you go to bed?"

"Of course."

"Will you wait a few minutes?"

Strouss nodded. Gertrude returned to the suite to prepare for bed. Freda, who had been waiting for her, followed Gertrude into her bedroom and helped her change to her nightgown and robe.

"I'll brush my own hair tonight," Gertrude said. "You may go. You must be tired."

"Yes, mistress Gertrude. Thank you, m'um. What time shall you be rising tomorrow morning, m'um?"

"I shall sleep in, I think. Tell the steward I will have breakfast in bed. I'll ring for you when I wake up."

"Yes, m'um."

Gertrude walked into the salon. Strouss greeted her with a glass of champagne.

"A nightcap, my dear?"

"Perhaps a glass of water."

Strouss put down the glass of champagne and fetched a glass of water from the bar and handed it to Gertrude.

"Emil, I would like to move to a different table at dinner."

"Of course, if you like. May I ask why?"

"It's that Mr. Ferguson. I should never have danced with him. He was crude." Gertrude looked up at Strouss as if she were making a confession. "He wanted to meet me later."

"I see," Strouss said. "Do you want to meet him?"

Gertrude took his hand and held it in hers. "Of course not, Emil. I do not find him in the least attractive, and he is most rude and irritating. And even if I did like him, which I most certainly do not, I am traveling with you — as your wife."

"Gertrude, dear," Strouss said softly, "although we are obliged to travel as man and wife for the sake of propriety, I respect our agreement completely. You are always free to do as you wish."

"But I wish to be with you."

"What did the young man say?" Strouss inquired.

"He said terrible things. He saw that I have no wedding ring."

Strouss sighed. "In the spirit of our understanding, I did not want to raise the matter of rings. Nevertheless, I did prepare for the possibility that we might encounter just this difficulty."

Strouss went to his desk and pulled a small velvet box from the right drawer. He presented it to Gertrude.

"Emil, what is it?"

Gertrude opened the box and gasped. Inside was a flawless, brilliant, ten-carat diamond engagement ring.

"Oh my God! It's beautiful, Emil!"

"As long as you wear this bauble, little princess, I am confident that no one will doubt your marriage status."

Strouss took the ring and placed it on her wedding finger.

For several moments, Gertrude held out her hand, admiring the huge stone.

"Emil, you know this wasn't necessary. In ten days we shall be in Paris."

"But you have allowed me to hope. I wanted to be prepared should the day ever come when you would consent to be my wife." He took a second box from his pocket, and gave it to her.

Gertrude opened it. Inside was a gold wedding band. Shaking her head, she let Strouss place it too on her fourth finger.

"Emil . . ."

"Say nothing now, my dearest. It is just for the voyage, to keep the drummers away — that is, if you want to keep them away."

"Of course, I do. But I fear that even these rings will not keep away Master Percival, although I do confess that I will feel more comfortable wearing them. Thank you from the bottom of my heart."

She leaned over and kissed him on the cheek.

"Do you still want me to change our dinner table?"

"No, it's all right. I think I can handle the boy now. But Emil, what about in Paris?"

"In Paris?" Strouss asked.

"I mean, will it be necessary to be man and wife in Paris?"

"Not at all, my dear. Indeed, students at Madame Loreac's school are not permitted to marry."

"Oh, I see."

"There is no rule against engagement, however. We can therefore be engaged if you like. It is entirely up to you."

"As long as you understand, Emil. You must not have any expectations of marriage."

"I have none. Only hope."

"Even that you must have very little of. You know that."

Strouss nodded. "Of course, dear. As per our agreement."

"Then I see no reason why we should not be, you know, engaged, in Paris if you think it best. Are there many drummers in Paris?"

"Paris is teeming with them. Quite aggressive ones too."

"Then I shall be in need of such stones I think."

Strouss kissed her hand. "You shall wear the diamond in Paris?"

"Yes," Gertrude said. "Happily."

At dinner the following evening, Gertrude exchanged seats with Strouss to extend the distance across the table between her and Percival. Strouss and Captain DeLemar dominated the male conversation with a long discourse on international business relations, and the Viscountess and Mrs. Phipps talked about the quality of the linen. Cut off from discourse with Gertrude, Percival reverted to his pouting mode despite a half-hearted attempt by Natalie to engage him.

Immediately after dinner, Gertrude excused herself and retreated to her room where she met Freda.

"M'um," Freda said. "This afternoon, a young man gave me this to give to you." She handed Gertrude a small white envelope.

Gertrude read the note:

G.S.

> *"I am desperate to see you. I cannot be responsible for my actions if you refuse me. I beg of you to meet me in the first class promenade after dinner. I promise you will not be sorry. P"*

"What is it, m'um?"

"Nothing, Freda. But I must show this to Emil. Are you ready to go with me to the Ladies' Salon?"

"Yes mum."

A popular travel book of the day described the Ladies' Salon on the Campania as the ladies "own reservation, into the precincts of which man is only admitted on a special permit. It is a club-house and boudoir combined; if any lady has a nervous headache, or wishes to escape the importunities of an ardent but obtrusive admirer, she steals in here, and here is sanctuary."

It was this latter feature that prompted Gertrude's visit, for Percival was only steps behind her when she slipped into the salon with Freda. As the door to the salon slammed shut behind them, a frowning doorwoman stared down Percival at the gates, and the latter retreated like a bear deprived of its elusive prey.

Thus thwarted, Percival retreated to the cocktail lounge where he consumed several strong drinks in rapid succession. A half hour later he staggered out of the lounge and ventured into the first class smoking room. At the table by the fireplace, five gentlemen in evening dress were engrossed in a game of poker. Percival recognized Strouss, Captain DeLemar, and Judge Charles Howland, an acquaintance of his mother. Still smarting from Gertrude's rejection, and inwardly seething at the sight of his detested rival piling up hundred dollar blue chips, Percival saw an opportunity to punish Strouss. Percival fancied himself a poker player because he had often won money in the fraternity poker games he played at school.

"I say gentlemen," Percival said, "would you have room for one more player? Five card draw, is it?"

Captain DeLemar threw in his hand and turned around. None of the players wanted to slight the son of Mrs. Ferguson but allowing him to play with them for high stakes presented the prospect of unpleasant complications, particularly if he should lose.

"Well, I don't know . . . " Captain DeLemar began to say.

"I'm over twenty-one gentlemen, in case that's what you're wondering, and I believe I have sufficient cash to buy in."

Judge Howland was particularly concerned that Percival's mother might disapprove. "We'd be delighted to have you join us Percival," he said good-naturedly. "But we've all bought in for five thousand dollars, and I'm not sure your mother . . . "

"Oh, my mother suggested I join you gentlemen," Percival lied. "Would you mind if I bought in for, say, ten thousand dollars?"

He reached into his coat pocket and pulled out a packet of hundred and thousand dollar bills.

"What about you, Mr. Strouss, do you have any objections?" asked Percival, looking at Strouss directly in the eye.

Strouss looked up only briefly from his cards.

"I defer to the other gentlemen. I have no objection, Mr. Ferguson."

"Then I accept your invitation," Percival said drawing up a chair. Now who's the banker this evening?"

For the next hour Percival racked up several thousand dollars despite his transparent play. He hit a series of unlikely draws consisting of a full house, two flushes, and several straights.

"Well gentlemen," he gloated as he pulled another huge pot, "I guess it's just my lucky night. But I promise not to tell your mothers."

To Percival's great annoyance, the man whom he most wanted to crush was entering few pots and making even fewer bets. Strouss had managed to stay even during Percival's winning streak.

It was two in the morning and Percival was forty-five hundred dollars ahead when he was dealt a pair of queens.

"Three cards, Captain," Percival said.

Percival looked down and saw that his luck was holding. He had received a third queen.

Strouss asked for one card.

"Well, gentlemen, just because I have more chips than I know what to do with, I'll open with five hundred dollars," Percival said confidently.

All the other players dropped out. They weren't going to fight this kind of lucky streak.

Strouss looked down at his cards. He thought for a long time and finally called.

Judge Howland raised five hundred dollars.

Percival finally saw his chance to whip the man he despised. Although an experienced player would have exercised caution in this situation, Percival flamboyantly pushed five stacks of hundred dollar chips into the pot. "I raise."

The other players knew that it was highly unlikely that Strouss would have called a five hundred dollar bet heads up with only a flush or straight draw. Judge Howland folded.

"Well, Mr. Ferguson, I have no doubt that I will regret this, but I am going to see your five thousand and raise . . . how much do you have in front of you, Mr. Ferguson?"

There was a hush at the table. Percival, suddenly quieted, counted his chips. "Nine thousand five hundred," he said with a disdainful smirk.

"Very well," said Strouss. "I raise nine thousand five hundred dollars." He removed five blue chips from one of his stacks and then pushed it along with nine other full stacks of blue chips into the pot.

Percival scrutinized his cards nervously and then looked around the table. All eyes were upon him. There was not a player at the table who doubted that Percival had three of a kind — including Strouss.

Percival had wanted desperately to crush Strouss, if for no other reason than to impress Gertrude. Now he saw that it was he who was in danger of being brought to his knees.

Percival looked at Strouss with undisguised hatred.

"Mr. Strouss took one card?" he asked the Captain, obviously stalling for time.

"Yes, Mr. Ferguson. One card," the Captain replied matter of-factly.

"I should have known," Percival said, throwing his cards across the table in disgust. "Take it, Strouss. I guess this is how your kind always do business."

Ignoring the ill-disguised racial insult, Strouss raked in his chips. The other players traded knowing glances. Percival had gotten what he deserved. To everyone at the table except Percival, it had been obvious that Strouss had had nothing before and after his one card draw.

It took only moments for Percival to realize that he had been bluffed out of an enormous pot. But he still had all but five hundred dollars of his original stake, and he was now seething and determined to punish Strouss at any cost.

During the next hour, Percival lost another eight hundred dollars. To his annoyance, he had not been able to engage Strouss, who, playing tightly, still sat atop a giant pile of blue chips.

It was a quarter past four in the morning when Percival opened his hand and saw to his delight that he had been dealt a pat straight to the jack. Determined to play this hand coolly, he checked, hoping for a bet from one of the other players. Judge Howland bet two hundred dollars. When Strouss and Captain DeLemar called, Percival resisted the temptation to raise, and just called. With luck, Strouss would bet into him after the draw, and he could raise with everything he had.

"I guess my luck has dried up gentlemen," Percival said, trying to appear forlorn. "But since this will have to be my last hand, I'll contribute two hundred to the cause."

The Captain asked each player how many cards he wanted.

"I'll stand pat," Percival said, transparently trying to make it appear that he was bluffing rather than disguising his hand.

Captain DeLemar took two cards, Judge Howland three, and Strouss again took one card.

Percival took one last look at his beautiful pat straight and smiled broadly when Strouss made a modest bet of two hundred dollars.

"Well, gentlemen. Nothing ventured, nothing gained," Percival deadpanned, pushing in all his remaining chips. "I raise."

"I believe you, Percival," Judge Howland said, throwing in his hand. Captain DeLemar too folded.

"Well, I guess that just leaves you and me," Percival said directly to Strouss. "What do you say? It's only money. Your kind knows all about money, don't they?"

"What was the amount of your raise?" Strouss asked.

Percival's mouth dropped. His hands visibly shaking, he counted out the chips in the stacks he had pushed into the pot. "Eighty-seven hundred dollars, Strouss. It looks like you can handle it," he said with the last bit of bravado he could muster, but his voice was breaking.

"Very well, eighty-seven hundred dollars it is." Strouss pushed out eight stacks of blue chips and counted out seven more blue chips. "I call."

Percival nervously looked around the table.

"You are called, Percival," said Captain DeLemar with just enough firmness to suggest that Percival had again been played the fool.

Glaring directly at Strouss, Percival turned over his cards and triumphantly revealed his pat straight.

None of the poker veterans at the table had any doubt that Strouss had him beat. Only Percival was surprised when Strouss turned over a full house of fours full of threes. Strouss had drawn to two pairs, a perfectly respectable hand before the draw, and filled his hand. Percival had obligingly bet right into him.

Flushed and visibly shaken, Percival stood up, pushing his chair back violently.

"You . . . you . . . " he stammered at Strouss.

"Terribly unlucky, my boy," Judge Howland said in his dry British accent, trying to console him. "Can't win every time, you know."

Enraged, Percival stalked out of the smoking room and back to the cocktail lounge where he downed another series of strong drinks.

"Not very lucky, is he?" deadpanned Judge Howland with a smile after Percival had left.

Strouss had taken Percival for the entire ten thousand dollars his mother had given him for his summer at Oxford. He could not imagine how he could explain this to his mother.

Inebriated, Percival staggered out of the lounge and up to the first class staircase to the Riviera suite. He started banging on the door.

"Gertrude! Gertrude! Come out here! I need to talk to you!"

The disturbance brought out the night steward who recognized Percival as a first class passenger.

"May I help you, sir?" the steward asked timidly.

"Go away!" Percival shouted. "I'm talking to a fellow first class passenger. Now go away, man!"

The pounding woke Gertrude and Freda who, putting on their nightgowns, rushed out of their respective bedrooms into the suite salon.

"Who is it, mum?" Freda asked, alarmed.

"I know who it is," said Gertrude with a grimace. She looked into Strouss' bedroom and saw that he had not yet returned. She rushed to the door.

"Mr. Ferguson," Gertrude said loudly enough to be heard through the door, "I know it is you. If you do not go away this instant I shall call the sergeant-at-arms!"

Percival started twisting the doorknob violently.

"Please, sir," said the steward. He took Percival's arm, but was obviously unsure how to deal with a first class passenger in this situation. "If you come with me we can assist you, sir."

Percival pushed the steward away. "I said get out of here!"

Percival raised his arm to bang the door when he felt a firm grip on his arm. It was Strouss.

"Oh, it's you, you fat, dirty . . . " Percival hissed.

"Fat, dirty, what, Mr. Ferguson?" Strouss said calmly, still holding Percival's arm tightly.

At that moment the sergeant-at-arms arrived with two men wielding billy clubs.

"It's all right gentlemen," Strouss said to them. "Mr. Ferguson has had a bit too much to drink. He'll be all right."

The sergeant-at-arms hesitated.

"It will be all right," Strouss assured them. "I'll call if we need your help."

"Very well, sir," the sergeant-at-arms said. "But he was disturbing the other First Class passengers. If there's any more disturbance we'll have to take him."

"I understand gentlemen. I'll call if we need you." Strouss spoke with such authority that the security men finally took their leave.

"Well, Mr. Ferguson," Strouss said in a low, soothing voice, "it's a bit late to be calling on Gertrude wouldn't you say? But since you seem so determined, why don't you come in? Perhaps you and I could have a chat."

Strouss unlocked the door and gestured for Percival to enter.

Somewhat calmed, but perplexed by Strouss' intervention on his behalf with the sergeant-at-arms, Percival entered the suite.

"Chat about what?" he asked testily.

Gertrude and Freda were huddled together by the divan in the suite salon.

"Ladies, it seems that Master Percival has graced us with a visit." Strouss said to them. "Would you excuse us while we conduct some business?"

Gertrude looked at the disheveled Percival and turned away.

"Come, Freda," Gertrude said, relieved that the crisis was resolved. "Let's go back to bed."

"Please, have a seat and make yourself comfortable," Strouss said after Gertrude and Freda had returned to their rooms.

Percival sat sullenly.

"I have a proposition to make to you, Mr. Ferguson," said Strouss as he sat down at the King Louis desk and took out pen and paper.

"I don't think I have any business with you," Percival replied, making an extra effort not to slur his words.

"You lost a great deal of money tonight, Mr. Ferguson," Strouss continued. "I am concerned about what your mother might say when she learns of your loss."

Percival stood up angrily. "You bastard, if you say one thing to my mother I'll kill you, I swear it!"

"Please calm yourself, Mr. Ferguson. I have no intention of saying anything to your mother. But you told us at dinner that you planned to live in Oxford for the summer. I trust you have additional funds and will not have to ask your mother for more money."

Percival sat down in silence.

There was a long pause before Strouss spoke. "This is my proposition, Mr. Ferguson. I will return to you the ten thousand dollars that you lost at the poker table. In return, you will stay away from my wife for the duration of this voyage. You will send your regrets for not being able to join your mother for dinner for the remainder of the voyage."

"My mother insists that I come to dinner with her," Percival replied with a tone that suggested entitlement to the return of his lost wagers.

"You must ask yourself whether it will be easier to account to your mother for your loss of ten thousand dollars, or for your absence at dinner." Strouss took out a pack of bills from his pocket.

Percival stood up and reached for the bills.

"There is one further condition," said Strouss, pulling back his hand. "I will ask you to sign this note for ten thousand dollars which, by its terms, will expire if not presented to either you or your mother prior to the time we arrive at Southampton. If you so much as tip your hat to my wife before that time, the note will be presented. Do you understand?"

Without a word, Percival scribbled his signature on the note, took the bills, and stalked out.

The remainder of the voyage passed without incident. At dinner, Mrs. Ferguson apologized for the absence of her son, explaining that he had found some school friends in second class and had met a young lady who demanded his full attention.

Gertrude spent much of her time in the Ladies' Salon, reading her books on Paris. After reading an advertisement in the ship's newspaper posted by a retired schoolteacher in third class offering to teach French, Strouss retained the woman to give Gertrude her first lessons in the French language.

Two days before the Campania's arrival in Southampton, a steward delivered to Strouss a large envelope. It was a portrait of Gertrude that a young artist in third class had painted. Standing on the third class deck below, he had seen Gertrude one evening on the first class terrace looking out at the sea. Enchanted by his subject, he had drawn the sketch at a distance. A student and disciple of Maxfield Parrish, he had then romanticized the painting by unleashing her hair in flowing waves and surrounding her in a surreal setting of an enchanted fairytale land. Inquiring about Gertrude among the stewards, among whom Gertrude had not gone unnoticed, the young man had learned that his subject's husband was Mr. Emil Strouss. He had the good manners to send the painting to Strouss directly, along with a note offering to give the painting to him if he liked it. Strouss was delighted with the painting and insisted on rewarding the artist with a handsome commission. Strouss placed the painting on his desk, intending later to have it suitably framed.

"Is that really me?" Gertrude asked when she saw it.

"It is indeed, my dear. The artist has painted you as an angel."

"It's amazing," Gertrude said, entranced by her own image. "Who is the artist?"

"It seems you have another admirer . . . "

"Oh, no!" Gertrude exclaimed.

"It's all right, my dear. I've met the man and he was most courteous. It seems that you were an irresistible subject one evening as you looked out to sea from the terrace. The painting captures your essence perfectly, and I will treasure it."

Gertrude gave Strouss a hug. "I'm glad," she said.

16

"What is the grand magasin? C'est l'immoralite. The Paris department store is an abyss, a Babel, a spider web, where with her little bird's head, the daughter of Eve enters into this inferno of coquetry like a mouse into a mousetrap, and easily victimized by fetishists, mashers, and sexual deviants."

Gustave Mace, Chef de Service of the Surete (1899).

Paris was nothing like Chicago.

There were the same crowds, the traffic jams, the clatter, and the smell of horse manure. But Paris was another world, and Gertrude was to love everything about it.

Strouss and Gertrude arrived by private railroad car at the Gare du Nord on the morning of the eighth of October 1899. It being a warm fall day, Gertrude asked that they ride to their hotel in an open carriage, the better to see the city. Two freight carriages carrying Gertrude's six trunks followed them.

Gertrude marveled at the grand boulevards, the Champs-Elysees, L'Imperatice, Saint-Marcel, Beaujon, and especially the Avenue de l'Opera. The department stores were as impressive as Marshall Field's, and there were so many of them: Au Bon Marche, the Grands Magasins du Louvre, Au Printempts, A La Ville de Loudres, and the Galeries Lafayette.

The carriages arrived at the Hotel d'Elyses in late morning. Strouss had maintained a suite at this historic hotel for several years. He planned for Gertrude to stay there with him for a few days until she was settled at Madame Dorleac's School for Young Women.

Madame Sophie Dorleac had first met Emil Strouss some ten years before. Strouss had substantial business dealings with her now deceased husband, Georges Dorleac, who was a partner in the Creipin-Dufayel department store on the Rue de Bac near Boulevard Raspail. At a dinner party at Maison de Dorleac hosted by Sophie, Strouss had made a substantial contribution to her Society to Restore the Hotel de Ville. She greatly admired his business acumen and developed an enduring affection for him, calling him her pet beast and philistine. They had remained good friends since that time, and Strouss had never failed to visit the Dorleacs when he was in Paris, bringing them his latest textile products as gifts. After George's death, Strouss and Sophie remained close friends. Although Strouss could speak only a few words of French, Sophie spoke excellent English.

When Strouss had asked his friend to find a place for Gertrude in her school, Sophie had welcomed the opportunity to return old favors. She had not told Strouss that she had a waiting list. To accommodate Gertrude, she had asked three of her students to share one of the larger rooms, and asked the student in one of the four suites, Anna Trubetskaya, to take a smaller room. This latter reassignment, it turned out, had not been an imposition as Anna's father, a Russian duke, had recently suffered financial reversals and had inquired about a smaller room for his daughter in order to reduce the tuition.

It was raining lightly and the first chill of autumn was in the air on the afternoon of October 11 when the caravan of Strouss's carriages entered the front gates of l'Ecole de Dorleac on the Boulevard DeVilliers. The driver of the lead carriage carrying Gertrude's trunks brought the carriage to a halt on the gravel driveway. He rushed over to Gertrude's carriage, pulled out a footstool, and held out an umbrella for her. Gertrude, dressed in a double-breasted tweed, fitted tailor-made coat with cape, stepped down from her carriage. Freda followed, as did Strouss who took Gertrude's hand and led her up the stone steps to the front door.

Madame Sophie Dorleac and her two assistant head mistresses, Helena and Cora, were waiting in the vestibule.

"Emil!" Sophie exclaimed, "so you have finally arrived. How wonderful to see you!" She put her arms around his neck and kissed him on the cheek. "And this is your fiancé?" she said turning to Gertrude. "Emil, she is charming."

"I am so happy to be here," Gertrude said, extending her hand.

"Cora, please show Gertrude to her rooms," Sophie said.

Cora led Gertrude upstairs and directed the movers to follow with their trunks.

"Emil," Sophie said, "you have outdone yourself. Now come and tell me all about it."

Emil followed Sophie into the salon and sat on the divan next to Sophie.

"What will you have to drink, Emil?" she asked.

"Vodka, thank you," Emil said to the waiting server.

"She's charming, Emil. Where on earth did you find her?"

"Well," Emil said, sitting back on the divan, "I met her last year in St. Louis at an art opening. Then in August I met her at a benefit at the Auditorium. She had arrived in Chicago at the beginning of the summer."

"A coincidence?" Sophie asked with a tone of skepticism, heavily accenting the last syllable as if she were uttering a word in French.

"Perhaps not, but in any case . . . "

"I can see it in your eyes, Emil. You adore the girl, and I can see why. You are the rascal. Is it true? You are engaged to be married?"

Emil shifted uncomfortably. "Yes, but it is to be a long engagement."

"A very long engagement. You know l'Ecole de Dorleac's rule about marriage, which I cannot break even for you, Emil."

Strouss nodded.

Sensing that her old friend was reluctant to give more details about the nature of his relationship with Gertrude, Sophie changed the subject.

"She understands, does she not, that our academic requirements are strict?" She handed him a handwritten schedule of classes.

Strouss took spectacles from his coat pocket and scrutinized the schedule.

"I have assigned her to Monsieur Fouquet's beginning French class," Sophie continued. "Does Gertrude know any French at all?"

"She has been studying on her own, but she has not had a chance to practice."

"Then we shall assign her to the beginning class. If she shows rapid progress, we can transfer her to the intermediate class. At present only Anna, who is from Russia, is taking intermediate French. All the rest are in the advanced classes, reading the classics."

"The classics?"

"We have a . . . ," and here Sophie paused to find the right word, "how do you say, a more liberal definition of the classics than you will see at the Universite. The girls read Les Miserables, it is true, it is mandatory; but they also read Dumas and Zola. If the arrogant savants at the Universite only know what our little girls read. Why just last week Monsieur Demongeot, our French literature instructor, had the girls reading Nana, if you can imagine! It is scandalous, n'est pa?"

In making a reference to this latter novel, Sophie hoped to elicit a response from her old friend, and perhaps convey a note of caution to this lovable beast for whom she had long nursed a sincere affection. She was aware, of course, that Emil was quite the philistine and that her reference was oblique to a fault; nevertheless, she satisfied her conscience by making it.

"No, no certainly not," he replied, clearing his throat. I trust that your Mr. Demongeot is the best judge of what the girls should read," Strouss said, mispronouncing the instructor's name so glaringly that Sophie could scarcely hide a grimace.

Exasperated, but not really surprised that her dear but uncultured friend could not appreciate her literary references, she decided not to press her concerns about her friend's relationship with Gertrude further.

"We don't shelter the girls from the world here. When they earn their certificate, they will know what challenges await them in life and will be well equipped to deal with them. But they gain their knowledge of the world from books, not from experience, for they are never permitted to leave the premises unless escorted by an assistant headmistress or me. Of course, there are frequent excursions to the opera, museums, and to the shops."

"Gertrude will enjoy all of that, especially the shops," Strouss said.

"Of course, the girls are not permitted to visit the department stores. We do not believe they provide a suitable environment for young girls."

"Of course," Strouss said, wondering how Gertrude might receive this particular restriction. He also was curious about a school policy that would permit girls to read scandalous literature but restrict them from setting foot in a department store. No doubt it had something to do with the distinction between learning from experience and learning from books.

"What other subjects will she study?" Strouss asked, not anxious to reveal further his ignorance of French literature.

"All the girls are required to take political economy with Monsieur Degranges, rhetoric with Madame Louvois, mathematics, botany, and physics under Monsieur Tallien, and Greek and Latin with Madame Divuvier — all areas in which most young women today are expected to be conveniently ignorant. All the girls play tennis, too — we have our own indoor court — and the girls ride, sidesaddle of course, every week on the Parc Monceau. Fencing is optional, but we have the most expert swordsman in Paris, Frederick Le Play. Would Gertrude be interested? Four of the girls here are passionate aficionados of the martial arts."

"Gertrude did express an interest, yes, although she may reconsider depending on whether her talent in that discipline develops suitably."

"I see. And music? All girls must either select an instrument or take voice training."

"She has expressed an interest in the harp."

"Mon dieu! No one here plays the harp any more, and I must confess I gave it up years ago. But I shall make inquiries. Could she perhaps be persuaded to pursue the violin or viola? Anna and Eugenie both take viola lessons from a distinguished retired member of the Opera orchestra."

"Perhaps. I wish all her interests to be accommodated, as I think her capable of great accomplishment."

"I have no doubt, my friend. Now before you go, may I make one suggestion, which you are, naturally, free to disregard?"

"Of course."

"I know you wish Gertrude to have the most comfortable accommodations."

"Yes, the very best you can provide."

"And that is why I have assigned her to my best suite, which takes up the entire third floor. She is there now. But it would be my suggestion that Gertrude live with one of the other girls in a second floor bedroom. I was thinking that Anna might be a most suitable roommate. By living with one of the girls, she would get to know her classmates more quickly and avoid the envy that the girls in the private suites sometimes engender among the other girls."

"I shall leave that entirely to you and Gertrude. I shall deposit with you a note for five thousand dollars to deposit in her account, which she may use for any purpose for which the school's rules permit. I know she is anxious to procure clothes that are in fashion now in Paris. Please wire me if she requires additional funds."

"Emil, there is one more matter. I see that a servant accompanied Gertrude. I can't permit her to stay. This is a restriction I place upon all the girls regardless of their station, and I can not make an exception for Gertrude."

"Of course. I told Gertrude not to expect it."

Strouss stood up, and handed Sophie the note. "And now I shall take my leave, trusting that Gertrude is in the very best of hands."

"You are most generous. How long will you remain in Paris?" Sophie asked.

"My business negotiations will take three or four days. Then I must be return to Chicago. I shall come back to Paris in early December. I have promised to take Gertrude on the grand tour for the Christmas holidays."

"How wonderful for her! But before you leave, Emil, may I ask one question of a personal nature?" asked Sophie, unable to resist the temptation to try once more to satisfy her curiosity about her friend's true relationship with Gertrude.

"Of course," Strouss replied.

"I know that you are . . . engaged. But you will be away for months at a time. There will be social occasions, and dances, visits from young men. What is it that you wish?" Sophie was unsure how to articulate her question, but Strouss understood.

"I have no desire that Gertrude live as a nun, nor do I want to restrict her freedom in any way. Our marriage, if it is to be, will be in the distant future."

Sophie nodded understandingly. This was Paris, after all.

"I have a small confession which I will make to you alone, if I may rely upon your discretion," Strouss continued.

Sophie nodded. "Of course, my friend."

"Gertrude and I are engaged in name alone. It is not a true engagement. Perhaps someday she will love me, but for now I treasure my time with her. I can think of no better way to lose her than to put her in a cage. We are engaged only to the extent that she wishes it to be so, and she may act as a free woman without concern that she is betraying me. That is our understanding."

"And what about you, my friend? What do you receive in return?"

"Aside from the special friendship which you and I have, and which I value most highly, I have only two consuming passions in my life now — my business, which I have spent a lifetime building, and Gertrude."

Sophie found this kind of unconditional devotion difficult to understand, and she was not sure it was natural. Looking at his unattractive physical features, which she herself had always found endearing even as others found them repugnant, she felt a deep sympathy for her friend; for she could not imagine a beauty like Gertrude ever returning his love in a romantic way.

"You are a most remarkable man," she said, squeezing his hand tightly. "And Gertrude is a most fortunate young woman. You may be assured that I will treat her as you would yourself."

"You have my gratitude." Strouss said.

"And you mine," returned Sophie.

"May I take a moment to say good-bye to her before I go?" Emil asked.

"But of course, Emil," Sophie said, releasing his hand. "Helena will show you to her room."

Helena led Strouss up the grand staircase to the third-floor suite. He knocked lightly on the half-open door. Gertrude and Freda were busy taking Gertrude's clothes from the trunks and hanging them in her closets.

"Oh Emil!" Gertrude said when she saw him, rushing to him and taking him in her arms. "It is so wonderful here! I shall be so happy and learn so much. It is a dream! I shall make you the very best interpreter, I promise you."

She took him by the hand and led him to the window. Below them was spread all of Paris. "Look!" she gushed excitedly. "The Eiffel Tower! Isn't it wonderful? Oh, Emil, you could not make me happier!"

"Would you permit me to make a small attempt to do so?" Strouss said, smiling broadly and taking from his coat pocket a small velvet box and handing it to Gertrude."

"Oh my, Emil, you have given me so much already." She opened the box excitedly. Inside was a diamond bracelet of thirty perfect stones."

"Oh, oh!" she exclaimed. "Oh, oh, my!"

"Allow me," Strouss said, taking the bracelet. Gertrude stretched out her wrist. Strouss clipped it on.

Gertrude looked at it and then threw her arms around him. "It's, it's . . . Oh, Emil! I don't know what to say!"

"You already have," Emil said, taking her bejeweled hand from his shoulder and kissing it.

In the weeks that followed, Gertrude quickly made friends with her classmates. Gertrude soon became especially close to Eugenie, Anna, and Paiva, all of whom were of royal blood. Although Gertrude did not agree to give up her lavish suite, she did ask Madame Dorleac if Anna could share it with her. In doing so, Gertrude not only endeared herself to Anna, who had been faced with a downgrade in her accommodations, but adeptly dissolved the envy of her other classmates.

Gertrude applied herself diligently to the study of French. By mid-November she progressed to Monsieur Fouquet's intermediate class and was soon speaking conversationally with her classmates at meals. Before bed every night she was even able, with the aid of a French-English dictionary, to read a chapter of a Zola's novel *Au Bonheur des Dames*, transparently based on the life surrounding the popular Paris department store, Au Bon Marche.

Sophie was impressed with how easily Gertrude learned to speak French and adapt to her new surroundings.

It was one cold November evening — the first chill in what had been a warm Parisian fall — when Gertrude, after a long day of classes, tennis, and fencing lessons, stepped out on her balcony and looked out at the lights of Paris and the Eiffel tower in the distance. The cold was refreshing, and Gertrude shook her head and let her hair flow in waves against the breeze.

She shut her eyes and took a deep breath. She had never dreamed that life could be so good.

And rich.

17

"The beauty of women, O Lord, has been a plague and tribulation to my eyes, for because of the beauty of women have I been forgetful of Thy great goodness and the beauty of Thy works."

Confession of Ramon Lull, *Book of the Order of Chivalry* (1257).

Over the Christmas holidays, Strouss took Gertrude on a grand tour of Europe — the most pleasant, rewarding, and educational experience of Gertrude's life.

Strouss had treated her like a princess. They had traveled as husband and wife — though in separate accommodations — by private rail car to the great cities and venues of Europe. Freda accompanied Gertrude as her servant and hairdresser, and Strouss had employed two full-time servants to attend Gertrude and run errands for her.

Their first stop had been to Nice on the French Riviera, where Strouss took a villa overlooking the Mediterranean. Gertrude had spent most of her time shopping for the latest French fashions. Because not a single electric was available in the entire city of Nice, Strouss retained a carriage to take her on her shopping expeditions and dutifully accompanied her. She had only to express an interest in an item that caught her eye in one of the fashionable boutiques to stir Strouss to initiate negotiations with the shop mistress to purchase it. If Gertrude demurred, Strouss would desist; if she did not, the item was hers and added to the inventory of dresses, hats, shoes, and accessories which filled her trunks. The chief limiting factor for these purchases was not money, but logistics, for the number of Gertrude's trunks soon expanded to more than could be handled by two porters. Since there were no accommodations for additional porters on the rail car, Strouss had to hire local porters, who more often than not proved unsatisfactory.

After a two-day delay occasioned by the breakdown of a steam engine near the French-Italian border, they continued on to Rome. With her trunks now filled and her passion for clothes temporarily surfeited, Gertrude expressed her desire to see the ruins that she had studied in her ancient history class. They spent one day at the Coliseum.

This great ruin had been sadly neglected and was overgrown with foliage. Nevertheless, the interior was romantically garden-like, and Gertrude spent a pleasant afternoon sketching the flowers that wound themselves around the crumbling columns. The porters were directed to fetch food from the local shops. When they returned, they set up a picnic table, and Freda prepared lunch.

The next stop had been Naples, where the couple enjoyed a sunny weekend on the island of Capri and an afternoon boat trip to the Blue Grotto. Mid-December found the pair ensconced at a villa on a sunny promontory of the Italian boot overlooking the Mediterranean. They spent Christmas in Venice, where Gertrude spent long hours in the art museums preparing a report on Renaissance art to be submitted to her art history instructor upon her return to school the following spring quarter.

On a starry Christmas Eve, after attending midnight service on St. Mark's Square, Strouss invited Gertrude to join him on the balcony of their apartments overlooking the Grand Canal. While she looked out dreamily at the flickering lanterns of the gondolas, he stepped behind her and tenderly placed around her neck a twenty-seven carat emerald necklace. Overcome with the magnificence of this gift and the romantic setting of soft lights and sounds in which it had been presented, she was tempted, though only for a moment, to let him take her in his arms and kiss her as a woman. But seeing him in the light after going inside to admire the jewels and herself in the mirror, she was determined to keep their relationship pure. When she offered her hand instead, he kissed it and knelt down to press to his lips the hem of her gown.

"I worship you," he whispered with both tenderness and passion.

"Emil, you mustn't," Gertrude said, taking his cheeks in her hands and pulling him up.

The couple brought in the new century on the grand new cruising yacht, the City of Rome. From the deck of this great ship, anchored in the ancient port of Piraeus, they viewed the fireworks over the Parthenon at the moment the clock struck 12:00. "Oh, I must have a picture!" she had exclaimed in excitement as she took in the awesome sight of the ancient monument in light. She was anxious to use her new Brownie camera to take her own picture of the spectacle, but settled later for an artist's rendition after Strouss explained to her that the aperture of the lens and speed of the film was not sufficient to record this once-in-a-century sight.

From Athens, the *City of Rome* returned to the city that was its namesake. Thence the pair traveled to Vienna, where, with much apprehension, Strouss agreed to accompany Gertrude on the largest Ferris wheel in the world. On their last night, after dinner at Maxim's, Strouss treated Gertrude to a private midnight revue of the Lippazanna horses at the royal stables.

"It was trip of a lifetime," Gertrude had said to Strouss as she embraced him at the threshold of L'Ecole de Dorleac on the wintry evening of January 9, 1900. "I don't know how to thank you, my dear, dear Emil. You have shown me so much, things that I could never have seen without you. And I have learned so much as well."

"You have allowed me to see those same things for the first time through your eyes," Emil replied tenderly, looking into Gertrude's eyes even as his own welled. "You are so beautiful. Every moment I have spent with you has been precious, and I shall remember each one."

"As I will. I feel so safe with you Emil. You give me everything, and I have so little to give in return."

"You give me more than you will ever know." He kissed her hand a final time and returned to his waiting carriage.

In the months that followed, Gertrude progressed in all her subjects. Although she fell far behind in Greek and mathematics, she received top marks in French literature and history. She became proficient at tennis and made a valiant attempt at fencing; however, when she realized she had no natural talent for swordplay, she took up ice-skating instead. By the late spring of 1901, she was doing spirals and completed her first double toe loop.

Strouss and Gertrude spent the early summer holidays at Strouss's chateau in Fountainbleau. When he was called back to Chicago on business, Gertrude invited Anna Trabatskaya to keep her company at the chateau, and the pair spent countless pleasant hours reclining on divans in the atrium by the pool reading French novels and playing backgammon, or "Nardee" as Anna called the Russian version of the game. Freda was reunited with her mistress during these times, and a staff of cooks, maids, chauffeurs and gardeners served Gertrude and her guests.

Although these periods away from L'Ecole de Dorleac presented ample opportunities for amorous adventure — neither Freda nor Anna would ever have betrayed Gertrude's confidence — Gertrude never considered using Strouss's Fontainebleau chateau for amorous liaisons. What amours did take place were discreet and took the form of an occasional cautious rendezvous at the Opera Garnier, at the Lumineres, or a small café on the Champs Elysees.

A passionate admirer had once or twice enticed her to the Moulin Rouge, a lively dancehall that had excited her and briefly captured her imagination. But Strouss had always returned to Fontainebleau before she could make such excursions a habit. In the end, she realized she was not comfortable in such places. She was always pleased to find an excuse to return to the comforts and security of Fontainebleau and her adoring benefactor.

The fact was that Gertrude never found a man who truly appealed to her. She found most of the young men who pursued her to be but versions of Mayweather and Percival — men who could never quite sweep her off her feet. Perhaps this was because they could never measure up to the male protagonists in the countless French novels that she devoured during her many hours of leisure; or perhaps — and she often considered this possibility — it was because of her deep affection and loyalty, if not romantic desire, for her benefactor. She knew that the day would come when she would exercise the freedom he had always promised her to find her own love, but she would not do so for the sake of these pale versions of her literary male fantasies.

Gertrude graduated with honors in French literature from l'Ecole de Dorleac in June of 1903. A beaming Strouss sat in the front row at the graduation ceremony. It was held in the Napoleonic room of the Hotel De Ville. Devotions followed in the northwest chapel of Notre Dame. As a graduation gift, Strouss presented her with a star sapphire pendant as big as a goose egg.

It was on a bright summer morning at the Fontainebleau chalet that Strouss and Gertrude, eating breakfast on the veranda, discussed their plans for the future. They would spend June and July in Nice. But with Gertrude's education completed, a decision had to be made as to whether Gertrude would stay in France or return to America in the fall.

"I am very much conflicted, Emil," Gertrude confided. "In many ways I feel more at home here than in Chicago or anywhere else in America. I think I could be very happy living here for the rest of my life."

"I always knew that you and Paris would fall in love with each other," Strouss said, taking her hand in his. "You know this place is yours if you wish to live here."

There was a long pause as Strouss considered whether to bring up the matter of marriage. But after four years of "engagement," he knew better. If Gertrude ever wanted to marry him, she knew he was hers. She alone could broach the matter.

"But what shall I do here?" she asked plaintively. "I am well versed in poetry and literature. I know some Greek and Latin, and I am well acquainted with French and Italian history. But what can I do?"

"You could teach."

Gertrude thought for a moment. Finally she shrugged her shoulders. "I don't know."

"You know I will always need you as a translator," Strouss said.

"Oh, yes, and I shall always be of service to you in that regard, Emil. But you are only in France a few months of the year. What shall I do the rest of the time?"

Gertrude sat back as one of the house servants, a slight man from India dressed in white robe and turban, replenished her coffee.

with a divided calf-length skirt, a double-breasted jacket edged with braid and velvet, and button-flap pockets with matching edging. She wore a new pair of Daghilov Russian boots. Judging from the admiring glances of two passing young gentlemen who tipped their top hats, her mannish blouse with stiff detachable collar and man's tie did not detract from her femininity, and she returned their gestures with a dazzling smile.

The fact was that Gertrude Gibson had reached yet a new crossroads in her life.

She was bored.

Like a bird that never had to worry about predators or its next meal, life presented no challenges that might stimulate and excite her imagination. There had been, in the years since Paris, many dalliances, flings, and frolicking with the frisky younger set that frequented the pubs of the better Chicago hotels; but she had always cut an adoring admirer short before he became obsessive, or threatened to throw himself off a bridge in to the Chicago River for love of her. It was always for his own good that she dismissed an admirer — before he did real damage to himself.

Materially, she lacked for nothing. Since returning to Chicago, Strouss had anticipated her every need even before she herself thought to reveal it. He provided her with a seven-room suite at the Auditorium Hotel and gave her the latest and most luxurious model of the Woods Brougham electric vehicle. He opened accounts for her at the most exclusive shops and stores in Chicago, including, of course, Marshall Field's. In addition to the staff assigned to her suite, Freda continued to serve Gertrude as hairdresser, maidservant, and companion and occupied her own room in Gertrude's suite. Every summer since 1903 Gertrude and Strouss had returned to Fontainebleau, which served as a base from which they made annual trips to the south of France, to Spain, Italy, and Greece. In winter, they traveled to Florida and to Bocard Key on the recently opened key train — the marvel of its day — where Strouss leased a villa on the west side overlooking the Gulf of Mexico.

In the fall and spring, Gertrude continued with her studies, auditing classes in French and ancient history at the University of Chicago. She kept her figure trim with daily exercise, biking or playing tennis, and becoming proficient in the latter under the tutelage of an instructor whom she was later obliged to dismiss for taking liberties.

In all this time there had been no change in Gertrude's relationship with Strouss, who never demanded any amendments to their original agreement and seemed resigned, if not content, with an arrangement under which he and Gertrude presented themselves as engaged when it was convenient to do so. It was convenient when they attended balls, concerts, or dinner parties together. When they traveled out of town, they traveled as man and wife as propriety demanded.

Each became more deeply attached to the other, although in different ways. For Gertrude, Strouss was not only her security but also her confidante upon whom she could always depend for unconditional love and slavish devotion. He gave advice only when she sought it, and he had not once, in all their years together, uttered a word of criticism or reproach — even when, Gertrude realized, she justly deserved it.

In return, she showed him gratitude in every way short of offering herself to him sexually, and she was loyal to a fault, providing comfort to him whenever he suffered any kind of reverse. Although such reverses in his business were rare, even during the frequent economic panics such as the Silver Panic that swept the country in 1901, there were many occasions on which she saved him from social ostracism and gave him solace when he was forced to endure insults to his race and religion.

Strouss never gave up hope of marrying Gertrude but never brought up the subject or pressured her. He had come to understand the cause of her recent malaise: her failure to find a man whom she could love as a husband and who could fulfill her as a woman. How he wished he could be the one who could do so — but he had long accepted that he could not.

Saturated with luxuries laid regularly at her feet, waited on hand and foot by a retinue of servants, endowed with every creature comfort, and showered with attention and admiration, what Gertrude longed for was the one thing she had never had — a normal life with a loving husband, children, and a warm and happy hearth. Many times she had sat in the secluded luxury of her Woods Electric and watched young families laughing gaily as they played together in the park or had a picnic.

It was a mark of her privileged existence that she felt, even now, that life had mistreated her. If life were fair, she told herself, she would find Strouss attractive and marry him; for in many respects he would make the perfect husband. He was kind, attentive, loving, able to provide for her most amply, and he held sacred the ground upon which she trod. But how could she marry someone who, for all his admirable traits, lacked that one essential combination of male charm and physical attraction that would sweep her off her feet, make her burst with sexual desire, and give her kisses and caresses that would send her to the moon and beyond?

And so Gertrude looked.

Had she considered the cause of her spinsterhood thoughtfully, it might have occurred to her that she had dismissed many young men who could have met her expectations if she had given them fair opportunity. Rarely had she experienced the joy of the chase or the exquisite torment of longing for someone forbidden to her. If she had, she might have recalled the fourteenth law of love in the first recorded responsum of the medieval Le Cours d'Amour about which she had studied at the Dorleac school: "Too easy possession renders love contemptible."

It was the man who always approached her, who desired and adored her, became desperate for her, but who inevitably always wanted something from her, caused a scene, or threatened to cause a scene if she did not return his passion in kind. She recalled bitterly how she had lost her best friend Bonnie because of the unwanted attention of Bonnie's betrothed and how she had lost her first job because she rejected the advances of her despised employer. She had always been so busy thinking of how to thwart such advances that she rarely gave any man who pursued her a chance to fairly woo her. She had no doubt that she could have any man she wanted, for that was the power that beauty gave her; but her curse was that she wanted no man, for any man won so easily could not possibly be worthy of her.

She imagined it to be the cruelest fate that at age twenty-seven she had never found love, while most other women her age, even the plain ones, were already happily married with children.

The two men who tipped their top hats could not have surmised Gertrude's melancholy from her flirtatious demeanor. But Gertrude never tired of being the object of admiration, for such admiration was always a consolation, if not a substitute for experiencing the thrill of passion in her own bosom.

The blinding light of her smile shone on them only for a moment, for she quickly cast her gaze beyond them to the intersection of Cottage Grove Avenue and Sixtieth Street where she had arranged to meet Tiffany Lake, a member of the hotel lounge whom set she had met several weeks before. She and Tiffany had a common interest in skating, and Tiffany had invited Gertrude to join her at the Sans Souci roller-skating rink.

This rink had opened seven months earlier, in time for Christmas the year before. It was part of a major $2 million facelift that began in 1906 and was not to be completed for some years. Additions to the park included a ballroom, a vaudeville theatre, and two roller coasters — the famed Aerial Subway and the Velvet Coaster.

Sans Souci Park itself had first opened in the summer of 1899 shortly before Gertrude's first trip to Paris, although Gertrude had not visited it then. The park consisted largely of grounds and exhibits left over from the World's Columbian Exposition of 1893. These included the commercial, industrial, and cultural exhibits of the "White City" in neighboring Jackson Park, so named for its neoclassical, white-colored buildings. The most profitable part of the Exposition had been the "Midway" — a mile-long strand of theaters, restaurants, and amusements such as the original Ferris wheel.

The most popular attraction along the Midway was a German beer garden known as Old Vienna. It was that venerable institution, along with surrounding buildings, that formed the core of a ten-acre park purchased by the

Chicago City Railway Company, operator of the Cottage Grove Line, and named Sans Souci after the palace of the Prussian king, Frederick the Great.

In 1908, Sans Souci Park surpassed even the Auditorium as a great wonder. The interior of its gardens rivaled the Hanging Towers of Babylon, with electric fountains, sculptured shrubbery and trees, and a Japanese tea garden. Its centerpiece was the Casino, an extravagant eatery that featured bands and orchestras playing the latest waltzes and ragtime music, led by the world's most renowned musicians including Don Phillipini, Oreste Vesella, and Guiseppe Creatore. In the late 1940s, in a post-war world that had little time for such simple turn-of-the-century pleasures, these magnificent gardens were razed and flattened by developers to make room for ticky-tacky housing.

"Over here!" Gertrude cried, waving to the slender, fashionably dressed young woman on the corner.

Tiffany Lake turned, waved, and trotted over, holding in one hand her hat of egret plume and satin-faced brim and in the other her satchel containing her skates and skating costume.

"Gertrude, I was afraid we'd missed each other," she said breathlessly as she approached. "Oh, I love your costume."

"I usually wear it for biking or tennis, but I thought it would be most suitable for skating as well."

"I daresay it shall," Tiffany said, strutting along the walkway in her tight hobble suit. "Oh, don't think I plan to wear this while I skate. I have a change of costume."

Tiffany's hobble dress, which clung so tightly around her ankles that she could barely walk in it without tripping, let alone skate, was one of the most fashionable though impractical fashions of the day.

Gertrude picked up Tiffany's energetic stride. "I didn't doubt it. I have a skirt like yours but wore it only once after I tripped on my face walking into the elevator."

"This shall be my last time as well. I nearly fell myself getting into the carriage."

"I would have been glad to pick you up in my electric," Gertrude said.

"I do so want to ride in your electric," Tiffany said, still hobbling in a most inelegant fashion along the walkway, "but I had to take a taxi from my hairdresser's. Oh, is that it?" she said, stopping to eye the gleaming Wood Trap on the street.

Tiffany stopped to admire the vehicle, running her hands along its side.

"Oh, I really want one of these, if only they weren't so expensive." She wanted to ask Gertrude the cost but stopped herself, hoping Gertrude would volunteer the information.

"I wouldn't know," replied Gertrude, unwilling to stir her new friend's envy or curiosity by telling her that this newest electric cost four thousand dollars. "Listen, I can take you home after we finish skating."

"Oh, that would be delightful. Gertie," Tiffany said, resuming her hobble toward the rink, "some of my friends will be at the rink. I'd like you to meet them."

"Not mashers, I hope."

"Oh, no, respectable kids, students from the university."

Gertrude smiled. "Sure, Tif, I'd like to meet them."

Because it was a weekday and most Chicagoans were at work, it was not crowded at the Sans Souci rink. Gertrude and Tiffany sat in the gallery and helped each other lace up the skates.

"You see those two kids standing over there?" Tiffany asked as they took to the rink.

Gertrude turned to look.

"No! Don't look! I'll introduce you to them in a while."

After twenty minutes of skating, Tiffany led Gertrude over to where the two young men were standing.

"Hi Tif, who's your friend?" the shorter man with sandy hair and freckles asked.

"Harry, Edgar, I'd like you to meet my very dear friend, Gertrude Gibson."

Harry Ellison and Edgar Farmington eagerly held out their hands. Edgar, a thin-as-a-rail nineteen-year-old with acne, gave her a distinctly moist handshake.

"Gertrude, why don't the three of you get acquainted," Tiffany suggested. "I'm going to go around a few more times." She skated off.

Diffidently, Gertrude stood back against the wooden wall surrounding the rink and watched Tiffany attempt a spiral.

"I think I saw you here a few weeks ago. Were you here then?" Edgar asked, lamely trying to initiate a conversation.

Gertrude never heard the question. She had shifted her gaze from Tiffany to an Adonis-like, athletic creature who was swirling around the rink with full graceful strides. The more she watched him, the more she could not take her eyes off him. When he swept close to her on a turn, she gazed intently at him, hoping to catch his eye. His jaw was strong, his eyes were deep blue, and the long sandy bangs of his thick crop of hair bounced carelessly yet luxuriously across his handsome face. Never had she seen a man so athletic, well proportioned, graceful, and stylish at the same time. She felt her heart skip a beat.

Edgar and Harry sensed her preoccupation and were ready to give up and return to their skating when Gertrude addressed Edgar, though without looking at him.

"Edgar?" she said.

Pleased that Gertrude had remembered his name from Tiffany's introduction, Edgar awkwardly inched closer.

"You are Edgar, yes?" she repeated, momentarily taking her eyes off the young man who had caught her attention. "May I ask you something?"

"Well sure you can. How can I help you, Gertrude?" asked Edgar, only too eager to continue the tone of familiarity that Gertrude had initiated by calling him by his first name.

"That fellow over there in the red bike sweater. Do you know him?

Edgar and Harry both looked across the rink floor.

"That fellow there, just passing Tiffany," Gertrude said, resisting the temptation to point but turning her body toward the young man who had just turned the corner.

"Sure, that's Chuck Patterson, a swell guy. He comes here a lot. Harry and he played on the football team at Englewood last year, didn't you, Harry?"

"Sure," replied Harry. "Best damn halfback we ever had. Scored four touchdowns against Midway High."

"He looks very strong," Gertrude said.

There was a long silence as Edgar and Harry looked at each other with a knowing expression. Though their friend Chuck had always been popular with the girls, they held him in sufficiently high esteem as the hero of Englewood High to not begrudge him the admiration he received from the opposite sex; on the other hand, they did not volunteer to introduce him to Gertrude and so jeopardize what chances they might have with her.

After several more unsuccessful efforts to engage Gertrude in conversation, the two youths conceded defeat, shrugged their shoulders, and took their leave. "Bye, Gertrude. Maybe we'll see you here again."

Gertrude smiled shyly without taking her eyes off Charles Patterson.

Gertrude had never had to approach a man to gain his attention, and she was not about to do so even on this most rare occasion when a man distinctly appealed to her. She held fast her gaze on Charles Patterson, flirting with her eyes as he skated by on each circuit of the rink. For a moment she thought his eyes met hers, but then he turned away and picked up speed. She was about to resign herself to asking Tiffany for an introduction, when, on the next circuit while passing her he turned around to skate backwards and gave her an unmistakable smile of appreciation.

Gertrude turned away. She had gone further than she ever had before to gain a man's attention, and now it was his move.

On the next circuit of the rink, Chuck Patterson turned his skates sharply and braked to a stop in front of Gertrude.

"I say, do I know you?" he asked with an innocent eagerness.

Gertrude paused to look more closely at the slim, tall, sandy haired youth whom she had been watching skate with such a splendid combination of grace and agility.

"Why I do not know, sir. I was just introduced to Harry Ellison, and Harry . . . "

"Harry Farnsworth?"

"Yes," Gertrude replied softly, looking down and feigning an awkward nervousness that belied her own eagerness and excitement. "They said they were friends of yours."

"Well sure they are. They're classmates. Say, did you see where they went? They were here just a few minutes ago."

"Oh, they left a little while ago. Perhaps they'll be back."

"Who introduced you?"

"My friend Tiffany."

"Tiffany Lake?"

"Yes. Tiffany Lake."

"Sure, I know Tiffany. A swell girl."

There was a long and awkward silence as Gertrude waited for Chuck to pick up the conversation.

"Well, I'd better see to Tiffany," she said turning to skate away.

"What's your name?" Chuck asked.

Gertrude stopped and turned around. "Gertrude. Gertrude Gibson," said she, extending a hand.

He took her hand eagerly. "I'm Chuck Patterson. I'm surprised I haven't seen you here before. I'm sure I would have noticed you."

Gertrude felt the first flush of victory at this hint of a compliment. "I don't come very often."

"Were you going to skate some more?"

"I don't know. Tiffany and I will be going home soon."

"Why don't you skate some more? Come on."

"I was watching you skate. I doubt if I could keep up with you. You're very good."

Chuck held out his hand. "Come on, I'll show you some moves if you like."

Gertrude astonished herself by taking his hand without hesitation. She felt a spark of electricity as she took his hand — a thrill she had never before experienced.

"Can you skate backwards?" he asked as he led her across the rink.

"A little," she replied modestly, though in fact she skated backwards with great aplomb when so inclined.

"Here," said he, taking both her hands and pulling her in front of him. "I'll push you."

Across the rink, Tiffany Lake watched the frolicking pair with a resigned shake of the head. "Why, little Gertie, you certainly move fast," she whispered to herself. Tiffany had once made a play for the football hero herself at a party at Old Vienna several months before. "But Gertie, it's a pity he's as poor as a church mouse." Tiffany let them skate alone for a half hour before she skated over to them.

"Hi, you two," Tiffany said cheerfully. "I didn't know you two knew each other."

"We just met," explained Gertrude, catching her breath. "Chuck here is showing me how to skate backwards."

"Why Gertie, you were skating backwards beautifully the last time we were here," giving the two of them a knowing smile.

"Not like Chuck," gushed Gertrude, giving Tiffany a playfully nasty look. "He's the best skater I've ever seen. He plays football too."

"Oh, I know," said Tiffany, giving Chuck a sly smile. "I saw him play against South last year. Scored a couple of touchdowns, didn't you, Chuckie?"

"Aw, football's easy compared to skating. All you have to do is run like hell. There's nothing to it."

"Well," Gertrude interrupted, "I really must get home. Can we drop you off somewhere?"

"Do you have a taxi waiting?" Chuck asked.

"Actually I have an electric. We'd be glad to drop you off somewhere."

"An electric! I've never been in one. You drive it yourself?"

"Sure. Come along if you've never ridden in one."

"Sure, sure." Chuck eagerly followed Gertrude off the rink floor.

Gertrude sat on a bleacher and reached down to untie her skating boots.

"Here," said Chuck, kneeling down, "let me do that for you."

"Why, thank you," said Gertrude as she took out her Diaghilev Russian boots from her satchel.

Chuck unlaced Gertrude's skates, and then slipped a Russian boot on to Gertrude's outstretched foot. As she watched this little ceremony, Tiffany rolled her eyes and exchanged a knowing smile with Gertrude, who was beaming most contentedly.

"Wow," said Chuck, suitably impressed as he sat back in the soft velvet cushion of the Wood Trap. "How fast can she go?"

"As fast as any horse on a paved straightaway," chimed in Tiffany, who was nestled in the back seat.

"I'll show you," Gertrude said. She twisted the accelerator wheel to its limit. The agile electric weaved around a startled horse pulling a hansom, passed one of the new Model-T's that was sputtering and clattering, and then passed an omnibus, drawing hoot and howls from the passengers.

"Whoa, I believe you!" cried Chuck who tightly grasped the electric's mahogany hand railing.

A traffic jam at the next intersection obliged Gertrude to apply the brakes.

"Sangamon Street, you said?" Gertrude asked.

"Yes, it's about five miles north. I'll show you."

"Would you like to go skating again tomorrow?" Gertrude asked.

"Yes, I would very much, but I have to work tomorrow."

"Oh, where do you work, Chuck?"

"I'm a clerk at the Lucas Print Shop. It's near my mother's house on Sangamon Street."

"You live with your mother?" Gertrude asked.

"Yes. I'm afraid the print shop doesn't pay me enough to get my own place. I hope to, though. I want to set up my own print shop some day."

"Perhaps in the evening then, after work."

"Well it's difficult on the trolley in the evening."

"I could pick you up," Gertrude offered.

"Oh you could? You wouldn't mind?"

"It's no bother. In return you can show me how you do your spiral."

"Hey, that'd be swell. Can you come about seven-thirty tomorrow night? I don't get home until seven."

Twenty minutes later the electric pulled up to a modest apartment building on Sangamon Street.

"Until tomorrow, then," said Chuck. He opened the door and got out but instantly returned and stuck his head in the window. "Hey, I enjoyed skating with you today," he said with a great smile.

"And I too, Chuck. I'll see you tomorrow."

Tiffany got out of the back seat and settled into the front seat vacated by Chuck.

"Well," said Tiffany after they were several blocks away. "I think you made a conquest today."

"Oh, isn't he just the most beautiful creature you've ever seen?" Gertrude gushed. "How well do you know him?

"I met him at a party a few months ago. He's a swell guy from what I've heard — football hero and all that. That's all I really know. All the girls are after him, though."

"How old do you think he is?" asked Gertrude, thinking of her own age of twenty-seven.

"Well, he can't be much older than twenty. He just graduated from high school a year and a half ago."

"Twenty," Gertrude said contemplatively. "He's so young."

"Well, Gertie, you're only . . . what, twenty-two or-three, aren't you?"

Gertrude shrugged. "About that."

Tiffany smiled. Tiffany had only known Gertrude for a short time, and Gertrude certainly looked no more than twenty-two or-three, but something about her — her confidence, a cosmopolitan air of a woman of the world, and not least her unexplained wealth — suggested to her that, just possibly, Gertrude could be older than she let on.

"Tiffany?" Gertrude asked.

"Yes?"

"Is there any possibility you could join us tomorrow? I mean, I think Chuck might feel uncomfortable if I came alone to pick him up."

"Why?"

"I don't know. It might not look right."

Tiffany shook her head. "I'd like to, Gertie, but tomorrow night I promised to meet some friends at the Grand Pacific. I was hoping you might join me there."

"Perhaps another time. I'll call a relative I know. She can accompany us."

"An aunt or something?"

"Well, an aunt of . . . " Gertrude pursed her lips for a moment, and then stopped the electric at the curb. She turned to Tiffany. "Tif, can you keep a secret?"

"Sure I can. Tell me."

"I know we haven't known each other for very long, but . . . "

"We're friends. You can tell me anything. I am the . . . " — and here Tiffany paused and groped for the right word, finally coming up with *epitome* — " . . . epitome of discretion."

Both women giggled.

"Tif, do you have some time to talk?"

"Sure, Gertie."

"I'd like to go somewhere where it's quiet."

"How about the pub at the Lakota?"

"Yes, that will do."

Gertrude parked the electric in the front of the Lakota Hotel. The two women got out and entered the lobby together. Minutes later they were seated at a cozy corner table.

"Wine?" Gertrude asked.

"Sure."

Gertrude rarely drank alcohol, but on this occasion she ordered a bottle of wine. She had had several glasses, and was quite tipsy before she came to the subject that she wanted to discuss with her friend.

"You're probably wondering where I got the electric," Gertrude began.

"No!" Tiffany said. After a pause she reconsidered. "Actually, yes I was," she giggled. "And your clothes, and your jewels."

Gertrude leaned forward so that her head was only inches away from her friend and whispered, "Tif, I think I really like Chuck. I mean, really, really like him."

"He's swell. I understand," said Tiffany in a normal voice.

"Shhhh . . . " Gertrude whispered. "Tif, I want to tell you something. I need your advice."

Flattered, Tiffany waited expectantly for a revelation.

"Tif," Gertrude said solemnly. "I'm kind of . . . engaged."

"To another man?" Tiffany asked with surprise.

"Well, not really engaged; you see, we have this understanding, and he . . . "

There was a long silence as Tiffany absorbed this information. "But you are to be married?"

Gertrude burped. "It's so difficult to explain. Yes and no. We are engaged, but he . . . well, you see he understands we can never be married."

"But why not?"

"It's so difficult to explain. You see, he knows I can't love him that way."

"What way?"

"You know . . . in a physical way."

"You don't love him?"

"Oh, I do. But not in that way. I'm not in love with him."

It was Tiffany who now took a deep breath and let it out slowly. "I see your problem," she finally said. "I think."

"No, it's not a problem in the way you think. Emil . . . " and here Gertrude bit her lip for she had not intended to let his name slip, but having done so went on, "Emil understands that I may marry someone else. He wants me to be happy."

"And he gave you all this, the electric, the . . . "

"He gives me anything I want," Gertrude said bluntly in the manner of making a confession. The wine was now acting as a truth serum and enabling her to confide all in her friend.

"Anything?"

"Yeah. Sometimes even before I know I want it."

Tiffany's mouth gaped in an expression of amazement mixed with envy.

"Your clothes?"

"He has accounts for me in all the stores. At Marshall Field's I just sign for what I want."

"I love your boots."

"These Daghilovs?" Gertrude held out a leg. "Do you really like them? They're so comfortable. They're lined with sable, you know. "

"They're to die for. They must have cost a fortune. I bet they cost a thousand dollars."

Gertrude shrugged. They had cost three thousand. "Something like that."

"And the electric?" Tiffany asked.

"All I had to do was point to it," Gertrude giggled. "Emil and I were walking out on Michigan Avenue one day, and we went by the Woods showroom. The Brougham was right there in the front window. I pointed to it and just said, 'I want that.' And the next day he bought it for me. He was so sweet. He put the keys in a little silver box and had my servant girl put it under my pillow."

"Your servant girl! Oh, Gertie!" said Tiffany, incredulous. "This Emil — he must absolutely adore you."

Gertrude sat up straight, held up her fifth glass of wine in the manner of a toast, and hiccupped.

"He worships me."

"I can believe it. You're in his will, I suppose," Tiffany said, now anxious to hear it all.

"Oh, sure. I get everything — his factory, business, mansions, chateaus, all his money, his stocks — everything," said Gertrude nonchalantly.

"Oh, Gertrude! You are so lucky! How I envy you!"

Gertrude sat back, gave her friend an inebriated grin, and burped. "Don't. I'm going to give it all up."

"Give it up?" said Tiffany incredulously. "Why on earth would you give that up?"

"Because after today, I know what I really want."

"You want more than you have? What more could you want?"

Gertrude again leaned forward conspiratorially.

"I want Chuck. I want Chuckie. I want a real marriage, a real family." Gertrude's expression became deadly serious, and she leaned forward. "I want children. I want a real home. I want what everyone else has. That's all. Is that so crazy?"

Tiffany shook her head. "Let me see if I understand. "This Emil, the man to whom you are engaged — he doesn't mind if you marry someone else?"

"Yes. Well, of course he would prefer to marry me himself, but he would understand. He does understand. He wants me to be happy, to have what I want. And I want Chuckie."

Tiffany could only shake her head in disbelief. "So why are you telling me all this?"

"Because I know that Chuck would never understand about Emil. I can't ever tell him. But I also can't see Chuck alone, not at first at least. It wouldn't look right. I want you to be with us, at least sometimes."

Tiffany shook her head skeptically. "You know Chuck hasn't any money."

Gertrude shrugged.

"Who is this aunt who will accompany you when you pick up Chuck tomorrow night?"

"He's Emil's aunt."

"Oh, Gertie, now I've heard everything!"

"She's a lovely woman, in her seventies. We often go shopping together."

"I still don't know why you're telling me all this."

"Chuck and I and you and others . . . we might be together, and, well, someone might ask some questions about me, and . . . "

"And you want me to cover for you."

"No, not exactly, just, you know . . . "

"I understand, Gertie. Your secret's safe with me."

Gertrude leaned over and hugged Tiffany. "Oh, thank you, Tif. I will be ever so grateful."

"But Gertie," said Tiffany, breaking her embrace, "you act as though you and Chuck are already, already . . . "

"Married? Oh, we will be, Tif, you can be sure. He's the man I've been looking for all my life. He's perfect, Tif! Everything I've always wanted! I want him! And I'll have him!"

"But you've only known him for one day. How can you be so sure?"

"Tif, I've never been so sure of anything in my life. He's the one."

Tiffany looked at Gertrude with a mixture of envy, concern, and apprehension for her friend. "Well, Chuck is swell. But if I were you, I would hang on to this Emil."

"But I don't intend to lose Emil," Gertrude said.

"Gertrude, you surely don't think he will support the both of you!"

"Of course not, silly! I never intend to ask Emil for another cent. Chuck can take care of me. And even if he can't I'll get a job. I wouldn't mind living in just a little flat for a while."

"And Emil?"

"Emil will always be my closest and dearest friend. You have no idea how much he means to me. I adore him, you know."

"Emil — you adore him?"

"Yes, and I admire him. And I owe him so much."

All of this was now becoming too much for Tiffany, and she wasn't even sure she believed all of it. She wanted to tell Gertrude how unrealistic her plans sounded, but given Gertrude's inebriated state, Tiffany thought it better to feign understanding.

"Well, Gertie, Chuck is swell, I know he is. And if anyone can land him, I know it's you."

19

"Every tragedy ends in a death; every comedy ends with a wedding."

Lord Byron

"'Peek-a-boo Dresses Hurting Suffrage' Says Lecturer; Grills Society Leaders."

"'Nothing Has Harmed Cause So Much as the Way Women Dress and Undress.'"

Mrs. Ida Husted Harper, author and lecturer, has at last discovered the real reason women haven't the vote. "Nothing has done so much harm to suffrage in the last fifty years as the way women have dressed themselves in the last year or two," she declares. "They have aroused general contempt and criticism and have made men say everywhere that they have neither sense nor judgment, and so are not fit to be trusted with the ballot. Their hats especially have made them the object of ridicule and burlesque from one end of the country to the other. No woman who enters a great movement can allow herself the same freedom she enjoyed before."

Rocky Mountain News, citing New York wire service,
November 10, 1908.

September 27, 1908

Gertrude Gibson sat at the window table of the Old Vienna and looked out at the gardens and neoclassical buildings of the old Midway. A freak, early frost had decorated the large elm trees lining the German beer garden below with glistening white crystals. She had asked for and gotten a table that offered a view and was close to the fireplace. Although such weather gave her an opportunity to wear her favorite ermine jacket, she disliked the cold weather of Chicago immensely. At this time of September in years past, she and Strouss would be planning their winter trip to Bocade Key in Florida. This year she had plans to travel to a place no less charming and balmy — but in the opposite direction and not with Strouss.

She had made a decision the very moment that she had first laid her eyes on Chuck Patterson. She would have him, and she would marry him in a place about which she had read in a recent issue of *Cosmopolitan* magazine — Carmel-by-the-Sea.

In a whirlwind courtship — if that's what it could be called, since it was Charles Patterson who had been courted, all the while thinking that it was he who was doing the courting — Gertrude and Chuck had become inseparable. Gertrude had always insisted that either Aunt Josephine or Tiffany, when she could be enticed from her frisky hotel set, act as chaperone during their meetings. She had done this for the sake of propriety, but also to allay the concerns of Chuck's stern and protective mother, Mrs. Mary K. Patterson, a retired Chicago public school teacher. The couple had dined at Chicago's finest eateries, taken in the last concerts of fall on the Midway, enjoyed long brisk walks along the Lake Michigan shore, and stolen kisses when their chaperone happened to look the other way.

The walks and kisses had cost nothing, but Gertrude had financed the concerts and meals at Kinsley's Castle because Chuck had no more than a dollar or two to his name. Charles had at first resisted the frequenting of establishments that he could not himself pay for; but Gertrude had always persuaded him that it was she who had certain expectations in dining, and that money was no object.

It was during one of these minor tiffs about money that Charles had insisted upon knowing where she got it, since she had no employment. Gertrude had considered deceiving him with some story of an inheritance or the like, but she had finally decided to tell him about Strouss. She did not relate the full extent of her relationship with Strouss or mention anything about a past or present engagement. Strouss was an old family friend, she told him, who had taken her under his wing, educated her, and frequently engaged her services as an interpreter when he made business trips to France. Surprised if not shocked by these revelations, Chuck Patterson did not press her for further details because such questions seemed to greatly upset her. In any case, he was by this time as infatuated with Gertrude as she was with him, and he had no desire to put at hazard the happy circumstances in which he found himself. The most beautiful woman he had ever seen was in love with him, and she seemed never to want for money.

Gertrude had never deceived Strouss in any matter, including her many affairs with suitors over the past eight years. She had confided in him about Charles Patterson the very evening of the day on which she met Charles at Sans Souci Park and had kept Strouss informed of the progress of their relationship.

Only hours before Gertrude was to meet Charles at the Old Vienna, Gertrude had come to the Standard Club suites to tell Strouss that she intended to marry Charles Patterson.

Strouss had known from the first that Charles Patterson would be different from the others. Before, when Gertrude confided in him about suitors, the question had always been about how she would deal with them or dismiss them. This time, as she lay curled before the fireplace in his study, she told him that she was in love for the first time.

"Do you hate me?" Gertrude had asked, apprehensive at how he might take this potentially shattering news.

But Strouss had always known this day would come, and he was prepared. "Of course not my dear. I wish only for your happiness."

"Oh, Emil," said she, rising up and falling into his arms. "I don't deserve you. You are so wonderful. You don't know how many times I have wished that I could . . . "

"Love me as you say you love this man?"

At this, Gertrude had broken into tears and hugged him tightly. "Yes," she said with a muffled sob. "Yes, like that."

Strouss had taken her by the shoulders. "I have only one concern, my dearest Gertrude."

"Yes, anything, please tell me."

Strouss offered Gertrude his handkerchief. "Is this man worthy of you? Does he have prospects?"

Gertrude took it and dried her eyes. "Well, he wants to open his own print shop."

Strouss raised his eyebrows. Not impressed, he asked: "What does he do now?"

"He works in a print shop. He's a clerk."

There was a long silence as Strouss carefully planned out his next words. He took Gertrude's hands and looked into her eyes.

"Gertrude, my dearest, dearest Gertrude." There was a long pause before he continued. "For the last eight years I have lived only to make you happy. You have become accustomed to a certain way of living. You have . . . "

"Oh, I know that, Emil. You have given me everything I wanted. But I need this! I need him! I don't have to live at the Auditorium. I would be happy just living with him in a little house, a little flat even. I want children. I will never ask you for anything, I promise you. I would never ask you to do that."

Strouss sat back and nodded.

"Gertrude, you know I would never stand in the way of your happiness. I will always be there for you if ever you need me, regardless of your circumstances."

Strouss looked as if he had something else to say but was reluctant.
"What is it, Emil? Tell me."

Strouss paused a long time and then said the words that were obviously weighing heavily upon him. "Will I ever see you again?"

Gertrude clasped his hands tightly. "Oh, Emil, of course you will. You know that no one is closer to me than you. Emil, of course you shall see me! Whenever I can come, I shall! I promise!"

Tears welled in his eyes.

"Oh, Emil," said Gertrude tenderly taking the handkerchief and wiping away his tears.

For many minutes they embraced each other as the fire cackled in the fireplace.

It was this last conversation with Strouss that Gertrude was replaying in her mind when she saw Chuck come up the steps to the Old Vienna. She took a sip of wine and waited for Chuck to arrive at her table.

He came up behind her and planted a kiss on her cheek. "Sorry I'm late, old girl. Old man Lucas made me stay late to write up the invoices. You look ravishing tonight, my love."

Gertrude smiled. "Have a glass of wine, Chuckie. This is going to be a very special evening."

"More special than every night the past two weeks?"

"Don't you notice something different?" Gertrude asked mischievously.

Chuck looked closely at Gertrude's evening gown in silk and lace and then at each piece of jewelry she wore. "It's your earrings. You have new earrings, and they look beautiful on you."

Gertrude laughed. "No, silly. I want you to notice something that is not here."

"Not here?" asked he, puzzled.

"Yes, who is not here tonight?"

"Ah!" Chuck said, finally getting the point. "We have no chaperone tonight."

"That's why I asked you to meet me here — so no one would see us alone together in the electric."

"Shall we always have a chaperone, then?"

"Well, you know why we always have one — except tonight of course?"

"No really, no."

"Well, your mother for one thing. She doesn't like me, does she?"

"Oh, she likes you well enough. It's just that she doesn't know where . . . " Chuck was about to go into his mother's concern about where Gertrude got her money and spent it so freely and why she never seemed content to visit places that he could afford on his own salary; but not wanting to begin the evening with any unpleasantness, he stopped short and changed the subject.

"Say," he asked, "what do you want to do this weekend? I was thinking we could go skating again."

"Actually, I was thinking we should try to get away from this cold weather."

"It's just a freak cold snap. Why it'll be back in the eighties next week. It's only September after all."

"I still want to get away."

"Get away from Chicago? But surely we can't . . . "

"I mean get away for good."

Stunned, Charles sat back in his chair, speechless.

"I have a railroad ticket for Carmel-on-the Sea," Gertrude continued. "It leaves tomorrow morning."

"Tomorrow morning? You're leaving?"

"Yes. But I want you to join me — later."

Gertrude was only mildly annoyed that Chuck was so slow in understanding the implication of what she was suggesting.

"But Gertie, we can't . . . "

"I'm talking about getting married, Chuck," she whispered impatiently.

"Married!"

She paused a moment to let this sink in.

"Chuckie, don't you want to marry me?"

"Of course I do. More than anything in the world. But how would I . . . I mean how could I . . . I make only five dollars fifty a week. How would we . . . "

"I have money, Chuck. We could get married in Carmel. Then we could go anywhere you want. You could open a print shop."

"Carmel. Where is that?"

"Oh Chickie, you've heard of Carmel-by-the-Sea. I've been reading about it. It's in California. It's a beautiful place. A beautiful place to get married."

Gertrude had taken to calling Chuck "Chick" or "Chickie" whenever she felt playful or wanted to express her affection.

Chuck reverted to his speechless state.

"But I must go there first," she continued. "It wouldn't be right for us to travel together without being married. You could follow in a day or so. I'll meet you at the station and we can go right to the justice of the peace and be married. Then we can have our honeymoon. There's a beautiful hotel, right on the beach."

There was a long silence.

"Well," said Gertrude softly, "if you don't want to get married."

Goaded into action, Charles leaned over the table and clasped her shoulders with both hands. "I do want to get married! I do! I love you, Gertie! I love you!"

"Chick," she whispered. "People are looking. Sit down!"

Charles looked around and awkwardly sat.

"Here's some money," she said, pushing a white envelope across the table. "A hundred dollars. Buy a ticket tomorrow and come the day after."

Chuck looked at the envelope and then, looking around the room, surreptitiously slipped the envelope into his coat pocket.

"Oh, Chick," she said. "We'll be so happy!"

Returning to her suite at the Auditorium, Gertrude, still blissfully walking on air, plopped down on the divan and rang for Freda.

"Oh, welcome home, m'um," said Freda, kneeling down to take off her mistress' shoes and rub her feet. "I was worried. It's so late, mum."

Gertrude sat up. "Not now, Freda. Please get up and sit."

Freda looked confused.

"Here, sit beside me," Gertrude repeated, patting the cushion on the divan.

Hesitantly, Freda sat down on the divan. "Yes, mum?"

"Freda, something very exciting has happened."

Freda's eyes brightened. She loved good news. "Oh, what is it m'um?"

"Freda, I am to be married!"

Freda's mouth gaped wide open and she clapped her hands with delight. "Oh!" she squealed. "I'm so happy for you! I always knew that someday you and Mr. Strouss would marry!"

Gertrude shook her head. "No, Freda. I'm not to marry Mr. Strouss."

Freda looked not only crushed, but bewildered.

"You know the young man I told you about, who I met at the skating rink? Mr. Charles Patterson? It is him I love, Freda."

"But I don't understand, m'um. Mr. Strouss, he loves you, m'um, he . . . "

"Freda, you know how much I care for Emil, and how grateful I am for everything he has done for me. But in marriage I must follow my heart, as you must do some day, Freda. Mr. Strouss knows this, and he understands. I hope you will too."

Freda wrung her hands and looked away. "I do, m'um. He wants you to be happy, as I do."

"Freda, you mustn't cry. I will be very happy, and I want you to be happy for me."

"Oh, I will, I do, m'um" Freda cried, stifling a sob and turning to embrace her mistress. For a long moment they hold each other. Gertrude hold Freda by the shoulders.

"Freda, I wish you could meet him. He's so wonderful. I know you would just love him!"

"When is the great day m'um? When shall you be married?"

"Freda," Gertrude said slowly. "I am going to California tomorrow, a little village called Carmel-by-the-Sea. Mr. Patterson is to follow me in a few days, and we are to be married there."

"Tomorrow? You are leaving tomorrow?" Freda asked anxiously.

"Yes Freda."

Freda started to say something, but held back.

"What is it, Freda? Tell me?"

"Am I to come with you, m'um?"

Gertrude took a deep breath. "No, Freda, and that is what I wanted to talk to you about. Mr. Patterson is not a wealthy man. In fact he is quite poor. But he has ambitions — to open up his own print shop, and I just know he will take good care of me. We will probably get a flat somewhere at first. Later, when he makes more money, we can buy a small house."

Freda thought for a long moment. "So you will leave . . . "

"Yes," said Gertrude, looking around the room. "I will leave all this. It has been wonderful, Freda. And you have been wonderful, and served me well. Mr. Strouss has been wonderful to me. But I have to go with my husband-to-be. I have made up my mind on this."

"But if I do not go with you, where shall . . . "

Gertrude took her hand. "Don't worry, Freda. You shall work for Mr. Strouss directly now."

"Shall we never see each other, then?"

"Oh, Freda, you silly goose. Of course we shall see each other, just as I shall come to visit Mr. Strouss as often as I can."

"Oh, mum," said Freda, fighting back her tears. "I want to be with you."

"I know Freda, I know," Gertrude said, again taking Freda in her arms and comforting her. "But we shall see each other, I promise you, and Mr. Strouss will take care of you. Now go on to bed. You can help me pack tomorrow morning, although I won't be taking much. We shall have to get up early as the train leaves at eleven."

"Yes, m'um. Is there anything else tonight?"

"No, Freda, you may go," Gertrude said. But then she had a thought. "Wait, Freda. There is something. I am going to go out for a while."

"Now, mum? It's so late."

"I won't be long. There's something I must do tonight. Fix my hair with a fillet. Then I want you to bring me my new wide-brimmed hat and my ermine — not the jacket, the coat."

"Yes, mum," said Freda, eager to serve her mistress if even for the last time.

Gertrude tipped the hansom driver handsomely. She strode up the icy steps of the stone staircase to the entryway of the Standard Club. The uniformed doorman recognized her instantly and waved her in with a tip of his hat.

Gertrude used her own key to open the door of Strouss's suite and quietly tiptoed down the hall to the study. She peered in. Strouss, deep in thought, was sitting on the divan in front of the fire sipping a cognac.

Gertrude, who rarely drank spirits, had consumed three-quarters of a bottle of wine in the Auditorium rathskeller before hailing a hansom.

It had occurred to her in the moments just before she had sent Freda away, that there was a truly momentous fact about her present state. For all the men with whom she had had brief but unsatisfying relationships, she had never once allowed a man to soil her. It occurred to her that at age twenty-seven she was very, very special.

She was still a virgin.

With this thought had come several others. The first was how much she owed Emil Strouss, who had taken her in when she was at the very limits of her endurance, given her everything, educated her, and loved her unconditionally without ever asking for anything in return. The second was whether any man, even a man as wonderful as her Chick, truly deserved to marry a virgin.

There had never been an adequate way for her to express her gratitude to Emil Strouss for all that he had done for her — until she had this one idea. It was an idea, a plan, that would require all the spirits she could consume to carry out.

Gertrude stood at the study door and for a few minutes watched her dearest Emil sip his last few drops of cognac.

"Emil," she said softly.

Startled, he turned around. There, in the soft flickering light of the fire, he saw the form of his beloved — her hair in ribbons, flowers, combs and feathers, wearing a wide-brimmed hat and red satin court-style shoes with waisted Louis heels. Her ermine coat was flung open, and underneath she wore nothing at all.

The words she spoke were uttered in French, but there was no mistaking their meaning, which, crudely translated, was

"Fuck me, Emil."

20

"Don't vote for Perry Newberry if:
 You hope to see Carmel become a city.
 If you want its growth boosted.
 If you desire its commercial success.
 If street lamps on its corners mean happiness to you.
 If concrete street pavements represent your civic
 ambitions.
 If you think a factory is of greater value than a sand
 dune,
 Or a millionaire than an artist,
 Or a mansion than a little brown cottage.
 DON'T VOTE FOR PERRY NEWBERRY"

Turn of the century Carmel campaign poster

October 3, 1908

Carmel-by-the-Sea was situated on a cove of Carmel Bay. Both seaside resort and woodland glen, its older section lay on hillsides of oak and pine covering the Black Hills, a spur of the Santa Lucia Mountains. Its newer section along the beach wound along a delicate crescent connecting Point Lobos and Pescadero Point. The beach was made of pristine white sand, upon which the tide sent showers of foam against the outcroppings of crags. The water was so clear and rich that no one could agree whether its color was blue, green, or even deep purple.

By the 1880s, the original Spanish town on this site, known as Mission San Carlos Borromeo del Rio Carmelo, had fallen into ruin. It remained a collection of tiny shacks along the pines until 1906, when refugees from the San Francisco fire began arriving.

These were mostly artisans — painters, artists, and writers. Some years later they would be joined by the likes of Jack London, Sinclair Lewis, and Upton Sinclair. It was these early artisans who created a world which author Mary Austin described as one of "tea beside driftwood fires, mussel roasts by moonlight. There was beauty and strangeness, beauty of Greek quality, but not too Greek, green fires, and billows tremulous with light, but not wanting the indispensable touch of grief; strangeness of bearded men from Tassajara with bear meat and wild-honey to sell; great teams from the Sur, going by on the high road with the sound of bells; and shadowy recesses within the wood, with the droppings of night-hunting birds."

In 1908, the great developer and later president of Stanford University David Starr Jordan had yet to pioneer the development of building lots to replace the picturesque cottages. Despite a new influx of professorial types from the universities, villagers still lit their homes with candles or old buggy lamps and entertained each other at barbecues and dinners of mussels and abalone. They left their empty bottles of milk on the "milk shrines" of Ocean Avenue along with coins for refills. The lone law officer was old Gus Englunder, who also served as tax collector, bailiff of the court, and janitor of the council.

It was also the year that a small elite of the leisure class began to "discover" this enchanted place. Some wanted nothing more than a temporary retreat from the bustling mobs of the great cities; others fancied that they could trade their riches for a more permanent "bohemian" lifestyle.

Gertrude Gibson Patterson stood on the balcony of the honeymoon suite of the Del Monte Hotel, looked out over the blue-green waters of Monterey Bay, and took a deep breath of the fresh morning air still moist from dew. She took out the note that she had found under her pillow the previous morning. She had read it a dozen times, but now she read it again:

> *Dearest Gertrude,*
>
> *This is, without a doubt, the happiest night I have ever lived; but perhaps the realization of the importance of this night has not dawned upon us. But I sincerely hope that in a few months, when all is ready for you and me, all our nights shall be spent in the same contented minds as this. Tomorrow, we will take a beautiful drive, and in our future lives may we "drive" through life with the motto "be on the square and win," and it will be a pleasure to some day come back to Del Monte and look back with this happy thought to this one evening. No matter whether it snows, rains, or the sun shines, I LOVE YOU. Your loving "Chick."*

Three years later, this letter would become Exhibit A in a murder case that would rock the nation.

Gertrude Gibson and Charles Patterson had been married two days before at the Carmel council building. Determined not to ask Strouss for anything more, and particularly determined not to ask him to finance her honeymoon to another man, Gertrude had hocked for four thousand dollars the diamond bracelet that Strouss had given her in Paris the night she arrived at L'Ecole de Dorleac some seven and a half years before. After arriving by Pullman car in Los Angeles, she had spent two full days in Los Angeles seeking the best offer for the necklace before proceeding to Carmel by motor coach. Chuck had followed three days later, and the happy couple was married the next day.

With the proceeds from the sale of the bracelet, she had paid for a full month in the honeymoon suite of the Del Monte Hotel, rented a modest but new Model-T Ford that had just come out that year, and set aside enough to travel to their final destination, wherever that might be.

Gertrude had brought only one trunk of clothes to Carmel. The rest of her clothes, with which she had reluctantly parted, still hung in the closets of her Auditorium Hotel suite. Although she had discussed with Strouss the possibility of placing them in storage, Strouss had persuaded her to leave them where they were. He planned to maintain the suite as a shrine to the woman he still loved in hopes that one day she might return. Based on what little he knew about Charles A. Patterson, he thought this possibility not unlikely.

Strouss had wasted no time on self-pity. In some ways he had even welcomed Gertrude's departure, for their relationship over the years since Paris had not progressed. He knew it needed more and had sensed her deepening malaise though he was at a loss at how to make her happy. Gifts and luxuries no longer excited her, and on those occasions when she sought his counsel he had had little to offer her other than himself — and that had not been enough. He had encouraged her to continue her education, paid for the best classes and instructors, and was satisfied that her studies in literature and archaeology had enriched her life. In the end, he had accepted her own account of what she needed — a man to whom she was sexually attracted and who could give her family and hearth.

During all this time, Strouss had never relinquished his hope, though faint, that Gertrude might reconsider her own feelings and marry him; he was now resigned to the possibility that he might never be able to provide what she felt she needed. He was not able to dismiss completely the possibility that only Charles Patterson had the power to make her happy.

Strouss plunged back into his business enterprises. He kept above the mantle piece in his study the painting of Gertrude that the apprentice to Maxfield Parrish had painted aboard the *Campania*. On those rare evenings when he allowed himself a respite from his labors, he would sit on the divan before the fireplace and gaze upon this image of her beauty. He would remember the little games they played before the fire, their late evening tête-à-têtes, and the way she laughed and teased him.

Some day, he thought. Perhaps, some day.

"I think we should go back to Chicago," said Chuck Patterson as he sipped his coffee on the veranda of the Hotel Del Monte overlooking Carmel Bay.

For the past three weeks, the happy couple had enjoyed the many attractions of this venerable hotel and its surroundings. Chuck had taken up golf, and they had attended the horse races at the nearby polo fields. They visited the newly opened art gallery devoted exclusively to California artists. Oblivious to all around them, they had danced until the early hours of the morning to the latest ragtime two-steps at the dances held in the hotel lounge. With only a week remaining before their honeymoon ended, it was time to talk of their future.

"Chicago?" Gertrude replied with some dismay.

"Sure," he said. "I know people there — classmates from school who can help me get started in my business.

"The printing business, you mean." Gertrude said.

"Sure, the printing business. I'm going to open up my own shop. You know, we've talked about it."

Gertrude poured a cup of tea and looked out at the bay. "Chuckie, what do you really know about the printing business?"

"I've worked at old man Lucas's shop for almost a year now. I've seen how he does the work."

"But you don't actually do any of the printing work yourself."

"No, I'm the clerk. You know, file the bills, send out the invoices, that kind of thing. But Lucas says he's going to start letting me do some of the typesetting soon. It won't take long to learn. Then I'll open up my own shop."

"What did you tell him when you left?"

"Well, the truth: I was going to get married, and I would be back in a month."

"You told him that?" she said sharply.

She and Chuck had never talked about where they would go after the honeymoon, and Gertrude was dismayed to now learn that Chuck had planned to return to Chicago all the time.

"Oh now don't be sore, Gertie. I told him that just in case we did go back. If we decide to go somewhere else, he'd just find someone else."

Not fully satisfied on this point, but feeling that they were slipping into their first real argument, Gertrude was willing to concede for the moment that they would return to Chicago.

"Where would we stay in Chicago?" she asked.

"Well, it'll be a while before I can earn enough to get our own flat. We could live at my mother's, and it wouldn't cost us anything."

This was Gertrude's first real dose of reality since becoming Mrs. Gertrude Gibson Patterson. It was also the first time in her life since the autumn of 1899 that money, or the lack of it, posed an obstacle to what she wanted. Living with Chuck's mother was not what she had envisioned when she imagined her life with Chuck. She had met Chuck's mother only once, and it had not been a particularly pleasant encounter. Mrs. Mary K. Patterson was stern, blunt, and overbearingly protective of her twenty-year-old son. On that occasion, she had demanded to know the exact hour that Gertrude would return Chuck home after skating.

"I don't know," said Gertrude, wondering how living with Chuck and his mother would work out.

"Gertie, if we love each other, it doesn't matter does it?"

Gertrude smiled. "I suppose not. As long as we're together."

"Now that's my Gertie. And I have another surprise for you."

"Oh, Chick, you know I love surprises!" said she, expecting a little gift of sorts.

"Just maybe I won't have to go back to the print shop, and just maybe I can make a lot more money — maybe fifteen dollars a week!"

Gertrude tried to act excited, even though, for the past eight years, such a weekly sum would not have paid for her pomades.

"Where?"

"The American Steel Company."

"What would you do there?"

"I'd still be a clerk, but I'd get paid a lot more. But with that money, if we didn't have to pay rent, I'd soon make enough to open my own print shop."

"But what about learning the printing trade?"

"Aw, I know how to do it. Besides, as the owner, I'd hire my own people to do the typesetting."

"I don't know, Chick."

Chuck got up from the table and came over to her, taking her by the shoulders. "Now don't you worry your pretty little head about such things. Your Chick will always take care of you. Now, let's get ready for the dance tonight."

One week later the couple was in Los Angeles staying overnight at the Clayton Hotel. They planned to catch the Pullman to Chicago the following day.

Chuck slept late, but Gertrude was up early and dressed.

"Chickie, I think I'll go out for a walk," she said, leaning over and kissing him on the cheek. " It's such a lovely day."

Chuck turned over and groaned. "What time is it?"

"Half past eight. Go back to sleep, silly. I'll be back in an hour, and we'll get a late breakfast."

Chuck pulled Gertrude close and kissed her hard on the lips.

"Alright," he said, relinquishing her, "don't be long. I'll be dressed by the time you get back." With that he turned over to go back to sleep.

Gertrude had not been gone more than a few minutes before it occurred to Chuck that he would like to read a paper before breakfast. He rose from the bed and leaned out the second story window in time to see Gertrude step out into the street and stride briskly up the avenue. He was about to call out to her to ask her to buy a paper, when he stopped short. He noticed that she was not taking a leisurely stroll but walking quite purposefully. He watched for several minutes as she walked up to the corner and entered the Ocean Bay Hotel.

Curious as to what business she might have there, he dressed hurriedly and walked up the street to the Ocean Bay Hotel. He immediately took a seat in the lobby, grabbed a newspaper from the coffee table, and pretended to read. Then he peered cautiously over his paper.

Gertrude was at the desk talking to the hotel clerk. He could not hear what they were saying, but a few minutes later the clerk brought out a letter and gave it to Gertrude. He heard Gertrude thank him and then heard the words that made him freeze:

"Anytime, Mrs. Strouss," said the clerk cheerfully.

"Mrs. Strouss!" The words struck him like a thunderbolt. His first reaction was to confront his wife and demand an explanation, but he needed time to think first. He waited until Gertrude had left the lobby and watched as she returned to the Clayton. Then, in a confused and dazed rage, he ran out to the park across the street.

It was midnight before he returned to the room. Turning the key in the door, he heard Gertrude within.

"Is that you, Chuck?" Gertrude cried, raising her head from the pillow. Thinking herself deserted, she had cried herself to sleep on the bed.

In speech slurred from the effects of a day's consumption of spirits, he spat: "You're damn right it's me! Open up the fucking door!" As Gertrude opened the door he kicked it hard, striking Gertrude and knocking her down.

"You god damn fucking whore!" he shouted, giving her a kick to her side as she struggled to get up.

Clutching her side and terrified at seeing Chuck in such a state, she retreated to the other side of the bed.

"Chuck, what is it? What happened? I thought you had deserted me! What's the matter?"

"'Mrs. Strouss!' That's what's the matter!"

"Oh, my God," sobbed Gertrude, falling back on the bed.

Chuck threw the flask of whiskey into the trash, sat down, and waited.

After several minutes of sobbing, Gertrude looked up.

"All right," she said. 'I'll tell you everything. Just please don't . . . "

Chuck calmed down. "I'm listening," he interrupted.

Gertrude wiped her hands with a handkerchief and sat up.

"I told you before about Mr. Strouss."

"Yes, I know. He took you to Europe to work as his translator. But you were more than his interpreter, weren't you?"

Gertrude stifled another sob, but continued. "No, nothing like that happened between us. He was always a gentleman. But it was very awkward traveling together. We didn't want to raise questions."

"I daresay."

"So we let people think we were husband and wife, so they wouldn't talk."

"Oh my God!"

Chuck put his head in his hands. Finally he looked up.

"Did he give you a ring?"

"Yes, but I sold it." Gertrude had now told her first lie, for the engagement ring Strouss had given her was locked in Strouss's safe at the Standard Club, along with several other items of her jewelry.

"And what about after you came back to Chicago? Were you 'Mrs. Strouss' there too? People must be laughing behind my back."

"No, hardly ever. Sometimes when we went to some society event . . . well, sometimes we let people think that."

"What about your parents? What do they think?"

Gertrude thought long about how to answer this but finally decided to answer truthfully. "They think I'm married to him."

At that, Chuck rose violently and kicked the side of the chest of drawers.

"Please, Chuck, try to understand! We had told my parents before we left for France that we were to be married. I've hardly seen them at all since then. I've been home maybe one or two times. I know it was wrong, but I couldn't tell them. I just couldn't. They'd never understand."

Chuck sat down and again put his head down between his hands.

"I don't understand either."

Gertrude stood up and came toward him to comfort him, but he held out his arm to stop her. Gertrude sat down on the floor in front of him.

"I'm so sorry, Chuck. I was so desperate when I came to Chicago. I was working in a sweatshop for pennies a day. I didn't know where my next meal was coming from. He took me in, helped me, and gave me an education."

Chuck looked up. "And you expect me to believe you never slept with him?"

Gertrude straightened up and looked at him. "Yes," she said firmly. It was almost the truth, Gertrude thought to herself. For eight years there had been nothing sexual between her and Strouss — until that last night before she left Chicago when she had finally given herself to him.

"I want to believe you," Chuck said. "I so much want to believe you."

"All that's in the past, Chuck. I'm married to you now. I'll never see him again. I promise. Can't you forgive and forget?"

"What about the letter?" he asked.

Gertrude pursed her lips. "Chuck, I sent him a telegram, asking for a little money," she said slowly. "We . . . I spent an awful lot of money in Carmel. There was the hotel, our meals, our Pullman tickets . . . "

"You said you had money," he broke in.

"I did, but I spent most of it, and I knew we'd need money when we got back to Chicago."

"We talked about that! We're going to live at my mother's so we can save our money for the shop."

Gertrude did not want to renew the argument about living with his mother. "Oh, Chickie, I'm so sorry," she said, breaking into another sob.

This time Chuck rose and put his arm around her in sympathy. "I believe you, little Gertie. I believe you." He now became tender. "How is your side? Did I hurt you?'

"No," she lied. "It's all right." Her rib was badly bruised.

"I'm sorry," he said, tears welling in his eyes, "I'm so sorry. I never meant to hurt you. I was just so hurt . . . "

"It's alright," she said soothingly.

That night they made love wildly and furiously.

The couple's trip back to Chicago was a leisurely one, with stops in Salt Lake, Pueblo, and Colorado Springs to visit family relatives. It was early January when they arrived back in Chicago and were met at Grand Central Station by Mrs. Mary K. Patterson.

There were only two bedrooms at the home of Mary K. Patterson, who lived at 5511 Sangamon St. in Chicago.

The older Mrs. Patterson rose by 6:00 a.m. and expected Gertrude and Chuck to rise at the same time and to be ready for breakfast at 6:30 a.m. She banged long and vigorously on their door.

"I could use your help prepar'n the eggs!" she shouted.

Gertrude and Chuck, still tired from their long trip, turned over. Their single bed took up most of the floor space in the small bedroom. There was more banging before Gertrude opened one eye.

"Does she mean you or me?" she whispered to Chuck.

"We'll skip breakfast this morning!" he shouted back to his mother.

"You'll do no such thing, son," came the loud reply from the other side of the door. "I'll not have the two of you sleepin' the day away. It's your first day at American Steel, and your little wife'll be wantin' to do the shoppin' for dinner."

"We'll be just a minute," Gertrude said, rising quickly and pulling up her hair.

"Fifteen minutes and not a minute more, or you won't be any help at all," came the reply from the kitchen.

"Chuck," whispered Gertrude as she hurriedly changed from her nightgown to a blue frock, "is it going to be like this every morning?"

Chuck threw his nightshirt into a corner in frustration. "Coming, Ma!" he shouted.

Forty-five minutes later, after Mrs. Patterson had left for school, Gertrude and Chuck sat glumly at the kitchen table sipping coffee.

"Chuck, I don't think this is going to work," Gertrude said.

Chuck nodded glumly. "What do you suggest?"

"I know a good hotel near Midway," she said. "Its' not too expensive. It's called the Lakota. We could live there until we find a flat."

"What about the money?" Chuck protested. "How will we save money for the print shop?"

"We can talk about that later," she said. "I was thinking that maybe we could lease a house and then rent out rooms to boarders. But you know as well as I we can't stay here. Why we'll never have any privacy."

This struck a cord. "Yeah," he said. "I know."

It was three weeks before Gertrude found a house suitable for boarding. It was on Racine, near Chicago Avenue, and had six small bedrooms. Gertrude leased the house for six months at one hundred dollars a month. It would take a lot of work, but if she took in five boarders at six dollars and fifty cents a week, she could provide free lodging for her and Chuck and make a small profit as well.

The bill for three weeks lodging at the Lakota came to one hundred and eighty dollars. When the bill came, Gertrude paid it with what remained of the proceeds of the sale of her bracelet. Chuck asked no questions. He had received two paychecks from American Steel Company totaling thirty dollars, but he had used all of it to purchase beer at the local pub.

In the weeks that followed, Gertrude fixed up the house, cleaned, prepared meals, advertised for and interviewed boarders, and settled all accounts. Chuck became dissatisfied with his employment at American Steel, and one morning he did not go. When Gertrude asked why, his response was succinct.

"It's boring. They didn't need me now, but they'll still pay me until business picks up."

When Gertrude expressed skepticism over this response, he said he would go out that evening and seek different employment.

"This evening? What employers interview applicants at night?" Gertrude asked.

" I won't know until I look, will I?"

"Well, I hope you find something. The rent of one hundred dollars is due next week, and we only took in three boarders this month, so we'll be short."

At this, Chuck kicked the table — something he had not done since that one terrible evening of violence in Los Angeles. "Look, I know the Jew gave you money, and probably a lot else. You admitted it! Now you're telling me you can't get your hands on twenty dollars to tide us over for a few weeks?"

Gertrude bit her lip. It was now apparent that the matter of Strouss would continue to be an issue in their marriage, and a poison in their relationship.

"I'll see what I can do," she said resignedly.

Chuck did go out that night and did not return until the early hours of the morning. Gertrude heard him come in and smelled his strong breath reeking of whiskey as he got into bed. She pretended to be asleep.

As she lay in silence, she thought of her life since she had married Charles A. Patterson. She had believed, or wanted to believe, that she was marrying a man who not only loved her but who had prospects. She had been prepared to give up her life of ease and luxury to make a new home for her husband and raise children. She had been prepared to scrub floors and spend hours over a hot stove if necessary to secure her home and family. It now occurred to her that her great mistake had been to let her new husband know that she had financial resources upon which he might rely. Chuck had simply assumed that she would pay the bill at the Lakota and pay the rent at the boarding house in which she now worked twelve-hour days. His meager salary had never been enough to support them. Now, as he lay next to her, snoring loudly and reeking with liquor, she realized she could no longer live like this. It would be tolerable, she supposed, if she did indeed have unlimited financial resources; but she had resolved never to ask Strouss to submit to the indignity of supporting her new husband. She had already sold one piece of jewelry. Next to the engagement ring that Strouss had given to her, it was the piece that meant the most to her. She could sell her other jewels, but what would she do when the price of those were gone? Chuck showed no promise of advancement at his place of employment, or even, for that matter, of being able to support her at a basic level — never mind in the manner to which she had become accustomed before her marriage.

For the time being, she resigned herself to selling another piece of jewelry — perhaps the star sapphire pendant Strouss had given her for graduation or the emerald necklace he had given her in Venice. But since the necklace and pendant were both locked away in a safe at Strouss's Standard Club suite, she would have to go and see Strouss to retrieve them. She had thought of going to see her old friend many times since returning to Chicago but had always checked herself — for what reason she was not quite sure, although the promise she had made to Chuck never to see Strouss again weighed heavily on her conscience. But now it was her husband who was urging her to seek out her old benefactor.

As she thought these thoughts, tears rolled down her cheeks. Why, she thought, does happiness always have to be so elusive?

It was eleven o'clock the next evening when the doorman of the Standard Club rang the intercom in Emil Strouss's suite to advise him that he had a visitor — not just any visitor, but one whom the doorman recognized instantly, despite the gray and worn frock that she wore.

Strouss waited with great anticipation at the elevator door. When it opened, Gertrude was at first startled to see him. Their eyes met for only a moment before Gertrude rushed toward him and fell into his waiting arms.

"Oh, Emil," she sobbed, burying her head in his shoulder.

Strouss gently stroked her hair, which was uncharacteristically dry and unkempt, and held her close. "Come in, little princess, and tell me all about it," said he, giving her a handkerchief and putting his arm around her. He ushered her in.

Gertrude dried her eyes and looked around the surroundings that had once been so familiar to her. "Let's go to the study," she said softly. "Can we go there and talk?"

"Of course, my dear," Strouss said soothingly. "Come in and tell me all about it."

Gertrude followed him into the study and went immediately to the fireplace and sat down on the floor. She wrapped her arms tightly around her knees.

"What can I get you?" Strouss asked.

Gertrude thought for a moment. "Wine please," she said. "Do you still have that French wine we used to drink in Paris?"

"Of course," he said. "I have some 1899 cabernet. Your favorite, as I recall." He poured a glass and gave it to her.

"1899? Was that a good year?"

"The very best, my dear." he said. "It was the year I met you. All my bottles in stock are that year."

Gertrude looked up, took his hand, and pressed it close to her cheek. "Oh, my dear Emil. You are always so good to me. How did you put up with me all those years?"

Strouss sat and watched her for several moments. Although amazed by the changes in her appearance since he had last seen her some two and a half months before — her frock was worn, her face dirty, and her hair sticky and knotted — her beauty shone through as it always did for him. He said nothing but savored this close moment with his beloved.

After some fifteen minutes of staring into the fire, Gertrude sighed deeply. "It's my marriage to Chuck," she finally said. "It's not what I thought."

"I'm very sorry to hear that, Gertrude," said Emil. "I was very much hoping you would be happy."

"Oh, Emil, you told me. You tried to warn me, but I didn't listen."

"Just tell me how I can help."

"It's not just the money. You see he . . . "

"He is employed, is he not?" he asked.

"Oh, Emil, I'm not even sure of that. He says he has a job at American Steel . . . "

""I know the company." Strouss said. "It is having some difficulties right now."

"He says he works there, that they like his work. He says they pay him even though they let him go home — where he just sleeps all morning, and . . . "

"And what?"

"And drinks all night."

There was a long silence He did not have to ask details. "You must let me help you," he said.

Gertrude turned around sharply. "No, Emil! I can't let you do that. It would never end. You would end up supporting us until the grave."

Strouss sat silent, for he couldn't agree more. He wanted to ask why she had come, but Gertrude was ready with an answer before he asked.

"I came to ask your advice, Emil. And . . . " She paused. "And because I miss you, Emil." She squeezed his hand.

"Is there any prospect of your husband's advancement at the company?" he asked.

"I don't know. But even if there were, he doesn't bring home anything. He's provided me with a total of thirty dollars since we got married, and I may be short next week in paying the rent on our boarding house."

Gertrude bit her lip. "I have to tell you something, Emil, and I hope you won't be too angry."

"I could never be angry with you."

"I sold the diamond bracelet you gave me in Paris."

Strouss sat back. He dared not ask how much she had gotten for the bracelet, but he was sure it was considerably less than the twelve thousand dollars he had originally paid for it.

"You're angry?" she asked plaintively.

Strouss shook his head. "No, of course not."

"I'm so sorry Emil, but there was no other way for us to have a honeymoon. And if I am to pay our rent next week, I think I shall need to sell more jewelry."

Strouss pulled her toward him and stroked her hair.

"Gertrude, the jewels are yours to do with as you wish, and you may take them any time you wish. But I beg you not to sell any more. They are for you."

Gertrude put her head on his knee and stifled a sob. "Oh. I don't want to, Emil, I don't want to."

"I want you to wear them," Emil said. "That is where they belong — on you."

Gertrude picked up her head. "I think I'd be a peculiar sight now wearing emerald necklaces and diamond bracelets while I clean our house with a dirty dust broom," she said.

"Gertrude, if you won't let me give you money, then let me at least offer you your old job."

"A job?"

"The same that you had before. Have you forgotten that you worked for me as an interpreter? I am going back to Paris next week, and I am just as much in need of an interpreter as I was when we first went to Paris back in '99."

"Oh, Emil!" Gertrude said with excitement as she thought of those wonderful days in Paris. "Do you think I could? I would be the best interpreter for you. Oh, it would be wonderful!" But her expression abruptly changed to one of gloom. "Chuck would never agree to it. He hates you."

"He knows about us?" asked Strouss.

"Emil, I had to tell him. He saw me in Los Angeles when I picked up the letter from you at the Ocean Bay Hotel. He heard the clerk call me 'Mrs. Strouss.'"

Strouss took in a deep breath and let it out slowly. "I see," he said. "Did you tell him everything?"

"Pretty much. Except for . . . "

Strouss knew to what "except for" referred and put up his hands. She didn't need to say it, even though he had thought about that night every night since she had left for California.

"Why don't you let me talk to him?" Strouss said.

"You? Talk to Chuck?" Gertrude asked, somewhat appalled by the suggestion.

Strouss shrugged. "He wants to be a businessman. And he sounds like someone who . . . " Strouss did not complete the sentence.

Gertrude thought for a moment. "I don't know, Emil. He's changed so much. He's not the man I knew. Ever since he found out about you and me, and that you had money. "

"I wouldn't want him to come here, of course," Strouss said. He thought the reason for this quite apparent.

"You would come to our house?" Gertrude asked apprehensively.

"Yes. Give me your address. Talk to him first and see if he will agree. If he will meet me, I will come to your house."

Gertrude nodded thoughtfully, still appalled by the whole idea of a meeting between Strouss and Chuck.

"But before you go," Strouss said, "there is someone here who would very much like to see you."

"Emil, who is it?" said Gertrude excitedly as she turned toward the door.

"Freda!" Strouss called.

Gertrude stood up as Freda appeared at the door. The two rushed toward each other and happily embraced.

"Oh, Mistress Gertrude!" cried Freda bursting into tears of joy. "I am so happy to see you, m'um."

Freda stood for a moment looking at her former mistress. "Oh, m'um," she said, "you must let me do something about your hair."

"You invited that bastard here?" Chuck said sharply when Gertrude told him about her meeting with Strouss. He raised his hand as if to strike her across the face but held back.

"I just happened to meet him on the street," Gertrude said, certain that the whole truth would be enough to trigger a blow.

"Gertrude, you are the worst liar I ever heard. Alright, you tell him to come here. Maybe we can do business. He owes me."

"Would you excuse us?" Gertrude asked one of the boarders who was reading a newspaper in the parlor room of Gertrude's boarding house. It was eleven in the morning, and Gertrude rose to answer the doorbell. The boarder left sullenly.

Gertrude answered the door. It was Strouss.

"Sit here while I get Chuck," Gertrude said as soon as she saw him. She led him into the parlor, took his coat, and laid it on the table.

"Sit down, Emil," she whispered. She went to the stairs.

"Chuck!" she called.

Strouss and Gertrude looked at each other quietly, saying nothing that might be overheard.

It was ten minutes before Chuck sauntered down the stairs. He took a chair by the piano and put his feet up on the table, pushing Strouss's coat to the side.

"So, Mr. Strouss, I understand you have a job for our little Gertrude," Chuck said without offering to introduce himself. "Here's my offer and you can take or leave it. Gertrude can work for you — interpreter, whatever, Europe, whatever. But first I want fifteen hundred dollars, in cash. Now. Today. No discussion. Capish?" Chuck slapped a pair of gloves against the table.

"You wish me to pay Gertrude's wages in advance, is that it, Mr. Patterson?" Strouss inquired.

"Yeah. Advance wages — if that's what you want to call it."

Strouss thought for a moment. "I shall require something in return."

"Oh yeah? What?"

"A signed release from you waiving any claims that you might make upon Gertrude or myself at any future time."

Chuck laughed. "Sure, I'll sign whatever you want."

"Very well. I'll have the release written up. It will take a short while to arrange for the funds."

"Shall we say four o'clock?" Chuck said, cutting off the conversation.

Strouss got up to take his coat and hat. "Four o'clock. Yes, I can have a check prepared by then, drawn on an account at the Illinois Trust and Savings Bank. Do you know it?"

"Yeah, I know it. Make out the check to Gertrude and give it to her."

Chuck turned to Gertrude.

"Meet me at the bank at four o'clock."

"Do you have the check?" Chuck asked.

It was four-fifteen in the lobby of the Illinois Trust and Savings Bank.

"Yes," Gertrude replied.

"Cash it. All in twenties. Then come back here."

Gertrude nodded.

Chuck watched her walk to teller's cage and cash the check. Ten minutes later she returned with an envelope.

"Well, you give me the money, and I am perfectly delighted that you are going with Strouss," Chuck said, holding out his hand.

Gertrude gave him the envelope containing fifteen hundred dollars in twenty-dollar bills.

Chuck counted the money. "Have a good trip," he said, turning away.

"Wait!" Gertrude said, handing him the release that Strouss had prepared and which Chuck had promised to sign.

Chuck took a look at the paper, ripped it up, and laughed. "Now you tell that Jew bastard to go to hell."

21

"There is no equality in love."

Leopold Sacher-Masoch, *Venus in Furs* (1869).

January 24, 1909

The *Mauritania* was a fitting successor to the *Campania*. Launched two years, before it eclipsed even its sister ship the Lusitania in power and luxury.

"When she was born in 1907," said Franklin D. Roosevelt some years later, "the *Mauritania* was the largest thing ever put together by man. She always fascinated me with her graceful, yacht-like lines, her four enormous, black-topped funnels, and her appearance of power and good breeding. If ever there was a ship which possessed the thing called 'soul,' the *Mauritania* did."

Theodore Dreiser wrote about the ship that it was "a beautiful thing all told — its long cherry-wood, paneled halls, its heavy porcelain baths, its dainty staterooms fitted with lamps, bureaus, writing desks, wash stands, closets, and the like. I liked the idea of dressing for dinner and seeing everything quite stately and formal. The little-be-buttoned call-boys in their tight-fitting blue suits amused me. And the bugler who bugled for dinner. This was the most musical sound he made, trilling the various quarters gaily, as much as to say: 'This is a very joyous event, ladies and gentlemen; we are happy; come, come; it is a delightful feast.'"

The woman who had registered as Mrs. Emil Strouss looked out over the ship's upper deck railing at the frothy waves of the Atlantic. She pulled back the collar of her ermine coat tight against her neck.

Although she had made the transatlantic crossing many times, none of them, until now, had been as exciting as her first trip on the *Campania* in 1899. The *Mauritania* was more luxurious than any ship on which she had sailed, and she felt once again a pampered princess.

She could not pinpoint the exact time that she ceased to love Charles A. Patterson. Looking back, it may have been the moment he first struck her three months before in the Clayton Hotel. She had not realized then that she no longer loved Chuck, for she took his rage as the jealousy that proved his love.

It was not until later that she entertained serious doubts about her marriage to Charles A. Patterson. Although she had briefly consulted a lawyer about the procedures for filing an action for divorce, she had resolved to save her marriage and perhaps allow herself once again to fall in love with the man to whom she was so strongly attracted. She still felt the raw chemistry that existed between them — the chemistry that had brought them together in the first place; and she still nursed the hope that he could provide a happy home for her. All she needed, she told herself, was time to get away, to think, and clear her mind. Nothing could be a sweeter balm than quiet time at Fontaine-bleau where she would be served rather than having to serve, and be relieved of the burdens and worries of maintaining a household and supporting both herself and a husband.

She had left the boarding house on Racine Street in the capable hands of a woman whom she had hired just days before leaving for Paris with Strouss. For a moment, she allowed herself to fret about how the house was being kept and whether the boarders were paying their rent. But then she checked herself and thought instead of the luxuries and pleasures that awaited her in Fontaine-bleau.

Strouss had outdone himself in preparing the chateau for Gertrude's arrival. Most of the work had been done before Gertrude had married, when Strouss had hoped that Gertrude might someday return with him to Fontainebleau. When Gertrude had agreed to return, he had rushed completion, completely remodeling Gertrude's bedroom. He had built for her, on a raised platform constructed in the manner of an altar, a magnificent canopied bed adorned with bedposts of gold leaf delicately molded into figures of cupids and angels. The pool had been enclosed in a great heated greenhouse that resembled a miniature crystal palace, with lush foliage, waterfalls, and a swimming grotto. On the south side of this paradise, he had recreated a sandy beach, bathed in the rays that shone through a crystal skylight, upon which Gertrude might stretch in her bathing costume on a beach towel and read, listen to music, or have her hair coifed. In addition to Freda, who accompanied Gertrude to Fontaine-bleau, Strouss retained a staff of eight.

Only two weeks after their arrival at Fontaine-bleau when Gertrude's idyllic existence was intruded upon in the form of a brown, wrinkled envelope. Strouss, recognizing the return address, delivered it to her personally as she swam in the grotto.

"For me?" asked Gertrude, walking up to the beach while Freda covered her with a robe. Usually when Strouss entered the beach in such a fashion it was to present her with some small gift, but Gertrude quickly saw from his expression that this was to be no joyous occasion.

"Emil, what is it?" Gertrude lay down on a beach divan while Strouss sat next to her on an alcove stone.

"It's from Chicago," he said gloomily, handing her the envelope.

He watched her expression as she read it and knew immediately that once again she would leave him.

Feb. 2, 1909

> *Dearest Gertrude,*
>
> *Gee! I must be a long way from Europe. Seems like a million miles to me. I love you in Chicago. I love you in Colorado Springs. Oh, didn't you hear Pikes Peak about my love in Denver? I love you in Pueblo. I love you in Salt Lake. I love you, honey, any old place at all. Please dearest, come home to me. Your Chick.*

"You must return to Chicago," said Strouss stoically.

Gertrude quietly folded the letter and returned it to the envelope.

"No," she said slowly, gazing down. "I don't know."

Several minutes passed.

"We have seats for the opera tonight," Strouss finally said, resisting the temptation to ask about the contents of the note.

Gertrude thought for a moment. "Emil, would you be terribly disappointed if we stayed in tonight. It's frightfully cold out, and . . . "

"But of course, my dear. I shall have the horses bedded. Shall I see you at dinner?"

Gertrude smiled and took his hand. "Yes, dear, at dinner."

A second letter from Chicago followed three days later. This time, Strouss had Freda deliver it to Gertrude in the privacy of her bedroom.

Strouss was at his desk in the study when Gertrude, face flushed, rushed in with the letter in her hand.

"Emil!" she cried in distress, laying the letter on his desk.

He quickly read the first two pages, which outlined in detail the deteriorating circumstances of the boarding house, the lack of new tenants, the resignation of the housekeeper, and the urgent need for money to pay the lease. It was the final few lines, preceded by a litany of obscenities that caught his attention:

> *I want you home now. If you are not on the next boat back to Chicago, I will do what any husband would do in my*

circumstances — I will come over there and kill the Jew,
and then I will track you down and kill you too. C.

"Oh, Emil, what shall I do?" Gertrude said in anguish.

Strouss laid the letter down and put away his spectacles.

"He could do it. I know he could!" said Gertrude, trembling.

"I could send him money, " Strouss said, "but I doubt if it would last very long."

"No, Emil, you shall do nothing of the kind. But I am afraid. Afraid of what he might do."

"My dear, I doubt if he would ever come all the way over here, or even *could* come here. Certainly he could not approach this house without being seen. "

"No, Emil," Gertrude said. "He has your address. You don't know him like I do. He could come here. I truly think he could."

She began to tell Strouss about the time Chuck had struck her in such anger that she was sure he could kill her.

"We could go elsewhere, to Nice, to Venice . . . " Strouss offered hopefully.

"No Emil. He is my husband, and I must resolve this matter with him."

"Before you left Chicago, did you give him a date upon which you would return?" Strouss asked.

"No, and that's just it, you see. I didn't think he cared if I ever returned. I just thought . . . "

"If it's just money . . . "

"No, it's more than that. Emil, I have to go back."

Strouss sighed. He knew that any decision must be hers.

"Perhaps you are right, my dear." he said. "This is a matter that will not go away on its own and must be resolved — perhaps sooner better than later. I cannot tell you what to do, but I support any decision you make. You know you have a home here for as long as you wish, and you know I would always take care of you. There is no greater happiness for me than to be here with you. But you have a husband, and he wants you home. In that one respect, I cannot say I blame him, for if I were your husband I would ask no less."

"The fifteen hundred dollars," she murmured. "It must be gone, and it bought me only three weeks' peace. I suppose I always knew I would have to go back. I just didn't know it would be this soon."

"If you must go, I will come with you," Strouss said when he heard her decision.

"No, Emil, I want you to stay here. You have only just arrived, and you have business here in Paris that must be attended to and which I know you have neglected. I will go back alone. I must try to patch things up with Chuck."

Strouss wanted to ask her: Did she still love Chuck? Instead he said, "I understand. I will procure a ticket on the next steamer — I think it is the Lusitania. But promise me you will call upon me if there is anything I can do to help you.

"Yes, I will, Emil. I promise."

February 17, 1909

At the gangplank of the Lusitania in Le Havre, Strouss kissed Gertrude tenderly.

"Goodbye," he said. "And here is some money. I hope it will be sufficient to resolve any difficulties.

"Oh, Emil," she said returning his embrace.

She put the envelope containing five thousand dollars in her coat pocket, walked up the plank, and waved goodbye.

Gertrude's homecoming at first promised to be a joyous one. Chuck met his wife with outstretched arms and tears of happiness at her return. For the moment, his passion and touch made her believe that she did love him after all.

On the first night of her arrival, they made love with all the passion that had first brought them together.

It was Gertrude who first turned a sour note upon learning about the state of the boarding house. Rents had not been collected, the house had not been cleaned, bills were unpaid, and the woman Gertrude had retained to run the house had left after not being paid her wages. Chuck still had no income and had little prospect of securing employment. It was not long before the few remaining tenants took their leave. They had no desire to stay in a place where their rest was constantly interrupted by the loud and frequent arguments of their landlords — arguments that often started late at night and continued until the early hours of the morning.

One evening in early March, Chuck came home with a hacking cough after a long night of heavy drinking. Within a week he was coughing blood. Putting their differences aside, Gertrude stayed up all night nursing him. His condition did not improve, however, and a belated visit to the doctor confirmed the worst — he had consumption.

"We have to have money for medicine, or I'll die!" Chuck cried in despair one day after learning the terrible news. "We need to sell your electric. I know a man who will buy it for six hundred dollars."

At this suggestion, Gertrude demurred in the strongest terms.

"No Chuck. I will try to get money, but the electric cost more than four thousand dollars and is still worth at least half that amount. I won't sell it for six hundred dollars!"

In response to this disobedience on the part of his wife, Chuck rose from bed with righteous indignation. "I lie here with the consumption, and you talk to me of the best price! I know where you got that damned car! You and I both know! And you'd rather see me die before you sell that bastard's car!" He came toward her, raising his hand to strike her before a fit of coughing overcame him and he fell back on the bed.

In the end, Gertrude agreed to sell the Brougham. Continued refusal, she feared, would give her husband grounds to suspect that she had other funds available, and she was determined to make the five thousand last as long as possible.

The months that followed were difficult. Gertrude alternated between feelings of deep compassion and sympathy for her ailing husband to fear and loathing when he lashed out at her and demanded money. Still, she took care of him, coddled him, made his meals, and stayed up nights to watch over him. Unable to both care for her husband and maintain the boarding house, she moved to a small flat at 120 East Sixtieth Street. This accommodation proved uncomfortably small when Chuck's sister and mother joined her. When Mary K. Patterson demanded that Chuck be sent to a private sanitarium, Gertrude at first demurred, angry with the presumption that underlay this demand — namely, that Gertrude would pay all his bills. She had resolved never to ask Strouss for another cent and had tried to hoard what was left of the five thousand dollars. In the end she relented, using the proceeds to pay all medical bills. What remained of the five thousand dollars she used to purchase some bank stock in hope that its appreciation would extend the life of her capital.

Within weeks, Gertrude felt her own health failing. When a doctor advised complete rest and a change, she told Chuck that she wished to return home to Sandoval for a visit with her parents. Chuck raged and forbade her to go, accusing her of abandoning him. One night when she was up all night nursing him, he began coughing blood. He demanded that she kiss him on the lips to prove that she loved him. When she kissed him on the cheek instead, he bit her.

In mid-September, she defied her husband and left him in the care of a nurse. In a state of exhaustion, she returned to Sandoval for a six-day visit to her parents. They welcomed her with open arms and nursed her just as they had done when she had come down with chicken pox as a little girl. When Gertrude's health declined precipitously and she had symptoms of a high fever, chills, and coughing, they feared that she too had contracted consumption. Under the care of her mother, however, Gertrude's health finally returned and she went back to Chicago to care for her husband.

October 1910

By October of the following year, Chuck had returned home from the Chicago sanitarium and returned to the flat where Gertrude, despite having consulted another lawyer about a divorce, resumed caring for him. His condition improved marginally, though he was still unable to work.

Gertrude wanted to visit home again, but did not want to leave Chuck with a nurse whom Chuck was convinced was incompetent. Gertrude asked her parents if she could bring Chuck home with her to Sandoval for a few weeks. Although this request was met with considerable consternation on the part of Gertrude's father, he relented against his better judgment and even built a porch for Chuck to sleep in during his visit.

Chuck mellowed considerably after he and Gertrude arrived in Sandoval. In the shadow of the watchful eye of Gertrude's protective father, Chuck stopped drinking and did not once give way to a violent outburst. Because there was no question of Chuck working in his present condition and there were no rent or bills to pay, there was less for Gertrude and Chuck to argue about. It was during this relatively happy period that Gertrude became more optimistic about saving her marriage. She thought often of their happy days in Carmel.

"I think we should go back to California," Chuck said one day as he and Gertrude reclined together on a hammock on the Pattersons' porch.

It was not an entirely disagreeable suggestion because it was not inconceivable that a return to California would rekindle the affection that they once had. The only difficulty was that by this time there was little left of Strouss's five thousand dollars.

"Chuck, we don't have the money," Gertrude said.

"You could get it. You could get it from that fat cow in Chicago."

This remark ignited the old animosities and when Gertrude indignantly refused, Chuck threw her from the hammock, pulled her hair, and hit her in the face with his fist. Chuck was tired of being on good behavior and wanted to leave Sandoval.

In the end Gertrude complied. She did what she had promised herself she would never do again — write Strouss for money. He sent it immediately.

Three days later the pair were on the train to California. It made a stop in Denver, Colorado, where they had made arrangements to stay with Chuck's aunt in Littleton, south of Denver. After five weeks at this home, Chuck made a fateful decision.

"Denver is a wonderful place," he said. "The doctor says Colorado would be the perfect place for me to recover. Let's stay here."

"I like it here, too," Gertrude agreed. She was willing to make one more go of her marriage in this new environment.

Once Gertrude and Chuck decided to remain in Denver, it remained to find a suitable facility to treat Chuck's consumption. After touring several facilities in the Denver area in the late spring of 1911, Chuck decided that the Phipps Sanitarium, located in a spacious park two blocks west of the Richthofen Castle, offered the best hope of favorable treatment. Unfortunately, it was expensive. The sanitarium directors demanded payment in advance and the purchase of a wardrobe. Demands by Chuck that Gertrude obtain the necessary money from Strouss brought about the first of many violent arguments that year.

Strouss did provide the necessary funds for Chuck's treatment, and Chuck entered the sanitarium. Gertrude rented a modest one-room flat on Colfax Avenue to live in.

When Gertrude wrote to Strouss about her living conditions, he offered to buy her a house. Anxious to escape from her dreary Colfax flat, she accepted this offer and found a comfortable three-bedroom bungalow at 1008 Steele Street for him to purchase for her.

In the months that followed, Chuck visited Gertrude several times a week at the bungalow. He never asked where she got the money to purchase it because there was only one place the money could have come from. Neighbors on Steele Street reported the sounds of violent fighting between the two, apparently followed by equally vigorous lovemaking. However, their relationship continued to deteriorate, and Chuck continued to demand money. When permitted to leave the sanitarium for short visits, he visited pubs, drank heavily, and began to accumulate a string of gambling losses playing poker.

Finally, on September 1, Gertrude decided that she had had enough and went to Willis V. Elliott, the district attorney of the City and County of Denver. Willis did not serve in that capacity full time and retained his own private practice. Gertrude went to retain him for the purpose of filing for divorce against her husband on the grounds of cruelty and threats to kill her on numerous occasions. Among the litany of complaints she submitted to her lawyer was that on August 15 of that year Charles Patterson had menaced her with a razor and threatened to kill her.

Perhaps anticipating future legal action, Chuck took to writing letters to his brother and writing a diary, making numerous entries declaring his undying devotion and love for Gertrude, and claiming that she had heartlessly "abandoned" him at the sanitarium.

When served with divorce papers, Chuck reacted angrily. He obtained an afternoon pass from the sanitarium, appeared at the bungalow where Gertrude was doing a wash of laundry, and yelled to her, "I am going to have ten thousand dollars out of this lawsuit, or I am going to have blood."

Several days later, another heated incident took place at the bungalow. Chuck came to visit Gertrude to try to talk her out of the divorce just at the moment that a certain George Strain was leaving the bungalow. Strain, in the company of his fiancée, had visited Gertrude several days before and had accidentally left his Kodak camera. It was Strain's misfortune to come alone to retrieve it at the very moment that Chuck appeared at the bungalow. Convinced that Strain had come for a liaison with his wife, Chuck reacted violently.

"I could kill you!" Chuck raged at the sight of a man on his bungalow porch. "I could shoot you down like a dog, and the law would never touch me because I have lung trouble!"

Alarmed, Gertrude ran into the house. Strain, who happened to have a pistol in his pocket, remained on the porch to confront Chuck. He brandished his pistol and chased Chuck away. When Gertrude returned to the porch, she told Strain how much she feared her husband and what he might do to her. Strain sympathized with her plight.

"Let me leave this with you for your protection," Strain said, putting the pistol on the table.

"Perhaps that would be a good idea," Gertrude replied, taking the gun and putting it away.

On September 20, after consulting with several lawyers, Chuck countered Gertrude's petition for divorce with a lawsuit against Strouss in the amount of twenty-five thousand dollars for the alienation of his wife's affection. This act was to trigger a sequence of events that would soon hold an entire nation in thrall.

Beecher, Beecher is my name,
Beecher till I die!
I never kissed Mrs. Tilton
I never told a lie.

Ditty chanted by children on New York City sidewalks (1874).

September 24-25, 1911

The common law tort of "alienation of affection" contained three elements, which if proven were the basis of legal liability: first, that there existed a marriage characterized by genuine love and affection; second, that this love of one spouse for the other had been destroyed or "alienated"; and third, that the wrong and malicious conduct of the defendant was the controlling cause of this alienation.

Such were the legal grounds alleged by Charles A. Patterson against Emil Strouss of Chicago, Illinois. In a twist that would later generate observations of great irony Chuck Patterson retained the legal service of W.W. Grant, Esq., the son-in-law of E.B. Hendrie, who lived at 7020 East Twelfth Avenue — also known as the Richthofen Castle.

In 1911, most states recognized the legal action known as alienation of affection. Prior to that year, the most famous lawsuit for alienation of affection had been that filed in 1874 by journalist and lecturer Theodore Tilton against his long-time friend Henry Ward Beecher, the renowned preacher and spiritual leader of the Congregationalist Plymouth Church, and first president of the Lane Theological Seminary. Beecher's baby sister, Harriet Beecher Stowe wrote Uncle Tom's Cabin, a work credited by Abraham Lincoln with triggering the War Between the States.

In late 1897, Tilton's pretty young wife Elizabeth had begun confessing to her husband that she had committed adultery with Henry Ward Beecher. These confessions were eventually leaked to the press, and newspapers around the country began publishing it on their front pages. It was in the midst of this national scandal and uproar that Tilton filed his alienation of affection lawsuit against Beecher.

In a celebrated 112-day trial, which in a day of television would surely have preempted such trials as that of O.J. Simpson or the impeachment trial of President Clinton, the details of scandal and illicit sex dominated the national news. After fifty-four ballots, a hung jury of nine supporting Beecher and three supporting Tilton threw in the towel, and a mistrial was declared. Four years later, Elizabeth Tilton got in the last word, declaring in a secret letter to her legal adviser that was eventually published in every newspaper in the country, that the claim of alienation of affection was true.

Many years later, in the 1930s, most states abolished the tort of alienation of affection on grounds that it encouraged mischief and blackmail. In declaring its reasons for its abolition, the Minnesota legislature stated that such suits have been "subject to grave abuses, have caused intimidation and harassment to innocent persons, and have resulted in the perpetuation of frauds." By the year 2000, only a handful of states retained the law of alienation of affection, including South Carolina. When a North Carolina jury awarded a jilted wife a million dollars against her ex-husband's secretary in 1997, newspapers in that state reported that "business dropped at motels renting rooms by the hour, and husbands came home from work on time."

Gertrude was deeply distressed when she heard news that Chuck had filed an alienation of affection lawsuit against Strouss — and she was angry. She now believed that Strouss had been the only man who ever truly loved her. It was Strouss who had come to her rescue in her hours of need, supported both her and Chuck, and paid for Chuck's medical expenses. She resolved that she could not repay her benefactor by allowing her husband to drag him through the mud.

On Monday, September 24, 1911, Gertrude made the fatal decision to call Chuck at the sanitarium to arrange a meeting with him. At 7:30 a.m. that day, she took the Fairmount streetcar to Twelfth and Madison Streets and asked the clerk to ring Chuck at the nearby sanitarium.

"Why didn't you call me on Sunday?" Chuck asked when he picked up the phone.

"I've been sick," she replied.

"I don't believe you. You're a liar. Meet me at 10:30."

"I can't. I have an appointment with my dressmaker. Maybe a little later. We could go Daniel and Fisher's for lunch."

"No," he said. "Why don't you withdraw this divorce suit and sign over the deed to the house over to me, as I have asked you to do, and I will withdraw my suit and come home."

"No, Chuck, I won't do that."

"Well, meet me in the front of the Peck School at ten o'clock, and we'll have a little talk."

Gertrude went to the appointed place and waited. Minutes later, she saw Chuck walking up Olive Street from the south.

"I have an appointment with my dressmaker. I can't stay very long," she said.

"Come on down the street with me; it's too public here," he demanded. "I lost twelve dollars playing poker, and I am three weeks behind in my board. I need some money."

"No," Gertrude answered sharply.

"Look, why don't you just put the bungalow in my name, turn over all your stock, and I'll come over tomorrow."

Gertrude, remembering how Chuck had refused to sign the release after receiving the fifteen hundred dollars in Chicago, was firm. "No, Chuck. I'm not signing over anything."

In heated argument, the pair walked down Twelfth Avenue toward the Richthofen Castle.

Within ten short minutes, four shots rang out.

Gertrude Gibson Patterson did not want to think about those four shots. She wanted to blot them from her mind. She wanted to think about something else — anything else. The loud crack of Judge Allen's gavel awakened her from her reverie of the past and brought her to the very real present.

"Your motion is denied, counsel. You may proceed with your opening argument."

23

"Foul Murder is Charged by Prosecutor in Opening."

The Daily News, November 24, 1911.

"When they saw her enter the courtroom, a quiet, submissive, gentle-looking creature, raising plaintive baby eyes from time to time, looking with somewhat wistful glances at the talesmen, there was indeed a murmur of surprise.

"A well-groomed, carefully-coiffured, smooth-skinned, faultlessly manicured young woman, listening attentively to a matinee performance of some problem play in which an erring wife is fighting out her life battle — might have been this prisoner — listening to the details of her own trial.

"'It isn't possible,' said an experienced newspaper writer, 'that Mrs. Patterson could have endured all of the degradations she alleges and still preserve that unsullied, exquisite, doll-like face.'

"Sin, however, does not always leave its blighting mark upon the face. There are those who, like Dorian Grey, retain their external loveliness though they descend deeper and deeper into the sloughs of degradation, while their souls, symbolized by the picture of Oscar Wilde's famous romance, bear the hideous marks of crime.

"Looking at the face of Gertrude Gibson Patterson, a face whose beauty is a tremendous drawing card for the defense, the wonder does grow, however, at the purity of its lines."

(Page one feature story, *Rocky Mountain News*, November 24, 1911)

Thursday, November 23, 1911
Day One of the Trial

"Thank you, your honor. I am ready to proceed."

Horace G. Benson, looking dapper in his single-breasted waistcoat, strode confidently to the front of the courtroom, and planted his feet firmly in a position no more than three feet in front of the jury. Behind him, half the student body of the University of Denver Law School watched in anticipation.

Horace Benson was not the district attorney for the City and County of Denver. He had been appointed as special prosecutor when Willis Elliot, the elected district attorney, was obliged to disqualify himself from the prosecution on grounds that Mrs. Patterson had previously retained him in a divorce action against her husband.

Years before, Benson had worked in the district attorney's office as a deputy. He was known for his aggressive tactics and was most famous for his prosecution of Guiseppe Alia in 1908 for the murder of Father Leo in the vestibule of St. Elizabeth's Church. Against one of the strongest insanity defenses ever made in the Denver courts, he had not only won a conviction but had sent the defendant directly to the gallows, where Benson watched the hapless Guiseppe consume twenty minutes in the act of being strangled to death.

In recent years, Benson had turned to the more lucrative practice of defense. His most notable victory was the acquittal of a man charged with killing two Denver policemen. In that case Benson had been greatly aided by the fact that the police had kept his client locked in a dungeon for seventy hours before making him confess.

Whether on prosecution or defense, Benson was known as a lawyer with an unquenchable — some said obsessive — desire to win. He insisted on trying cases alone, so that any credit or blame fell on him alone. Because he almost always won, it was the credit he enjoyed alone. If he was a bad loser, as his detractors claimed, there were few occasions on which he was obliged to reveal this less than admirable trait.

The trial of Gertrude Gibson Patterson was his kind of case — it was high profile, enjoyed national publicity, and best of all in his view, it was a sure winner. The facts in the case would surely speak for themselves: a weak and consumptive victim with two shots in the back (two shots had gone wild) and a defendant who, after first being caught in several transparent lies, admitted bringing the gun to the scene of the crime and shooting her estranged husband. Benson didn't much care whether her defense would be insanity or some trumped-up self-defense theory. He knew that the defendant had already eschewed an insanity defense, and as for self-defense — two bullets in the back was all the evidence he would need. It would take nothing less than the sight of sweet, pretty little Gertrude swinging, choking, gagging and kicking at the end of a rope to quench his thirst for justice.

Benson presented a stark contrast to his opponent, O.N. Hilton. Equally skilled and zealous in representing a client, Hilton's style was less aggressive and more folksy. He had won acquittals in no less than a hundred homicide cases and made a national reputation in 1907 when he stood by Clarence Darrow and successfully defended George Pettibone on a charge of complicity in the assassination of Governor Frank Stunenberg in a trial of worldwide notoriety. Not surprisingly, he commanded the highest fee of any lawyer licensed to practice law in Colorado.

Although Benson and Hilton were known to be close personal friends, having served together in many fraternal orders, neither was known to have ever held back in the combat of trial. In their only previous courtroom battle against each other, Benson had won a murder conviction against Hilton's client, Frank Cavanaugh.

The press was at odds over whether the trial of Gertrude Gibson Patterson would be a battle between these two great titans or a simpler, more colorful contest between "Gertrude's beauty and Benson's brains." Though the front pages of the Denver newspapers played up the latter contest, less sensational articles on the back pages predicted that "there is no law, rule, principle or trick in criminal law or practice that is unknown to either Benson or Hilton, and in this trial there will be no omission of effort on either side."

With a fierce expression of fire and brimstone, Horace Benson waited until every eye in the courtroom was upon him. Even then he waited for absolute silence before beginning his opening statement:

"Gentlemen of the Jury.

"Vampire! Wise in the ways of this world, this pure innocent woman, after her fancy Paris education, met, proposed, and married this young Chicago lad. Vampire! She taught him the ways of love. She trained him the way he should go and when at least, after four years of devotion, he protested her taking more and more money from her so-called 'protector' Strouss, she called him by telephone from the sanitarium where he was sick unto death and shot him in the back!"

"On that morning, September 25th, Mrs. Patterson, this defendant, had called her husband by telephone — several hospital attendants swear to this — and asked him for a meeting. He agree to meet her near the sanitarium as he was too feeble to walk further. She had dressed herself carefully in a blue tailored suit and turban for the tryst. Patterson, pale and emaciated, met in a quiet spot and they started toward a small park near East Twelfth Avenue and Pontiac Street. Nearby was a stately mansion, the home of the socially prominent E.B. Hendrie, known as 'the Castle' since it had been erected in boom days as a monument to the vanity of a German Baron named Von Richthofen. Between 'the Castle' and the street was a stonewall and behind this was a tool shed. From the door of this tool shed, George Schramm, caretaker, heard a man and a woman quarrelling. He saw the woman hand the man a slip of paper, saw the man read the clipping and hand it back. As he handed it back, according to the evidence of the defendant, he struck her in the face, spat at her, struck her again and again until he knocked her down."

Benson turned toward Gertrude, his face crimson with rage, and pointed in her face.

"And you! Down on the ground, as you claim, opened your purse, took out Strain's gun and with it shot your sick husband in the back! Shot in the back! The shooting over, as the poor man sprawled on the ground, you stepped on him and after a brief moment rushed toward the gate in 'the Castle' wall, calling 'My husband has committed suicide! Help!

"The murdered man's mother will testify that her son was a gentle, kind boy. He never carried a gun and had never quarreled at home."

"Gertrude's mother, Mrs. James Gibson, her son James, and her daughter, Mrs. Farsham, have come from their home in the east to testify

Chicago Detective J.J. Hopper, who testified at the Patterson murder trial.

to the goodness, sweetness, and purity of the daughter and sister. They agree that 'Gertie' had accompanied Strouss to Paris as a daughter would accompany a father on their last trip to act as his interpreter in his dealings with the French.

"I believe the evidence will show that Charles A. Patterson, husband of the defendant in this case, was a consumptive. In September of this year he was living at the consumptives' home commonly known as the Phipps Sanitarium in this city. The defendant was living at her bungalow at 1008 Steele Street, this city.

"On Saturday night, the twenty-third of September 1911, a young unmarried man who had been in the habit of calling at the Patterson bungalow called again. Patterson told this young man, a Mr. Strain, of the temper possessed by her husband. Because of what she had told him, on this night Mr. Strain put a double action-pistol in his outside right-hand coat pocket. He had arrived at the bungalow around seven o'clock that evening. Mrs. Patterson and Mr. Strain took seats together in a nice easy swing chair hanging from the ceiling of the porch.

"About the hour of nine o'clock a man was seen to approach the bungalow. Mrs. Patterson cried out, "There comes my husband," or "There is Chick"; then she left her partner in the swing and rushed into the bungalow. Her husband walked to the steps leading to the house. The husband walked on the porch, and leaning over, looked into the stranger's eyes and asked him if he did not think he had gotten into the wrong house, or words to that effect. He leaned over with his hands in this position and said, 'I am going to fix you,' or 'I will fix you now,' or something to that effect. Strain jumped up from the swing chair and pulled his revolver and put it against the throat of Patterson and told him to throw up his hands and for him to keep on going and not to stop. Patterson threw up both hands and went.

"No shot having been fired, Mrs. Patterson came out of the house and saw her husband going away with both hands in the air.

"Mr. Strain had a Kodak at the home of the prisoner, which he left there in some previous visits, and he had not called at the Pattersons' bungalow in some days, on account of certain divorce proceedings instituted by Mr. Patterson against his wife, but on this occasion he called to secure his Kodak. He was about to leave with the Kodak when Mrs. Patterson said, 'I am afraid of my husband, and I want that pistol; let me have it; you leave it here with me.' Strain left the pistol with her that Saturday night between ten and eleven o'clock.

"Monday morning, Mrs. Patterson telephoned to the Phipps Sanitarium to her husband to meet her — I think the evidence will disclose this — and on Monday morning she sauntered over with this pistol which she had secreted about her person. She waited in a certain place for a considerable length of time, walking back and forth and looking.

"The evidence will disclose that her husband appeared at the scene, and when he saw her she called to him to stop or come to her, or words to that effect. He did stop, and she went up to him and took hold of his arm with one hand, with her other hand about her clothing or in her handbag, and she walked off with him, holding onto him. They walked around to the house of E. Hendrie; they went down the south side of the building, then the west side and then the east side and then along the wall on the north side of the building. On the north side of that building there are some stone pillars higher than a man's head. At this point they were obstructed from the view of the Hendrie home and the nearest building in a northerly direction from that point was something like three hundred feet. A shot was heard.

"As that shot was fired, which was the first shot fired, a man looked up or turned his head, and this is what he saw:

"A man on his hands and knees at the foot of one of the tall stone pillars, Mrs. Patterson standing over him with a pistol pointed at his back. He was struggling and trying to rise. The witness made an outcry to prevent, if he could, further happenings. Following his outcry the second shot was fired into the back of the man who was on his hands and knees, and he fell forward on his face and stiffened out. The witness ran around his house, and when he ran around the house he went out of sight of the tragedy; when he came back out he saw this woman leaning over with pistol in her hand and just about to fire another shot. The witness cried out to her again, and she thrust the revolver under the body of the man she had killed. How

Charles Patterson in happier times.

many shots were fired when this man was going around the house and was out of sight is uncertain.

"The evidence will show, I believe, that she stated to one witness that Patterson took this pistol from his hip pocket and handed it to her and told her to kill herself with it. To another witness she denied she had a pistol, and she made various contradictory remarks with reference to this pistol and how she happened to have it.

"I believe the evidence will show you, gentlemen of the jury, that this woman borrowed a pistol, secreted it on her person, went out to find her husband, and finding him, took him to a secluded spot with this borrowed deadly weapon concealed about her person, that she shot him twice in the back, then hid the pistol under the dead body, denied that the weapon was hers and that she killed him under these circumstances. We think we have the right to ask at your hands a verdict of murder in the first degree, with as high a penalty attached as the law provides — which is death."

The verbatim transcript of Benson's opening statement, together with pictures and drawings of courtroom images, filled the entire second page of the November 23 issue of *The Daily News*. Columnists filled the front page with their own spin on Benson's oration:

> *Is the languor of the tear-forbidden eyes of Gertrude G. Patterson with which she faces the juror hearing her case in the West Side court, a badge of childish innocence, as sometimes accredited to her, or a screen for the viperous scowl of a vampire?*
>
> *The State has begun its answer of this interrogation, which as a huge question mark envelops the woman for whom the prosecuting attorney, Horace G. Benson, yesterday asked the highest penalty, hanging for the slayer of her husband.*
>
> *This answer of the State seeks to remove the screen, which the unsophisticated expression is declared to be, and reveal the cool, calculating mind of a woman who not only led her husband to a secluded place for his death, but had plotted details and explanations to a nicety.*
>
> *In the solution of this question the state presents a series of circumstances to show that the hand that held the pistol fatal to the young invalid was directed by a scheming brain. These circumstances date from the Saturday before the morning of the shooting, when Patterson was compelled hastily to back away from his home on Steele Street by a stranger to him, who the State declared,*

Montage of characters in the Patterson murder trial: left, Gertrude Patterson dressed in her smart blue suit and wearing a velvet toque, leaving the courtroom during a recess; top, crowd waiting for the trial to begin; middle, Horace A. Benson, zealous special prosecutor of Gertrude Patterson; bottom middle, trial judge George Allen; right, Gertrude Patterson sitting demurely at counsel table next to Deputy Sheriff George McLachman, who attentively poured glasses of water for Gertrude during the trial.

labored under fear of injury from Patterson through tales told him by Mrs. Patterson.

Gertrude had listened to Benson with no apparent emotion, but she was shaken. Court was recessed until the following morning.

"That's not what happened," she whispered in anguish to Hilton as the sheriff came to take her back to her cell.

"Don't worry," Hilton assured her. "Tomorrow it's our turn. Don't worry. Get a good night's sleep if you can."

What Hilton did not tell her was that he had a very important witness waiting in his office to talk to him.

24

"It's Thirty for Gertie,' Predicts Court Observer."

"'Oh, God, Save Me! Don't Let Him Hang me' Cries Mrs. Patterson in Jail."

"Self-Defense Sole Hope of Escaping the Gallows."

"Don't Worry, Little Girl, We're For You' Declares Weeping Parents."

(*The Daily News* headlines, November 24-25, 1911).

The man who sat in O.N. Hilton's Denver law office on the evening after the first day of trial was not distinguished looking. Indeed, he appeared quite ordinary and homely. He was large, and balding and he wore a well-worn suit of clothes. A soiled gentleman's hunting hat covered the upper portion of his face.

Hilton took his hand and was about to greet him as "Mr. Strouss," when he caught himself. Hilton had been sworn to secrecy about this visit.

"You are Mr. Hilton?" Strouss asked.

"Yes, sir. And you are Mr. . . . ."

"Myers. Mr. Abraham Myers," replied Strouss.

"Yes, of course, Mr. Myers. Please come in," Hilton said as he looked around the outer office to see if any secretary or clerk had lingered after closing time.

Strouss entered Hilton's cluttered office and took a seat.

You can rest assured that no one knows of your presence here in Denver, Mr. Myers — least of all the press," Hilton said.

"Are we alone now?" Strouss asked in a hushed tone.

"Yes, my staff has all left for the evening. We may talk in strictest confidence, I assure you."

Daily News *sketch of Gertrude Patterson's life entitled "Visions of the future that haunt the sleep of Gertrude Gibson Patterson." (November 30, 1911)*

Strouss cleared his throat. "Yes, well about the press. They have set up a vigil around my hotel in Chicago — five or six of them waiting outside all the time. I can't even leave my own home without being hounded by them. I was only able to slip out last evening through the back kitchen door in this disguise. How is Gertrude?"

"She's holding up quite well, considering. Her parents arrived last night, and Gertrude was upset with me for not allowing them to visit her in jail, but I thought it would be better to spare them having to see her in a cell."

"I have come to do what I can for Gertrude. I would like to help in any way I can. I will pay all your fees, through an intermediary, of course . . ."

Hilton held up his hands, palms out.

"Yes, yes," Strouss said, understanding.

Hilton sat back in his chair, carefully choosing the words he was about to utter carefully.

"You think highly of Mrs. Patterson, I think."

"Yes, most highly, and I am prepared to do anything, I repeat anything, to extricate her from the unfortunate circumstances in which she finds herself. I believe that she did what she did in order to protect me."

"Protect you, Mr. Strouss?"

Strouss shifted in his chair uncomfortably.

"It's alright, Mr. Strouss," Hilton continued. "As I said, everyone has gone home. There is a way you can help. But, I am afraid, not in the way you think. In fact, I fear that the way in which you can most help is one which you may find distinctly distasteful."

Strouss looked puzzled.

"You are paying me a great deal of money. A great deal of money. I intend to give Gertrude the best defense that money can buy."

"You are by all accounts the most accomplished lawyer in the state."

"Thank you, Mr. Strouss, and for that reason I must ask you to trust me without question in regard to all matters relating to the defense of Mrs. Patterson."

Strouss nodded. "Of course."

"I know this city very well, and the people who live here. If you have been reading the newspapers, you know that Gertrude's fate will lie in the courtroom of public opinion shaped by those newspapers."

"I understand."

"You may have already read some of the speculations that have been printed about you in the press."

Strouss shifted uncomfortably. "Regrettably."

"Well, here is how you can best help Gertrude."

Strouss listened intently.

"Stay away, Mr. Strouss. Go back to Chicago. Do what you have been doing. Say not one word to the press."

"But couldn't I testify, say something on Gertrude's behalf, that she . . . "

Hilton put up his hands. "Absolutely not!"

Strouss sat back.

"In fact you love Gertrude, do you not Mr. Strouss?"

"Yes, I do."

"Then that is what Mr. Benson would eventually pry out of you on cross-examination, and that would not help Gertrude at all. Indeed, it would hurt her because Benson could then argue that she might indeed have killed her husband in order to protect you — although I'm sure he would frame it as protecting you because you were her benefactor rather than protecting you because you loved her."

"But . . . " Strouss looked truly hurt.

"You see, Mr. Strouss," Hilton said, regretting that he had to lay out the matter so directly, "there has to be another villain in this picture beside the victim, who in this case was a ninety-pound skeletal consumptive at death's door. I can tell you that the jurors, in any case, will not look kindly on the relationship you had with Gertrude before she was married to Mr.

Patterson. They will never believe that it was not a meretricious relationship or that . . . "

"But it wasn't like that," Strouss protested with even greater indignation.

Hilton thrust out his hands forcefully in the manner he often used to make a final point to a jury. "It doesn't matter!" he said most firmly, for in fact he himself did not believe that Gertrude had not been his mistress in the usual sense. "Because I will tell you the only thing that will save her is if she can be seen as the innocent young girl seduced and taken advantage of by an older, rich . . . "

The word "Jew" hung in the air even though it was not spoken.

"I see," Strouss said, finally understanding.

"In short, the best thing you can do for Gertrude is to abandon her and be perceived as abandoning her."

Strouss shook his head. It was the old story. The defense could only use his money — and even that only if its source was not revealed. Hilton allowed this to sink in before going on.

"I will be putting out press releases, and I have advised Gertrude that it would be best to denounce you as her seducer who took away her innocence to satisfy your lust."

Strouss rose in indignation. "Satisfy my lust! Denounce me? She would do that?"

"I can tell you the idea is abhorrent to her. But she will do it upon my firm advice — if I can persuade her that you will understand. "

"You think this course is necessary to save her?"

"I do not think she can be saved if she does not."

Hilton looked down to avoid Strouss's tearful gaze.

"She must be saved," Strouss said, "whatever the cost."

"Then you will understand what she has to do."

There was a long silence.

"Perhaps it would be better if you took a trip, didn't read the papers," Hilton continued.

Strouss had never denied Gertrude anything. Now he was being asked to sacrifice his reputation for her.

"Very well," said Strouss, rising from his chair. "Tell Gertrude I understand. Do whatever you think will help her. If there is anything else you require in her defense, anything at all . . . "

"I will call upon your intermediary," Hilton said, "as I think it would be wise if we did not meet again."

"Is there any chance I might see her?"

Hilton shook his head.

"Just for a short while . . . "

"No. Absolutely no. If you were seen visiting her, the press would . . . "

"I understand," Strouss said sadly.

"Mr. Strouss?"

"Yes," he replied, turning around.

"I am truly sorry. But it is the only way. Mrs. Patterson is a most fortunate woman indeed to have you behind her."

"And you," said Strouss as he took his leave.

Gertrude Gibson Patterson had waited all day for her mother to come visit her. She stood for several hours and watched out the window of her cell at the streetcars that ran on Kalamath Street every seven minutes in the yard below. At seven o'clock, an attendant brought her a tray with tea and toast.

"Take it away, please. I don't want anything tonight," Gertrude said. "Where is my mother?" she asked plaintively. "If I had a child, nothing on earth could keep me from her."

It was only moments later that the warden came with a message from her attorney. In it Hilton notified her that her parents had arrived but that he had advised them not to see her until the next day.

After reading the message, Gertrude stood perfectly still, and was on the verge of crying. Then she turned about and fell on to her bed.

"It's been this way always," she said to the matron. "In all my life I never had one little truly real thing; it's been all the sham and unreal things. Perhaps my mother won't come because she knows I lied about being married to Mr. Strouss; perhaps she doesn't want to see me; perhaps she doesn't care."

Matron, who had just entered her cell, tried to comfort her. "Oh matron," Gertrude sobbed. "I want my mother so! I've waited so long!"

25

"Mrs. Patterson Expects No Aid from Man Who Bought Her."

"Tragedy Shows to What Infamy Man Will Sink to Gratify His Vices."

"Defense Appeals to Chivalry In Effort to Win Leniency for Beautiful Slayer of Husband"

"Attorney for Slayer Tells Jury He Will Prove She Fired Fatal Shots in Self-Defense."

(*Rocky Mountain News*, November 24, 1911).

Mrs. Patterson confidently expected, at the first, that Strouss would come straight to Denver, confirm her story of Patterson's mistreatment, and put the Strouss millions at her service in the effort to escape conviction of the charge of murder. But Strouss apparently has no such intention — never had. All he has done has been to dodge. Instead of coming to the rescue of the woman who was his comrade for many years, when he was recognized in a Chicago hotel the other night, he leaped from the table, ran to the elevator and went to his room.

Guards have been established about Strouss's suite, and every effort is made to prevent anyone asking him questions, or even approaching him. When he leaves the hotel he has a taxi-cab drawn up in front of the door, makes a run for the elevator, and has the chauffeur start immediately, so that nobody may speak to him.

In her cell in the county jail, Mrs. Patterson has given up all hope of help from the man who once claimed all her time and affection. Newspapers all across the land have given much space to the story and especially to the conduct of Strouss in deserting Mrs. Patterson in her hour of need instead of taking his share of the blame and helping her.

Dorothy Dix, the famous writer of New York, pours words of vitriol on the head of Patterson. What she will say of Strouss when his behavior is known remains to be seen. Here are Dorothy Dix's remarks:

'The other day in Denver a young and very beautiful woman turned upon her husband and killed him because, she claims, after having been sold to another man as if she had been a horse, or a dog, he was trying to extort more money out of her purchase.

'Never was there a story stranger or more terrible than this tragedy reveals, for it turns a searchlight upon some of the dark places of modern life and shows into what sin a folly a girl's love of luxury and fine clothes may lead her and to what depths of infamy a man may descend to gratify his indolence and vices. Two summers ago, Gertrude Gibson met Charles A. Patterson, a former football hero. She appears to have fallen in love with him almost at first, and thereafter they were much together, riding every day in the electric Brougham Strouss had given her as a gift.

'When the season was over, she told Patterson she was going to California and gave him $100 on which to go along with her. Soon after, they got married and returned to Chicago.

'Patterson did not work and drank heavily and spent half of his days in bed. After a bit, money began to run low in the household. Mrs. Patterson sold her jewels and her Brougham and then, when the price of these was gone, began to be in want. Then it was, according to Mrs. Patterson, that her husband went to Strouss and offered to sell her back to her old lover, and a bargain was struck between these two loathsome creatures in the form of men for a woman's honor.

'But Patterson was a welcher who could not even stick to his own dastardly trade. In less than a month after Strouss had gone abroad with Mrs. Patterson, he wrote threatening to kill her unless she returned at once. And when she did come back he began a course of unending abuse and vilification. He lived on her shame and then derided her for it and beat her until she was black and blue.

'In the meantime, Patterson had fallen sick with tuberculosis, and it is typical of this woman's contradictory character that she should have nursed him with the most wonderful tenderness and devotion. She was young and beautiful, and she

knew that she ran the risk of death in a dreadful form by attending him and being constantly with him, yet she hung over his
sickbed like a mother over a sick child: she cooked for him, pet-
ted him, coddled him, did everything possible to smooth the hard
path he was treading.

'At last they went out to Denver. Things were no better
between them and his treatment of her was a cruel as ever. At the
advice of a lawyer she applied for a divorce from him. In retali-
ation — although he had but a few months left to live — he sued
Strouss for alienation of his wife's affection and for taking her on
a trip to Europe — that ghastly trip for which she had been sold.

'Mrs. Patterson does not pretend to be a good woman, but
she has her code of honor, and part of it is the sacredness of
abiding by the bargain she had made. According to her lights,
Strouss had dealt fairly by her husband, and she wanted to save
him if she could. She begged her husband to come and see her
and to talk matters over, hoping she could persuade him to withdraw his suit against Strouss.

'They met at a sanitarium. It was a weirdly inappropriate
place, this house of the dying, for this husband and wife whose
souls were charnel chambers. The husband came, nothing alive
in him but hate and vengeance. The wife came, all blooming
beauty and health and strength. She begged him piteously not
to prosecute the suit against Strouss and so publish her shame
to the world. The husband, for reply, spat in her face and called
her a vile name, and she shot him dead.

'This is Mrs. Patterson's story, and if she can substantiate
it, no jury on earth can convict her, for a million leagues lower
than the most bloody-handed murderess is the man who trades
in the bodies of woman. There are some crimes that are past
human forgiveness, and the man that sells his wife is beyond the
pale of mercy.'"

(*The Daily News*, November, 1911).

Friday, November 24, 1911
Day Two of the Trial

O.N. Hilton read the front-page headlines of *The Denver Post* with satisfaction — particularly the remarks of Dorothy Dix. He felt that his
strategy of vilifying Strouss and keeping him away was being vindicated.

He sipped his coffee and, grabbing his briefcase, hurried out to the
courthouse.

By 8:00 a.m., the frenzied mob of railbirds, many of whom had been waiting in line for a seat since three in the morning, had been brought under control. The courtroom was packed in anticipation of O.N. Hilton's opening statement in which he would lay out the defense of Gertrude Gibson Patterson.

Hilton began: "Gentleman of the jury, we shall show you in our defense of this prosecution, the following facts: "That this young lady, Mrs. Patterson, was married to Mr. Patterson, the deceased, on October 1, 1908, in California. She had met him a short time before and, following the marriage, she returned to Chicago, where she had lived. During that time immediately subsequent to the marriage, and after their return to Chicago, Patterson, who had no employment, committed many acts of cruelty on Mrs. Patterson during the first two or three months of her marriage, beginning with the ensuing month after they were married and sometime during the early part of November. Sometime about the fifth or sixth of that month he said to her on one occasion after he had importuned her for money, "I'll tell you how we can fix it up so that we won't either one of us have to worry about any money'"; for he did not care who she went with or what she did, providing only he was in on it, and we will introduce a letter in evidence written by the defendant in which he so states directly to his wife.

"In the next month, which was December, and about the middle of the month, following a quarrel with his wife in relation to money, being out of employment and drunk and abusive most of the time, he said: "You make a proposition to Strouss that he take you and live with you, providing I live under the same room and enjoy the same privileges."

A.E. Shuggart, star prosecution witness who testified that he saw Gertrude Patterson deliberately take aim at her husband, Charles, at the gates of the Richthofen Castle, and shoot him four times.

Denver Post *sketch montage showing: 1) Gertrude Gibson being introduced by a mutual friend to her future husband, Charles, at a Chicago roller skaing rink, 2) Gertrude accompaning her benefactor and admirer, the millionarie Emil Strouss, to Europe on a luxury ocean liner, 3) Gertrude nursing her tubercular husband, Charles, 4) A drunken Charles Patterson striking and abusing Gertrude during one of their frequent arguments, and 5) Gertrude shooting Charles in the back at the gates of the Richthofen Castle.*

"Mrs. Patterson resented this and stated that she would not be a party to any such arrangement as this.

"A few days later, Mrs. Patterson left for New York to take the steamer for Europe with Mr. Strouss. Her husband accompanied her to the train and saw her off. Mr. Strouss was on the steamer, and the two sailed for Europe and went to Paris.

"Before she left her husband, Patterson made her promise that whatever money she was able to get from Strouss she would send to him.

"Upon their arrival in Paris they found a letter at the hotel in which Patterson said: 'Now I think you are not intending to come back home, but you are going to stay with that fat cow, and if you don't come back on the next steamer, I will make Strouss trouble.'

"So Strouss sent her home on the next steamer, and before she left he gave her five thousand dollars in cash.

"Upon her arrival in Chicago, Mr. Patterson, her husband, met her at the train, and after they had gotten to the house, he said, "How much money did you bring home with you?" She replied that she did not bring any money home with her except the little she had left over from her expenses, concealing from him the fact that she had five thousand dollars.

"At that he flew into a rage, cursed her, and called her all kinds of names, and seized the plates from the plate rail and threw them at her. Finally, taking her by the neck, he threw her on the bed, and, in an effort to strike her, hit the cord that held the art lamp and smashed that. As a result of all this she was confined to her bed for two or three days.

"We shall show that, about this time, gentlemen of the jury, this man's relations with his wife as a husband were of a most unspeakable character. I cannot detail to you in the presence of respectable and decent people the details of the treatment of the wife by her husband, but insofar as I can, I will endeavor to give you an idea. We will show you that he was a sexual degenerate.

"We will show that about February, 1910, he contracted pneumonia, and he was removed to St. Bernards' hospital. I think it was in Chicago. A trained nurse was called in, and doctors examined him and found that tuberculosis had set in, and they instructed the nurses that he should be careful in his relations with his wife or with anyone else, not to breath in their faces, as there was danger of communicating the disease.

"Mrs. Patterson left the flat and went to the hospital to assist in taking care of her husband; she assisted the nurse while she was there, and afterward, took care of him alone. We will show you that frequently, as Mrs. Patterson would give him his medicine and at other times, he would seize her around the waist and pull her over on him and kiss her in the mouth, against the nurse's protestations.

"They came here together on their way to California, arriving here on the twentieth day of October 1910, as I think the testimony will show. They got room and board with a private family, and during the first few weeks that they were here Patterson's treatment of his wife was again renewed as it was before in Chicago. She could not go downtown without being accused that she had some vicious purpose.

"She then went to the district attorney of this city, Mr. Willis V. Elliott, and told him her story, and he prepared divorce papers for her. Mr. Elliott will testify as to the condition of this poor girl's face and neck when she came to his office — that they were so swollen and discolored that she could hardly turn her head.

"Mr. Patterson came to the house on the Saturday evening preceding the homicide on Monday. A young man by the name of Strain, whom Mrs. Patterson had met at the house in a social way, was there — he having called with a Miss McDowell.

"While she was inside, Patterson came to the house, and Strain, who had a revolver in his pocket, without any knowledge of Mrs. Patterson or his situation, and in a silly and braggadocio manner, pulled out his revolver and, using a vulgar expression, "stuck up" Mr. Patterson and his companion, more in a spirit of silly bravado than anything else and made him put his hands over his head and back away from the house.

"On Monday, the day of the homicide, at about seven thirty in the morning, or at about that hour, Mrs. Patterson went to a drug store nearby and had the clerk call up the sanitarium. The testimony will show that she did not call up the sanatorium herself, but that she had the proprietor or clerk call up for her.

Patterson answered the phone, and then she answered, and she talked to him over the phone. He asked why she did not keep her appointment to meet him on the day before, Sunday. She told him that she was sick. She said that she could not meet him at any hour that morning, but suggested a later hour at Daniels and Fisher's for luncheon, to which he would not agree, and he said "Why not withdraw that divorce suit you have begun? Meet me in front of Peck's School at ten-thirty this morning.'

"Mrs. Patterson relented and went out there at about that time to meet him, pursuant to his own arrangements.

"To show you that they were walking along on Pontiac Street, having come up from Olive Street, we will show you, gentleman of the jury, that there was a witness here who crossed over to Pontiac Street behind them, and followed them around during the walk down Pontiac Street. We will show that this witness was behind Mr. Patterson and his wife some fifty to seventy-five feet, and as Mrs. Patterson said 'I will give you no more money,' Patterson replied, 'you fucking whore!' and then grabbed her and bit her on the shoulder with his teeth.

"She screamed out and swerved out into the middle of the street and they both proceeded along Pontiac Street, followed by the gentleman we will introduce as a witness. As they came to the corner of East Twelfth Avenue, quarrelling all the time, and he cursing and abusing her, they turned the corner of East Twelfth.

"As they walked along Twelfth Avenue, Mr. Patterson said, 'I want to know if you are going to give me the deed to that house?' She said, 'No, I have told you I am not, and that is final as far I am concerned.'

"He then pulled from his watch pocket a clipping from a newspaper which was the notice of a suit he had filed against Strouss, claiming, so the article said, twenty-five thousand dollars for alienating his wife's affections.

"Mrs. Patterson stopped and looked at him and said, 'Don't you know that is blackmail?"

"'Well,' he said, 'I don't ever expect it to come to trial. I have given my lawyer here fifty dollars if it doesn't come to trial, and I am going to give him one hundred dollars if it does come to trial, but I don't ever expect it to come to trial. Now, I want to know if you are going to give me the bungalow and the stock."

"And she said, 'No, no, no!'"

"They were standing at that time just in front of the gate. As she said, 'I will never give it to you,' he struck her with his fist on the left side of her face, knocking her down, and she struggled to regain her feet, and then he struck her again and knocked her down completely and kicked her brutally.

"Fearing for her life from such a beating, she opened her Boston bag and fired — she didn't know how many shots — and we will bring you a witness who saw all the blows that were struck and every shot fired by her while she was lying on the ground as she recovered.

"This is our case, and we will show you, gentleman of the jury, by every rule of law that governs the doctrine of self-defense, that it was in defense of her person from not only apprehended but actual danger and by terrible necessity shown by every rule of jurisprudence, as the court, I think will charge you at the proper time."

It being only 8:30 a.m., Judge Allen called no recess but asked Benson to begin calling witnesses for the prosecution.

"The State calls George W. Strain to the stand," bellowed the bailiff.

The twenty-year-old youth took the witness box and was sworn.

"Mr. Strain," Benson asked, "on or about the twenty-third of September 1911, did you have occasion to visit the Patterson house at 1008 Steele Street?"

"Yes, sir, I did."

"I show you Exhibit A and ask if you ever saw it before."

Benson handed Strain the pistol found underneath Patterson's body on the day of the killing.

"Yes, I have."

"Whose revolver was that?"

"It was mine."

"Are you in the habit of carrying a pistol?"

"No, sir."

"Did you carry it on the night of September 23, this year?"

"I did."

"Where did you carry it?"

"In my right-hand coat pocket."

"Why did you go there that night?"

"To secure my Kodak."

"Why did you take the pistol with you that night?"

Hilton objected, and his objection was sustained.

"What, if anything happened?"

"Why, Mrs. Patterson and I were sitting there talking and Mr. Patterson came up. 'My god, there's Chick,' she said, and ran into the house. Mr. Patterson stepped out in front of me and said, 'I guess you're in the wrong house, aren't you? Now you beat it out of here damned quick! I've got a good notion to fix you right now,' or 'I'll fix you,' or some such words. I said, 'There's no occasion for that.' Then I pulled my revolver and told him to hold up his hands and walk away from the house, which he did."

"Where was Mrs. Patterson all of this time?"

"In the house I believe."

"What did she say?"

"I don't remember everything that she said — she was very angry for my having driven her husband away from the house and informed me that I would certainly be brought into the divorce case after what had occurred that night."

"Then what happened?"

I got my Kodak and started home, and I informed Mrs. Patterson that myself and my young lady friend would not be back until after the divorce proceedings. Mrs. Patterson said she was in constant dread of her husband and was afraid to stay alone any of the time, and she asked me if I would leave my revolver there."

"Do you remember now what she said to you as to why she wanted you to leave this revolver there?"

"She said she was afraid to stay in the house on account of her husband — that is, she was afraid to stay there alone."

"No further questions. Mr. Hilton, your witness."

Hilton had only two questions.

"You put the pistol in your pocket, as I remember your testimony, before you left your house?"

"I did."

"For what purpose, Mr. Strain — any particular purpose?"

"No, no particular purpose."

"Thank you. No further questions."

Benson next called Dr. C.A. Taggart to the stand to testify as to the height and weight of Mr. Patterson.

Hilton objected to this testimony.

"This might be proper evidence on rebuttal," he argued to Judge Allen, "but not at this time. How can it be material at this point to show the size of the deceased? It could only be competent where self-defense was being proved — where disparity in weight and those other factors relating to self-defense were being shown. As we have not yet even presented our defense, there is no indication at this time that this case is one of self-defense."

Although the objection was technically a sound one, Judge Allen, who had no doubt that the defense would be self-defense, overruled the objection, and Dr. Taggart was permitted to testify that the deceased was 110 pounds at the time of his death.

Benson next called Dr. J.W. McNamara, one of the physicians who performed an autopsy on Charles Patterson. He testified that a bullet through the heart caused death.

"How many bullets entered the body, Dr. McNamara?"

"From the external wounds?"

"Yes, from the external wounds."

"Two."

"You say one of these bullets entered the back near the point of the left shoulder blade?"

"Yes, sir."

"The other bullet entered the back near the point of the right shoulder blade?"

"Yes, sir."

"This bullet that entered the body near the point of the shoulder blade went through the body at about what angle?"

The doctor indicated an upward angle.

"Cross-examine, counsel."

Hilton stood up but did not step forward.

"You say the course of the bullet you last described went upward, did it not?" Hilton asked from his standing position.

"Yes, sir."

"How much higher was point of exit than entrance?"

"About two inches."

Hilton sat down, and Gertrude gave him a look satisfaction. He had scored a critical point by establishing that the shot had been fired from a position lower than the victim.

The prosecution's star witness was A.B. Schugart.

Benson established that the witness was a carpenter who lived at 1216 Pontiac Street.

"About how far is your house from the Richthofen Castle?

"About three hundred to four hundred feet."

"On the morning of September 25, 1911, were you at home?"

"Yes, sir."

"Was your attention attracted by anything at that time?"

"It was."

"What was it that attracted your attention?"

"Shots in rapid succession, just as I stepped to the door."

"How many shots?"

"Two."

"What, if anything did you do?"

"I looked out and saw a man on his hands and knees crying out, 'Oh, my God! My God!' And a woman was at his back with a revolver in

Daily News *re-creation of Gertrude Patterson's direct examination at trial in which she knelt down to show to her attorney O.N. Hilton, the position she was in when she was forced to shoot her husband in self defense. Trial observers noted that every neck, particularly male ones, craned at the sight of Gertrude kneeling on the courtroom floor.* **(November 26, 1911)**

her hand taking deliberate aim for the third shot. I hollered to her and as I hollered, she fired the third shot. He fell on his face, and I never saw him move again."

This testimony was demonstrably wrong, since in addition to the two bullets that entered Patterson's body, two bullets that apparently went wild were found at the scene, for a total of four shots fired. Benson, not being inclined to impeach his star witness at this point, moved on.

"Did you make any outcry before she fired the third shot?"

"I did."

"In what position was the man when the third shot was fired?"

"He was on his hands and knees."

"After the third shot was fired, what did you do?"

"I ran around to the front entrance."

"When you got in front of your house, you then came in view of the man and woman again, did you not?"

Benson, who had assiduously avoided asking improper leading questions up to this point, was now asking a clearly objectionable question.

Hilton, an experienced trial attorney, did not waste an objection on a matter that he did not intend to dispute.

"Where was the man?"

"He was lying on his face where I had seen him fall."

"Where was the woman?"

"She was stooping over him."

"Just what, if anything, did you do?"

"I called to her again."

"When you called out the second time, what did she do?"

"She jumped and ran into the yard of the Richthofen Castle, then turned as if coming out, then turned back again."

"Was there anything in the woman's right hand?"

"I couldn't see anything."

"What did you do then?"

"I went over to the body of the man; he was still gasping. I spoke to him; he did not reply. I turned him over on his side and asked him what was the cause of the trouble, and he did not reply."

"When you turned him over, what if anything did you observe?"

"There was a revolver lying under him."

"What did you do then?"

"When I found I could not help him . . . "

"Just what did you do with the revolver?"

"I picked it up and put it in my pocket."

"How long did the man live after you arrived?"

"I don't think over two minutes. He was still gasping when I left him and another man had come up."

"You could not get him to speak to you?"

"No, sir."

"And after you had taken the pistol and put it in your pocket, what did you do then?'

"I started after the woman."

"Where did you find her, if at all?"

"In the sitting room of Mr. Hendrie's home."

"Who did you give the gun to, if anyone?"

"To police sergeant McIntyre."

"Do you remember how Mrs. Patterson was dressed at that time?"

"She was dressed in a dark suit, and I must say she was dressed most beautifully."

There were titters in the courtroom at this seemingly gratuitous observation of Gertrude's dress.

"Do you remember whether she had her hat on?"

"Yes, sir."

"What did you say, and what did she say?"

"I asked her who that was out there, and she said, 'My husband, he has wronged me.' Then I asked her name, and where she lived, and she did not answer me."

"Then what happened?"

"I asked them if she brought a gun with her, and they said no. I picked up her handbag and put it in my pocket, and opened her coat and searched to see if she had more weapons on her, and did not find any."

"Did anything happen while you were searching her?"

"Yes, sir, she opened her eyes and looked at me."

"Was there anything about her face to attract your attention?"

"Nothing that I noticed. There were no marks on her face."

This testimony was obviously devastating, and on cross-examination Hilton did not attempt to get the witness to retract it. Rather, he tried only to soften it, while at the same time lighten the atmosphere in the courtroom that by now had become oppressive to the defense.

"I take it that you took Mrs. Patterson's purse for your own protection?" Hilton asked.

There were titters, and Hilton, not expecting an answer, sat down in dismissal of the witness.

Benson next called W.G. Mudd, the police surgeon who had made the run in the ambulance to the Richthofen Castle.

"Doctor Mudd, did you make an examination of the body of the deceased?"

"I turned the body on the side and saw the gunshot wounds in his back on the left side and also looked at the front, opened his shirt, and saw the blood. That was all the examination I made."

"When you saw the bullet wounds about which you speak, did you observe the condition of the clothing?"

"I believe there were powder burns around the bullet wound in the clothing."

"Where?"

"Surrounding the bullet wound."

"Front or back?"

"Back."

There was a collective gasp in the courtroom as this answer was made.

"Did you see Gertrude Patterson, the defendant in this case?"

"Yes, sir."

"On the way to the hall, did you have any conversation with her?"

"Yes, sir."

"What did she say, and what did you say?"

"I asked her how it happened and she replied she did not know, and she repeated it two or three times and said she did not know whether she fired the shot or whether he fired it."

"Did she say anything further than that?"

"She told me this man struck her and knocked her down. She also stated, that he handed her a gun and said, 'Now, whore, you kill yourself.'"

"Your witness, counsel," said Benson, turning to Hilton.

"Did you notice she had a reddened cheek?" Hilton asked.

"Yes, sir."

"On which side was it?"

"I think it was on the left side."

"Thank you Dr. Mudd."

Sergeant Joseph McIntyre was next called to testify about another statement Gertrude had made after her arrest.

"Did you see Gertrude Patterson in this case?"

"Yes, sir."

"State what was said by you and her in this conversation that you had."

Montage of witnesses who testified at the Coroner's Inquest, including those who later testified at the trial: (counter-clockwise) Adie Shuggart, Charles Logston, Lawrence Fleckenstein, and Louis Shramm. (Daily News, September 30, 1911)

"When first I went in, she was sitting with her head on the table, and I asked her who did the shooting. She said, 'He shot himself.' Then she raised her right hand. I waited a few minutes, and she said, "Oh, he was abusing me. I said 'How many times did you shoot him?' She said, 'Oh, I don't know.'"

Sarah Kenzie, a servant at the Richthofen Castle, testified that she heard the shots.

"When you first saw the woman she was at the entrance way?"

"Yes."

"Had all of the shots been fired when you first saw her?"

"Yes, sir."

"After she raised up and started for the house, what, if anything, did she say?"

"She said, 'Murder, murder, help!'"

A series of minor witnesses followed, confirming that Gertrude had told a series of contradictory stories about the shooting. Others testified as to Gertrude's demeanor and behavior after the killing. Charles Sims and Thomas Van Reimer corroborated the testimony of Sarah Kenzie — that the first two shots were in rapid succession, followed by a long pause, a third shot, another pause, and finally a fourth shot.

Chief of Police Armstrong took the stand to relate Gertrude's version of who had brought the gun to the scene.

"About two weeks after the killing did you have a talk with Gertrude Gibson Patterson?"

"Yes."

"What did she say?"

"I asked Mrs. Patterson if she knew whether she had the gun before she went to the sanitarium, and she said, 'No.' I also asked her if she had seen this gun prior to that time, and she said, 'No.' Then I said to her, 'Now, you are not telling me the truth about the gun,' and I said, 'I know the owner of this gun, and I know where you got it and I am going to give you the chance to tell me the truth'; and I said, "Do you know a young man by the name of Strain?" and she said she did. I asked her how she got acquainted with him, and she said through a young lady friend of hers. I asked her how often he had been at the house and she said twice. I said, 'Now, as a matter of fact, is this not Mr. Strain's gun? Was it not his gun that was used, and did not Mr. Strain give it to you?' and she simply replied by saying, 'That's a lie.' I said, 'All right, but I think I can prove that is the truth.' She still said it was her husband's gun."

This testimony was particularly damaging, because it revealed the facility with which Gertrude lied. No one doubted that Gertrude's testimony at the trial would be crucial, and any damage to her credibility would therefore be of even greater damage to her case. Benson had no difficulty proving the murder weapon was in fact Strain's gun, because Strain himself had identified the gun as his. In any case, Hilton had no plans to dispute the fact that Gertrude had obtained the murder weapon from Strain.

Benson's case might easily have rested on a strong foundation at this point. He had already introduced medical evidence that the victim died from gunshot wounds to the back. Gertrude had admitted shooting her husband, Strain had admitted giving her the murder weapon, and Schugart had testified that he saw Gertrude shoot the victim while he was down on his hands and knees.

Benson then made a mistake common among prosecutors: He endeavored to gild the lily. He proceeded to clutter his case with an odd assortment of weak witnesses whose testimony was only marginally relevant. Because the order of his witnesses had been dictated at least in part by their own availability, and not by his strategic plan, he had the misfortune of calling as his final witness a certain Cornelia Jones, an obese servant woman who was washing windows at 765 Olive Street on the day of the killing.

On direct examination, Cornelia identified Gertrude as the woman she had seen on the morning of the killing with a man in a gray suit. The reporters at the trial did not miss Gertrude's hearty laugh at Cornelia's testimony that the hat Gertrude was wearing in the courtroom was the same hat as the hat she wore on the day of the killing. Hilton brought out on cross-examination that the hat Gertrude was wearing in court that day was a velvet hat of Bulgarian trimming which she had purchased only the week before — thus revealing Cornelia's inability to distinguish between fall and winter styles. Cornelia's lack of fashion sense appealed to Gertrude's sense of humor, as well as many of the lady railbirds who joined her in thunderous laughter and giggling.

Cornelia's cross-examination prompted a blaring headline in the following day's *Daily News:* "Slayer of Husband Laughs Merrily In Court At Ignorance of Witness."

After the State rested, and the case was recessed until the next day, Hilton took Gertrude aside and advised her not to provide any grist for the press mill by making any expression that could be interpreted as one of happiness or good humor. He cautioned her softly, however, as he was aware that the incident with witness Jones was nothing more than a release of nervous tension, and that Gertrude was in fact under great distress and fear of her fate. In any case, he wanted her to be as relaxed and composed as possible for court the following day when she would be called upon to give the testimony of her life.

26

"Court in Tense Stillness as Slayer, With Face Blanched, Fists Clenched, Enacts Tableau in Battle for Her Life"

"Gertrude Patterson Tells Horror Tale of Slavery"

"Murder Trial Awfully Funny; Mrs. Patterson Laughs Merrily!"

"Witness Couldn't Distinguish Between Fall And Winter Styles of Hat."

"Epidemic of Murder by Wives Sweeps United States; Criminologists Compare Outbreak of Tragedies to Slaughter of Sisterhood of Death."

(Headlines, *The Daily News,* November 25, 1911).

Not within the memory of police officers and criminologists has there been a period in the United States when so many women have killed their husbands as in the concluding months of 1911. Experts in criminal matters are struggling to solve the riddle of the cause of this practically wholesale murder of husband. Criminologists are wondering if it is the altitude of Denver that affects the nerves of women that is the cause of the slaughter.

By many students of criminals it is declared that not since the Middle Ages when 366 women banded themselves together in the fearsome Roman sisterhood of Death and most of them poisoned their husbands has there been such a murdering of husbands as in the last six months in the United States.

Criminologists call attention to the fact that murders by women are invariably remarkable for cold deliberation and lack of feeling. Since the early days of the Bible when Jael herded Siser, her friend, to her house to hide him, she said, from his enemies, and then drove a nail through his temples into the floor, murders by women have been particularly cold-blooded.

(*The Daily News,* November 24, 1911).

Saturday, November 25, 1911
Day Three of the Trial

"Good God!" muttered O.N. Hilton, shaking his head in disbelief as he read the feature story about the "Sisterhood of Death." "Now they're bringing in the Middle Ages."

He was not pleased with the day's headlines. He grew even more apprehensive as he began to read an interview Gertrude had given to *The Daily News:*

> *"Gertrude, why did you ever get mixed up with a family like the Pattersons?" Gertrude's mother asked. "It's just as I told you when you were at home. They are an awful nest to be with.*
>
> *"My mother is all broken over my trouble," said Gertrude Gibson Patterson from her prison cell, "but I told her she must be brave. She wanted to stay all evening with me, but I told her that I had not slept all of last night and must be alone so I would be fresh for the courtroom in the morning.*
>
> *"I was sitting on my bed with just a skirt and dressing gown on when I saw my mother and father come in the door. I was out in my dad's arms in a second. He held me for five or ten minutes, stroking me on the head and telling me not to worry, that he was going to stand by me. It was hard to face them, because I had never told them the truth about Strouss. But they never mentioned his name.*
>
> *"My mother said the same things to me today as she did when she came to visit me in Chicago, and that was" 'Gertrude, why did you get in such a nest as this?'*
>
> *"While she was there in my house all the Patterson family would get together and talk in an undertone. I am sure that at that time, which was two years ago, they were plotting to file this alienation charge against Strouss."*

*"This is the first time I have eaten today,' she said.
'I have not had any appetite."*

Relieved that Gertrude had said nothing that might damage her case, Hilton went back to his trial notebook to go over the all-important direct examination he would conduct that morning. Slurping the last drops of his coffee, he told his secretary Rosalie to follow up on a call he had gotten from a potentially important witness for the defense, a certain Francis J. Easton.

"Find out what he knows and make an appointment," he said to her as he rushed out. "I'll be tied up all day."

"Yes, Mr. Hilton," came the reply.

The early morning mob at the courthouse was the biggest Hilton had yet seen. There were several groups of women chanting slogans supporting Gertrude, and another group chanting, "Shot in the back! Hang her!"

O.N. Hilton was almost never late to court, but on this morning he had tarried in his office a few minutes too long, and the chanting crowd had delayed him more than he anticipated. When he finally arrived, everyone, including the judge, was waiting for him.

After laying down his brief case and giving Gertrude an encouraging smile that exuded confidence, he announced with a clear voice that reverberated around the courtroom: "Your honor, the defense calls Mrs. Gertrude Gibson Patterson to the witness stand."

The bailiff shut the courtroom door tight against last minute railbirds hoping for a seat. Judge Allen announced that no one would be permitted to enter or leave the courtroom until after the direct examination. Hilton, however, knew this was not the big show, but only the prelude to the big show — Benson's cross-examination to come.

"You are the defendant, Mrs. Patterson, in this case?" Hilton began.

"I am."

"When were you married, Mrs. Patterson?'

"October 1, 1908, in Carmel-by-the-Sea, California."

"And from thence where did you go?"

"We went back to Chicago."

"You first met your husband in Chicago, did you?"

"Yes, sir."

"Did you and your husband go to keeping house in Chicago?"

"We went to a hotel first."

"What hotel?"

"To the Hotel Lakota."

"How long did you remain there?"

"About one week or so."

"Was your husband engaged in any business at that time?"

"He was employed about two months."

"What was Mr. Patterson's course of treatment of you, Mrs. Patterson, after you married him and during the month of November."

"He incessantly demanded money."

"The next month, Mrs. Patterson, you were living in the same place. Do you recall any conversation with your husband during the month?"

"He wanted me to make a proposition to Mr. Strouss."

"What did he say — tell the jury — tell his exact language?"

At this point, Benson rose with a roar.

"Incompetent, immaterial, and irrelevant, your honor!" It was a nonobjection, lacking in specificity, and therefore too broad. Judge Allen overruled the objection.

"You may answer the question. What followed, Mrs. Patterson?"

"I told him to leave the house; that I would not stand any more of his insulting proposition, and then he cursed me, and . . . "

Combination sketch photograph showing O.N. Hilton exhibiting a document to his client, Gertrude Patterson, during his direct examination. (Daily News, November 27, 1911)

"What did he do — tell the jury."

"He knocked me down with his fist, knocked me down and beat me with his fist after I was down on the floor. I was in bed for two days as a result."

"You knew Mr. Strouss at that time, did you not?"

"Yes, sir."

"Did you meet him?"

"I just casually met him on the street."

"Did you subsequently accompany him to Europe?"

"Yes, sir."

"State to the jury how and why."

"I told him my trouble, and he said he was going to Europe, and that he pitied me and wished he could take me with him. I told Mr. Patterson of this that evening — before that he had asked me why I did not see Mr. Strouss and get some money to pay the bills — when I told him of this meeting, he became very delighted and he said, 'Tell him he can take you if he will come through.' I asked what he meant by 'coming through,' and he said to come through with the cash — he said, 'Make it fifteen hundred dollars.' I told him I would never make such a proposition to Mr. Strouss, and he flew at me and called me vile names."

"What did he call you, Mrs. Patterson — just state to the jury — what he called you. Did he call you a bad name or a bad woman?"

Gertrude stammered. "He called me a vile name."

"What else did he say and what did he do?"

"He took hold of me and nearly threw me into the grate iron; he then went out and came back intoxicated."

"At what time did he come back?"

"About two o'clock in the morning."

When did you next see Strouss, if at all?"

"I saw Mr. Strouss again after that and told him all that had transpired and he gave me fifteen hundred dollars. I gave this to Mr. Patterson, and he put it in the Illinois Trust and Savings Bank in Chicago."

"Did your husband meet you at the bank?"

"He did, yes, sir."

"What did your husband do then?"

"He said, 'Now you tell that fat Jew to go to hell.' He then went over to the window and said that he wanted to open an account, and he deposited the money."

"And from thence where did you go?"

"I sailed for Europe; I met Mr. Strouss on the steamer, and then when I went aboard he asked for the paper which Patterson was to have given him. I told him what had transpired, and that Mr. Patterson had made me swear that I would send him any money that I might get on the trip. When we arrived in Paris, I received a letter from Mr. Patterson, saying that he had come to the conclusion that I did not intend to return and that if I did not come at once he would follow me and kill me."

Benson rose. "I ask that answer to be stricken out unless the letter is presented in evidence." He was raising an objection under the best evidence rule, and the motion to strike was granted by Judge Allen.

"How long did you remain in Paris?"

"I took the next boat on the seventeenth of February, 1909. Mr. Strouss gave me five thousand dollars and told me to go back, and I took the next boat and went and I have never seen him since."

"What transpired between you and your husband when you got home?"

"When we got home that evening, he asked me how much money I had, and I said I did not have any, and he said, 'Why don't you bring me back some money — there are a lot of bills that must be paid.' I asked him what he had done with the fifteen hundred dollars. At this he got very angry and flew at me. I tried to run into the bathroom and lock the door. He came in and knocked open the door and hit me with his fist. In doing this, his arm caught on the cord of an arc lamp and he knocked it to the floor and broke it. I was in bed two or three days as the result."

"Did you at that time own an electric?"

"Yes, sir."

"State to the jury under what circumstances you disposed of your electric."

"Mr. Patterson always wanted money; he always had an improper proposal to make me go and get money, and he wanted me to sell the machine for six hundred dollars. I did not want to sell the machine for six hundred dollars and I told him so. He then hit me in the face with his fist and knocked me down."

"Did you sell the car?"

"I sold it about two weeks later for six hundred dollars, and I gave the money to Mr. Patterson. He deposited it in the bank in his own name."

"Mrs. Patterson, I call your attention during the same month to some property at the corner of Seventy-first and Palmer Avenue in Chicago. State to the jury an incident which took place with your husband concerning that."

"That was in September."

"Very well, in September."

"Mr. Patterson saw an ad in the *Chicago Tribune* regarding some property at Seventy-first and Palmer Avenue. He said it was a snap and wanted to get some money to buy it. He said, 'I think I will sue that Jew bastard for taking you to Europe with him. I want this property.' I then confessed to him that Mr. Strouss had given me five thousand dollars before I left Paris. I gave him $3250. He deposited that money in the bank and took the deed to the property."

"Did your husband about this time commit any other assault which has not been described?"

"Yes."

"When was it?"

"It was in October."

Gertrude related events, later deleted from the transcript printed in the newspapers, showing that Mr. Patterson was a sexual degenerate.

"When was he taken sick, Mrs. Patterson?"

"He was taken sick in February of 1910."

"Where did he go? Where was he taken at that time?"

"The doctors . . . "

"Never mind the doctors — where was he taken?"

"He was taken to St. Bernard's Hospital."

"Where is that hospital?"

"At Sixty-third and Harvard streets. I broke up housekeeping and went to nurse him and help take care of him. After months of caring for him, he demanded that we take a trip to California. I told him we didn't have the money. He said, 'Why don't you get it from that fat cow in Chicago?' I told him that I did not intend to communicate with Mr. Strouss, and he said, 'Well, I'll go back to Chicago and start suit against him if you don't write him for five hundred dollars.' I refused. We were sitting in a hammock. He threw me on the ground, pulled my hair and hit me in the face with his fists. I then wrote to Mr. Strouss for $250 as I had $250 there. Mr. Strouss sent $250 without any comment, and we left a few days later for California via Denver. When we arrived in Denver, Mr. Patterson liked it so much that he wanted to remain here for the winter."

Gertrude related her visit to Phipps Sanitarium, their demand for payment in advance, and her husband's demand that she again write Strouss for the money.

"How much did he send you?"

"Two hundred dollars in the form of a check without any comments. I gave Mr. Patterson fifty dollars, bought his wardrobe and went with him to the sanitarium on May 11, 1910. Then I bought the bungalow on Steele Street."

"How often did you see Mr. Patterson after he was admitted to the sanitarium?"

"About four times a week."

"I call your attention, Mrs. Patterson, to an interview with your husband, when you were sitting on a curb at Tenth and Madison some time during the earlier part of August. Do you remember that occasion?"

"I believe I do."

"State to the jury the particulars of that interview."

"Mr. Patterson wanted some money that day. He said, 'I want fifty dollars. I have been playing poker and I want a month's expenses.' I told him I did not have it. We went on home, and after we got there, he grabbed a razor. I ran into the bathroom and locked the bathroom door; he said he would kill me. I stayed in there for some time, until I thought he had gone. Later when he came home, he told me he wanted the fifty dollars. He said he did not care how I got it, or who I went with, just so I got the money, that he wanted it and had to have it.Then he slapped me twice and hit me with his fist and knocked me down."

"What else did he do?"

"He bit my fingers."

"Which finger did he bite?"

"He bit my thumb nearly off."

"Show your thumb to the jury."

Gertrude described other beatings and how her neck was still black when she saw the district attorney, Willis Elliott, about filing an action for divorce.

"What did your husband say about the divorce proceedings?"

He said, 'I'm going to have ten thousand dollars out of this divorce suit, or I am going to have blood.' He said this with his right arm raised. Then he said, 'I am coming back after it and have it ready for me, or I will kill you.'"

Gertrude described how on the evening on which George Strain had come to call, her husband had happened on the scene, prompting her to run into the house. Moments later Strain chased her husband off with a gun. Gertrude said that she then chased after her husband.

"What happened next?"

"Mr. Patterson struck me a blow under the chin, and I fell to the sidewalk. He helped me to my feet, then raised his right hand, and said, 'I am going to kill you, you fucking whore, so help me God.' The Fairmount car was coming. He grabbed me by the shoulder, shaking his fist in my face and saying, 'Call me tomorrow morning; let me know what time you will meet me, and we'll talk this matter over.' Then he took the car."

"What did you do then?"

"I went back to the bungalow and told Mr. Strain to leave the house. I also told Mr. Strain how Mr. Patterson had threatened my life and how he had threatened me and said, 'I could kill you. I could shoot you down like a dog, and the law would never touch me, because I have lung trouble.' Mr. Strain pulled out the gun and said, 'Let me leave this with you for your protection,' and I said, 'Perhaps that would be a good idea.'"

"What did you do with the gun?"

"I put it in my purse."

Gertrude then described how, on the following Monday morning, the twenty-fifth of September, she called her husband at the sanitarium and asked to meet with him to talk about their situation.

"You said that after you had been waiting in front of the Peck School for five minutes that Mr. Patterson came up. Tell the jury what direction he came from and how he was dressed."

"He came up from Olive Street from the south, and he had on a light suit of clothes; he came up to me. I did not leave the bench."

"What happened next?"

"He came up to me, and I asked him to sit down, and I told him that I had an appointment with my dressmaker and could not stay very long. He said, 'Come on down the street with me; it's too public here.' We had gone about one and a half blocks, and he said, 'I lost twelve dollars playing poker, and I am three weeks behind with my board,' and he asked me if I would help him out. I said no, I would not give him any more money."

Daily News sketch by artist Ramsey of Gertrude Patterson weeping on the witness stand as she confesses to her relationship with the millionaire, Emil Strouss, and the events which led up to her shooting of her husband, Charles Patterson (upper left, in high school football uniform) (November 27, 1911)

"What other conversation did you have at or about that point?"

"He said, 'Why don't you give up this divorce, put the bungalow in my name, turn over your stock, and I'll come home tomorrow?' I said I would not sign anything over to him and would not give him any more money. He then grabbed me by the throat and said, 'You'll do it,' and he called me a vile name, 'or I will choke the life out of you.' Then he bit me with his teeth on my arm."

"Where?"

"On the shoulder. I screamed and began to cry. We then turned onto Pontiac and when he was about thirty feet from the entrance of the premises, Mr. Patterson stopped."

"What did he do?"

"He pulled out of his vest pocket a clipping."

"What kind of clipping?"

"A newspaper clipping, and he said, 'Have you seen this?' and he handed it to me and I read it."

"What was it?"

"A suit against Strouss for twenty-five thousand dollars."

"She often attacked and scratched me."

Denver Post *artist's conception of Charles Patterson's claim in a letter to his brother in which he claimed Gertrude had attacked him during an argument.*

"What did you do with it?"

"I read it and handed it back to him."

"What did you say to him?"

"I said, 'Don't you know this is blackmail and aren't you afraid you will get into trouble?' 'Well,' he said, 'I don't ever expect it to come to trial. I am giving my lawyer fifty collars if it does not come to trial and one hundred dollars if it does come to trial. I only want to scare him out of about $5,000.00" — and here he called Mr. Strouss another vile name — "but I will give it all up and come home if you will sign over the bungalow, put the deed in my name, and give me all your stock.' With that he struck me a

Denver Times *montage showing Gertrude Patterson surrounded by the twelve male jurors who will decide her fate. Many of the jurors did not disguise their admiration of her, and columnists suggested that the jurors were being seduced by Gertrude's beauty.*

blow in the face. I said I would do nothing of the kind."

"You say at this time he struck you on the left side of your face; what hand did he strike you with?"

"The left hand."

"What effect did this blow have on you?"

"I staggered backwards."

"What then took place?"

"He then hit me with his fist under my left ear, and I fell to the ground."

"Describe to the jury how you fell."

Gertrude left the witness box, walked over to the jury, and knelt down to show the position she was in when she fired the gun in self-defense. The jurors stood up and craned their necks to see Gertrude bending down and acting out this final scene on the courtroom floor. On the other side of the courtroom, the University of Denver law students also stood up to get a better view.

"I fell back when he struck me with his fist, and when I was on the ground he kicked me on the side."

"Had you ever had a revolver in your hands before?"

"No, sir."

"Have you ever fired a revolver before?"

"No, sir."

"Why did you fire the revolver at your husband?"

"I thought he was going to kill me."

For several moments there was total silence in the courtroom.

"Your witness," said Hilton.

Daily News *photograph of Gertrude Patterson surrounded by a* Daily News *artist's recreation of salient events in the life of Gertrude Patterson, including her rise from poverty to being the mistress of a millionarie, her studies in Paris, meeting Charles Patterson as the San Souci skating rink, the trip on an ocean liner to Europe with Strouss, and finally the shooting of her husband (September, 1911)*

27

"Hundred Defy Gale and Stand in Line to See Slayer."

"Pretty Slayer Defiant Under Cross-Fire."

"'Please Let Me Rest,' Begs Pretty Slayer on Witness Stand."

(Headlines, *The Daily News*, November 25, 1911).

Horace Benson strode confidently to the podium. It was time to cross-examine the defendant on the stand, and Benson was determined to make the most of it.

"Where were you born?"

"In Indiana."

"In what year?"

"In 1886."

Benson had drawn first blood, as he was prepared to show that Gertrude was born in 1881, and was in fact thirty years old — not the twenty-five she had reported to the police when she was arrested. O.N. Hilton squirmed in his seat. It was not a good beginning.

"At what place of Indiana were you born?"

"I don't know."

"You don't know at what place in Indiana you were born?"

"No, sir, I do not."

"Were you not born in 1881?"

"No, sir, absolutely not."

"You don't know where you lived in Indiana?"

"No, when I was born I don't remember."

"Your memory is not that good? Well, you lived there after you were born, didn't you, and still you do have no idea where you were born?"

"None whatsoever."

"You lived in Sandoval, Illinois, didn't you?"

"Yes, sir."

"Your father worked in the coal mines there, didn't he?"

"He was an engineer."

"You went to school there, didn't you?"

"Yes, sir."

"You ceased attending school there when you were thirteen or fourteen years of age, did you not?"

"Yes, sir."

"Were you expelled from school?"

"I quit school."

"Were you not, Mrs. Patterson, at about the time you were thirteen or fourteen years of age, expelled from the public school of Sandoval, Illinois for immoral conduct?"

"No sir, I was not."

"You were not?"

"I was not. My mother took me out of school."

"For what reason?"

"Not for immoral conduct, no sir."

"You were not expelled from school? Answer yes or no."

"Yes, sir."

"What year did you arrive in Chicago?"

"I don't know."

"You have no idea?"

"No sir, I have not, Mr. Benson."

"Do you know whether it was 1889 or 1909?"

"No, sir."

"You were married to Charles A. Patterson in 1909 weren't you?"

"No, in 1908."

"I know, but you were still married to him in 1909, weren't you?"

"Yes, sir."

"Well — then you did go to Chicago from Sandoval, didn't you?"

"I beg your pardon?"

"I am asking you if you know when you went to Chicago?"

"I don't remember."

"You don't know whether it was 1897, 1889, 1905, or 1908?"

"I don't remember the year."

"You don't know whether you went there in 1898?"

"I was at home in 1898."

"When you were at school in Sandoval, isn't it true that you were expelled?"

"I was excused for tardiness."

"Were you not living in St. Louis on Lucas Avenue or Chestnut Street in a house of prostitution, conducted by yourself and another woman, whose name was Kupples?"

Gertrude Patterson on her way to court.(Denver Post, *November, 1911)*

This time it was Hilton who rose in furious indignation. "Your honor, this is outrageous."

"Overruled. The witness may answer."

Gertrude shook her head vigorously. "I don't know where Lucas Avenue or Chestnut Street is, and I have never lived at either."

"Were you in a house of prostitution at that time?'

"Never!"

"And you were not at that time going under the name of Georgie or Birdie Knight?"

Hilton stood up, but made no objection.

"No, sir!"

"When did you go to Chicago?"

"The last time I left St. Louis. I went to Chicago from my home."

"Did you meet Strouss?"

"When?"

"Anytime in your life."

"Yes, sir."

"Was he a married man?"

"No, sir."

"You went to Paris with him, did you?"

"Yes, sir."

"Then you took up the study of French, did you?"

"Yes, sir."

"And Strouss was a clothing manufacturer in Chicago?"

"Yes, sir."

"Did you gain a speaking knowledge of French?"

"Yes."

"And in 1908, you met Charles Patterson at a skating rink in Sans Souci Park, did you not?"

"Yes."

"At the time you met him he was working for American Steel Foundries, was he not?"

"No, sir, he was not."

"Do you remember just before you were married, Mr. Patterson asking you if you had ever been married, and you assured him that it was a falsehood?"

"Yes, sir."

"Did you ask him if he would go to California and you would give him one hundred dollars for expenses, and did you ask him to meet you there?"

"I never gave him one hundred dollars, and I did not ask him to go there."

"You knew he was without means, didn't you?"

"He said his mother was rich."

"Now, after you returned from California, that is when the brutalities that you speak of occurred, is that right?"

"Yes, sir."

Benson spent the two hours grilling Gertrude as to the exact times and dates of each alleged beating and brutality. After a luncheon recess, he picked up the cross-examination by introducing a series of love letters allegedly written by both Gertrude and her husband to each other during the same period as the alleged brutalities. Then he moved on to ask about the money Gertrude had received from Strouss.

"And is it not an untruth, Mrs. Patterson, that your husband sold you to Strouss for fifteen hundred dollars?"

"No, sir."

And after he sold you and after you had given Mr. Patterson the money, you packed your trunk, and you went with Mr. Strouss to Europe?"

"Mr. Patterson packed my trunk."

"And you went to Europe?"

"Yes."

"And when you got on board the vessel and it sailed away you went as Mr. and Mrs. Strouss, did you not?"

"I didn't buy the ticket, and I did not register."

"You were known as Mr. and Mrs. E.W. Strouss, were you not? Just answer yes or no."

"Yes."

"And then, after you went to Europe and got another five thousand dollars, and after that you got $250 and then again you got $250 from Strouss, and after that how much from Strouss?"

"Not any, Mr. Benson."

"Not a cent?"

"Not a cent."

Here, Benson missed an opportunity to ask Gertrude where she had gotten the money to buy the Steele Street bungalow.

After confirming Gertrude's direct testimony that Strain had given her the pistol she used to kill her husband, Benson asked about the morning of September 23 on which Gertrude prepared to go meet her husband.

"You said you went home and prepared to meet with Mr. Patterson, didn't you?"

"Yes, sir."

Montage highlighting the features of Gertrude Patterson's
acclaimed beauty, including her eyes, ears, and nose. (Denver
Post, *November 23, 1911*)

"And you got the handbag that morning, did you not?"

"Yes, sir."

"And that is the preparation that was made to meet your husband, is it?"

"What do you mean by preparation?"

"You said you went home and prepared to meet him, didn't you, and I understood you to say you got the handbag with the pistol in it, and you went to meet him. Is that correct?"

"I combed my hair and dressed myself and put on my coat and went out to take the streetcar."

"Well, those were the preparations that you made — dressed yourself, combed your hair, put on your hat, and took your handbag with the six-shooter in it; these were the preparations that you made to meet him, were they not? Answer yes or no."

"Yes."

"Did you say at that time, over the phone in conversation with your husband in substance as follows: 'I will meet you at the Shultz corner; I have four thousand dollars and the house, and I want you to go to California or Kansas, and we will start all over again where we are not known?'"

"No, sir!"

"You said nothing of the kind?"

"No, sir!"

It was late in the day before Benson finally got to the actual circumstances of the killing.

"There, in front of the Richthofen Castle, he struck you?"

"Yes."

And he knocked you down?"

"Yes."

"Did he knock you down twice?"

"No."

"And he kicked you?"

"Yes, sir."

"And then you were on the ground, and he had his hand raised to strike you, as you testified, you took the pistol out of your handbag, did you?"

"Yes, sir.

"And you were still on the ground were you, Mrs. Patterson?"

"Yes, sir."

"And you shot him while you were still on the ground, did you?"

"I was on my knees, yes sir. He had his right hand raised to strike me."

"Can you tell the jury, how it happened that, with your husband standing facing you, as you have indicated while you were on your knees, can you tell the jury how it happened that you shot him in the back?"

There was a hush in the courtroom. This was the critical question of the cross-examination, and many in the courtroom were sure that her life would depend upon her answer.

"No, sir. As he tried to strike me with his right hand raised, I shot him. I don't know how many times I shot him."

"Did you not state that you were on your knees and he was facing you? Now, do you mean to say he turned his back to you and you shot him in the back?"

"Did I say that?"

O.N. Hilton cringed inwardly at this answer by his client, but he did not let it show.

"I say, do you mean to say that when you were on your knees and your husband was facing you, that when he turned his back that you shot him in the back?"

"No, sir."

"Then he did not have his back to you?"

"I don't remember."

"And, Mrs. Patterson, did you not say to your husband that if he would not dismiss the suit against Strouss that you would kill him, and did he not start to run?"

"No, sir."

"And didn't you tell him the Saturday before that the Jew was not wrong, that you were the one who was wrong, that the fault was yours, and that if he persisted in the suit that you would perjure your soul to save Strouss?"

"No, no, that's a lie!"

"And did you not then shoot your husband, and when he ran he cried, 'Oh God, Oh God!' and did you not then walk up to him and shoot him through the heart?"

"No, sir, that's a lie!" Gertrude sobbed.

"If that's a lie, can you explain to the jury how the bullet went into his back?"

"I cannot."

"Did you say in the presence of Alma Bodie in the kitchen of the Hendrie home, just after your husband had been killed and the pistol found under his body, did you say, 'My husband has committed suicide?'"

"I told you, Mr. Benson, I don't remember anything that happened in the Hendrie home."

"And did you tell Sergeant McIntyre that after your husband was shot and the pistol had been found under his body, 'Oh, he shot himself?'"

"I don't remember."

The cross-examination had been a disaster for the defense, and no one was more aware of that than O.N. Hilton. At its conclusion, an eerie hush fell over the courtroom, and there were few who doubted that Gertrude Gibson Patterson would very soon be hung by her neck until she was dead.

Montage of a demure Gertrude Patterson gazing serenely out from her jail cell and appearing to contemplate the faces of the twelve male jurors who will decide her guilt or innocence. **(Denver Post, November 29, 1911)**

28

"Women Jam Trial to Aid Fallen Sister."

"Mrs. Patterson Contradicts Self On Stand"

"'Benson Murdering Me With Lies' Sobs Mrs. Patterson."

"Pretty Slayer Sobs as Sin of Past is Laid Bare."

"Slayer Denies Conducting St. Louis House of Ill-Fame."

"Mrs. Patterson Admits She Wrote Love Letters."

"Please Do Not Mix Me Up, She Pleads With Benson."

(Denver Newspaper headlines, November 24-26, 1911).

To the Rocky Mountain News:

On behalf of our oppressed sisters everywhere, I would like to ask the News why the devil takes down with such greed the names of women only at the Patterson trial? Is it because of the absence of man? No, indeed!

Can you conceive of a situation more trying to a man than sitting before a jury composed of women, a woman judge, women lawyers, a courtroom full of women spectators. Would he not cast his eyes about wildly for the sight of the face of a brother? But why try to imagine such a situation? Man would never give up his long considered 'natural rights of supremacy,' under which is cloaked curiosity as wild and all consuming as ever dwelt in a feminine breast.

(*Rocky Mountain News*, Letter to the Editor, November 27, 1911).

Monday, November 27, 1911
Day Four of the Trial

Gertrude had been caught in numerous transparent lies, not least of which was her own age. But the most devastating feature of the cross-examination was Gertrude's inability to explain how it was that her husband had been shot in the back.

The day following her grueling cross-examination was a Sunday, and court being recessed, Gertrude spent the day with her family and friends in her cell.

The following Monday morning, the defense's first witness, Willis V. Elliott, was most extraordinary for the fact that he was the district attorney of the City and County of Denver.

"When did Mrs. Patterson come to see you?" Hilton asked.

"Mrs. Patterson came to see me in August about a divorce."

"What were the grounds for divorce?"

"Cruelty."

"Describe to the jury the condition of Mrs. Patterson when she called to see you: the condition of her face and neck."

"There were black and blue spots on the neck. There were abrasions of the skin and the neck was swollen. She told me how she had obtained the bruises and marks. They were inflicted by her husband."

"Thank you, Mr. District Attorney."

Benson had no questions.

Hilton next called Mrs. Nettie White, who testified that the previous July she had overheard the Pattersons quarrelling and had seen Mr. Patterson strike his wife and slam her against a telephone pole.

Then Hilton called Mr. Thomas S. Peatee, who testified that immediately after the shooting he had examined the stone wall at the Richthofen Castle and determined that the bullet from Mrs. Patterson's pistol had penetrated the stone wall horizontally, thus confirming Mrs. Patterson's account that she had fired the bullet from a position lower than that of her husband who was standing over her. On cross-examination, however, Peatee was forced to concede that the bullet might not have entered the wall first but might have ricocheted into that position after hitting a nearby crevice.

Believing that Mr. Peatee was the defense's last witness, Benson sat back in great satisfaction, for the case appeared to be won for the prosecution.

"I have one final witness, your honor," Hilton declared.

Benson turned around, puzzled because he knew of no other witnesses in the case.

"I call Mr. Francis J. Easton to the chair."

"Who?" Gertrude asked Hilton when he sat down.

"Don't you worry, Mrs. Patterson," Hilton reassured her as he sat down to await the entrance of the witness. "He is a witness who just came forward yesterday."

Everyone in the courtroom looked at each other, the reporters looked befuddled, and there was a general murmur of amazement.

"I must object, your honor!" Benson thundered. "No such Mr. Easton has been brought to the attention of the people."

"Approach the bench," Judge Allen instructed.

"Your honor," Hilton explained, "this witness came forward just yesterday afternoon. He is an eyewitness to the killing of Mr. Patterson, and I submit that justice demands that he be heard even at this late hour."

"Your honor, I have never heard of his person and have had no chance to examine him!" Benson hissed.

Judge Allen scowled. "There is no requirement of which I am aware that requires the defense to make any witness available in advance to the prosecution in a criminal case. You will have a chance to examine this witness after Mr. Hilton is through with him. Have your witness sworn, Mr. Hilton."

"A rabbit in your hat, Mr. Hilton?" Benson whispered angrily to Hilton as he returned to his seat.

The **Rocky Mountain News** *portrait of Gertrude Patterson which filled the front page on the first day of her trial. (November 20, 1911)*

"Counsel!" Judge Allen admonished. "Return to your seats, and have the witness sworn."

"Do you swear to tell the truth, the whole truth and nothing but the truth, so help you God?" the clerk asked the tall, hardy-looking man on the witness stand.

"I do."

"State your name for the record," Hilton instructed.

"Francis J. Easton."

"Where do you live, sir?"

"I did live in Tacoma. I have taken up residence in Denver."

"When did you come to Denver?"

"September 24, 1911."

"How do you remember that date?"

"I arrived that evening on the train from Tacoma by way of Laramie, Wyoming. Upon my arrival, I went to a hotel on Larimer Street and went to bed."

"And what did you do the next morning?"

"I woke up and decided that I needed a constitutional. I didn't know much about the town but decided to go out toward the plains. After a while I found myself far out on Colfax Avenue. I got off the streetcar and walked south to where I saw the towers of a building. I think they call it the Richthofen Castle. I walked on, and suddenly, a couple of hundred feet away, I saw a man and a woman. They were walking fast, so they must have been young. They were making gestures, so they must have been excited."

"What did you see next?"

"Suddenly, I saw the woman hand the man a slip of paper. I saw him read it. There were a lot more gestures, and I saw him hand back the paper and strike the woman a blow and another blow, and she went down. I heard shots, and he was down."

Benson looked as if he would burst with apoplexy, but there was no legal objection he could make. The witness was simply stating what he claimed to have seen.

"Your witness, Mr. Benson."

Benson strode to the podium with an expression of outrage that now seemed permanently etched on his face. His face was red.

"At what hotel did you register on the twenty-fourth of September?"

"I don't remember the name, or if it even had a name. It was a fifteen-cents house."

"And you came from Tacoma?"

"Yes."

"Is that where your parents live?"

"My parents are dead."

"Where are your parents buried?"

Easton paused to think.

"I don't know."

"You don't know where your own parents are buried?"

"No."

"Are you married"?

"I was. I was divorced several years ago."

"Where does you former wife live?"

"I don't know."

"Well, where were you married?"

"I don't remember."

"Do you have any children?"

"I have one son. He lives in Tacoma."

"What is his address?"

"I don't know that."

"And you just happened to arrive in Denver on the twenty-fourth of September?"

"Yes, that is the day I arrived, yes."

"So we would expect to find your name in the register book of that hotel on Larimer Steet?"

Easton thought for a moment. "I'm not sure I actually signed in that night. It was very late, and the desk clerk dispensed with the usual formalities, as I recall."

"How convenient," Benson muttered.

"You say you were three hundred feet away from where this man and woman were quarrelling?"

"Yes."

"Did you go toward them, did you try to offer help and find out what was happening?"

"No sir. I didn't want to get my foot into that affair."

"So you just turned and went away?" Benson asked with a disbelieving snarl.

"Yes, but I saw enough. That woman's life was in danger!"

"And you never reported what you had seen to the police afterwards, or come forward until now?" Benson asked with an expression of incredulity.

"As I said, I didn't want to get my foot in this affair, but I'd been reading the papers, and decided I should come forward and tell . . . "

"Just yesterday, you decided!"

"Yes, sir."

"No further questions!" hissed Benson with disgust, cutting off the witness in midsentence and dismissing him.

In five short minutes, the momentum of the case had shifted to the defense. Gertrude, who had been listening intently, seemed as surprised as anyone else about Easton's dramatic testimony.

Hilton looked at Benson. He was aware of Benson's one fatal weakness. He knew from prior experience with Benson that he could become aggressive, overbearing, and nasty when angered or roiled. During his cross-examination of Gertrude, Benson had caught her in many lies and inconsistencies and reduced her to sobs and tears. But the contrast between Benson's disdainful, oppressive demeanor and the vulnerable, childlike sweetness of his witness-victim had been stark, and Hilton had no doubt that this contrast would lead the jury to sympathize with her. The testimony of Easton, incredible though it was, had damaged Benson's case, and Hilton was now hopeful that this setback would trigger Benson's obnoxious and imperious side.

"The defense rests your honor."

"Very well," said Judge Allen. "Mr. Benson, do you have closing argument?"

"I do indeed, your honor."

"We might recess, if you like, counselor."

But Benson was raging like a lion and desired to give no quarter. "I am ready to proceed now, your honor."

"Proceed, then, Mr. Benson."

Benson slipped his thumbs under his suspenders, cleared his throat, and took a position only two or three feet in front of the jury. Looking at each juror intently, he began his closing malediction by citing verses from Rudyard Kipling's poem, "The Vampire":

There was a fool, and he made his prayer,
Even as you and I,
To a rag and bone and hank of hair,
And we know there was a woman who did not care,
But the poor devil called her his lady fair —

"That's the heart he had, gentleman, of the woman he loved. He wrote her, in a letter which, according to the defense, was too vile to be read: 'My love may find you in that far somewhere.' God bless him, he thought that she was his:

And a fool there was, and he made his prayer,
Even as you and I,
To a rag and a bone an a hank of hair,
But the poor devil called her his lady fair.

AND SHE SHOT HIM IN THE BACK!"

Benson swirled around and in histrionic fashion pointed directly at Gertrude. "And it is she, I submit, this vampire who sits before you now!"

Benson paused for several minutes to let his accusation of vampirism sink into the minds of the jurors.

"The time is now at hand when we are going over the opening chapter of the closing scene in this tragedy. I deem it the first and highest duty to make an appeal to our own consciences and to look into our own hearts and do that which would satisfy our own judgments.

"We are advised by the defense that the defendant is a sweet, beautiful, unsophisticated, and unsullied girl, the daughter of poor parents living in a little mining village, who went to a great city and became the victim in Chicago of wicked men of the world. What do you twelve men think about this statement?

"However unpleasant it may be to present degrading facts to you gentlemen, and however unpleasant it may be to speak of human degradation, it is the words and actions and demeanor of Gertrude Patterson herself that appeal to you.

"At about the age of eighteen or twenty we find her in Chicago living at the Auditorium Hotel. He is paying her bills, a rich man, and oh, the glory of it! The Auditorium Hotel is so different from the boys at Sandoval. And then she went to Europe. After years of living in luxury, she returns to Chicago from Paris. She goes to the Sans Souci skating rink, and there she meets Charlie Patterson, a boy five or six years younger than she is, and she deigns to look at him, and her looked settled it. And from that day to the day of his death, he paid out the right tribute of his heart to the woman that he was insanely in love with.

"Every sentence, breathed in every letter that has been introduced here, shows nothing but love and worship and adoration and infatuation. He believed her against the world, against his own judgment, against his own heart, against his own eyes.

"Let me say to you that this woman had taught Charlie Patterson everything he knew — everything of the iniquities of this life that he knew she had taught him. Is there a word or a breath of a suspicion in this case that Charles Patterson ever at any time had anything to do with another woman except the woman whom he loved and who killed him?

"And my good friend on the other side will try to paint this woman, who lived in Paris as the mistress of Strouss, as a pure, unfortunate, and unsullied little girl at the time of her meeting with Charles Patterson, this monster, this devil. Here are some of his sentiments, which will speak for themselves, and which my friend will say were written by the most degraded, dishonorable wreck of humanity that ever stood on two feet:

Could I find words as pure as the rose,
Half hidden in the wayside grass,
That rose not right of itself known,
That word is the word I would say to you;

"Oh, the monster! The degraded monster, to have written such words in a letter to the woman he worshiped and adored! Here are some more of his thoughts:

Could I make a song,
Careless of art,
As the robin's thrill,
That should seem a part,
Of my life, a blessing from my heart
That song I would sing for you.

"This letter is dated June 1910, and in that he speaks to her about the song 'When a Fellow's on the Level with a Girl That's on the Square.'

"In the letter, he speaks of having hurt her on the arm. Of course I suppose this evidence is offered to convince you that no married man ever put on mark on his wife's arm or neck or cheek; yet in the same letter he sweetly and kindly sends her a poem. Was he not a consummate scoundrel?"

Hilton visibly rolled his eyes at Benson's histrionic sarcasm.

"Let's talk of the defense's first witness," Benson continued. Consider the contradictions:

"She denied being expelled from school, then admitted it; she admits that she lied to Hamilton Armstrong, chief of police, and she swore that Strain suggested leaving the gun with her, and Strain swore she asked him to leave it with her. She admits she lied to Chick about the five thousand dollars upon her return from Paris. And she wants you to believe that she did not shoot this man in the back, when the suit worn by the dead man proves the contrary. Doctors McNamara and Brown and Mudd also testified that he was shot in the back.

"Let's talk then of the defense witnesses.

"There came this man from Tacoma, who had just happened into Denver from Cheyenne and went into a ten and fifteen cent house on Larimer street upon his arrival in Denver — and this man just happened to get on a car and just happened to go out to the sanitarium. And this man didn't know where his father conducted his business and he didn't know anything definite about anything that we could put a hand on, and he stated that his father and mother were dead, and he didn't know where they were buried and finally said they were buried in a cemetery. He did know he had a son who lived some place in Tacoma, but he didn't know the number. He testified that he saw the defendant knocked down twice and had seen her shoot Charles Patterson, that he did not go to her assistance and did not tell any officer of the law of the shooting. And when she went into the house, the people testified that there were no marks on her clothing and no bruises on her face, all of which give the lie to the story of this man who was brought here from Chicago, or wherever he was brought from.

"And this is the defense's star witness!"

Hilton winced at Benson's transparent suggestion that Strouss had bribed Easton and sent him to Denver to commit perjury.

"Mr. Shugart testified that he saw a woman leaning down over a man who was on his hands and knees, and then he heard shots fired and the man pitched forward on his face, and there are bullet holes in the back of the coat in mute evidence of the fact that he was shot in the back.

"This same witness also testified that after the shooting he ran up to the body and found the revolver the woman had used in the killing under the body of the dead man; that the woman ran into his house and said, 'My husband has committed suicide;' whereas she had said to her husband, 'I want you to dismiss this alienation suit against Strouss, and if you don't I will kill you' — and why didn't she want him to sue Strouss? Because it was her source of revenue and he would cut her off, and she said ' I will give you the house and four thousand dollars if you don't sue him.' And why did she do this? Because she could get more money from Strouss and she had reason to believe that Strouss would cut her off if this suit came to trial.

"When the argument took place and he saw the gun and started to run, she shot him in the back, and when he was down she shot him again, and then she came on this witness stand, her tears have been for baring of her shame but never tears for the memory of her dead husband who was insanely in love with her, and she smiled and laughed and sneered at the sight of his blood-stained garments and at the mention of her husband's name as he called out in his agony.

"This is a crime worse than adultery, gentlemen of the jury. It is the crime of using honored words, of taking this boy, her husband, in her arms, of fondling him, of embracing him, and telling him of her love, while at the very time she loathed him and was planning to rid herself of him so that her luxuries and pleasures should not be interfered with.

"I ask you gentleman to bring in a verdict of guilty of murder in the first degree and to sentence this vampire to be hung by the neck until she is dead!"

Denver Post *photographs of Gertrude Patterson taken during various periods of her life (September, 1911)*

29

"Prosecutor, Flaying Slayer, Compares Her to Vampire."

"'He Called Me A Vampire,'" Mrs. Patterson Sobs: 'That Hurts Worse Than Anything. That isn't Justice.'"

"Contradiction in Testimony Arrayed Against Beautiful Defendant"

(*The Daily News*, November 29, 1911, p. 2).

It was a merciless, pitiless, overwhelming, crushing steamroller that he ran over the character of Mrs. Patterson which he tore into little shreds and incinerated with his biting scorn.

With the strong, vile, and brutal brush of the realist, Horace Benson — special prosecutor for the state — painted the picture of a woman so debased, so low, so degraded, that long before she had met her aged and licentious paramour, Emil W. Strouss, she had been the initiate into the infamies of life in her home town, Sandoval.

With the harsh brush of the realist, he painted in crude colors this picture of a young, unsophisticated boy trapped into the sapping and enervating, the degrading dregs of passion, where his life's blood was sucked away from his very soul by a vampire woman. The Burne-Jones picture which inspired Kipling's lines might have been inspired by the word picture drawn by Horace Benson.

In the words of attorney Benson, Mrs. Patterson is a vampire, and in the words of his opponent, a poor child ruined by a bad, unscrupulous man, and led into the intricate maze of the forest of life.

*In the words of attorney Benson, Charles A. Patterson was
an unfortunate boy, lured to shame and death by a siren voice.
In the words of attorney Hilton, Patterson was as vile a reptile
as ever assumed the form of man.*

*One grand debauch of vitriol and gall, one magnificent
revel of word-sensationalitis, blacksmiths of thunder phrases,
was this contest of these attorneys, and when they ran out of
words to brand with ignominy and shame the living and the
dead alike, they turned like kilkenny cats upon one another.*

(*The Daily News*, November 29, 1911).

*Vampirism filled the very air in the West Side Court. It
sucked the little freshness frrm the atmosphere and left it lifeless
and poisonous. With finger extended toward the white-faced
woman, from whose fragile beauty, all the color, all the defiance
and airy nonchalance of preceding hardships had been wiped
out by this kind of personal suffering, Prosecutor Benson recited
dramatically the lines of Kipling's poem.*

*Around this theme Benson made a gout-baring address
that painted the woman before the bar as a vampire more deadly
than those Hebraic and later Slavonic creatures of superstition
that frequent the legends of those peoples. Charles A. Patterson
he painted as a young boy only a few years out of school who,
flattered by the attentions of this vicious vampire woman, young
and beautiful, fell a victim before her.*

*It was Robert Hilliard, appearing in the Denver Playhouse
production of A Fool There Was, who, after being seated incon-
spicuously among the spectators, did seat himself at the press
table and distribute opinions of whether Mrs. Patterson was
indeed a vampire woman.*

*Ah, but Robert, who nightly falls beneath the spell of the
vampire woman, is somewhat of an "expert" on those soul-
destroying, life-sucking creatures. Therefore, as a connoisseur,
and with the idea of press-agenting himself (far be it from us to
suggest such a thing) he did stalk into the presence of sordid
tragedy in the West Side Court.*

*Although Robert disclaimed ever having seen Mrs.
Patterson before entering the courtroom yesterday afternoon, he
was not overlooking the chance to express his opinion on vampires. Even so far as suggesting that he might give pointers to
Mr. Hilton on the case did his altruism lead him.*

Shrinking from the reporters' gaze by taking a chair in

*their midst, Benson rose with rebuking air at the question of an
impertinent reporter person.*

"*Mr. Hilliard, is it true that you have offered Mrs.
Patterson the place of the vampire woman in your play?*"

"*Nay, forsooth, quoted the actor: "I fain would elevate my
art, not drag it into cheap sensationalism. Mrs. Patterson is not
the vampire type. She is but a poor little creature, the victim of circumstances. I have no contract for her, only love and sympathy.*"

"*Can you tell the vampire type at a glance?" the actor was
asked.*

"*Nay, nay," quoth he, "but I could not say anything . . ." *

*At this point the exchange of courtesies between counsel
for the defense and prosecution killed the actor's speech.*

(Alice Roche, *Denver Daily News*, November 29, 1911).

O.N. Hilton looked at the headlines and threw down his newspaper
in disgust.

Ten minutes later he was in front of the jury making the closing
statement of his life:

"It is one of the misfortunes of our illustrious profession that sometimes court, counsel, and jurymen are compelled to witness such an exhibition on the part of the gentleman who sits opposite me, and I sincerely
trust that there is no one here who has seen it and heard it that will take
away from Denver the story that a Denver lawyer came into court and acted
like a drunken Indian who had taken about two drinks too much.

"He has said that we should state the facts, and when during the
long hours of this trial he has struck out at this shrinking woman his wrath,
he reminds me very much of a story that I once heard of a man who used
to come home to his wife at night and she would beat him with a black-
snake whip — he being a henpecked husband — and when some of the
boys heard of it, and asked him why he stood for it, he said, 'Well, it don't
hurt me very much, and it does tickle Mary Ann.'

"And in considering the case of this defendant, gentlemen of the
jury, I want you to put yourselves in her place with Strouss, to put yourself
in her place when she did not exceed seventeen years of age — in short
clothes and her hair in a braid down her back. Put yourself in her place for
the purposes of this inquiry as a father or a brother. Consider her as your
daughter if you will, and as one whom you have loved and as to one whom
you would wish the natural joy of wife and mother.

"Is it not, gentlemen of the jury, a travesty upon man made in the
image of the Great Father that there never blooms a lily in this world so

fair but there is some vicious heel to crush it, some sooty hand that reaches to destroy?

"Oh, the shame of this horrible thing. A man fifty years of age and old enough to be this girls' father, rich in the world's goods, ruins her life and her home and surrounds her with every material luxury, gives her an education in French, a special tutor in music, and brings her home without marrying her.

"And this is the position Mr. Patterson *finds her in, and he marries her.* Now society damns a woman and praises the man. When this is done, gentlemen of the jury, when after a girl has been dragged into this kind of sin by all of the allurements of that path, and the courts and counsel and society in general damn that girl, I say to you that we have all confounded justice. I will also have the honor to show you, gentlemen of the jury, that Patterson knew of the fact this girl wife had been unfortunate, that he after their marriage continued to receive money from his wife for her disgrace, and I say to you when he did all of this, that he was a blacker monster than Strouss ever pretended to be, and if she had then and there slain him it would have been justifiable homicide.

"Patterson knew what his wife's relations with Strouss had been, and he knew his purpose in taking her to Europe. He knew that Strouss was the man who had seduced her, and a husband who packs her trunk and takes her to the train, and who tells her when she gets there, if she gets the money to send it to him, must have known, gentlemen of the jury, of Strouss's purpose in taking his wife to Europe.

"Shortly, he said to her,' I'll tell you how we can both get along nicely, how we can both have plenty of money.'

"Do you think that story was manufactured? If a man is capable of making that kind of a request for his wife when he needs money, is he capable of allowing her to go to Europe with Strouss in the first instance? Will any man on the jury not agree with me when I say if he will do one thing, he will do the other?

"I don't believe it is necessary to spend much time on this subject, when the attacks are admitted by the husband himself in letters over his own signature. She said to him, 'Where is the fifteen hundred dollars that you got in the first place?' — and you will remember that he got fifteen hundred dollars. He said to Strouss, you will remember, 'I will let you go, if you will pay a certain sum of money, and if you will come through,' and she did not know what he meant by coming through; and so she told Strouss about it when she casually met Strouss on the street and when she very naturally told him about her unhappy lot and that her husband had said to her that she could go to Europe if he would come through with the fifteen hundred dollars, Strouss said, 'If Patterson will sign a paper absolving me from any harm, I will give him the money.'

"And after the money has been deposited in Patterson's name, she then said to him, 'Where is the statement that you promised to give Strouss to exonerate him?'

"And he said, 'You tell Strouss to go to hell, will you?'

"Oh, I would like to have anybody do this man up as a loving and wronged husband, a man who did not know why Strouss had taken his wife with him to Europe.

"We will start out now, gentlemen of the jury, with this affair one month after the marriage of this man to this defendant here, and we will see whether this wronged and loving husband proved to be such things all through their married life.

"If there is anything in this whole wide world of ours more despicable and abominable than this form of white slavery, I would ask you to tell me what it is. I have said that it was very astonishing, to my mind at least, that this girl was seduced and wronged by Strouss. You have understood from her story the circumstances, and she was perfectly frank in telling you. You have heard how he turned her into a plaything.

"We have heard it repeated here and again that this defendant is degraded and a wanton, and we sometimes notice that those of the same sex as one of those unfortunate girls will draw their skirt about them and pass them by.

"I want to know, gentlemen of the jury and everyone who is within hearing of my voice, how many of you could have your lives bared to the world — unless it is counsel for the prosecution — without some man pointing his finger at you and saying, 'Thou hypocrite!'

"And so I say that when Strouss found this butterfly for his pleasure and after he had desecrated this lovely innocent creature, it is only the old story of such is life and such is lust. We are such grand creatures, aren't we? We sort out and pursue until our feet are weary. We hunt down innocents. We must satisfy our whim. We then toss it aside, and we point to the river or to the street or to borders defied, and the woman turns her face and meekly steals away from us lords of creation.

"There is nothing new in this story — it only exemplified the fact that for a woman the wages of sin is death, and I am reminded as I have listened to the denunciation of counsel for the past six or eight days, of a jury at another trial — and we read of it in Holy Writ, when a woman was brought before our blessed Lord when he died to redeem the souls of men and women, and you remember that she was to be judged by the Mosaic law, and they said, clamorous and resentful and anxious to catch her, 'Judge her! Judge her!'

"They wanted judgment, and there they stood above the woman awaiting judgment and the verdict of the Lord. They were thirsty for her blood — for the blood of a woman who had become the victim of a man.

And the Lord knelt down, and in the extremity of His confusion and embarrassment, He raised His face, and oh, the sweetness and melancholy of the music of His voice, and He did not speak as the crowd had hoped for, but he turned to the woman and said, 'Who are these accusers — do any of these men accuse you?' and she said, 'No, No!' and he said, 'Neither do I. Go and sin no more.' And I want to ask you, as jurors, when her case is closed and when this distinguished gentlemen who has preceded me rants again and glares at you, and pounds this railing and throws in your face this code as he shouts, 'My God! My God! She shot him in the back!' I want you to remember that time that our Lord said: 'Let him who is without sin cast the first stone.'

"Gentlemen of the jury, I want to call your attention to the question that was put to Mrs. Patterson as to whether she was ever in a house of prostitution in St. Louis. The name of the house was given, the name of the proprietress was given, and then, gentlemen there were promises made that proof on this subject would be forthcoming. Did we see any proof offered? Did we? I have never seen such a cowardly attack upon character in my life! If you had a sister as a witness in a court of justice and she were asked those questions under a promise to make them good to the jury, and when the case was closed, the prosecution was silent, put yourself in the place of the brother of that girl. You all have a sister or a wife or daughter that you love and respect, and, gentlemen of the jury, there should be a line drawn as to insulting remarks made by counsel into the jury box, a poison to make them think that perhaps all of these denunciations were true; and I will say to you right here and now that that was only an assault on the chastity and purity of this women. After all, gentlemen of the jury, even if this woman had been the infamous woman that she has been painted, what has that to do with the merits of this case? I want to ask you if she is being tried for the indiscretion of her early life or for the homicide.

"The nurse who testified has said that Mr. Patterson put his hand under his pillow at different times when sick in bed and said, 'If I ever get out of this bed, I will kill you.' Have you heard anyone contradict this testimony?

"Mr. Willis Elliott, the district attorney, took the stand and testified that the defendant came to him to file suit on the grounds of extreme cruelty; he testified that her was face was black and blue and swollen when she was in his office. I say, gentlemen, that Mr. Elliot's testimony alone is enough to prove that this woman had been assaulted by this man. What put the marks on her face? She didn't put them there herself, did she?

"Dr. Mudd also testified that he saw two marks on her face, as did also the two girls from the city jail, so here we have corroborated Mrs. Patterson again in her statement that her husband had struck her and inflicted injuries on her.

"There was a witness to what transpired in front of the castle immediately before these shots were fired. You will remember that there was a bullet hole in the stone wall fifteen or sixteen inches from the ground, and you can readily see that this shot was fired while the defendant was in a kneeling position or down on the ground. The first shot evidently missed; he saw that he was up against the real thing, he turned, and the next two shots struck him in the back. The last shot missed him.

"The credibility of Mr. Easton was attacked and for no other reason than that he was unable to tell where he was married. Is that strange? The reason that he did not go over to the couple, it was because he was a stranger in a town — and when a witness is a stranger they are put under bond, and when they cannot furnish bond, they are locked up. If Patterson acted as this witness has testified, she had reason to believe that he was going to do her bodily harm, and she was justified in taking his life and the jury should so regard it.

"What were the circumstances? He asked her to deed him the property on Steele Street. Do you blame her? He said to her, 'I want you to sign to me the stock and put the house in my name. When she refused, he said, 'I think I will sue that Jew bastard,' and she said to him, 'That would be blackmail.' But he said he did not intend to push the suit.

"The only fault I find with this woman is that she did not do this years ago. She would have been justified in my opinion. She ought to have shot him the first time he abused her and compelled her to get money for him.

"So, gentlemen, I thank you for your attention. I conclude, and I submit to you that the facts compel a verdict of not guilty in this case."

30

"Harsh Realism or Sentiment: Which Will it Be With the Jurors?"

"Fate of Mrs. Patterson Rests tonight With the Jurors."

(The Daily News, November 29, 1911).

In contrast to Horace Benson's tirade of innocent boy falling victim to the vampire woman, O.N. Hilton went back to the greatest of works, the Bible, but from its pages he drew only those somewhat trite and conventionally appealing illustrations, the story of Magdalen and the story of Adam and Eve.

According to the picture related by O.N. Hilton, Gertrude Gibson Patterson, instead of being the vampire portrayed by Horace Benson, is a down-trodden lily, a child-wife, a shrinking girl caught in the fowler's net, and the fowler's name was an elderly libertine. A picture of a lily spotted by the mire of the world, spotted by mire from the hands of two men, was the picture painted in those smooth oils of O.N. Hilton and between the two — the one brutal and harsh of the realist, the other saccharine and sentimental.

(Alice Roche, Denver Daily News, November 29, 1911).

As the jury retired in the case of the People of the State of Colorado vs. Gertrude Gibson Patterson, an entire city held its breath.

There was one final dramatic scene as Judge Allen banged his gavel and recessed until the jury reached a verdict. As Gertrude was being escorted out of the courtroom by the sheriff, she came face to face with the other Mrs. Patterson. The mother wore black; Gertrude wore a long fur coat over a blue frock. The mother's lips were shaking, and, for moments that seemed an eternity, she stood and gazed into the eyes of the woman who had slain her boy. Then, both women passed each other without acknowledgment.

Back in her cell, Alice Roche interviewed Gertrude for her column the following day in *The Daily News*. "What do you think of this experience and your chances?" Alice asked.

"What do I think of things now?" Gertrude replied. "I am sure that never has a woman been subjected to such persecution. As a woman of the world, I thought I knew the meaning of the rules which make for decency and kindness and truth. I find that one's mistakes, even those made in thoughtless youth, are used as instruments of torture by those in power to insist the mistake was a crime. Those mistakes are tossed into the balance against life and death. So I have learned more during these days than I could ever have learned in ten lives such as I have lived. Almost, I do not care what happens."

The life of the city of Denver came to a virtual halt as its citizens waited for the jury to reach a verdict. The next morning after enjoying a final late morning brunch courtesy of the taxpayers of Denver, the jury announced that it had indeed reached a verdict.

The biggest mobs the City of Denver had ever seen began immediately to form outside the West Side Court House, blocking traffic and bringing all traffic to a standstill. As Gertrude and her entourage, consisting of her attorney, the sheriff and deputy sheriff, and family members entered the courthouse, there arose a cacophony of cheers for "Good old Gertie" mixed with whistles, catcalls, and blood-curdling screams from groups of young women.

Francis Wayne described the scene:

"Dressed in a brand new blue frock, which fit her lovely figure closely to the waist then spread out in soft folds, with a wide-brimmed hat, which cast shadows on the pale, lovely face, she sat poised as a statute and waited the news."

Gertrude held the hand of her attorney tightly as she awaited the verdict. The gallery, which on previous days had had to be admonished by Judge Allen to be quiet, was silent. The wailing from the crowds outside diminished to a hush as everyone strained to hear the verdict.

"Has the jury reached a verdict?" Judge Allen asked.

"We have, your honor," said the foreman, stepping forward and offering the jury verdict form to the clerk.

The clerk, no doubt relishing being the focus of attention as well an instrument of suspense, read the form slowly, enunciating every word: "We, the jury find the defendant . . . "

It seemed as if time itself stood still as the clerk paused, looked up, and then read the final fatal word on the jury verdict form.

31

"Mob Cheers Patterson Verdict of 'Not Guilty'"

"Sensation-Crazed Mob Overruns Courtroom."

"Beauty Conquers Evidence and the Law."

"Four Jurors Visit Defendant After Trial and Shower Her With Roses."

"Beauty Carries Off Laurels in Patterson Murder Trial"

"Women Worshippers in Riot Claw at Acquitted Slayer; Bailiffs Fight for Order.'"

"'Jury Flim-Flammed!' Mother of Victim Wails Bitterly; Verdict a Disgrace Cries Mrs. M.K. Patterson."

"'We Love You, Gertie,'" Shout Courtroom Railbirds Who Jam Each Other In Effort to Congratulate."

(Headlines, *Rocky Mountain News*, November 30, 1911).

Yesterday afternoon at the West Side Court, Denver witnessed a sight the like of which has not been known in the history of trials. Mrs. Gertrude Gibson Patterson, who shot and killed her husband, the sick-unto-death consumptive, Charles A. Patterson, was acquitted by a jury of Denver men, four of whom later ran to her hotel room to pour out their personal feelings of admiration at the feet of beauty.

When Mrs. Patterson, her hands clasped together in an expression of joy, started to leave the courtroom, a cheer rang forth from the crowds of men and women. Mrs. Patterson, bowing to right and left like royalty, a smile upon her beautiful red lips, acknowledged the plaudits of the crowd of court hangers-on with the joy of living that had sprung up now in her being.

The departure of Mrs. Patterson was the occasion of a scene paralleled only by the one in her hotel, when four of the journeymen, smooth-shaven and unembarrassed before those languorous eyes that had looked into theirs so appealingly for eight days, held the hands of the husband-slayer and obsequiously congratulated her upon her freedom. The acquittal of Gertrude Gibson Patterson was predicted by this writer the second day of the trial when the psychology of beauty began its deadly influence upon the twelve men of the jury.

A pair of beautiful brown eyes looking appealingly and alluringly across the intervening space in that courtroom was the thing that worked its subtle influence in the Patterson case and marked, as one of Denver's most prominent legal authorities said upon learning of the verdict, "the most startling miscarriage of justice ever witnessed in the history of this state."

Beauty conquered evidence and the law. A woman's pretty face, clouded by sorrow, lightened by joy, whited by personal suffering, was the hypnotizing influence that made arguments of both counsel and defense a useless thing.

When Mrs. Patterson entered the courtroom yesterday afternoon awaiting the verdict, she was gowned for the occasion in a stylish new blue broadcloth suit. Later, in her cell, while packing her belongs, she tore a panel of her skirt and this accident caused the jauntily dressed, pretty butterfly almost as much distress as the verdict of acquittal had given her joy.

"Never mind the dress," said the matron, Mrs. Normile, her kind eyes filled with tears of joy at the acquittal of the young and pretty prisoner whose conduct had endeared her to the matron during her stay in jail.

The visit of four jurymen, F.J. Crane, Charles Oppenlander, F.S. Perry, and S.E. Berkett, to Mrs. Patterson's hotel, where they clasped hands and received the glowing looks of gratitude from the brown eyes and smiles from the red lips was a scene that made its impression on those who had been watching this trial from the very first.

"What was the dominant thing that marked your decision?" F.S. Perry was asked. "Was it the vehement attack of Prosecutor Benson upon the defendant?"

"No," Perry replied.

"Then it is true is it not, that it was this woman's beauty that caused you to free her?"

Perry's pale eyes glanced toward the flower-like face of Mrs. Patterson, who was still holding the hand of one of the other admiring jurors.

"No, I can't say that," replied Perry. "We decided purely upon evidence," he said, making his way to Mrs. Patterson to kiss her hand.

(Alice Roche, *The Daily News*, Thursday, November 30, 1911 at page 3).

As the words 'not guilty' fell from the lips of the clerk there was an audible gush from Mrs. Patterson. Convulsively she leaned forward, pressing her lily-white hands against her lips to keep from crying aloud for joy.

From the crowd came the gasps and cheers of women, intermingled with boos, and there was a quick, loud rustle of people rising from their chairs. The bailiffs tussled hard to handle the sensation-crazed mob from overrunning the courtroom and trampling all before it.

When the verdict was relayed to the crowd outside, there were cheers of Hurray for Gertrude!"

(*The Daily News*, November 30, 1911).

Flushed with victory and happiness, Gertrude first hugged her attorney and then walked over to Horace Benson.

"No hard feelings?" she said sweetly, offering her hand.

"No thanks," replied Benson gruffly. He turned away, grabbed his briefcase, and pushed his way impatiently through the mob cheering his defeat.

O.N. Hilton granted a brief interview immediately after the trial: "Benson need not have talked of vampires. He is a vampire himself. I never saw such a relentless, bloodhound prosecution as that. It was disgusting."

As Hilton had hoped, Benson had indeed overplayed his hand.

Hours later in her cell as she gathered her belongings, Gertrude was surrounded by admirers and well-wishers cheering her victory. She granted her first open interview to members of the press who hung on her every word. For the first time since Gertrude had retained him, O.N. Hilton harbored no apprehensions. Every word she uttered was duly recorded verbatim in the November 30 Thanksgiving issue of the *Daily News*:

"I am so happy that I just can't tell you how I feel! Isn't it grand the way the people cheer me! When I heard the words 'not guilty,' I wanted to scream with joy, but I don't believe that I could have spoken a word if I wanted to. I did not want to be disappointed, and I knew that if I went over to the court with the feeling that I would be convicted, I would not have felt too bad. But when the words 'not guilty' rang out over the courtroom, I felt a tingle go through my body, even to the tips of my fingers. It was a sensation that I had never experienced before in my life and I hope that I will never have to experience again.

"I prayed on my knees all morning long in my cell. I prayed that the jurors would believe my story. They did, and I am so thankful to them.

"I wore a Sacred Heart medal during my trial that was sent to me by a friend. My friend is Catholic, and I wore the medal. I am sure it had something to do with my acquittal.

"Just think, I am free and will be able to eat my Thanksgiving dinner with my people. Oh, you don't understand how happy I am! This world seems so bright and big now, and I am going to make the best of my life. I am through with men. Yes, forever. I have had enough trouble, and men have been the cause of it all. They are all worms as far as I am concerned.

"Do you know I had a dream Tuesday night about my trouble. I dreamed that I was on a boat and the water was a dark blue and beautiful. I was standing on the boat and was throwing Patterson's letter into the water, and the last thing that left my hand was the bankbook with the fifteen hundred dollars entered in it. After this left my hand, I said, 'I am through with them forever.' Then I woke up and found that it was all a dream, but it was more than a dream; it meant that I was going to be acquitted and that I was through with them forever.

"I never in all my life expected to see so many people cheering me when the trial was over. I was overwhelmed. I did not know that the people of Denver were on my side. But I guess Benson's attitude toward me turned them against him, and then they were in my favor. I wanted to shake hands with him, but he turned up his nose and walked away. It was terribly funny. I just couldn't help laughing at him."

That night, O.N. Hilton took Gertrude by carriage to the Brown Palace Hotel, where he had reserved the best suite in the hotel for her. It was nine in the evening when she heard a light tapping on the door. Apprehensive, she went to the door.

"Who is it?" she asked softly.

"The jurors, Mrs. Patterson."

Gertrude opened the door. There at her doorstep were four of the jurors in her case, including a beaming F.S. Perry, who held in his hand a grand bouquet of three dozen roses.

"For you," F.S. Perry announced, "with congratulations and our sympathy for the ordeal you have sustained."

"Oh, they are just beautiful! Come in gentlemen!" she exclaimed, ushering them all in to her room. "Gentlemen, you have no idea how grateful I am! I am simply overwhelmed. I must put them in a vase."

Gertrude rang for a bellboy, whom she instructed to fetch a vase of water.

For the next half hour, the jurors showered her with congratulations and compliments.

"The night before your verdict, I was so afraid of what you might do," Gertrude confided.

"Well," said Charles Oppenlander, "we never doubted your innocence. After all the wrongs that had been done to you, you did only what you were obliged to do to defend your person and your honor. But of course we couldn't say anything until they asked us for a verdict."

"And to think I was so worried, gentlemen. And I needn't have been. If I had only known! After the verdict, did you see me try to shake hands with Mr. Benson?"

Daily News *photograph of a jubilant Gertrude Patterson in the moments following her acquittal of murder (November 30, 1911).*

"Yes, we saw," said Perry.

"Well, then, you saw him turn away. He wouldn't shake my hand. And did you see his ugly face turn red? Why when he just slinked away, he looked so funny I couldn't help but laugh at him. He was just so pathetic, don't you agree?"

"Oh, absolutely!" said Charles Oppenlander.

"Did you hear the crowd cheer me?" asked Gertrude.

"Oh, yes," said F.J. Crane. "They loved you, Mrs. Patterson. Everyone loved you."

"Yes, it was just wonderful, and I had no idea, truly I didn't."

The four jurors who, as Alice Roche observed the next day in *The Daily News*, came to "pour out their personal feelings of admiration at the feet of beauty," might have stayed all night had Gertrude not pleaded exhaustion.

"Thank you so much for coming, gentlemen," said Gertrude, rising. "You have no idea how much your visit means to me, and to know that you believed in my innocence all along. And the flowers are just beautiful. But now I do hope you will excuse me, as I am very tired."

"Of course," said F.S. Perry, standing up, bowing and kissing Gertrude's hand. Tipping their hats, the four jurors shuffled out.

Alone at last, Gertrude attended to the roses and held them before the mirror as she gazed at her image in the mirror for several minutes, smiling happily. Then she quickly changed into her nightgown, tumbled into the freshly ironed sheets, and fell into her deepest sleep since that first fateful night in Carmel-by-the-Sea.

Although the newspaper headlines had heralded Gertrude's victory as one of "Beauty Over the Law," Horace Benson took it more personally than any defeat he had ever suffered. His only consolation was that the woman who had so thoroughly tram-

Gertrude Patterson leaving the courtroom after what appeared to many observers to be a vicious cross-examination by Horace Benson. (November 28, 1911)

pled upon his dignity would never know what he was now being driven to do. After fleeing the railbird mobs cheering Gertrude's victory and his defeat, he rushed home in a delirious fever, brushed aside his sympathetic wife who met him at the door, secluded himself in his study and locked the door. Cursing the power of the beauty of the woman whose neck he had tried so hard to string from a rope — a power to which even he had not been immune — he took from his briefcase the most alluring of the newspaper pictures of the woman he had denounced as a vampire, and found release, succumbing, in rage more than passion, to the images laid out before him.

When Alice Roche described the exhibition of the jurors paying court to Gertrude and showering her with roses after acquitting her of murder — surely unprecedented in the annals of jurisprudence — it prompted an outraged editorial cartoon depicting Gertrude as Snow White patting the heads of her cooing and submissive juror-dwarfs.

It was midafternoon when a tapping at the door awakened Gertrude, who was still sleeping.

"Who is it?" Gertrude called out, rising lazily from her bed.

"My name is David Lodge," came the voice from behind the door. "I have a message for you."

"Do I know you, Mr. Lodge?"

"The letter will explain, Mrs. Patterson."

"Please wait a moment."

Gertrude put on her robe and opened the door a crack.

"What message?"

The man, tall and slim and dressed smartly in a black wool suit, handed her an envelope. Gertrude took the envelope.

"Just a moment," she said, closing the door.

As she read the note, she smiled broadly. She opened the door.

"Come back in an hour," she said. "I'll be ready."

"Yes, Mrs. Patterson. Mrs. Patterson? Members of the press are downstairs in the lobby waiting for you. I know a back entrance if you want to avoid them. I have a hansom waiting."

"Thank you. David is it? Wait. Is it cold outside?"

"Quite brisk, yes, Mrs. Patterson. A touch of frost."

"One hour, then," she said, shutting the door.

Gertrude dressed quickly into her blue broadcloth suit and ermine coat, put on her wide turban hat, and slipped into her Louis heels. She discarded several outfits with which she didn't care to be burdened and packed the remainder of her belongings, including her jewels, shoes, and clothes in three large suitcases.

Half an hour later, before she had finished her packing, there was another knock at the door. Thinking it was David, and annoyed that he had returned before the hour, she opened the door to ask him to give her more time.

"Mr. Lodge . . . "

But it was not David Lodge. To her surprise, she recognized one of the four jurors who had visited her the evening before.

"Why, Mr, Mr..."

"Perry, Mrs. Patterson. F.S. Perry. I do hope you will forgive this intrusion, Mrs. Patterson, but, but . . . " the wide-eyed young man stammered.

"Yes, Mr. Perry, I remember you well, and, as I said last night, am very grateful, but you see I'm about to leave . . . "

"You are leaving Denver, Mrs. Patterson?" said Perry, obviously crushed.

"I'm sorry, Mr. Perry, but I really am in a hurry . . . "

Awkwardly, Perry took out a small leather box from his coat waist pocket and held it out. "For you, Mrs. Patterson."

"Why, Mr. Perry . . . "

"It's a small token of my esteem and admiration, Mrs. Patterson."

"Mr. Perry, I couldn't possibly accept a gift like this . . . "

Perry looked crestfallen, and Gertrude was anxious to get back to her packing.

"Very well, Mr. Perry," she said, taking the box. "But you understand that I am leaving."

"I want you to have it," Perry said, still stuttering nervously. "In compensation for the ordeal you have sustained. Perhaps if you return to Denver . . . "

Despite her impatience, Gertrude flashed a broad smile. "Thank you, Mr. Perry. And now I really must go."

Perry bowed as Gertrude shut the door.

Gertrude laid the box down beside her grip on the bed as she resumed packing. Then, curious, she picked it up and opened it. Inside was a thin gold bracelet. Shaking her head in amusement, she took the bracelet in her hand and gently bent it to see if it was solid gold. It was not. She put the bracelet back in the box and carelessly cast it into her grip. Though the bracelet paled in comparison to her other jewels, she would later wear it from time to time as a souvenir and symbol of the power that had saved her.

Moments later, David returned.

"Is that you, David?" Gertrude said, putting on the finishing touches of her eye makeup as she leaned forward toward the mirror.

"Yes, Mrs. Patterson.

"Come in, then. The door's unlocked. My bags are ready."

"Yes, Mrs. Patterson," said David, entering. He took one grip under his arm and carried the other two in his hands. "If you will follow me."

He led her down a back staircase where a two-horse hansom was waiting. David helped her into the back seat and tucked a fluffy blanket over her legs as she snuggled into the back seat. It was dusk by the time the hansom, unseen by the waiting press corps, departed the Brown Palace Hotel for Denver Union Station. It being the Thanksgiving weekend, the streets were deserted, and the ride to the station took less than ten minutes.

The hansom bypassed the main station lobby and crossed behind the station across several tracks to a waiting train consisting of a locomotive and two rail cars.

Brining the hansom to a stop, Lodge helped Gertrude from the cab and escorted her to the last car on the train. He helped her up the steps and ushered her into the car.

Gertrude's mouth opened as she stepped into the threshold.

The private car was lavishly appointed with Louis XVI furniture, brass fittings, and a crystal chandelier. At the far end, next to a door that opened into a private galley, was a walnut table, set with silver and china. The central feature of the car was a queen bed covered with a silk comforter and cushions. At the foot of the bed was a trunk-sized mahogany box brightly wrapped with a golden bow.

"Oh, oh! Is all this for me?" Gertrude asked excitedly.

David, who was entering with the bags, set them down by the door. "Yes, Mrs. Patterson," he said. "Here is the key to the box."

Gertrude took the key and excitedly opened the giant box.

"Oh, my!" she said as she withdrew a full-length sable coat. Then she opened the small envelope attached and read the note:

"Dearest Gertrude,

I'm so sorry for everything. If you will permit me, I want to make you happy again. You have endured so much, but your ordeal is now over. I hope you like the coat. It is quite chilly back here in Chicago. E.S.

P.S. Be sure to look in the right pocket."

Shaking her head in happy amazement, Gertrude pulled out the coat and reached into the right pocket. She withdrew a glittering necklace set with flawless diamonds the size of marbles.

As Gertrude gasped at this dazzling treasure, David pulled a signal line. The train lurched forward.

"I am to escort you to your home in Chicago," he said.

"Home?" Gertrude asked. "To my apartments at the Auditorium?"

"Yes, Madame, if you wish. But there is also a house on South Prairie Avenue in Hyde Park . . . "

Gertrude covered her open mouth with the back of her hand. "Oh, I know it — the white Victorian at Prairie Shores, the one with the red gables?"

"Yes, Mrs. Patterson. I believe that is the one."

"Oh, Emil knew I loved that house! It's magnificent! I can hardly believe it! I have always wanted to live in such a house. It's on the 2200 block of South Prairie Avenue, isn't it?"

"Yes, Madame. Mr. Strouss thought you might prefer living there as it can accommodate a full staff of servants."

Gertrude shook her head in disbelief.

"And what about you David? Are you a member of the staff?"

"There is a new automobile — it's called a Pierce Arrow, and I am to be your driver if you are agreeable."

"But of course I shall be. You are an excellent driver, David."

"Thank you," said David, bowing. "And now, Mrs. Patterson, there are two people on board who are quite anxious to see you."

Gertrude turned as two figures emerged from the galley. She recognized both Freda and Herbert instantly.

"Freda!" Gertrude cried, rushing to her former servants and embracing them.

"Oh, it is wonderful to see you both! You have no idea how happy I am!"

The tearful reunion was followed by a dinner of pheasant and champagne prepared and served by Herbert.

"Oh, m'um," said Freda "I have missed madame so. We shall all be happy again, won't we?'

"Oh, yes, my dear friends. Just promise me that we shall talk only of the future, and nothing of the past."

After dinner, Gertrude excused Herbert and David who retired to the adjoining service car for the night. Gertrude and Freda found themselves alone.

Gertrude took Freda's hand. "You still wish to serve me, Freda?"

"Oh, yes, m'um, more than anything."

Gertrude smiled. "Freda, I don't deserve you, and you must not think of yourself only as my servant. I think you are my best friend in all the world, and I have missed you terribly."

There was a long silence as mistress and servant gazed fondly at each other and held each other's hands.

"Oh, m'um, please try on the coat," Freda pleaded, bringing the sable to her. Gertrude stood up while Freda undressed her, released her corset and wrapped the sable around her naked shoulders. Gertrude walked over to the mirror.

"How do I look?" asked Gertrude, twisting and turning in self-admiration before the mirror.

"Oh, you look exquisite, m'um, so elegant!" Freda gushed.

"I just love sable, Freda," Gertrude said, stroking the fur and hugging herself. "It's so much softer than the ermine." It will go splendidly with my sable Daghilovs. I think I should just like to sleep in it."

"It's from Russia, m'um. Mr. Strouss brought it back from his last trip to Paris. He was so afraid that he might never be able to give it to you. Now shall you try on the diamonds, m'um?"

"Yes, yes," said Gertrude eagerly, picking up the necklace and holding it to her throat. As she sat down on the Queen Anne chair in front of the mirror, Freda knelt down to take off Gertrude's shoes and rub her feet in prelude to a more intimate ceremony of gratification. Gertrude, whimpering with pleasure as Freda attended to her, lay back on the chair and held the gems up to the light, admiring them from every angle.

"Look how they sparkle!" Gertrude marveled.

"It shall be like before, m'um?" asked Freda after some while.

Upon release from the tension that had weighed so heavily upon her for the past two months, Gertrude reached down to stroke Freda's hair.

"Yes, Freda. It shall all be just like before."

EPILOGUE

In 1946, when Frances Wayne wrote her chapter on the Gertrude Patterson trial in her book on Denver murders, she concluded her chapter with this passage:

> "As for Gertrude Gibson Patterson, the star of Denver's super murder melodrama, she went off to Europe. For a bit of gaiety for her homeward voyage, she took a passage on a brand new ship — the Titanic. She was young, she was pretty, she was mistaken, and as Alla Wheeler Wilcox might have remarked, 'Karma finally caught up with her.'"

Denver Post *headline of the Titanic disaster showing the Titanic's size in relation to downtown Denver. Gertrude Patterson, who had travelled frequently on luxury ocean liners in the company of her admirer and benefactor, Emil Strouss, was rumored and believed by many to have been one of the disaster's victims. (April 16, 1912).*

Certainly, this was an ending that would conform to the conventions of the morality plays of the period, and in the days after the sinking of the *Titanic* on April 15, 1912, the Denver newspapers did indeed report Gertrude as having gone down on the *Titanic*. These reports were apparently based on letters received from Gertrude's relatives in the days prior to the sailing of the *Titanic* stating Gertrude's intention to sail on the Titanic's maiden voyage.

If Gertrude had been a passenger on the *Titanic*, she would have traveled under an assumed name. It is doubtful that she would have been among those who perished, however, because as a first-class woman passenger, she would have been among the first to board the lifeboats. It is possible that Strouss, also traveling under an assumed name to avoid press scrutiny, did perish. In this case, Gertrude would have inherited his vast wealth, including his factories and estates, making her one of America's wealthiest women. It is more probable, however, that neither Gertrude nor Strouss was on the *Titanic*, and that Gertrude finally agreed to become Mrs. Emil Strouss by another name.

In May of 1912, members of the Denver press launched a search for her and claimed to have found her living in a palatial mansion in Chicago. Articles in *The Denver Post* later concluded that Gertrude was using the reports of her voyage on the *Titanic* to drop out of sight and assume a new persona. On May 12, 1912, the following story appeared in the *Rocky Mountain News:*

"Has Mrs. Gertrude Patterson Used the Loss of Titanic to Disappear and Start Anew?"

Gertrude Gibson Patterson, the young woman who shot to death her consumptive husband in Denver, Colorado, and was later acquitted of the crime, is living in Chicago. The death tragedy linked the woman's name with the name of Emil W. Strouss, Chicago millionaire, who, she asserted, paid her $1500 to take her to Europe.

Mrs. Patterson today is living in expensive and luxurious style on the South Side. That fact became public today.

This discovery comes but a few weeks after a story was given circulation to the effect that Mrs. Patterson was numbered among the victims of the Titanic disaster. It was said that she had been in Europe and that she was returning to this country on that vessel under an assumed name.

She is today mistress of a pretentious mansion in an exclusive neighborhood. Mrs. Patterson has luxuries.

She has money. Her clothes, of the finest texture and fashion, have created comment in the neighborhood. She wears sables and ermine. She has a large retinue of servants who cater to her every whim and bow and scrape before her. Frequently an automobile, a limousine, takes her out driving. Her luxuries, it is said, are the fruits of the labor of thousands who labor in textile factories. Inadvertently, Mrs. Patterson dropped her secret. In a commercial transaction she used a name which recalled the tragedy of her life.

Today a representative of a Chicago newspaper visited her. When the fashionably dressed woman stepped into the drawing room and asked quietly the visitor's mission, he asked in return: "Are you Gertrude Gibson Patterson?"

The woman, whose every feature tallies with that of the woman of tragedy, seemed startled, and gave the name under which she is going.

The visitor persisted. Then the woman sharply exclaimed: "I have nothing to say."

"Have you remarried?" was the next question.

"That is a very impertinent question," she responded. Then she became frenzied.

"What if I am Mrs. Patterson? Whose business is it?" she cried, and then slammed the door.

On May 1, the *Denver Times* in a front page article, reported:

"Denver Friends Believe Beautiful Slayer Has Taken Advantage of Reported Death."

The parents of Gertrude Gibson Patterson claim that they feel certain that their daughter did not sail on the Titanic, as at first was her intention.

When Mrs. Patterson embarked for Europe she took passage under an assumed name. In the European cities she visited, among them Naples, when she was resting preparatory to beginning a four months tour of the Mediterranean, she passed under this name, which was known only to her parents.

Denver friends of Mrs. Patterson declared that there is but one conclusion to be reached in explaining her disappearance. As Gertrude Gibson Patterson she wished to retire into seclusion when she left Denver.

> When Mrs. Patterson learned that her name was mentioned among the victims of the Titanic, say her friends here, she determined that the disaster should be her opportunity to forever drop out of sight.
>
> According to advice from Europe, Emil Strouss, the Chicago millionaire, whose name figured in the Patterson trial, is now in Paris.

The last article published in the Denver newspapers about Gertrude Patterson was published in the *Rocky Mountain News* on November 12, 1912:

"Gertrude Patterson Writes Book on Tragedy of Own Life."

"Slayer of Husband in Letter to News *Tells of Sordid Romance Penned in Shadow of Historic Fountainbleau."*

> Out of the historic forest of faraway Fountainbleau, once scintillant with the ribald court life of gay Louis XVI, that still whispers lovers' woes, dark intrigues and deep tragedies, there comes like a voice from the grave, a message penned by Gertrude Gibson Patterson, central figure in the sordid episode of love and violent death that one year ago held Denver in thrall.
>
> While The Denver Post *was deliberately faking stories that she had perished with the Titanic, Mrs. Patterson, slayer of her youthful husband, was basking serenely in the shadow of the home of the great Napoleon.
>
> She was engaged in writing a book which she styled a romance from the threads of the tragic crime in which she played the leading part. Her book is soon to be published.
>
> In a letter to the* News, *received yesterday, Mrs. Patterson tells of her life abroad, of her plans for the future and her hopes of returning to Denver. The book, she says, is to be the story of her own life, a recital of the grim tragedy, the sinister fate that wrecked her life, and culminated in murder and disgrace.
>
> The beautiful heroine is to be simply Gertrude Gibson Patterson in disguise. Denver will form the setting of the story, the climax of a life as thrilling as it is unusual.

Mrs. Patterson says she left America last December and traveled over Europe until seized with the resolve to write the book.

Then she sought out the beautiful little suburb of Paris, haunted by the ghost of past glories and sorrows — even as hers had been for the work.

Mrs. Patterson writes:

"I shall not return to Denver or America immediately, as I intended, as I am writing a book on which I have working for some time, and expect to have it ready for publication in the spring.

"I left America at once after my trial. I spent some time in Warsaw, in Russian Poland, and Turkey and spent most of the summer in Vienna. I expect to make mention of this in the second part of my book at the very end.

"I am now living in Fontaine-bleau, one of the most charming places in the world. I will remain here until spring, when I shall return to America and back to dear old Denver again.

"It's beautiful and delightful over here, but I long to return home.

"Yours sincerely,
Gertrude Gibson Patterson.'

Although Mrs. Patterson made no mention in the letter of Emil W. Strouss, the multimillionaire clothing manufacturer in Chicago, against whom her dead husband once filed suit for $25,000 for the alienation of his wife's affection, he is known to have gone to Europe about the time of Mrs. Patterson's departure abroad and from latest accounts was in Paris.

Since this article was published in 1912, not a single subsequent account of Gertrude Gibson Patterson has ever been found.

If Gertrude lived to her life's expectancy, she would have lived into the 1950s. One can only wonder how she might have fared during the turbulent periods of World War I, the Great Depression, and World War II.

If karma caught up with her, it seems fated to remain forever a secret to the world.

Was Gertrude Gibson Patterson guilty of the murder of her husband?

There was no question that she shot her husband, but was it self-defense? There was ample evidence presented that Gertrude Patterson was an abused spouse. Several unimpeachable witnesses, including the district attorney of Denver, so testified.

On the other hand, there can be little doubt that the testimony of Francis Easton was perjured. His testimony was critical to Gertrude's defense, as revealed by one juror's disclosure after the trial that he had voted for acquittal based on Easton's testimony that he saw Gertrude fire in self-defense while being assaulted by her husband.

Immediately following Gertrude's acquittal, Horace Benson, still smarting from a defeat he declared to be the greatest miscarriage of justice in the history of Denver, sent an investigator to Denver's central railroad station to track Easton down. The investigator reported that he saw Easton stashing a wad of one hundred dollar bills into his pocket before boarding the train. Despite efforts to follow Easton, the trail grew cold at the Canadian border where Easton disappeared without a trace. He was never seen again.

Did Gertrude's beauty influence the jurors in the manner suggested by the sensational headlines and articles of the Denver newspapers? Certainly the unseemly spectacle of the male members of the jury paying court to Gertrude after the verdict and presenting her with roses and congratulations suggests that it played a role. Nevertheless, one must ask whether any system of justice can screen out the influences of appearance — or in such more recent cases as the trial of O.J. Simpson — the influence of celebrity and money. On the other hand, it was not uncommon in the early twentieth century American courts for wives to be acquitted of the murder of demonstrably and chronically abusive husbands. Whether abused spouses are as likely to be acquitted today is not an easy question to answer, because each case carries its own unique set of facts, and generalizations are misleading. Certainly where an abused spouse has no realistic option of escaping an abusive spouse determined to stalk or kill them even at the expense of their own life, acquitting a spouse who takes the only realistic course of preemptive action can not be said to be a violation of basic principles of fairness and justice.

Whether Gertrude Gibson Patterson acted in self-defense to an immediate threat of violence, took justifiable preemptive action against a demonstrably abusive spouse, or, as Benson claimed, killed her husband for no other reason than to prevent the filing of a lawsuit — is left to the reader who has read the testimony as it was presented in the courtroom some ninety years ago.

It is probably a fair observation that under twenty-first century standards of ethical conduct, neither attorney in the Patterson case was beyond reproach. Benson's strategy of vilifying Gertrude and calling her a vampire was in the end a counter-productive one. On the other hand, O.N. Hilton's strategy of casting Gertrude as the innocent girl corrupted by a millionaire Jew cynically and blatantly played upon the anti-Semitism so virulent in turn-of-the-century America. Playing upon the racial prejudices of society in defense of a client is an ethical question deserving of more scrutiny than it has thus far received in the legal profession.

In fairness to Hilton, he did present sufficient competent evidence to enable a jury so inclined to reach a finding of self-defense. The upward angle of the bullet that passed through Chuck Patterson's body, together with the bullet found in the wall, suggested that Gertrude fired from a position beneath her husband. The victim turning away at the last moment could explain the shots in the back.

Benson was never entirely convincing in establishing a motive, and apparently could suggest nothing better than that Gertrude killed her husband to prevent him from pursuing an alienation of affection lawsuit against Strouss. As a matter of trial strategy, he was encumbered throughout the trial by his initial decision to charge Gertrude with premeditated, first-degree murder. Had he charged her with second-degree murder, or manslaughter, he could have avoided the difficulties of explaining why, if Gertrude did act with malice aforethought, she chose to commit her act on a public street before witnesses in front of one of Denver's most well-known mansions. The evidence at trial revealed that it was Chuck Patterson who insisted on taking a walk around the Richthofen Castle — not Gertrude, who suggested a lunch meeting at a local eatery.

What is most intriguing about the trial of Gertrude Gibson Patterson is not the story of sex and scandal, but what it tells us about the role of culture, gender, and racial prejudice in the evolution of American justice at the turn of the century. It is that lesson which makes this a story worthy of telling.

One hundred years from now, the trials conducted today will no doubt provide similar lessons to legal historians about the effects of culture and society on the evolution of law in our own times.